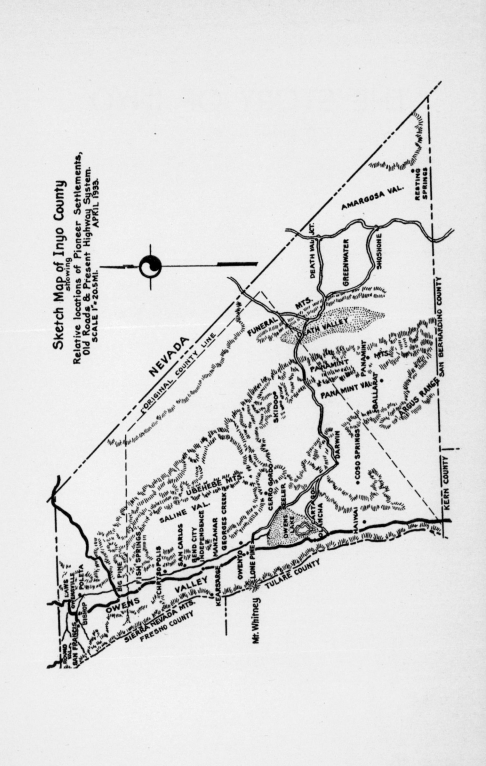

Sketch Map of Inyo County
showing
Relative locations of Pioneer Settlements,
Old Roads & Present Highway System.
SCALE 1"=20.5MI.
APRIL 1933.

THE STORY OF INYO

REVISED EDITION

❖

BY

W. A. CHALFANT

Willie Arthur ,1868-1943

❖

Author of

"OUTPOSTS OF CIVILIZATION"

"DEATH VALLEY: THE FACTS"

❖❖
❖❖

1933

To the Pioneers
and especially to the honored memory of

PLEASANT ARTHUR CHALFANT
Forty-Niner
Pioneer of Inyo and pioneer in endeavor
for her moral as well as material growth
this volume is dedicated

TABLE OF CONTENTS

FOREWORD TO FIRST EDITION

California has furnished probably more themes for books than has any other American State. The easy-going romantic years of Mexican rule, the padres, the Argonauts, the golden era, the wonders of this Empire of the West, have had generous attention from both masters and amateurs in prose and poetry, fact and fiction. The flood of writing hardly diminishes, for magazine literature and still more books add to it month by month. Yet few of the writers on California subjects look outside of the boundaries coined by a phrase-making politician, "from Siskiyou to San Diego, from the Sierra to the sea." Even such historians as Bancroft and Hittell deemed it hardly worth while to inquire into the annals of the borderlands, though the wilds were conquered through many hardships and wars bloodier than some on which volumes have been written.

Those who ventured into the unknown regions seldom thought it worth while to set down for the future any extended record of their trials and achievements. While they lived history, it all came to them as part of the day's work. Being more familiar with implements of livelihood and of offense and defense than with the pen, they wrote little. Before a succeeding generation fully appreciated the closing scenes of a drama of high interest, most of the actors in it had gone on the journey pioneered when time began. Therefore much has been lost.

This book's purpose is to preserve, particularly, the record of Inyo County earlier than 1870, when a printed record began. Gathering data for some such purpose began more than twenty years ago, while many of the pioneers still lived. It was the author's good fortune to know personally every early-day Inyoite then in the county. Each of them gladly gave his help. Personal interviews when possible, and correspondence with those who had moved to other parts of the country, elicited their recollections. All narratives were checked and rechecked with each other and with other sources of information. Public records were searched, as were also the files of pioneer newspapers in different libraries.

One of the most valuable sources of information was an extensive manuscript collection in the private library of Henry G. Hanks, in San Francisco. Mr. Hanks was an assayer in San Carlos and Chrysopolis mining camps, Owens Valley, in 1863. In later years he became State Mineralogist of California. He was a man of education, and when age caused his retirement from active labors his library received his whole attention. His interest in Owens Valley continuing, he kept and arranged many letters, diaries and other writings relating to this county's history. When the collection was examined for the purpose of this compilation, in 1902 or 1903, it had become an almost complete though disconnected history of the more strenuous pioneer years in Inyo.

Everyone who took any prominent part in the Indian war has passed on. The Hanks library was burned in the fire of 1906. As those sources of information are thus forever lost, there is some justification in believing that a service was done in getting what they had to impart; and also, that these chronicles, having that advantage, give the only fairly complete record of the county's beginnings that can be compiled.

Much of this material has been published in serial form in the *Inyo Register*. The idea of putting it into book form had been virtually abandoned when in the spring of 1921 the Federation of Women's Clubs of Inyo County, desirous of having the record preserved and made available, gave the publication their co-operation; and the Board of Supervisors later extended support that made the book a certainty.

Material has been procured from more sources than can be fully noted here. A general list of those sources follows:

Personal accounts of T. F. A. Connelly, Alney L. McGee, S. G. Gregg, J. S. Broder, A. Van Fleet, Milo Page, Thomas W. Hill, John L. Bodle, Thomas E. Jones, Henry G. Hanks, T. H. Goodman and others.

Correspondence with L. A. Spitzer, J. A. Hubinger, F. W. Fickert, John C. Willett, Gen. J. H. Soper, Dr. S. G. George, William B. Daugherty, George Otis Smith (Director U. S. Geological Survey), the Smithsonian Institution, Willard D. Johnson, Dr. A. L. Kroeber (Director Department of Ethnology, University of California).

Many manuscripts in the collection of Henry G. Hanks.

Articles by P. A. Chalfant, Mrs. J. W. Brier, C. L. Canfield, J. B. Colton, E. C. Atkinson, W. L. (Dad) Moore, and others.

Files of the San Francisco *Alta California,* San Francisco *Bulletin,* San Francisco *Call,* Sacramento *Union,* Los Angeles *News,* Los Angeles *Star,* in some instances as early as 1852; also of the *Inyo Independent, Inyo Register,* Bakersfield *Echo,* and other papers of subsequent years containing narratives of pioneers.

Addresses by Henry G. Hanks in San Francisco in 1864 and by James E. Parker in Lone Pine July 4, 1876.

Official reports of Warren Wasson and several other Indian agents; field notes of A. W. Von Schmidt's survey of Owens Valley; journals of the California Legislature; records of the Independence land office and of the Inyo County government; and sundry other official documents.

"Death Valley in '49," by W. L. Manly; "Death Valley," by J. R. Spear; "California Men in the War of the Rebellion," by R. H. Orton; "History of Nevada," by Thompson & West; histories of Kern, Tulare and San Bernardino counties; "Official Documents of the 38th Congress"; "The Panamint Indians," a government report by F. V. Coville; Bancroft's "Native Races"; Fremont's "Memoirs"; "Botany of Death Valley."

And many more not here set down.

As the reader is to infer from a preceding sentence, the aim of this undertaking has been to collect Inyo history that has not been printed. The principal matters since 1870 are presented by subjects, rather than with special regard to the order of their occurrence.

Bishop, California, December, 1921.

Justification for a reissue of this book is found in a continued demand, and even more in the desirability of having an available outline of events of the decade since "The Story of Inyo" first appeared—history vitally momentous to the region most concerned, and unique in American annals.

When the chapter on "Los Angeles Aqueduct" was written for the first edition, there was expectation that Owens Valley development would not be ended, and that its communities would continue as free, ambitious and progressive entities. The subject was treated from that standpoint. But absolute disaster impended, more complete than the most pessimistic then dreamed. It is well that there should be preserved an authentic record of these happenings and consequences without parallel.

Much has been added to the chapters on Indian life and lore, material as accurate as care could compile and confirm, chiefly from dependable Indian sources.

Continued research has added somewhat to the facts given in many of the original chapters, and has furnished a very few unimportant corrections. Files of the Visalia *Delta* have produced most of such material. Southern Owens Valley was a part of Tulare county preceding 1866, and up to 1870 the *Delta* was its newspaper spokesman. Those files, sought in preparing the first edition, were not then available, but since becoming so have been closely scanned for all information bearing on this purpose. Other new sources of information are generally credited as their facts are quoted herein.

Bishop, California, April 1, 1933.

CHAPTER I

SOME GEOLOGICAL FACTS

MOST DIVERSIFIED TOPOGRAPHY ON THE CONTINENT—ALABAMA
HILLS NOT THE OLDEST AMERICAN MOUNTAINS—A MILLION
YEARS THE TIME UNIT—WIDE RANGE OF SCIENTIFIC ESTIMATES
—VOLCANISM AND GLACIATION—A NOVELTY IN STREAM GORGES

No other equal area in North America approaches Inyo
County in diversified topography; in one respect it is
matched by no other on earth, in having in neighborly proximity the extremes of elevation within a vast national
boundary. The loftiest Sierra peak is but waist high compared with the Himalayas. The deepest American depression has a floor much nearer to sea level than the shores of
the Dead Sea. But those Asiatic extremes are very far
apart, while here Mt. Whitney*, highest point in the
States proper, is visible from the rim bounding Death
Valley**, lowest dry-land level on the continent; both are
in the one county.

Nature has written here, in bold strokes, studies more
fascinating than the little affairs of humanity. Since we
are noting briefly what geologists have deduced, and also
giving some attention to matters not strictly historical, this
is "The Story of Inyo," rather than its history alone.

To an English geologist was attributed the declaration
that the Alabama Hills, in southern Owens Valley near the
base of the Sierras, are the oldest mountains on the continent. This has been so often repeated and accepted as fact
that it should be set right. George Otis Smith, Director

---

*Mt. Whitney's summit bears four Geological Survey markings, respec-
tively engraved: "Mt. Whitney, lat. 36-44-44, long. 118-17-29, elev. 14,501";
"14,495.079"; "14,494.682"; "14,495.811"; the last, made in 1928, is the most
recent.

**The lowest U.S.G.S. measurement in Death Valley is –276 feet. Un-
official measurements by engineers at an obviously lower point establish the
extreme depth as –310.

of the United States Geological Survey, pronounced the assertion wholly erroneous. He said that while presumably some Archaean rocks are exposed in the Alabama Hills, their elevation above the water or the general level is a comparatively recent geologic event. A geologic map of California, compiled by the State Mining Bureau, classifies that patch of hills as Triassic, which is a long way back in world-building but far from the beginning. The most extensive examination was made by Adolph Knopf, whose "Geologic Reconnaisance of the Inyo Range and the Eastern Slope of the Southern Sierra Nevada" says:

The opinion that the Alabama Hills are "the oldest hills in the world" is in no respect tenable, either as to the age of the rocks composing the hills or as to the age of their uplift as a range. This opinion is probably fostered by the peculiar and fantastic weathering of the granite that makes up a large part of the hills, because this weathering lends them an ancient appearance in contrast to the Sierra Nevada. The fact that Lone Pine Creek flows across the range, which appears to have risen athwart its course, and the recent fault scarps that parallel its eastern front indicate that the Alabama Hills are of recent origin.

"Recent" in geologic parlance is a vague term. One geologist writes that "the million of years will remain the time unit." An interesting diversity of opinion is found as one searches for some idea of how long ago this region took its present general form. Schuchert, in "Historical Geology," says the globe was a molten mass between 20,-000,000 and 400,000,000 years ago, and further: "Now geologists are told they can have 1,000,000,000 or more years since the earth attained its present diameter." H. G. Wells, in "Outlines of History," diagrams the successive ages thus:

Azoic, or Archaean, possibly without life, 800 million or 80 million years ago.

Proterozoic, age of jellyfish, 600 million or 60 million years.

Early Paleozoic, sea scorpions, 360 million or 36 million years.

Later Paleozoic, fishes, 260 million or 26 million years.

Mezozoic, Triassic, Jurassic, Cretaceous, reptiles, 140 million or 14 million years.

Cainozoic, Tertiary, Quaternary, 40 million or 4 million years.

Wells not only takes a wide range but he enlarges that privilege for his readers: "It is quite open to the reader to divide any number by ten or multiply it by two; no one can gainsay him."

A National Research Council which has been studying this subject since 1927 announces:

The earth's age is in round numbers 2,000 million years; or more specifically, its age exceeds 1,460 million years and is probably less than 3,000 million years.

So long as the scientists differ so widely, the rest of us may well be satisfied to limit our convictions to the undeniable fact that most of the great changes, even the "recent," were made a very long time ago. Referring to this region more directly, they find evidence of different periods, and one of them states that the successive events cannot be guessed even by ages.

It is generally accepted that at the end of the Paleozoic period of world building an immense inland sea, comparable with the Mediterranean of the present, covered much of what we know as the Great Basin. Then came the rise of the ranges, among them the White Mountains and Inyo Range with a division between them east of where Big Pine now is, and the Sierra. Knopf does not theorize on the ancient sea. Instead, he begins with Owens Lake, the highest shore line of which he decided to be 220 feet higher than the level of the lake within our own generation. Another well defined shore line 100 feet lower, and still others, marked the recession of the waters. The lake overflowed its southern barrier, he says, cutting a channel 30 feet lower than the maximum surface of the greatest lake spread. Through this channel, which existed for a long time (as usual vague), flowed a stream which filled Searles and Panamint basins and probably Death Valley. H. S. Gale, of the Geological Survey, estimates that the stream ceased to flow about 4,000 years ago. Precipitation upon and leaching of wide areas, and evaporation during the many changes of surface and climate produced the saline deposits we now know. In our own time, Owens Lake was gradually diminishing even before diversion of its main feeder, Owens River, into the Los Angeles aqueduct; the latter has changed most of the age-old bed to a dry area, coated with minerals which have been held in solution or had precipitated through unnumbered years.

C. D. Walcott, former Director of the Geological Survey, gave the name of Waucobi to the old-time Owens Valley lake, apparently using an Indian word more commonly spelled Waucoba. He traced the shore in places on the White Mountains, where fresh-water fossils and shells were found 3000 feet above the valley floor. He dismissed the theory that the lake was 3000 feet deep because of the lack of a sufficient southern boundary, and believed that great changes had carried the old shore upward.

These great inland lakes were produced by the ice age. At least two of the five major periods of glaciation are well defined in the Sierras, where after earth folding had elevated towering summits the glaciers played their part in titanic sculpturing. A recent writer finds evidence of four glacial epochs in the region. Canyons and gorges were chiseled out, rock floors were polished to almost mirror-like smoothness, as the slow rivers of ice moved, year by year, to lower levels. Peaks were riven, mountains shattered, by nature's forces. It took long to remove the armor of ice from all the land above the 4000 feet elevation; but as it receded melting torrents poured into the lower basins and gathered in inland seas. Nature's chemistry was at work, leaching from the rocks the salts which were to concentrate in the lowlands, to be left in huge beds as with the passage of centuries the unrenewed waters were drawn off by summer suns.

Willis T. Lee, of the Geological Survey, remarks:

The present form of the Owens River system is due largely to changes of climate in recent geologic time. Throughout a part, at least, of Quaternary time Owens River flowed southward through Salt Wells Valley, and the portion of Owens Valley north of Bishop probably contained a flowing stream. During the changes toward aridity of climate which took place later, the water supply was cut off from the upper part of Owens River and one of its main tributaries was left as the head of the stream. At the time evaporation in the valley equaled or exceeded the inflow, that part of the river south of Owens Lake ceased to flow, and the tributaries from the White Mountains became dry from lack of sufficient rainfall, if indeed they had been permanent streams.

The observer traveling through the upper end of Owens Valley, north of Laws, cannot fail to note a deeply cut channel with banks still so sharply defined as to indicate that it must have carried a large stream, one would say within the last hundred years.

The viewer of evidence of volcanism east of the Sierras is inclined to believe in periods of intense activity, and to accept that the last of these was "very recent"—say not a great many centuries ago. The greatest of these appears to have been midway of Owens Valley's length, where cinder cones and widespread lava fields cover much of the surface. There were eruptions from both ranges, and plenty of them. A cinder cone near Bishop known as Red Hill is said to be later—possibly not far from the time when an immeasurable volume of volcanic mud poured forth to cover the north end of Owens Valley under hundreds of feet of tufa. Perhaps, too, this may have happened while the craters south of Mono Lake were active.

Proof that the layman can appreciate that volcanic periods came at widely separated intervals was disclosed in artesian borings near Big Pine. Lava was encountered at more than 100 feet depth, under alluvial soil, while not far away were products of eruptions so recent that lava strews the surface. Whoever can figure out how long it took the valley to fill that hundred feet can guess the least time that passed between those outpourings of molten matter.

Clarence King painted a striking picture of the California of the volcanic, formative days:

From the folded rocks of the coast ranges, from the Sierra summits and the inland plateaus, there poured a huge deluge of molten rock. . . . All along the coast of America blazed up volcanic chimneys. The rent mountains glowed with outpourings of molten stone. Sheets of lava poured down the slopes of the Sierra. Rivers and lakes floated up in a cloud of steam and were gone forever. The misty sky of those volcanic days glowed with innumerable lurid reflections, and at intervals along the crest of the great range great cones arose, blackening the sky with their plumes of mineral smoke.

This is the picture our beliefs imagine—a world on fire, shaken with earthquakes that rent landscapes asunder and raised up towering mountain ranges. Physical evidences along the eastern slope of the Sierras suggest the idea that surely here was the great furnace of the world, some time.

Yet Sir Archibald Geikie, eminent authority, tells us:

The assertion that volcanic action must have been more violent and more persistent in ancient times than it now is has assuredly no geological evidence in its support. . . . There is an overwhelming body of evidence to show that from the earliest epochs in geologic history volcanic action has manifested itself much as it does now, but on a less rather than a greater scale. . . . The oldest sediments like the youngest, reveal the operation only of such agents and such rates of activity as are still to be witnessed in the accumulation of the same kind of deposits.

We consider this old earth a more settled sort of habitation than Sir Archibald's assertion would indicate, but consider: There is today a 1700-mile front of volcanoes, beginning in Alaska and extending into the North Pacific, "a titanic parade, smoking, muttering, quiescent, reaching nearly to Asia." Explorer Bering recorded flaming mountains there in 1741, and the reconstruction of that part of the earth is still under way. It has not been thirty years since Mt. Katmai blew off its top and created the Valley of Ten Thousand Smokes. Elevation of new islands, subsidence of land and sea coasts, are occasionally reported or discussed. In our own region, Sierra fault scarps as high as twenty-five feet are attributed to the earthquake of 1872. A geyser forty years ago shot a fountain several feet higher than the surface of Hot Creek, in southern Mono county, sending its outburst upward through a strong flowing stream. A few miles to the northwest the caldron of Casa Diablo boiled considerably higher than the general level surrounding its rocky cup. Today the geyser is hardly perceptible, and Casa Diablo, while still boiling, is several feet below the top of its vent, while other springs in the same neighborhood have ceased to flow. More to the westward, a long rift in the mountain surface proves an earth readjustment some time in the past; that occurrence, certainly geologically recent, was rather remote as our history goes, for large pine trees, which are said to require 150 years to reach their present size, are growing inside the crack. A fault line nearer the coast had its part in the San Francisco earthquake of 1906. Thus considering the inconceivable time that has passed, it is not difficult to credit that perhaps the scientist is right in saying that the world is changing as rapidly today as ever in its existence except perhaps in the first few millions of convulsive years. Perhaps our home pyrotechnic displays, whenever they happened, came when it was the turn of this part of the globe to carry forward the constructive work that is now going on near the shores of the North Pacific. One is tempted to rashly wonder, too, if another climatic change, such as those repeatedly occurring in the course of time, is portended by a succession of years of decreased rainfall.

Evidences are that the mountains originally towered far higher above the valleys than at present. Whitney's pinnacle was higher above sea level and has worn and broken away. On the other hand, while internal influences may have raised or depressed them, the valleys have been filling with alluvial deposits for countless years. Borings to a depth of more than 1000 feet south of Owens Lake penetrated only sedimentary gravels and soils. At the lake, deep borings cut successive layers of gravel, sand, volcanic ash and gravel. Near Big Pine, a 576-foot well encountered only clay and fine sand, in several alternations. Other evidence of the same kind is derived from the many wells drilled by the city of Los Angeles in Owens Valley, where soil was found to depths of hundreds of feet. River mud was brought up from one well from far below the present river channel.

Willard D. Johnson, of the Geological Survey, spent months examining Owens Valley's geologic details, and wrote of it:

Owens Valley had a lively history in the recent geologic past. The mountain forces have been extraordinarily vigorous. For example, the broad embayment in the Inyo Range, opposite Big Pine, has been lifted at least 1800 feet, possibly 3000, since glacial times.

The Black Canyon region was lifted nearly as much. This great deformation was local, dying out rapidly from Black Canyon northward and southward from Waucoba Canyon. But the Bishop lava field, which had been spread only a little earlier, was warped, folded and shattered in an extraordinary manner. The display of faulting effects has had no parallel anywhere that I know of.

In volcanism, cones are built by explosive eruptions of molten lava. The coarser particles fall back vertically, to build the cone; the finer particles are drifted far on the wind, to fall as ash deposits. With excess of water and less heat, the steam-expanded lava is welled out and spreads as "lava flows." Owens Valley has record of volcanism of all types. There have been many ash showers in the Black Canyon section; many are preserved and exposed, one of which is five feet thick. There have been many cinder cones. Most of them have been in large part washed away, but several miles south of Big Pine one stands nearly perfect, embraced by glacial moraines, in evidence of post-glacial or "recent" volcanism. Rude cones of built-up lava flows are numerous. The largest is the black mountain immediately south of Big Pine. There are at least a dozen others. Flows of molten lava cover large areas.

In some time of the far past, Owens Valley was larger than at present, for a mighty spread of volcanic matter now covers its northern end, north and east of Owens River. A mesa of many miles square is full of such evidence. The gorge of Owens River, eroded to more than 800 feet depth, in places, below the general level, with some vertical cliffs of more than 400 feet, discloses only an unvarying tufa mass.

Mr. Johnson wrote of the river gorge:

For six miles it has a remarkably straight course. Has the river, in cutting its course, followed an earthquake crack? There is some reason to think so. This long section is not only exceptionally straight, but it runs at a considerable angle across the general slope of the lava plain surface. That is, fill the canyon and turn the river upon its surface above the Mono power intake and it would discharge into Round Valley. Furthermore, the lava plain is extensively faulted, in two systems of breaks approximately parallel. On the other hand, none of the recognizable faults parallel this long stretch of canyon. There are old river courses on the lava surface. There is evidence, finally, that the river took the long six-mile course following a tilting of pronounced grade in that direction. After it had cut down enough of a canyon to hold it, another tilt toward Round Valley occurred.

The really striking physiographic fact of this region, however, receives no comment. It is Birchim Canyon. Rock Creek cuts a deep canyon across a rising slope, in order to become a tributary of Owens River. If Birchim Canyon were filled, Rock Creek would pond up, only a few feet deep, and pass easily around the south end of the lava plain slope. What deflected it in this unnatural way? Early heavy glaciation, which, filling Round Valley in large part, crowded Rock Creek aside, up grade, and then left it permanently intrenched.

Johnson concluded that many of the great natural changes here mentioned happened but yesterday, so to speak, in the world's making. He believed that they occurred since man made pictures of the hairy mammoth and other mammals belonging to glacial times on the walls of caverns in southern France. While, say, the valley of the Euphrates has been standing still, and while on its plains of silt myriads of humas beings have time and again busied themselves in erecting brick temples on the moulded ruins of uncounted other brick temples, Owens Valley has been in the making.

CHAPTER II

WHO WERE THE FIRST FAMILIES?

NO TRACES OF ANCIENT MAN—VARIED ANIMAL LIFE WHEN OWENS VALLEY WAS WOODED—ROCK MARKINGS FOUND AT MANY PLACES THROUGHOUT THE COUNTY—NOT UNDERSTOOD BY EITHER WHITES OR INDIANS

Before the white man, the Piute; before the Piute, what people, if any, and for what duration of time?

Geologist Gilbert Bailey remarks that the remains of spear and arrow heads of obsidian, and the fossil bones of mastodon, horse and camel, mingled together, tell the story that elementary man lived along the shores of these ancient lakes.

Dr. A. L. Kroeber, of the University of California, took direct issue with this, in writing:

The age of most of the animal remains is to be reckoned by tens of thousands of years. The age of the human finds, whether they consist of skeletons or implements, probably does not extend beyond hundreds or perhaps thousands of years. Such at least is the consensus of opinion regarding all properly authenticated human discoveries yet made on this continent. In Europe and Asia the history of man seems to go back nearly half a million years, but he seems to be a very late comer in America.

He said that in no case investigated was there certainty that the remains of animals and indications of the presence of human beings were actually associated, without chance of their having been shifted together by later human or natural intent or accident. The scientific tendency is to be exceedingly skeptical in advance regarding any such discovery. The opinion of Professor Bailey is matched by even more startling reports of Professor Whitney and Clarence King, but recent examination has led to a general disbelief in their reports.

Dr. Kroeber wrote this to the author over ten years ago. Since then discoveries in eastern Nevada show that man was co-existent with the nothrotherium, or sloth, and give support to the contentions of those who hold that humanity was in western America earlier than has been generally believed.

That a varied animal population roamed the wilds east of the Sierra unguessable centuries ago is certain. Near Owens Lake, bones of some unidentified animal were brought up from 110 feet depth. Near Independence, men digging a well in 1863 found, under a cedar log, the thigh bone and forefeet of what was reported in print as being a "tremendous large horse." Still nearer to us in point of time was a mastodon, the bones of which were uncovered at a depth of only twelve feet, east of and near Owens River in the same part of the valley. The San Francisco Academy of Sciences, to which the exhumed bones were sent, estimated that the animal when alive measured twenty-five feet in length and fourteen in height. Not all of the bones were taken out; the Academy offered $25 for the rest of them, but the diggers did not seem to think the reward justified the work. Near Shoshone, east of the southern end of Death Valley, a great many bones and teeth have been found at a depth of about six feet, embedded in volcanic ash which was being mined for the manufacture of a well-known household commodity. Chas. G. Brown, of Shoshone, one of the finders, states that the bones were undoubtedly those of animals of the elephant family, as one tusk seven feet long was uncovered. It was perfect in form in its earthy bed, but crumbled on removal. Bones of several animals, seemingly of the same kind, have been removed from near the surface at a place twelve miles southeasterly from Olancha, at Owens Lake. If other animals shared the region with those, as is probable, traces of them are still under ground or have mingled with kindred earth.

Similar finds, in quantity, have been made in western Nevada, just across the State line. It appears that many ancient animals must have browsed on the luxuriant vegetation which in that day mantled the plains and hills of the Great Basin. No extensive investigation of fossils remaining from that prehistoric period has been made, or if made results are not available. Some individual specimens have been identified as belonging to the elephant, camel and horse families.

Discoveries in well drilling indicate that in olden times and at different periods Owens Valley was more or less wooded. The cedar log which apparently crushed the life from the "tremendous big horse" already mentioned probably toppled over untold years later than the growth of a black willow of which fragments were brought up from 281 feet depth near Big Pine; and many more centuries separated it from the life of a four-foot log, also of the willow species, bored through 447 feet underground in the same artesian well. In this well fourteen distinct changes of natural conditions were indicated by as many strata of soils. In the clay beds there penetrated, mass after mass of tules (rushes) was found.

Nearly 150 wells were drilled in Owens Valley for the Los Angeles aqueduct, some of them reaching to over 850 feet depth. Among so many, along a distance of approximately 70 miles, there must have been discoveries revealing something of the ancient facts of the valley; but unfortunately the drillers' logs noted nothing but the varieties of soils encountered.

Not a dependable indication of man's settled, or even occasional, existence in Inyo County in ancient times has ever been reported. A discovery, a few feet underground, of arrowheads of flint (not obsidian) and other articles not associated with the Piute tribe has been reported, probably indicating only that a wandering warrior from another region once filled a grave at that point, probably within hundreds of years. There are many petroglyphs, but no proof of their great antiquity.

Indian tradition reaches back to a time when groves and meadows abounded in these valleys, instead of the familiar sagebrush, and farther east desert and desolation. Fish and game were plentiful, and the tiger was an inhabitant, say the story-tellers of the campfire circle. That happy period came to an end when the mountains burned and the lakes dried. While this tallies with scientific conclusions, it is unbelievable as continuing tradition. It merely testifies to Indian powers of deduction and imagination.

Those who believe that a great aboriginal migration through Owens Valley once occurred cite the fact that a chain of petroglyphs, or rock carvings, extends from the Columbia River southward, into and through Inyo County, and into Arizona. Examination weakens the evidence. Pictured rocks are found at many points in the West; and while they can be traced northerly and southerly, so can they be traced easterly, and they are found west of the Sierras. "The pictures are not the work of any one roaming people," says one authority; "they have been made by all tribes, everywhere, at all times." The vague resemblances between those found in different localities may be only such as would come from the possibility that different tribes or bands, all lacking artistic conceptions, might chance to draw somewhat similar crude and simple designs.

Indian markings are of two kinds: petroglyphs, in which the design is cut into stone, and pictographs, in which it is put on the surface with some coloring substance. In a very few instances, some trace of color is found in the markings in Inyo and Mono, but those are so rare that it may be said that the petroglyph was the sole method of expression of the aboriginal artists of this region. Those found in the San Joaquin valley and in southern California are more frequently pictographs, and more ambitious in design than the stone carvings. It was easier for the primitive painter to daub on color with a crushed stick end, or whatever he used for a brush, than it was for the sculptor to express his idea by the use of a stone for a hammer and a sharper one for a chisel. He may have used but a single stone, but the usual absence of misdirected cuts points to the hammer-chisel probability.

One noteworthy example of color work is found in Owens Valley. On a stone within a few rods of the State highway, at the eastern edge of Round Valley, are a number of small handprints, such as a woman or child might make by coating the palm and fingers with paint and pressing it against the rock. One is very distinct; there are others, to the number of a dozen or more. They are red in color, fairly bright and undimmed notwithstanding considerable age. The first white men to locate in that locality, over sixty years ago, reported seeing them when they first came.

The largest area of petroglyphs is on the mesa north of Bishop. Collections found at different points show some variation of design. Seeming attempts to delineate deer and human footprints are visible. Sinuous lines which may mean snakes or streams, oval drawings with connecting lines suggesting lakes and creeks, upright marks branching as trees rarely do, many-legged bugs and gridiron figures are the most common. One group contains a roughly-drawn circle, with a central figure such as a child might make to represent a skirted woman. In general, the designs are crude geometrical figures, coils and seemingly aimless chippings.

Present-day Piutes disclaim any knowledge of the meaning of the petroglyphs and their origin, except as later will be told in a legend. Dr. Kroeber considers this fact immaterial, remarking:

I should be disposed to agree with your conclusion that the pictographs are comparatively recent, and very likely made by the ancestors of the present Piutes. The ignorance of the present generation would prove very little. Since the traditions of most Indians are most fragmentary, knowledge of that kind would be almost certain to die out in three or four hundred years and might be lost in a century.

Julian H. Steward, in his book "Petroglyphs of California and Adjoining States," says:

Innumerable attempts have been made to ascertain the meanings of petroglyphs and pictographs from Indians living at present in the regions where they occur. They have invariably met with failure. The Indians disclaim all knowledge of their meaning or origin. This can hardly be due to reticence, for intelligent Indians have themselves made efforts to ascertain something about the inscriptions, with no success.

The markings are generally found in soft material, such as tufa. A few are dim, but may have been only lightly cut. It is said that westerly from Benton, Mono county, petroglyphs are found cut to a depth of an inch and a quarter. This writer has never examined any reaching to half that depth.

The bottoms of the carvings are usually lighter in color than the surface of the stone; cuts made by white men show similar differences of shade, and the investigator will get like results if he chips off the surface. This tends to prove comparative recentness. Corroborative evidence that the work was done at no remote day has been found in Indian graves in which bones were in fair preservation, and with them bits of slate or other stone with carved markings.

Northern Owens Valley, Deep Springs, Keeler, Darwin, Coso Springs, Deep Springs Valley, the Death Valley region, some of the canyons of the White Mountains and the vicinity of Little Lake have groups of petroglyphs. One of interest is found near Fish Springs, about the middle of Owens Valley. Steward writes of that group:

About a quarter of a mile from the main highway, just before the road crosses Red Mountain Creek, there is a low lava hill between 50 and 100 feet high, to the west of and adjoining the road. Large and small boulders on the western and southern sides of this hill are covered with petroglyphs. Along the crest of this hill are innumerable circles of stone, belonging to ancient house sites, and abundant fragments of obsidian, many of which are worked. The petroglyphs have the appearance of great antiquity, for in nearly every group the lines have weathered so as to approach the dull black color of the untouched rock surfaces. As the depth of the lines is usually very slight, one-sixteenth to one-eighth of an inch, and as the rock surfaces are generally very rough, this weathering has rendered most of the figures very indistinct.

The opinion has been advanced that petroglyphs are found at camping places where there are or were springs or streams, and on natural routes of travel. There are exceptions to this, for some exist in mountain nooks quite devoid of indications of the presence of water at any time.

As at Fish Springs, where a considerable aboriginal village existed at some time, the Bishop area pictographs are not far from old-time camp sites. Natural conditions must have been different at that period, for one such site is on the top of the mesa high above Owens River, and with no nearer water. The villages themselves existed not so many hundred years ago, for digging within the stone circle which had formed the base of a dwelling brought to light bones which time had not destroyed. They were, however, not those of a complete skeleton, some portions being missing, indicating a probability of their having been carelessly reinterred at that place. They were not over a foot under the surface. In the same vicinity were found fragments from which were reconstructed a pottery bowl about fifteen inches high.

It is not an unreasonable conclusion that the pictured rocks offer no evidence of great tribal antiquity in the region, and possibly that they have small value except as illustrating a diversion of an idle people. Our archaeological and ethnological friends take issue with this, principally on the ground that the native was not given to such exertion as the carvings would necessitate. Mr. Steward is of the belief that

the primitive artist must have made the inscriptions with something definite in mind. He executed, not random drawings, but figures similar to those made in other parts of the same area. . . . We can probably never know precisely why many of the petroglyphs and pictographs were made, but we can guess that many of them were made for a religious or ceremonial purpose. . . . The elements were undoubtedly a more or less definite system of symbolism.

It would appear that the petroglyphs date back at least to the periods of the early beginnings of Pueblo culture in the southwest. Perhaps some are Basket Maker culture, which dates back to 1500 or 2000 B.C. Most groups are probably as recent as early Pueblo.

In some of the groups the markings are on rock faces twelve or fifteen feet above the ground and sometimes much higher, in situations wholly out of reach except by ladder, or by the artist being suspended by some means from the top of the rock.

It is reliably stated that near Greenwater canyon, on the Shoshone-Furnace Creek road, are petroglyphs cut in stone so hard that its marking with cold chisel and hammer is difficult. How the Indians did the carving is a matter for conjecture.

CHAPTER III

RELIGION AND MEDICINE

BELIEFS AS EXPLAINED BY A NATIVE—A WORLD PEOPLED WITH SPIRITS — BANISHING EVIL INFLUENCES — DESTINY CONTROLLED BY DREAMS—FANCIFUL AND PRACTICAL TREATMENTS—A BONA FIDE INDIAN SPEECH—CEREMONIES AND CUSTOMS

That the Piute is essentially a child of nature is nowhere else so manifest as in his religious beliefs. To get some understanding of those beliefs, appeal was made to Harry Bluebird Cornwell, an Indian who after graduating from the Carson Indian school did some studying in an eastern trade school. The quoted paragraphs which follow are as written by him, with no more editing or smoothing up than would be required by the writing of the average white person.

The Indian religion is difficult to comprehend at first study unless one speaks their language and lives and reasons with their customs in mind.

It is untrue that the Indians worship their "happy hunting grounds."

Somewhere beyond the dark curtains that shut off our conscious understanding, there seems to be a mighty power of some nature (Te-lu-gu-pu, meaning "our Creator") that the Indians plead to for their health and happiness. This same power is believed to control the whole universe and every living being. Perhaps this power is in what we may term the spiritual world. If we were to ask an Indian in his own tongue what he was talking to, he would answer "Tu-vaw-bu," meaning the creation, nature or universe.

It is common for an Indian to pray or plead with the unknown power to guide him safely through all danger while hunting in a dangerous country. He asks for safety by speaking direct to the things that he may fear may harm him. It is believed that when one is in danger nature or the unknown power gives a warning by having some strange or unusual thing to happen; this is believed to be true every day, as certain birds foretell sickness in the family or the death of a relative.

Often we may hear as Indian talking to himself when he is out alone, and not aware of any one else present. When we understand his language we learn that he is talking to some plant or animal life, or rock, water, the sun, star or moon. They believe all things have their own language and understand what is said, and are capable of transmitting any message to the unknown power.

The Piute Indians seem to try to live within the scope of nature's laws. They say "To nah-luh-gah gah-poo-zoo," meaning "rules laid down for us by the unknown power."

We may ask, in English, an Indian where the dead go. He would likely say he does not know. This is because he does not care to discuss this question, as he is superstitious, and perhaps does not know just how to explain his belief. But if you understand his language he will tell you that he believes the soul (moo-gah-ah) leaves the living being at death and goes on to the unknown world. He believes this soul is sometimes in this world and roams its old tramping grounds, invisible to all except supernatural persons or mediums who are able to hear and sometimes see them. These mediums are called "poo-o-ah-gah," meaning doctor or sometimes called medicine men.

Living in a world peopled with spirits, of which many appear to be evil, the ascribing of every illness or misfortune to them is a natural consequence, and from that comes belief in the powers of their medicine men who assume to banish malevolent influences. Cromwell states:

When hard luck comes to the family, the grandmother or some elderly person goes out just after dark with a handful of food of some kind with which to feed the bad spirits of the night. She argues with the darkness that brings evil and sickness, and relates dreams and strange instances that may have happened that she believes to have brought on sorrow. After she feels that she has shamed the evil spirits she throws out the food at intervals. This sort of prayer is known as "shame the evil spirits of the darkness." Then she pleads with the unknown power to send health and happiness with the following daybreak; this is known as "nah-ne-ja gaw-e te," meaning "call for help."

Oftentimes when the ill person is troubled in mind, her dreams seem to haunt her. They hire some person who is recognized to have developed power to converse with the unknown powers; this person we may term the priest or medium. He is known as "Tuh ya-lu-ha che-e-vo-gah-lu," meaning "one who speaks for another." When he comes to perform his duty, he sits down by the sick person's bed and the ill one tells him all of her dreams, bad or good, and such visions, impressions and thoughts as have come to her in the darkness of the night or in the day. After he has gathered all the evidence he is given some food with which to feed the bad spirits, to whom it is pay, or a sacrifice. He goes out in the darkness, and carries on a regular debate, picking points here and there from the story given him by the ill person. He accuses the evil spirits, and concludes with a plea.

Being thought to possess supernatural powers, medicine men, and sometimes medicine women, were important members of the community. Since the holder of the honor seldom lived out the normal life span, it might be supposed that the distinction would not be popular. Yet strange to say it was the individual himself who created his status. There was a strong belief in what we term "second sight," and a vivid dream became a vision. If therein were pictured strange events, or common events which thereafter came to pass, he became a doctor. He could not be silent about his visions, for malignant spirits were ready to inflict condign punishment on him for any such shirking of responsibility. His part in the drama of life was determined, whether he resented or approved it. Once in a great while there was rebellion against fate's decree. In one instance, a certain Jim, medicine man, constantly carried a "sixteen shoot gun," prepared at all times to "heap kill um" if attempts were made to force him to treat the sick or to fasten on him the results of some other person's lack of skill in exorcising evil spirits. If this had happened before the white man's gun had been available, probably Jim would have fled to other parts.

The medicine men had time-honored methods of treatment as precedent, but each one, having his own revelation, developed his own system. Incantations and weird dancing were the chief means of driving away the evil spirits. On occasion the absent treatment figured, for either good or evil. John Kieth, an intelligent English-speaking Indian who gave much of our information, told of an instance, with a seriousness indicating complete faith. A woman was gradually failing in health, and a relative went to a distant place to consult a learned medico. The latter stuck an arrow into the ground, and it gradually leaned more and more toward the horizontal. The relative was told that the decline of the arrow meant the decline of the sick woman.

He was instructed to go home and bury a stick in moist ground, and the patient would get well. He did so, and our authority assured us that the woman is now alive and well.

The medicine man was paid for his services, but if his work were a failure he might be called on to make restitution. His pay was given through a third party, or otherwise indirectly, for to accept his compensation directly would be an affront to the spirits that might undo his efforts.

Loss of his income was not the only penalty the unsuccessful doctor paid. The standard of professional success may be said to have been higher among the Indians than it is among the white people, for while a white doctor is in no danger of violence whatever his (or his patient's) luck, the Piute healer did wisely to arrange his earthly affairs immediately after the demise of his third lost patient. Relatives of the deceased considered that they had sufficient proof that the doctor did not know his business, and by common consent they attended to his unceremonious removal. Clubs, stones, arrows or any means sufficed to carry out the sentence, whenever and wherever opportunity offered. It was approved tribal law.

Even though his patient recovered, the doctor was not necessarily safe. If when called he predicted death, and the patient perversely recovered, it was a failure of prophecy, and counted in the record against the medicine man. If, regardless of prophecy, the sick person died, accuracy of forecast did not count, and losing the patient was the offense. The doctor's best chance to round out his years was in having no professional calls.

The *Inyo Independent,* 1876, mentioning an epidemic of measles from which red as well as white people were suffering, said that it was particularly severe on the natives, and no less so on their medicine men. Nearly all such "doctors" in the vicinity of Big Pine had been killed as a result of their unsuccessful practice.

The paper said also that after the medicine man had been slain, the custom was for the women in the camp to take his body out to one side and burn it. During the progress of this cremation, a circle of them stood all about, armed with willow whips, ready to deal with any evil spirit which might emerge from the burning body. At intervals they made many dashes after imaginary spirits, and concluded the ceremony with a general belaboring of the air in the vicinity.

The family of the unfortunate doctor was in no happier plight than he. Besides being subject to dreams which made them witches, the sisters, cousins, aunts and other female relatives of an unsuccessful doctor had a special liability to powers of witchcraft, and might suffer accordingly. The *Independent* article, herein referred to, told of the then recent burning of a young Indian woman near Owens Lake. A buck of the tribe accused her of having "witched" him, and she was wrapped in straw and burned to death.

Nearly all the threatened clashes between Indians and whites, after the close of the war, came from the white men's inability to appreciate the propriety of killing medicine men who had proved themselves failures, and a determination to stop murders of that character. There were a number of such killings long after the white people came into control of the region. In 1916 barbaric incantation was used to treat a belle of the tribe for some illness, until in the last extremity a physician was called, unavailingly. In another case as recent, a girl's sore eyes were treated by some campfire beldame who rubbed the eyeballs with a piece of stone until the blood started, in order to release the evil spirit that caused the distress.

So recently as September 1932 an Indian, aged but 25 and of weak mentality, had somewhat proudly accepted the designation of medicine man, near Aberdeen, in mid Owens Valley. A neighbor Piute concluded that the medicine man had "witched" his family by burying an eagle feather in the vicinity. The accusation was accepted, it appeared, by the young man, who went with the accuser to dig up the feather. It was not found; and the irate parent killed the offender. When this paragraph is written he is awaiting trial for murder. That the slate of superstition has not been wiped clean in that vicinity is shown by the satisfaction expressed by other Indian residents there at the removal of the medicine man.

The winter of 1900-1901 brought an unusual amount of illness all over the nation. Its effects on the Indians, living under unfavorable housing conditions, were specially disastrous. Killing their medicine men had apparently fallen into some disrepute, but this epidemic brought old superstitions to the fore. The natives appealed to the whites to be allowed to slaughter a few medicine men in the good old-fashioned way, and managed to create quite an excitement. White men addressed their meetings, pointing out the effects of their ways of living, and advising recourse to white doctors and healthier conditions. Still the elders shook their heads; they were not convinced. Finally Johnson Sides, Nevada Indian leader, came to Inyo to help to quell the agitation. He and some of the local chief Piutes came to the writer's office and explained the situation at length. Johnson proudly wore a silver medal as large as a small saucer, given him years before for service to the government, and inscribed with his name and the title Peacemaker. As a conclusion to the interview, he requested that his words be written down exactly as he gave them—being apparently doubtful about newspaper accuracy. At his dictation, a lengthy speech was written; from it are taken the following extracts:

They sent for me to come up and see what they been disputin bout doctors. After I get here they want me to talk law—Unite States law, State law. I told em since we meet we want ejcation. Get white doctor. Same sickness mong white people. Long time go, white doctor lose people account sickness, got to be strung up, same as murder. Next, Congressmen decide shouldn't kill anybody account sickness. This how people whole Unite States say; stick to it yet. Thas history. Us fellows we not got ejcation, no wonder we talkin bout same thing. . . . I don't think anything in killing doctors. I tole we better drop this. So many sickiness over ocean; blockade whole Unite States; thas what I tole em. Long John says we better drop this. Even if we die off we got die anyway. These doctors they protect by policemen. Doctors mustn't drink whisky, because when they drinkin they dunno what they say; thas what

makes Injun spicious gainst them. Thas orders—not drink whisky.
Quite long while this talk mixed up—only today decide it. We better
send our children given em ejcation. Old times pass way—no use
talk old times.

You sign um Johnson Sides, Unite States Peacemaker.

There were ten medicine men in the valley at that time,
and Johnson's peacemaking doubtless saved the lives of
at least some of them.

The writer has wondered, in reading, and in using a
reputed Indian speech in another chapter of this book, how
the many specimens of Indian eloquence were reported and
saved for the future. It was his privilege to transcribe one
genuine Indian speech, even though it lacks the imagery
usually a part of such alleged speeches.

In later years, the sick native usually calls a white physician, and the medicine man has become practically non-
existent, because of lack of patronage, of voluntary withdrawal from professional life, of involuntary withdrawal
from life of any kind, or more general tribal enlightenment.
Still many of the older natives, at least, retain some faith
in the mysterious and supernatural, and shreds of that belief may persist into future generations.

Use of the mooza, or sweathouse, was standard for
some complaints, especially those in which a rash appeared
on the skin. The victim went into an airtight wickiup with
suitable accessories for heating. When sufficiently warmed
up, and perspiring freely if possible, the invalid ran out
and plunged into a pool or stream of cold water. It undoubtedly made a difference in his condition; but as the
system was used for many ills, whether the difference was
an advantage in all cases may be doubted.

A few infusions were known and used. A decoction
which some white people regard as having merit is known
as "squaw tea" or "Mexican tea." It is made from a plant
of the yew family, usually Ephedra nevadensis, called joint
pine by the whites, chu-lupa by the Indians. It is an erect
olive-green bush, from a few inches to two feet high, leaf-
less in appearance and with jointed stems. Another of the
several varieties of the plant, Ephedra viridis, is also used.
A stomach medicine is made from the leaves of the creosote

bush, Larrea tridentata. Baked parts of the barrel cactus, Echinocactus cylindraceus, are said to be used for burns, after being ground to powder. A medicinal tea was made from the upper parts of the stems and flowers of the cotton-batting plant, Gnaphalium chilense. The coast-wide standby yerba mansa, Anemopsis californica, furnished roots which were cooked and used for various ailments, and leaves which were made into a poultice; the Piutes named it cha-wan-eba.

A white man who spoke Piute fluently was authority for the statement that heads of ants were used for stitching together the edges of open cuts, when practicable. The lips of the cuts were pushed together, and a certain kind of large ant was so held that it grasped the edges. The insect was then pinched in two, leaving its head in a death grip on the flesh. As many as necessary were thus applied, thus making quite a fringe, which unless torn off lasted until the wound healed. An Indian who was asked about this practice said he never heard of it; however, the white informant said it was a fact. A scientific exploration a year or two ago reported finding the identical practice among the mountain Indians of Peru, so we shall give our own aborigines credit for equal ingenuity. Pitch and fir balsam were frequently used as a dressing for wounds.

Ants figure also in a rheumatism cure given by an Indian to a white friend: "Make um sick man sit down on ants' nest. Bimeby (by and by) heap holler—puty good; maybe so git well." This has a parallel in the white argument that stings of bees help to cure the same complaint; and the parallel is not diminished by the uncertainty expressed in "maybe so git well."

The Panamints had a tribal custom which Owens Valley Piutes say did not exist among them. It disposed of aged members of the tribe in heartless fashion, but it is said that the individuals in question were willing parties to the arrangement. The one who had become "old and only in the way" was taken to some lone spot and left with a limited supply of food and water. There he or she starved, if some earlier termination of misery did not give release.

Malarango, chief of the Panamint (or Coso) Indians, had attained the ripe age of (supposedly) ninety years when with many bodily ailments he supervised preparations for his own removal in this way, in 1874. Supplied with a small stock of pinenuts with which to gradually "taper off" on a lifelong habit of eating more or less as circumstances had happened to control, he was located at a spring, with the expectation of going into his last sleep in three days.

The house of a dead person was burned, together with at least part of his personal belongings. No evidence appears that goods or chattels of any value were buried with the body. After the Indians came to possess horses, it was a custom to kill the dead man's favorite steed, skin it and use the hide for a shroud for the deceased. The practice of destroying goods was changed some fifteen or twenty years ago, when some of the wiser heads got together and agreed that it was a useless waste of property that people needed. Now the practice is for the relatives to keep such possessions, except probably clothing, of the departed for a a year, untouched; at the end of that time they are given to some one who appears to have just claims. The bodies of the dead were not burned, as in some tribes, except in disposing of slain medicine men and with this further exception: if the dead person were of importance, in relationship or worldly goods, and died at a point distant from his home, the body and the goods with him were burned, and the solid remnants were sent to the home place for burial.

Graves were unmarked, and were leveled off. They were sometimes covered with brush. Some time later, the friends assembled and gave their "cry song." The dry brush was burned, and the ground was seeded, if practicable, so that all trace of the grave would be hidden. That is another old custom that is being abandoned; coffins are now usually used, and graves are marked.

A sort of funeral ceremony was used, those near of kin standing beside the grave and telling the spirit of the departed that as his troubles were over and he had gone into the other world, he was to keep on going and not return to make trouble for those who remained. Finishing his adjuration, the speaker stepped over the body, or in later years the coffin, and walked away from the place without looking back.

One of the ceremonial customs among the older Indians is to sing to the morning star. Waking before it rises, he starts his song and continues until the star appears, and gets up with it. This is believed to stimulate enthusiasm, efficiency and good health, and to keep in harmony with the laws of nature as ruled by the unknown power. This custom may be popular in an Indian camp; one can imagine how much it would be approved in a camp of white people.

When a birth is to occur, what may be termed a hotbed is constructed for the mother by digging a shallow hole, making a fire in it and covering the fire with earth, or filling the hole with coals and ashes and using a blanket for a covering. Before the availability of blankets, sagebrush and leaves were used to modify the warmth from below. Before the mother leaves the bed, she makes confession of her sins, evil thoughts, dreams and laziness. Mother and child leave the bed with new life, and with the sins buried in the hole.

The father is purified by bathing. A quantity of water is heated; the father arises before dawn, and stripped he faces the coming sun. As he confesses his sins and short-comings a friend drenches him with the water. His confession and pleas for blessings of good deeds, good luck and a happy future are believed to purify his mind, body and soul. He is then fitted with his friend's clothing. He is never allowed to take back his own clothing, no matter what valuables may be contained therein; it is customary to leave something of value in the garments, as a sacrifice, the friend who takes them profiting accordingly.

As in most tribes, the entrance of the youth into manhood or womanhood is an occasion for special rites. The boy is wakened at the first sign of the morning star. A few morning songs are sung to him. He then goes to a nearby stream, where he asks the unknown power to guide him to a noble manhood and bless him with the power to overcome all hardships. He then plunges into the water regardless of season. This signifies his leaving childhood and taking up a manly life. He is then required to make a run of several miles up hill; sometimes he must do this every morning for several days. This is believed to develop endurance and speed. He is taught virtue, the laws of nature, facts about different kinds of game and their habits and cautioned about dangers. He is never allowed to skin or eat his first kill of game, for it is believed that if he does so game will be difficult for him to get in the future.

The girl at this period takes her early morning dip and makes her run. She gives up her doll days and is taught womanly arts. Her lessons begin with the gathering of food, kinds of food, ways to prepare and preserve it, weaving, respect for older persons' ideas.

The Piutes have their weather omens, among them these:

When the new mah-ah (moon) first makes it appearance over the western horizon the old Indians study the degree of dip or slant of the crescent. When it is very nearly on its round back or nearly horizontal, watch for heavy storms. When near vertical, the weather will be very dry. The degrees between are judged accordingly. Some practice is needed in judging the degree, to tell the amount of storm from one new moon to the next. Our informant thinks it is a fairly good guide.

Bright circles around the moon or sun indicate to the Indians a cold spell within a week. The time, nature and degree of the storm are judged by the color and size of the ring.

Flying spider webs or cobwebs sometimes foretell rain the following day.

A certain breeze foretells a storm. The Indians call it "o-so-ja-pu," meaning "its breath."

Though the natives believed in rainmakers, few if any among them ever attained the requisite proficiency. When the season required services of that nature they employed a "way-up" rainmaker from another tribe.

CHAPTER IV

PIUTES AND THEIR NEIGHBORS

PIUTES LITTLE STUDIED—THEIR ABORIGINAL NEIGHBORS—CLAIM TO
HAVE ALWAYS POSSESSED OWENS VALLEY—PROBABLY DECREASING
SLIGHTLY IN NUMBERS—GOVERNMENT A LOOSE CONFEDERACY OF
COMMUNITIES—WARFARE

Students of ethnology have given very little attention
to the aboriginal inhabitants east of the Sierras. Dr.
Kroeber's "Handbook of the Indians of California" dis-
cusses those nearer to the coast at length; those of this slope
are referred to but briefly. F. V. Coville published a few
pages on "The Panamint Indians of California," in a report on anthropology. Bancroft's "Native Races" mentions them incidentally. It is not for a layman to question
the general conclusions that these experts, though they
wrote at long range, have reached; but their records of
details of Piute living are negligible.

Bancroft assigns the western part of the Great Basin
to two "great nations," the Shoshones or Snakes, and the
Utahs. He designates the Piutes as a subtribe of the
Utahs, and holds them to be a different people from the
Pah Utes, making a distinction between the two tribal
names. Different writers have spelled the name Piute, Pah
Ute, Paiute, Paiuches, and otherwise, according to their
individual fancies. No reason appears for not writing it
Piute; the long *i* and *u* give the exact pronunciation. The
Indian himself adds a short final *e*.

Kroeber classifies the Inyo Piutes as Eastern Monos.
Whatever the scientists may figure out, the Indians themselves recognize no such naming; they are Piutes and
nothing else, except for subtribal designations. The Mono
Basin Indians are sometimes referred to as "Cozetica,"
from their use as food (formerly if not now) of the

"cozaby," a small worm found by millions on the shores of
Mono Lake. There are the "Toy" Piutes, dwelling among
the "toy" or tules of Carson Sink; the "Ah-ge-ed-i-ca,"
trout-eating Piutes of Walker River; and other minor distinctions based on food habits or places of residence. There
are designations meaning only the direction from which
the individual came. A Mono Indian coming to Owens
Valley is a "Que-ne-hah-gwat," or a northerner, and one
who goes from northern Owens Valley southward is similarly styled in his new location. An Inyo Piute going into
Mono is a "Pit-ah-nah-gwat," or southerner; one from the
east is a "Se-ve-hah-gwat," easterner; the westerner is
"Pah-na-gwat."

Many names appear in a listing of the western neighbors of the primitive Owens Valleyans. Tularenos appears
to have been a general designation for those from the Tulare region, including the Chunut, Tahche, Kokohiba,
Wechucket, Tuliu, Antumpits, Yokuts, Wik-tshum-ne,
Potwisha, Wokno, Wuksache, and others. The Notonatoes
were on Kings River; the Kaweahs on the stream of that
name, and many more. Bancroft gives the names of more
than two hundred California tribes, with the remark that
in many cases the same people took different names, from
their chiefs, or merely after going to a new locality. Kroeber gives other names, though reducing the number of
tribes, and says that one hundred and four languages or
dialects were spoken in California. The origin of the name
Olancha, borne by a locality at the foot of Owens Lake, is
not known. It cannot be identified by those familiar with
west-side tribal names. The place took its name from a
mining company once operating near there.

The Owens Valley Piute paid little attention to the
confusion of tongues, or of tribal names. He referred to
the Indians west of the mountains politely as Pahnagwat,
or more contemptuously and usually as Diggers.

Kroeber says the Monos referred to themselves as
Nu-mu, meaning "the people." An earlier writer said they
called themselves, and were called, Nut-a-a. A word not

unknown on this slope is Monache, the west-side designation for all on this side of the Sierras.

Kroeber assigns most of the southern and eastern part of Inyo county to the "Kosos" or Panamints. Why "Kosos" is not clear, since the same author includes the "Coso" mountains in their territory. He prefers Koso to Panamint as the tribal name on the ground that the latter may be confused with Vanyume, another tribe. The similarity of name is not sufficient to prevent other writers adopting Panamint.

Coville, visiting the Panamints in 1891, said they then numbered about twenty-five. It has since been stated that the last descendant of the original population, which evolved a subsistence from a barren land where a white man would starve to death, died some years ago. Whether that forbidding region now contains hereditary residents or not, other aboriginal blood was added. Among those who made their homes there were not only commendable citizens, red as well as white, but also those who did not court inquiry into their past before a hasty change of scene.

Note is found in the writings of a French priest, Domenich, who spent seven years among the Indians and wrote in 1860, of a tribe called the Benemes, inhabiting the Mojave desert and some of the territory later southern Inyo. The name also appears in Bancroft's listing. The only information about them is Domenich's observation that " the only prominent trait of these people is a character of great effeminacy. They are very kind to strangers." Accenting "Van-yu-me" and "Ben-e-me" on the last syllables, as is probably proper, indicates that both names refer to the same tribe.

Dr. Kroeber mentions different named subdivisions, all few in numbers, inhabiting the desert ranges. The Inyo Piute recognizes no special distinctions. To him the red inhabitants south and east of Owens Lake, in Saline, Panamint and Death Valleys, and in adjacent mountain ranges, are "Toboni," Shoshone. Indians of Fish Lake Valley, in western Nevada, are both Piutes and Shoshones, and those north of Benton, in Mono county, are Piutes and Monos, those localities being the borderlands wherein the tribes mingle.

Owens Valley Piutes claim to have been the overlords of this region from the dawn of tribal existence until the coming of the whites. Intelligent English-speaking natives say there is no knowledge or tradition of any other people having lived here. They fraternized freely with their neighbors east of the Sierras, regarding them as of equal social status, but seldom mingled with those across the Sierra summits.

Indians say they are decreasing in numbers. Statistics are uncertain, being in some cases mere guesswork, in others incomplete. Von Schmidt in 1855 estimated that Owens Valley contained a population of 1000. When Indian captives were taken to Fort Tejon in 1863, 906 started from Camp Independence, and the military commander said he thought twice as many were left in the valley. It is certain that many outside Indians had come into the valley for the war, and the guess is unreliable. Major H. C. Egbert, reporting in 1870 on the Piutes, estimated the population by localities at 150 in Round Valley, 150 at Bishop Creek, 200 at Big Pine, 400 to 500 at Independence, George's Creek and Lone Pine, 150 at and near Cerro Gordo, 250 in the Coso and other southeastern localities. He questioned an estimate given to him that there were 1500 more in the territory within a three-day ride east and north of the Piute monument.

United States census records give totals as follows for Inyo County: 1870, 311; 1880, 637; 1890, 850; 1900, 940; 1910, 792; 1920, 632; 1932, 736. The 1870 census is valueless even for a poor comparison as the foregoing may be, for the county at that time did not include the area north of Big Pine Creek, in which there was a considerable Indian population, and it did not include the southeastern half of the present county, the southern boundary then running northeasterly to a point about midway of the present eastern line.

The Indians themselves took a count of their people in the vicinity of Bishop, about ten years ago, finding about 400.

During 1930 the Indian Service sought to enroll all Indians eligible as claimants against the national government for recompense under treaties made early in white occupancy of California. A preliminary survey of results showed 970 having Inyo County addresses, with probably some absentees enrolled elsewhere and to be credited to the county in the final checking.

From the several sets of figures and estimates it would seem to be a fair conclusion that Inyo Indians, while not changing greatly in numbers, are probably decreasing slightly.

Dr. Kroeber's "Handbook" says: "When Troy was besieged and Solomon was building the Temple, the native Californian already lived in all essentials like his descendants of to-day"—ignoring white influence, of course. How far this applies to the Indians of Inyo is a point on which proof is lacking; but archaeological discoveries in eastern Nevada, proving aboriginal residence there in remote times, lead to the surmise that the red men were probably nearer the Sierra as well, at a time when the physiographic characteristics of the region were quite different from what they later became, and probably some details of Indian life were also different. This theory finds support in the ancient village sites now wholly unsuited for human habitation.

Owens Valley Piutedom was a very loose sort of confederacy, in which each community was a law unto itself. The population was grouped into communities, in localities substantially corresponding to those now occupied by the whites. Each had its own name, derived from some natural characteristic; for example, a settlement on meadows northwest of the present town of Bishop was "Pah-mah-hah-be-ta," because of a kind of grass found there; one southwest, "Tu-bu-tah-gee," took its name because of the adobe ground on which it stood.

Each community had its own chief, or Po-ko-nah-be. The position was to some extent hereditary, provided the next in line on the chief's death measured up to chieftain-ship qualifications, in the opinion of the elders of the tribe. Decisions were on a rather democratic basis, for momentous questions were usually submitted to a council of the leading men of the camp. The pokonahbe seems to have had authority to choose his counselors. On occasions of special importance, proclamation was made throughout the village calling a "pah-mu-e-tu-ah-te," or general gathering, on the town meeting order. Decisions so reached were absolute.

There was nothing resembling a court. Punishment for offenses rested largely in the hands of the aggrieved parties, and there was little interference with personal vengeance. If an inhabitant of one community trans-gressed against one of another place, the pokonahbe sent a runner to the chief of the offender's village with a state-ment of the facts. Either the pokonahbe or the pahmuetuahte considered the matter, and usually sent word to the injured camp to handle the case to suit itself—which in many instances guaranteed that the offense, if serious, would not be repeated by the same individual.

We are told that there were no wars between the communities; the people were of one blood and substantially the same speech and traditions. When one of the settle-ments foresaw war with another tribe runners were sent to all the pokonahbes. Each chief who thought it was a good war sent an indefinite number of volunteer warriors to take part. They were not warriors, in individual bravery, even though they were feared west of the Sierras. Their military strategy was similar to that of a free lance Civil War leader who believed in "gittin' that fust with the most men." Overwhelming numbers constituted the chief reliance of combatants.

An Indian acquaintance has told the writer of a foray made by the Piutes against the Diggers. His grandfather, who died at a venerable age, told him the story, and as the grandsire was one of the combatants it would seem that this event must have occurred in the earlier half of the last century. A party of Piutes made a big hunting trip, leaving their women and children in camp in northern Owens Valley. A band of Diggers came across the mountains and destroyed the unprotected camp, either killing or carrying off all the helpless occupants. When the hunters returned, they took the trail and found that the marauders had gone westward through Mammoth Pass. Messengers were sent to all the valley villages, and each chief voted that it was a war in which his braves should take part. The enlarged war party again took the trail and followed it to some "big river," doubtless the San Joaquin. The "spyers," as our informant called them, found the Diggers in fancied security in camp. Attack was made at daybreak the next morning, and the murderous band was completely wiped out. Word was craftily sent to others of the offending tribe, and when they came to the scene to gather up their dead they were ambushed and likewise massacred.

CHAPTER V

NATIVE LEGENDS

A PEOPLE WITHOUT A HISTORY—LOCALIZATION OF TALES—PREVA-
LENCE OF THE SUPERNATURAL IN PRIMITIVE LORE—LEGENDS OF
THE CREATION—ACCOUNTING FOR WINNEDUMAH—THERE WERE
GIANTS IN THOSE DAYS

Indian history may be said to be non-existent back of the preceding generation, or the one before it. What the old people experienced and could recall might be known to their children, but within another generation would be certain to become tinged with romance. The simple sons and daughters of nature were prone to read portents and personal meanings in happenings around them, and to see the supernatural in their own experiences. Pope used but simple truth in writing that Lo "sees God in the clouds and hears Him in the wind."

Being without standards of time, they were unable to know their own ages, or to definitely indicate long periods. Their stories of the past are usually dated "a long time ago," even though but two generations back. Details are lost, elaborated, or colored by the incredible. A flood of purely local proportions may become all-enveloping, in narrations of later years. A legendary migration may have had, originally, some actual basis in the movement of a small number of individuals.

Nearly all Indian legends appear to have their scenes in the vicinity of the tribes that tell them. The world of each people was limited by its own horizon. This is well illustrated by the statement, from some source not now recalled, that when Indians from Yosemite first crossed the Sierras and found other red men at Mono Lake they were greatly surprised, for they had believed themselves and their neighbors west of the range to be the only living people.

The supernatural prevails in practically all Indian tradition. The native found it easy to ignore laws of nature when it became preferable to improve his tale. The story teller had plenty of time, and when he had the center of the stage he made the privilege last. Consequently a great amount of detail was woven into each narration. For example, "The Dove's Romance," given in this chapter, filled three newspaper columns in the form in which it was written for the author by Harry Cornwell. That length was after Cornwell had, as he wrote, "condensed it to a practical story. It was often told in details, taking several evenings to end the story." Bearing this in mind, the reader may be willing to forgive the Anglo-Saxon directness with which some of the tales have been here summarized.

In the more definite tribal life of long ago, there were undoubtedly special individuals who entertained at the campfires with oft-repeated tales of "the brave days of old," when there were giants and when each created being had power to assume such other form as might best suit the immediate purpose. But such occasions have faded, since civilization has provided so many counter attractions. One can imagine the youthful Piute of to-day remarking in English to a comrade: "What's the use of listening to all that hooey? Let's go to a picture show." We were told last year that only two Indians in the northern end of Owens Valley now know the old stories; one of those has died since.

Probably legends transcribed half a century ago are more authentic, if such a term can be used—nearer to being genuine antiques, we might say—than those learned to-day. Indian narrators may act on the urge to improve their stories, and by the time white people have taken their turns at embellishment the finished product is far from agreement with the original version. In a known instance, an enthusiastic gatherer of legends made many notes of fantastic tales told by Piute women who consented to talk freely. After his departure, the Scheherazades fairly rolled about in merriment, as much as to say: "He wanted stories; we gave them to him."

Bearing this in mind, the legends which follow are not offered with guarantees of antiquity, further than that they have been derived from sources believed to be dependable and are believed to correctly represent the native trend of legendary thought, less many details omitted for the sake of brevity.

Occasionally a myth is secured at first hand from a native source with some degree of presumed reliability. Such an instance is one of several Piute versions of the Creation, told by an Indian to D. L. Maxwell, then of the Indian Service, and by him recorded thus:

THE CREATION

"The word Piute signifies 'people who come and go in boats. These people originally lived along the shores of Lake Lahontan. Their descendants now live near the mountain lakes of eastern California and Nevada.

"According to their legends, at the beginning the world was all water. At that time the Great Wolf God, the God of Creation, with the assistance of his little brother or son, the coyote, planted the rock seeds in the great water, and from them the rocks and land grew. The rock plants were helped in their growth, and cared for while growing, by the Pot-sa-gah-wahs. The Pot-sa-ga-wahs were the ministering spirits of the wolf god, and were supposed to have the form and physique of a beautiful child about ten years old. They could walk about on land, but lived and hid themselves from human eyes in the water, where their movements were rapid—almost instantaneous."

(Any one who is critical of this legend because of the introduction of human beings at this stage is requested, before he comments on the Indian story, to inform us where Cain got his wife.)

"When the earth became habitable, the first man to be created was Hy-nan-nu. His mother was a winged creature, a spirit or bird, perhaps Hai-wee, the dove.

"The Piutes were created from the rocks. A particular rock which is far up on one of the creeks west of Owens

Valley, and having a resemblance to a human form, was
the mother rock.

"After the Piutes had become numerous in Owens
Valley, Hy-nan-nu came from the southeast to teach them
better modes of living. He was not a Piute, but came from
some other tribe, and remained here for many years. He
was not only their Adam but also their Moses, writing laws
for them on tables of stone. They believe the picture
writings on the rocks of this valley are the work of his
hands. They were at one time able to read those writings,
but that art has long been lost. They have legends telling
what each of the different writings signify.

"Hy-nan-nu was also their Methusalah, Enoch,
Solomon and Samson. They have legends which tell of his
feats of strength and daring. He is to them more than that,
for they say of him as was said of the humble Galilean,
'He went about doing good.'

"Hy-nan-nu taught the Piutes to be happy; not to
worry or be concerned about this world's goods. He would
sometimes break a basket in the maker's hands or dig up
the growing taboose in order to teach them that work was
not of so much importance as a happy disposition. So work
took a secondary place in the minds of the Piute fore-
fathers.

"He was one day walking through Long Valley when
he saw several Pot-sa-gah-wahs who had left the waters of
Owens River and were walking on the side of the mountain.
He desired to catch them, and being between them and the
river he chased these little creatures far up the mountain
and was about to take them when the Wolf God sent water
up into the mountains to save their lives. A lake was
created for their benefit; they plunged into it and were
safe.

"The lake which originated on that memorable
occasion is now rudely called Convict Lake, instead of its
Piute name Wit-so-nah-pah, which means 'spring up,' or
perhaps 'spring up to save life.'

"The writing on a rock near Rock Creek in Round
Valley is the story of a little child and how it was taken by

the Pot-sa-gah-wahs into the spirit world and became a
Pot-sa-gah-wah. Hy-nan-nu taught that people might be
changed at death into those little beings. The qualities
essential to winning that reward are strength and bravery.
There must be no fears for the future—and here the idea
of trust and faith becomes part of their religion.

> " 'That in even savage bosoms
> There are longings, yearnings, strivings,
> For the good they comprehend not;
> That the feeble hand and helpless,
> Groping blindly in the darkness,
> Touches God's right hand in that darkness
> And is lifted up and strengthened.'

"Hy-nan-nu, while teaching in Inyo County, was always
looking for his mother, whom he had never seen or had but
glimpsed. Having finished his work here, and being sure
his mother was not in this valley, he one day walked up
Bishop Creek and passed over the mountains, to renew his
work with the people he might find there and to continue
the search for his mother.

"Thus according to Piute traditions was created the
earth and things that dwell therein."

Harry Cornwell records another northern Owens
Valley legend of the Creation as follows:

"Ow-wah-ne is the Indian name for Mt. Tom. It has
no special meaning other than to denote this noble
mountain.

"Long, long ago, on the peak of Ow-wah-ne (old Mt.
Tom) many beings lived on a pah-to-o-vo (island) when
this country (yo-ko-o-bu, general name for a region) was
under water (pah-ya). For a period of time these beings
pleaded with Nature (tu-vah-buk) for land, and in their
efforts dived in the depths of the eastern surrounding
water to find soil (tu-ve-e-pu). All kinds of waterfowls
(pu-yu) attempted to reach bottom, except one who is
known as the Helldiver, who took no interest in what was
going on. The coyote (e-sha), distrusted and hated by
most every one, was taking an active part in the diving. He
would plunge into the water and bring up a grain or two
of sand and offer it as proof that he had dived to the bot-

tom, while there was no doubt he had placed it under his fingernails before making the plunge.

"After every other being had tried, they called on the Helldiver. He told them it was impossible to reach bottom but he would try, so he plunged into the deep blue water and stayed under longer than any one else who had tried. When he came up he assured them it was no use to try; but others pleaded with him to try again, so he did. This time, after drawing a deep breath, he was gone for a long time, and the crowd felt sure he would come up with some evidence. At last the little Helldiver popped up, about worn out. After he had rested, he told his hopeless story and refused to dive any more, stating that there was danger of drowning. After several days of coaxing by his friends and others the Helldiver promised to make his last dive (pah-ku-we-e) at dawn the following day.

"When light began to break in the east (se-e-va), beings (nu-mu) gathered to witness the dive. As the morning star (ta-vah-ha-a) peeped over the horizon, the Helldiver stood facing in that direction over the silvery water, pleading with Nature for strength and endurance. Then he relaxed to draw several deep breaths to fill every cell in his lungs. Each time Pu-yu, the Helldiver, drew a deep breath, E-sha the coyote, even though resentful, would coax "A little deeper, a little deeper, deeper, deeper." When the morning star ascended high into the sky, the Helldiver plunged easterly and straight into the deep water.

"While the crowd waited patiently, the sun (tah-va-lu-lu) came up salmon colored, and painting the water's surface and horizon in tones ranging from golden pink to deep salmon, soon changed the water to dancing crystals.

"It was near noon when the anxious crowd concluded that the Helldiver had drowned. The coyote cried and sang funeral songs; they carried on a regular funeral ceremony. Suddenly the diver came to the top and made his way to shore. He offered a handful of fertile soil, and distributed it over the great water a little at a time, as if sowing grain. Soon the water began to lower. Islands and valleys here and there popped up as water pooled into lakes (pah-che-at-ta), rivers (pah-tah) and creeks (pah-ya-hu).

"The mountains (tah-ya-ve-e) and the whole country seemed to turn green over night; so vegetation grew. Man and beast lived; sun shone and water ran. The land will remain until some day nature will once more fill this country with water and destroy every living kind. Then when the water goes away again we will see new country, and there we will meet our relatives who have died long, long ago, and we will know them as we know each other.

"So distinct in the memory of the aged Piutes is this legend of old Ow-wah-ne (Mt. Tom) and their loved soil of Owens Valley that they really believe this country will some day be flooded with water."

TA-NA-DO-WA-MU-LUP

This legend, the title of which means "Our Birthplace," is another transcribed by Cromwell:

"On the north bench of Wa-ko-o-hu (Pine Creek) Canyon To-ve-e-e (our mother) gave birth to her do-wa-mu (children). Shortly after, E-sha, the coyote, was instructed to go down the canyon and bring up some water and to hurry back with it, while the mother stayed with her children.

"E-sha found a good place to skate (se-e-ko-e) on the ice (pah-tu-ah-zu-pu). After he had tired himself (se-e-ko-e-ne) skating, up the canyon he went. When he reached the bench he found all the children were departing; some walked and some flew. He excitedly called them to come back, but none returned. Then he hunched down by the side of the weeping mother.

"The prettiest of the children went que-we (north), the next prettiest went se-e-ve (east), pah-me (west) and pe-ta (south), and the ugliest remained. So the Owens Valley Piutes were to be the ugliest of the tribe.

"Near the mouth of Pine Creek Canyon is the mother of our tribe, a boulder about three feet high, facing south across the canyon. Another peaked rock site to the rear and to the left, and the small bedding of pebbles form the bed in which our tribe was born."

Hon. Guy C. Earl, of Oakland, California, spent part of his boyhood in Owens Valley, and in that period fellowshipped with Indian youths to such extent that he learned how to speak their language fluently, and heard many of their campfire tales. Many years later he returned to the valley for the special purpose of recording such legends as he could obtain. He has a notable collection of myths, and those credited to that source are used herein by his kind permission. All his recordings are tales told by the Indians south of Black Rocks, in the middle of the valley; and here again we note the constant localization. He notes a Creation version differing from the preceding, thus:

"Long ago there was no land; there was nothing but water. The coyote and the tiger were brothers, and had lived forever. The coyote said to the tiger: 'We need land. There is too much water. Let us make land, so we can go about on the earth.' But the tiger said: 'There is the vast sky full of air through which you can go anywhere. Why not fly?' So the coyote flew one whole day throughout the heavens, and on returning to the tiger said: 'Flying is not enough. There is no place to alight, and we must have land with its plains and valleys, its hills and mountains and streams, with grass and plants and trees and animals.' The tiger replied: 'All right; we will make land in the morning.'

"The tiger had in each ear an earring of cane, about three inches long and a quarter of an inch thick. The next morning he removed one of the earrings and blew upon it, and then holding it over his palm he shook out its contents in the form of dirt and threw it into the water. The dirt itself immediately created other dirt. The coyote urged the tiger to keep on, and asked him to throw the dirt to the east all the time and leave water to the west. By night the land was made, leaving the great sea to the west.

"From the waters and muds and slimes came all grasses, plants and trees, vegetables of all kinds, and all creatures but man.

"After their creation many of the animals went down to Coso Springs, the land of mystery. There the tiger and coyote saw and talked with two captains who had no bodies and were not flesh and bone, but just evil spirits. The two captains then made a great round pit, very deep, with a great fire at its bottom, and two men and two women sitting beside the fire.

"But the two captains seized one of the men and one of the women and threw them into the fire and burned them up. This made the coyote so angry that he declared he would burn up the sun. Though the other animals protested that if he did there would be no warmth and they would all die, he pulled down the sun and burned it in the fire in the pit. So there was no sun for a whole year, only darkness and cold everywhere, and great suffering, and the coyote ran about crying in the dark.

"At the end of the year the duck said to the coyote: 'You have made trouble enough, but if you will let me alone and just listen I will call back the sun.' Accordingly the duck quacked for a long time, and suddenly the sun appeared, and all were happy, at the light and the warmth and the knowledge that they would again have grass and wild fruits and berries and taboose for food.

"The tiger took the form of a duck, and taking with him two big red frogs went back to Coso Springs, where there are still deposits of red moist earth. Out of it he fashioned two beautiful red images, one a man and one a woman, and the Great Spirit made them to live. They were the first Indians and the first human beings, and from them all men have come."

Still another Creation legend is from the western Nevada branches of the same tribal stock:

"At first the world was all water and remained so for a long time. Then the water began to go down, and at last Ku-rang-wa (Mt. Grant) came up from the water, near the southwest end of Walker Lake. There was fire on its top, and when the wind blew hard the water dashed over the fire and would have extinguished it, but for the sage-hen nestling over it and fanning away the water with its wings. The heat scorched the feathers of the sagehen's breast, and they remain black to this day. Afterward the Piutes got their first fire from the mountain with the help of the rabbit." (Most Indian legends of the preservation of fire credit it to the coyote.)

"As the water subsided other mountains appeared, until at last the earth was left as it now is. Then the great ancestor of the Piutes came from the south past Kurangwa, upon which his footprints can still be seen, and made his home in the region of Carson Sink. A woman followed him; she became his wife. They dressed themselves in skins and lived on the meat of deer and mountain sheep. They had children, two boys and two girls. The father made bows and arrows for the boys, and the mother taught the girls how to dig roots.

"When the children grew up each boy married a sister, but the new families quarreled until the father commanded them to separate. One family went south and became fish-eaters, the Piutes of Walker Lake, and the others went north and became buffalo-eaters, the Bannocks. After the children had left them the parents went into the mountains and from there into the sky."

With the legends of the Creation may be placed one explaining the origin of fish and pine nuts:

A mountain rocked violently, and a mighty rift appeared in its side. As a dazzling light shone, a gigantic Indian, dressed in buckskin and decorated with beads and feathers, stepped forth. He fired an arrow at the hillside, and on the slope arose many trees laden with pine nuts. A shaft was shot into the water, and the stream swarmed with fish. He pointed to the mountain, and the awe-stricken natives followed his direction and found a cave floored with silver.

HY-NAN-NU

Hy-nan-nu, or Hi-nan-no as a young Mono Indian wrote the name, appears to have been quite a figure in legendary lore, for he appears in another narration which the Indian himself wrote out and is here briefed:

Once there lived two orphan boys; the younger, Hy-nan-nu, was so small that he was yet in his basket cradle. The older brother carried him when he went hunting for deer and quail. The infant grew fast, and the older boy built a tight wigwam in which to keep him. One day Hy-nan-nu got out and went to the end of the world, where he found many smooth rocks. He returned, and the brother bade him go and bring some of the rocks from the end of the world. The brother made a bow of wood and arrows from the rocks, and Hy-nan-nu used the weapons with which to kill a bear. The next day he saw his grandmothers and tried to shoot them; when they fled into their wigwams he smashed their baskets. When they came out again and saw his mischief they pursued, and waylaid and killed him. The brother knew what had happened, and on coming to where the boy's body was he struck it with a stick. Hy-nan-nu thereupon jumped up, good as new, and with his bow and arrows slew his grandmothers. They came to life, and the brother told him to go back, and he again found them. He broke their new baskets again, and when they pursued he jumped into "a cave twisted up in the air." When they tired and went home, our young hero emerged and killed them again.

Then the brother took him to see his grandfathers, the bears. The bears were pulling down the tops of pine trees, and then by holding on as the tops sprang back they were thrown high into the air. Hy-nan-nu wanted such a ride, but he could not sing so as to protect himself, and he came down changed into a rock. The brother made him alive again. Hy-nan-nu induced the bears to be shot into the air from the tree, and they became rocks as they fell. Soon the rocks again changed to bears, who chased Hy-nan-nu and caught and killed him, leaving only a small drop of blood under the leaves. The brother again restored Hy-nan-nu, who forthwith killed the bears.

The brother asked him to go and see his grandmothers, who were now tiny creatures in the water. On the shore of a lake he found a tiny woman, who seized his hand and tried to pull him into the water. He grasped a pine tree, but the woman's pulling took it out by the roots. He escaped with the loss of his finger nails. The lake began to rise up to the tops of the trees. He ran up the mountain, but the water followed. His brother told him to throw a rock into the hole in the air. As Hy-nan-nu threw the rock he caught hold of it and was drawn upward. The water continued to rise, and fell on him through the hole in the air; finally, beaten, it went down.

When night came the brother built a fire, on which he put a deer. When they looked again the deer was gone. One after another they killed all the deer and put them on the fire, and one after another the deer went under the fire and disappeared. They took a great stick and moved all the deer from under the fire. Out came a great man who chased them all over the world until they fell down dead. Then they went to the happy hunting ground.

Hy-nan-nu figures in a legend of the Western Monos, somewhat corresponding to the foregoing. Cornwell states that there are several Hy-nan-nu legends, forming a continuous narrative of the doings of the mythical character in his progress through the country. One of his stories also pertains to Convict Lake, the Indian name of which he spells Wu-cho-nah-pah, meaning "water in the dent."

Hy-nan-nu and his brother started from southern Owens Valley northward to take revenge on a tribe which had killed their mother when Hy-nan-nu was a baby in his basket. In Long Valley the brother warned Hy-nan-nu about Wu-cho-nah-pah, u-u-pah-ya, dangerous water, or su-ta-pah-ya, bad water. Hy-nan-nu wanted to see it, and promised that he would only peer from the top of the high peak.

Hy-nan-nu climbed the mountain and barely showed his eyes as he peered over at the calm water. He could see no difference between it and other water, so he said to himself: "Hah-tee-you cow-hoo su-e-na-we-ne me-he-u-ne-te evah-ve-oo su-ta pah-ya, too-we-pu-wa-oo du-ah, pah-ya che-e." (My brother is crazy, this water would hurt no one.) He yelled at the top of his voice, sending an echo far across the mountains.

When he yelled his second challenge the water began to rise. Hy-nan-nu continued his challenging yells. The water formed a huge wave and rushed up the height. Hy-nan-nu leaped to the opposite peak, where the water again pursued. He was driven from peak to peak until he leaped through the ceiling in the sky. He peered through the opening and saw that Wu-cho-nah-pah had subsided. Returning to earth he again taunted the lake, boasting of his cleverness. This time the water wasted no time, but caught and devoured him just as he was entering the ceiling of the sky.

The brother felt sure that disaster had come to Hy-nan-nu, so he sought the top of a peak and peered over, finding the pah-che-ah-ta (lake) quiet and calm. But he saw a pah-o-hah (water baby) in the water, so he carefully aimed an arrow and killed the pah-o-hah. When the pah-o-hah's body had floated to shore, he found bits of flesh in its teeth. From these he revived Hy-nan-nu, who remarked that he must have fallen asleep. They went on their journey.

Now Wu-cho-nah-pa is no longer su-ya (bad water). Hy-nan-nu is said to be the little whirlwinds that dash over the snow-covered Sierras during the winter and on the sunny sides of the foothills and canyons during the summer. He is said to be cold in summer and warm in winter, and he is watching the people who ascend the high mountains.

The legend, says Cornwell, has been told from time immemorial among the Piute people. He states that each of the legends he gives has been told to him by different persons and is a genuine part of the tribe's lore.

The Western Monos (those west of the Sierras) have a somewhat similar legend of Hy-nan-nu, in which it is explained that the grandmothers with whom he had so much trouble were the winds.

Tribal legends seem to be as varied as tales of the Thousand and One Nights; there is one, however, that is common, in general outline, to many tribes. That is of a flood which covered all the land except some very elevated point. Each tribal narrative selects the highest elevation in its own vicinity. As already noted, the western Nevadans designate Mt. Grant, near Walker Lake. In southern Owens Valley, Olancha Peak was chosen, the legend alleging that it was then higher than any other in the Sierras. Northern Owens Valley Indians name Mt. Tom. The story is that all living creatures took refuge on the mountain. In the Olancha instance, neither cattle nor horses were included among the refugees, and from this Senator Earl, whose collection includes this legend, concludes that the myth has been handed down from days before Europeans arrived in America. In due time the waters disappeared and the world was as it had been before.

Among the many myths collected by the author few account for general physical features of the country. Indians west of the Sierra crest explain the Sierra by an order from the Great Spirit that made them pile up all the earth to make the mountains, clear to the top of Mt. Whitney. They have never fully recovered from the weariness caused by performing this task.

On this slope there lived an enormous giant, whose home was at Black Rocks, according to a legend in the Earl collection. He could be seen for many miles. Indians who refused to do his bidding were killed. They built the Alabama Hills at his command. One day the giant stepped into an old crater and fell to the bottom. The crater began to erupt, and the cinders of his body are still to be seen around its base.

Another giant there imposed on the natives until they resolved on his death. His home was under a great rock. A potent medicine man went there and chanted a magic formula at each of the rock's four corners, whereupon the rock split and enabled the medicine man to make his way inside. He cut off the giant's head. The monster's blood turned pale, and it was as plentiful as the rain in the clouds or the water in the ocean. It still gushes forth from beneath the stone, forming Black Rock Spring.

Other constant menaces to the Indians were a giant and giantess whose only weapons were their long tongues, with which they licked up the natives. Determined to rid themselves of the scourge, the Indians attacked the creatures. With their obsidian hatchets they cut off the man's tongue. When it came to removing the woman's tongue the Indian women refused to help, and some of them even went to her assistance. While the warriors finally succeeded in severing the too-active member, some of its power passed on to the Indian women, who (the story says) still have long and mischievous tongues.

WINNEDUMAH

One of the most striking landmarks visible from Owens Valley is called Winnedumah, or the Piute Monument. As described by Geologist W. A. Goodyear, it has "an irregular trapezoidal base, 52 feet in length, southwest end 45 feet, north end 12 feet, angles and sides irregularly rounded and smooth; summit inaccessible; about 80 feet high; a solid block of weather worn and storm-beaten granite." Located on the exact skyline, centrally in a long relatively smooth dip of the range east of Independence, it has the appearance of a slender heaven-pointing finger. One would expect it to figure in Piute legends, as it does in at least three.

One of these, to which first place is given because it was written out as long ago as 1874, runs thus:

"Long, long ago" the great medicine man of the Piutes was Winnedumah, brother of Tinnemaha, war chief of his people. The principal stronghold was in the Black Rocks, a great field of tumbled lava in middle Owens Valley.

One day hordes of Diggers poured across the passes of Pahbatoya, the Sierra, to raid the Piute hunting grounds. The owners resented the trespass, and then began a battle such as no Piute has since witnessed. It lasted through days of the fiercest fighting. At last the Piutes were beaten and forced to flee. Many found refuge in the caves and recesses of the Black Rocks—which same cavities to this day may be viewed by whoever may doubt this tale. Others fled across the rugged mountains to the eastward. Among the fugitives was Winnedumah, whose medicine had been useless against the invaders. Sorely pressed, exhausted and alone he gained the summit, where he stopped for a final view of the domain which he deemed lost, and to await the coming of his warrior brother. But Tinnemaha had fallen in the fray; and while Winnedumah invoked the aid of the Great Spirit for his stricken people, a great convulsion of nature came, and one of its effects was to transform him into a pillar of stone. The same natural manifestation so frightened the Diggers that they forthwith went back across the mountains, never again to dispute the ownership of Owens Valley. There to-day stands Winnedumah, faithful to the end of time.

Two Winnedumah legends are found in the Earl collection. One of these, now inscribed on a brass plate in the lobby of the Winnedumah hotel at Independence, is substantially as follows:

Long ago there lived in what the white man calls the Owens River Valley two tribes; one, the Piutes, occupied the Inyo Range; the other, the Waucobas, the western side and the slopes of the Sierras, and in particular the region around Mt. Williamson and extending westward to the valley now called San Joaquin.

The roaring ocean backed up the waters and flooded the wonderful valley, so that the Indians had to signal to each other by fires.

The tribes were at war. One day, from a lookout on Mt. Williamson, a Waucoba brave spied twin Piute brothers ascending to the crest of the Inyo Range. He set to the sinewy string of his mighty bow an arrow made from a tree growing only in the western mountains. The arrow, released from the twanging bow, winged its way fifteen miles across the valley and pierced the body of one of the Piutes, who fell dead, his body turning to stone, and lying face downward across the crest, head to the east, feet to the west. Terrified, his brother started to run, but the Waucoba warrior, in a voice of thunder, shouted the command: "Winnedumah!" which means "stay where you are." Lo, the Piute instantly became the granite shaft, and still stands there awaiting release by the Great Spirit.

Marvelous to tell, the fatal arrow took root in the stone body of the slain victim and grew into a tree of its own kind, the only one in that range of mountains.

This, also from the Earl collection, is the third story of the occurrence:

The Shoshone Indians occupied Saline Valley and the region east of the Inyo Range, and the Piutes the Owens River Valley. The Shoshone chief had a very beautiful daughter, and the Piute leader had a wonderful son. These two met and fell in love, and asked their parents' permission to wed. Neither father would consent; in fact each felt himself insulted at the suggestion, having only contempt for the offspring of the other chief. The matter led to war, and a battle lasting a day and a night occurred at the boundary summit. While this was going on, the young people saw a happier solution, and ran away. When the warrior chiefs heard the news, the tall and splendidly formed Piute leader was instantly changed into the upright granite shaft, while the less stately Shoshone became a smaller stone which stands near by.

THE DOVE'S ROMANCE
(Transcribed by Harry Cornwell)

Among the people at the Creation was Haiwee, the most charming young lady in all the land. She was dressed in a soft gray gown, and we now call her the dove. There were also E-sha, the cunning and tricky coyote, who was a doctor in general practice. His principal rival was Que-da-goy-goy, the magpie. Another little old man, in bright green and blue, named So-ah-hi, we call the humming bird. Near the lake lived an old hermit, the mudhen, with unbelievable healing powers.

Esha tried to meet Haiwee, who avoided him. When a chance came he offered her everything, even a pearl necklace, a most valued possession because it guaranteed ownership to the owner's descendants. Dove declined his gifts.

By chance, while hunting, Esha saw Quedagoygoy place a bronze-blue necklace around Haiwee's neck, in token of their marriage. Enraged, he later sought the campfire, with arrows dipped in rattlesnake venom. He drew his arrow on one whom he took to be Quedagoygoy, but as the eagle and the sagehen interrupted his deed he saw that he had aimed at the crow.

The next day he sought the dove, who asked him for a knife to remove a sliver from her finger. He gave her a poisoned arrow instead. She became ill, and Coyote was called to doctor her. She got worse, and Coyote blamed Rattlesnake for her condition. Then Humming Bird was called in, and blamed Coyote. Coyote decided that he didn't want Dove to die, so he went after Mudhen. But Mudhen knew he was coming, and filled his tepee with so dense a smoke that when Coyote plunged in he was almost suffocated. Mudhen refused to go unless Coyote would give up the precious pearl. At last Coyote agreed to give the pearl if Dove were saved. Under Mudhen's ministrations she recovered.

Coyote was blamed for her illness, but denied his guilt. He challenged Magpie to a test of marksmanship, the winner to take Dove as his bride. The crowd objected, but Magpie was willing, and gave Coyote the pick of his arrows. Coyote shot at the mark and missed, then claimed that he had slipped and it was not a fair test. Magpie magnanimously gave him two more arrows, taking only one himself. Coyote shot again, almost piercing the center of the mark. Magpie shot, striking the center exactly. Magpie again gave Coyote a chance, leaving it to Dove to make her choice. Magpie was chosen.

Then came a great change, and every one except Coyote, who was despised by all, was permitted to choose his way of living. Mudhen announced that he would always bear the pearl on his bill, in token of Coyote's disgrace. The glossy necklace is still to be seen on Dove's neck.

OTHER TALES

Man made friends with some of the animals in this wise: A dog had a bear at bay. While Bruin sat on his haunches waiting for an opportunity to slap the dog into oblivion, the first man sneaked up behind the bear and killed it with a club. He skinned the bear with his strong fingers, and as he ate he threw portions of the meat to the dog, establishing a lasting friendship. A little later the first woman appeared, and while she was eating flesh from the bear the cat joined the party. She fed it, which accounts for the intimacy between women and cats ever since. When the dog saw the woman feeding the cat he became jealous and tried to drive pussy away. The woman protected the cat, and dog and cat established a lasting enmity.

Basketry was acquired by the Indians thus: From the union of a bird and a rattlesnake was born a beautiful Indian girl, and also two brothers, Hainolu and Popnaquz. The girl could fly everywhere, and as she did so she sketched on the rocks the form and method of making baskets. After she had thoroughly taught the Indians how to make and decorate baskets, the older brother turned into a snake and the younger into a bird, and carried away their sister, who was never seen again. The wavy or snaky lines and the designs of birds or feathers on baskets commemorate their learning the art.

WHY PO-HA-VE-CHE HAS A SHORT TAIL

(As written by Cornwell)

One day Pohaveche, the bear, met E-sha, the coyote, and saw that E-she had many pah-ga-we (fish). Pohaveche asked: "How did you catch them?" E-she said: "That's easy; I'll tell you how you can catch some. Go down to the river and find a still pool and stick your qua-che-e (tail) deep down into the water; and when you feel something biting you jump and pull it out. That's how I caught these."

Pohaveche hurried to the river and found a still pool. Then he put his tail into the water and sat very still. While waiting for a bite he fell asleep. When he was suddenly awakened by something biting his tail he thought he had a fish and made a long leap. When he looked back to see what he had caught he found that his tail had frozen off in the ice. So the bear has a short tail.

Not to further tax the endurance of the indulgent reader, this chapter will close with a tale which has some possibility of foundation. It was told by a Mono Indian, and was also known to Owens Valley Indians to whom it was mentioned. It is of a winter so severe that it virtually wiped out the population.

"Long time ago, my grandfather—him grandfather—him grandfather—him grandfather" and so on for many generations, this devastating winter came. Deep fell the snow, and continued to fall until the whole region bordering the eastern Sierra was under a covering that did not melt away until midsummer. All animal life was killed off, or sought pleasanter climes. The natives, banded together at the warm springs, were without food. In this extremity the aged of the tribe sought their own deaths, that the younger ones might thereby be able to eat and live. It was long after that, the narrator said, before there were any number of Indians in the region, for those who had survived the trials went away.

CHAPTER VI

HOME LIFE AND CUSTOMS

VOCABULARY LIMITED—FEW MANUFACTURES—BASKETWORK—IRRI-
GATION WITHOUT AGRICULTURE—OMNIVOROUS MENUS—VILLAGES
—SOCIAL OCCASIONS—A PEOPLE MOVING TOWARD THE LIGHT

The Piute vocabulary, like that of most tribes, is limited. A vocabulary of some 600 words has been compiled, but is obviously incomplete, as some common articles or actions are not indicated in it. Some words must be of recent coinage, since they designate objects wholly unknown in primitive days; such are "nah-bo-vo-no," scissors; "tah-be-dwa," clock; "pe-po-ne-ve," book; "tu-ze-pu-nu-he-nu," key. Some are adaptations of English, such as "dah-dah-ah," dollar; "co-so-wy-geen," firewagon, or railroad train, a combination of "co-so," Piute for fire, and the English wagon. The Indian tongue does not readily handle the "ag" sound, as in flag, hence the "wy-geen."

Dr. Kroeber's "Handbook of the Indians of California" asserts that the several sounds given to each vowel in our speech makes phonetic writing of Indian words impossible, and that several hundred diacritical marks would be required to meet the needs of all the California languages. There are quirks in Indian pronunciation that cannot be indicated by common letters; for example, some words end with an abrupt stop in a half-spoken guttural syllable. "Nin-nih," white man—perhaps not always a poor designation— is pronounced as "nin-nick" choked off without voicing the final ck. Assent, or yes, is expressed by a guttural "huh-huh."

There are fewer vowel sounds in Piute than in English. "Hai-wee," dove, is the only instance in the author's list in which the long sound of a is found; that letter is almost without exception as ah. E has the long sound; seldom the one in set. O is always long. U is equivalent to oo; when used otherwise it can be correctly indicated only by preceding it with e as a separate syllable. The white man's guess at indicating Indian vocalization produces some remarkable spelling, arbitrary and variable.

Many words given as such appear to be really phrases. Bad is "kah-du-u-tsa-u-du," "kah-du" being no or not and "tsa-u-du" good. Weak is "kah-du-u-tso-no-du-gwa-te," not strong. This construction accounts for words of seven or more syllables.

The sounds of f, l and r are difficult to the untaught native; "flour" to them is "pnowa."

Wickiup, campoodie, tepee, pappoose, mahala, familiar to readers of Indian stories, are words unknown to the Piute except as he has learned them from the whites. His house is a to-ne, e-no-vi (home) or if of importance a moo-za. His children are tu-ah-mu-be, a general term, or nah-tse-e, boy, or tse-u-u, girl. His women are he-u-pe, generically; su-zu or su-ah-du-mah, young woman, or he-u-ve-che-e, old woman.

Col. Geo. W. Stewart, for half a century a resident of Visalia, California, kindly supplied information about the Indian speech of that part of the State for comparison with the Owens Valleyans. Similarity of the languages of the Piutes and the Wuksaches, of Tulare County, supports his belief that the latter people were once a subtribe of the Piutes, taking their separate name from their most noted chief. Inyo Piutes visiting the Wuksaches have little difficulty in understanding their talk. The closeness of the two languages, or dialects, is shown in this list:

	Piute	*Wuksache*
One	Se-mah	Se-mah
Two	Wah-he	Wah-he
Three	Pah-he	Pah-hil
Four	Wah-tse-gwe	Wat-sin-gwe
Five	Nah-nah-ge	Nah-nah-ge
Six	Nah-ve-te	Nah-fe
Seven	Ta-tsu	Ta-tsu-e
Eight	Wo-se-we	Wo-sin

	Piute	*Wuksache*
Nine	Kwa-nu-ke	Kwa-nik
Ten	Se-wan-ne	Se-wan-ne
Eagle	Quing-ah	Quing-ah
Pine	Wau-ko-be	Wo-ko-be
Mortar (stone)	Pah-hah	Pah-hah
Woman	He-u-pe	He-e-pe
Coyote	E-sha	E-sh-wich
Fire	Co-so	Cos
Swim	Na-ba-ke-ya	Na-ba-ke-ya
Dove	Hai-wee	Hai-wee
Man	Na-na	Na-na
Drink	He-be	He-be
Come	Ke-ma	Ke-ma
Sick	Kah-maht	Kah-nah-te
Hot	U-du-wit	U-du-wit
Small basket	Ah-po	Ah-po
Star	Tah-che-nu-pi	Tah-che-nop
Acorn	We-ah	We-ah
Snow	Ne-vah-be	Ne-vah-be
Willow	Su-he-be	Su-he-be

There are, however, many meanings for which the words of the two languages are not similar in the least. It is probable that if the same person were to transcribe both languages the similarities would be more pronounced. The difficulty of indicating whether the sound is to be written b or v is puzzling—in fact the Piutes seem to use those sounds interchangeably in many cases. Col. Stewart wrote his vocabulary with the use of the Spanish i to indicate the long sound of e; the liberty of changing it to e has been taken here.

There was no system of family names, except that given names were often carried from one generation to another, the child being called as had been some progenitor or other relative. Some names were arbitrary and meaningless; others were taken from colors or natural objects, for example "Ohiono," yellowish; "Wongata," striped, and so on. For some reason, superstitious or otherwise, the Piutes are most reticent about stating their tribal names. Almost without exception, they now bear the names of white people, though retaining the native designations among themselves to a considerable extent.

The elders use their own language in addressing one another, but younger tribal members commonly use English, and in some of the families the children habitually employ white men's talk except when speaking to the aged.

There was no established week or other time period beyond the day, and no means of designating an exact time far in the future or the past. For immediate needs, the Indian designated a day since or preceding a known event by numbering it so many suns or so many moons from that time; but one of them says they did not count the winters or other seasons enough to know their ages in years.

Pottery making is not an attainment of what may be called the present age, nor do their traditions run back to a time when there was knowledge of that art. Some specimens have been found, nevertheless, tending to show that their distant forbears had some such rudimentary knowledge of the kind, or else acquired specimens of pottery from other peoples. Such potsherds show that plastic clay was rolled into a continuous string and coiled into the desired shape, and baked. Specimens recently found indicate Saline Valley to have been the last habitat of the pottery makers.

Manufactures were crude and simple, pertaining only to the chase, to war, or to the no less serious question of obtaining subsistence. Though they knew of gold deposits, the metal did not mean even ornamentation to them. Rough beads were sometimes worked out of soft stone.

The bow and arrow formed the chief weapon. The best bows were made of tough wood, mountain mahogany seldom or oak frequently being used. These, seldom over three feet long, were steamed and bent into an arc with reverse end curves. The strip was backed with sinew from deer, fastened with glue. Other bows were simple arcs, five to six feet long. Arrows were made of a species of cane, of the straight-growing arrowweed, or of willow. Arrow material was cut before fully mature. Bends were straightened by holding the slender rod in contact with a groove in a heated stone. Many examples of such stones are found in collections of Indian relics, and in old graves. While Piutes tell us they sometimes had arrow heads of flint, the material was undoubtedly obsidian. Such arrows were chiefly for war use; for hunting, the point was commonly made from the tough root of the sagebrush, scraped to a dull point. Writers on Indian customs have told how obsidian heads were shaped by being heated, then subjected to the dropping of cold water so as to chip away the stone. Others may have followed that method; the Piute plan was different. The maker chose a fragment of obsidian approximating the desired shape and size. This fragment was held in one hand, which was protected by a buckskin covering; then a sharp bit of bone was used to laboriously pry off chip after chip until the point was shaped to suit. Arrow and spear heads were fastened into place with threads of sinew, the blunt end of the point being put into the cane shaft so that it rested against a natural partition in the tube. The sinew, wet and soft, was wound firmly around the end to dry and hold the point securely. Halves of split feathers, similarly secured, were placed spirally at the other end of the arrow; there were sometimes two feathers, sometimes three, we are told on inquiry, but what decided the number has not been learned. War arrows bore smaller feathers, so that they might be less easily seen by the foe. An arrow with a special point was carried by each brave for firemaking, its use being the world-wide plan of placing the point in inflammable wood and revolving the shaft between the palms.

Glue used in bow making and otherwise was made by the Panamints, says Coville, by boiling mountain sheep horns and hoofs, pitch from pine trees, and a reddish-amber gum found on the creosote bush. A pulverized rock was mixed in, and the whole thoroughly pounded. It was heated before using, and made a durable cement. Valley Piutes appear to have used the glue from horns and hoofs, with fewer other substances added.

Part of the personal outfit of each brave was an obsidian knife.

Rabbit nets were woven from the fiber of the narrow-leaf milkweed, the stems of which were broken off and dried and the fiber twisted into a creamy white cord. The nets were less than three feet high, but of any length, and were stretched across rabbit runways. A community rabbit drive being announced, lines of men and boys herded the animals to the nets. Bunny had no difficulty in putting his head into the meshes, but his body would not go through. His long ears prevented his backing out, and he became easy prey for the clubs of his hunters. Rabbits as well as larger animals were sometimes caught in covered pits.

Domestic utensils were wickerwork, in shapes and sizes according to intended use. Plates and small sieves were nine to twelve inches in diameter. Water baskets and cooking utensils were closely woven, and finished with an inside coating of pitch. They were frequently urn-shaped, with a conical or rounded bottom. The pot basket was the most useful utensil. Bowl-shaped, with curving sides and a slightly flattened bottom, it served many purposes—a bowl for dry substances, a container in which to boil food by the hot-stone plan, and between times it made an excellent headcovering for the owner.

Winnowing baskets, for separating chaff from seeds, were shallow, two to three feet long, with one end brought to a point.

The infant Piute was cradled in a wickerwork contrivance called a hu-va or he-u-ba, with a Y-shaped tree fork as a foundation. The part of this basket which rested against the mother's back was flat; the rearward portion was rounded and extended perhaps two-thirds of the length, diminishing to a point at the bottom. A curved framework extended from the top to shade the infant's face. Bundled in robes, he was lashed in, and spent most of his time there, whether being carried about or in camp.

All wicker articles were made by the squaws at the cost of much time and skill. Willow was the usual material. Withes were gathered at a certain stage of growth; the bark was stripped off and protuberances scraped away. The basketmaker used her teeth to split the sticks unless they were small or to be used for large or coarse baskets. Each strand was scraped into a thin pliant strip and stored away until wanted, when it was soaked in water before using. A fine tough grass gave the thread-like effect in some of the weaving.

Finer baskets, such as are included in white people's collections, were ornamented in various ways. Bark was sometimes left on for this purpose, and withes were stained. Quail plumes, yellow feathers from the meadow lark, and other colored plumage were added in orderly arrangement. The black used by Owens Valley Indians was a natural growth; that in Panamint baskets was from the use of a black-fibered plant, called by Coville devil horns, but more often known as devil's claw. The red in Panamint work was from the yucca. Coville says that some baskets took a month in the making.

Clothing was a minor consideration, except for comfort. No fabrics of any kind were produced. Rabbit skins, sewed together with sinew or milkweed threads by the use of bone awls, served as warm robes for the women, who also wore buckskin skirts. Men wore breechclouts, or deer or other skins. The children, in their earlier years, got through the warmer weather in complete nudity. Early white visitors to the region found the natives clad in little more than primitive simplicity and bright face paints. Moccasins, worn as occasion required, were of animal skins, sewed with buckskin thongs. When deerskin was used, as was most usual, the thicker hide found on the animal's head was used for soles. The women wore their potbaskets for head covering; the men wore none.

Julian H. Steward, then of the University of California, published a monograph, "Irrigation without Agriculture," after studying the subject. One Indian authority disputes some of his findings, and is here given the preference. Steward's conclusions not questioned state:

The Eastern Monos (Owens Valley Piutes) were in most respects among the most primitive of the American Indians. In one respect, however, they stood unique: In certain localities they took the pains to increase the yield of several of the more prolific seed plants by irrigation. They did not till the soil, plant or cultivate. They merely intensified by irrigation what nature had already provided.

The greatest development of irrigation had been worked out at the northern end of Owens Valley, in the vicinity of the present town of Bishop. There the population was the most dense and the natural facilities were greatest. On each side of Bishop Creek were extensive plots of wild seeds and tubers, chief among which were tupus [taboose], a small bulb of the lily family, and mahavita, a seed-bearing brush. The largest of these plots, on the north side of the stream, was approximately four miles in length and from a mile to a mile and a half in width. The western half of this abounded in tupus, the eastern half in mahavita. The southern plot, approximately two miles square, had a large plot of mahavita and a smaller one of tupus. The irrigation system comprised two ditches, one running to each plot.

Steward's account makes the selection of an irrigator and the beginning of his work a ceremonious affair. Our Indian informant says all there was to it was a proclamation by the pokonahbe that it was time to begin the irrigating and a statement that each could go and help if he wished to do so. The only tool used was a long stick. Again to quote Steward:

Of particular interest is the alternation of the two major plots each year. The explanation given was that it prevented exhaustion of the soil. A more accurate explanation would be that it enabled the plots to reseed themselves. In the spring the water was turned on one plat (and the stranded fish gathered from the creek bed). In the fall when the seeds and tupus bulbs were ready for harvesting the dam was destroyed and the water allowed to flow down the main channel (and the fish gathered from the irrigation ditch).

The Eastern Mono used a species of wild tobacco which they assisted by burning off the land each spring and trimming away the poorer leaves on the plant in the summer so as to favor the larger leaves. They neither irrigate nor planted it, however.

Other localities in Owens Valley practiced irrigation, but it has not been reported elsewhere in California or Nevada.

Any systematic spring burning is open to question. "Indian tobacco," Nicotiana trigonophylla, is a perennial growing only on sandy plots, which harbor little other vegetation. The plants are usually well separated, and burning would in most cases require individual attention to each plant. The growth is one to three feet high, leaves hairless, flowers small, white and trumpet-shaped, odor disagreeable.

Coville found in the Panamint mountains small Indian gardens of corn, potatoes, squashes and watermelons. While such gardening in Coville's time may be attributed to knowledge and productions obtained from white people, Manly's party in 1849 found in that region small patches of a sort of squash which seemed to be more than chance wild growing.

Taboose, mentioned in quotations from Steward, is a tuber rather than a bulb. The nut resembles a miniature potato, and is pleasant in taste. We question its identity with the chufa or rush nut, Cyperus esculentus, of the eastern States, but it is certainly of the same sedge family. The nuts grow on rootlets; the triangular bright stems grow from several inches to a foot or more in height, in comparatively moist soil. While the natives may dig it out plant by plant, their preference is to locate the hoards stored by gophers; sometimes a quart or more of the nuts are taken from a single cache.

The pinenut, or pinon, seed of Pinus monoyhylla, was a reliance for food for the Piutes as for other tribes in whose territory the trees are found. Harvesting the nuts, called "tu-ba" by the Indians, caused an early autumn migration to the hills. Whole villages sprang up in the scrubby pinon forests while the crop was being gathered. The season comes as the nuts mature, but before the cone scales open. The cones are beaten from the trees and spread in the sun until the scales become dry and spread apart. Artificial heat is sometimes used to expedite the process, after which the seeds are shaken out or beaten out with sticks. The primitive plan of roasting was to put the nuts into baskets with live coals and shake or stir them until the cooking was completed; now other means are frequently used. When properly prepared the food remains fresh and edible for long periods. They were eaten either in the roasted condition or ground up with other seeds and made into mush or soup. A cold-weather dainty was made by mixing pinon meal with water into a fairly thick mush and allowing it to freeze; an Indian informant tells us it was "just like ice cream." While the native commonly gave little thought to his future food supply, the shortness of the nut-gathering season and the frequent abundance of the crop led to some degree of conservation. Some of the harvest was cached; sometimes the supply was piled up, cones and all, on the mountains and left through the winter snows, to be taken out in spring, or when other supplies became distressingly scarce.

Owens Valley Piutes exercised jealous watchfulness over their nut forests, as against outside tribes. In a season of food shortage in the Saline Valley region the Shoshones there came over the mountains and began to stock up from the trees in the vicinity of the Piute Monument. Learning this, the valley natives rallied and drove the trespassers away.

Paceta, wye and kuha were among the standard meal substances. The first is botanically Salvia columbariae, known as chia in other parts of California and in Mexico, where it has been systematically cultivated. It is an odd-looking bit of vegetation, with a purplish stem almost two feet high, projecting from a rosette of dark green leaves as wrinkled as the back of a toad. Small bluish flowers ornament purplish head clusters, and produce the seeds that were used by not only the Piutes but other tribes as well. Meal from them is said to be extremely nourishing. No information has been found that the Piutes ever put the plant to medicinal use, as was done by the Mission fathers in treating gunshot wounds and for fever, for which it was considered "muy bueno"; it has also some favorable repute as a water purifier.

Wye is classified by Prof. Jepson as Cryzopsis hymenoides; less scientifically, as Indian mountain rice.

It carries a crop of seeds which should have been no trouble to harvest, as they drop profusely from the dry plant on the least agitation.

Kuha, in formal rating Mentzelia albicaulis, is a white-stemmed yellow-flowered plant, appearing early in the spring.

Other seeds, which like the foregoing, were made into meal included those of side-oat grama, Boutelis curtipendula; common sagebrush; the common sunflower. In all cases, so far as inquiry has confirmed, the seeds were used only when ground to meal.

Buds of the wild rose, and of the squaw thorn, Lycium torreyii, tender roots of the cat's-tail and California bulrush, tender leaves of the Joshua tree and young shoots of the columbine were all edible and helped the food cause along.

Grinding was done in what English-speaking investigators term a metahte, but that name is not in the Piute vocabulary. A shallow, almost flat, grinding surface was a mahte; the grinding tool was a tu-su. A deeper bowl-like vessel was a pah-ha; its pestle was a pah-ha-gu-nu. The vessels were generally stone, though wood served at times.

When there happened to be a surplus of meat that could not be devoured without waste, it was made into jerkie— that is, dried.

Wild onions and a root resembling the parsnip (but not the wild parsnip, a deadly poison) were used, and so were the wild berries, such as elderberry, strawberry and currant.

The Panamints were without many of the plants found in Owens Valley, but had some foods peculiarly their own. Their stocks of seeds included those of sand grass (Oryzopsis membranacea), a form of cactus, the evening primrose and others. The prickly pear, Opuntia basilaris, furnished large flat stems filled with sap; these were well rubbed to remove the thorns, and dried in the sun. They were kept indefinitely, and boiled when wanted for eating. Sometimes they were prepared in another way. The gathered pieces were piled into a stone-lined cavity, with grass next to the stones. Cactus and hot stones were piled in, alternately in layers, and the whole was covered with vegetation and moist earth. After steaming for ten or twelve hours, the nah-vo, as it was called, was ready to be eaten or to be dried. The dried material is said to have resembled dried peaches in texture and appearance.

Plants botanically known as cruciferae, having large juicy leaves and with a cabbage-like taste, were gathered and thrown into boiling water for a few minutes, then taken out, washed in cold water, and squeezed. This process, repeated several times, removed bitterness and ingredients known to produce effects unpleasant to the eater. Frank Kennedy, an old-timer in the Panamint region, said that in periods of food shortage almost any green herbage was used in the same way.

The honey mesquite, Prosopis juliflora, furnished the desert Indians a food resource not available in Owens Valley. The ripe pods contain a small amount of sugary nutritious matter. They also made use of the undeveloped buds of the yucca. Though as the buds age they become very tough, in the early stage the stems are brittle and easily broken by one who understands the knack of giving the proper twist and sidewise pull. In preparing this food the outer leaves and tips are discarded, leaving an egg-shaped solid juicy mass. This is roasted and eaten hot or cold.

The nearest approach to bread was a hard cake of some of the mush materials, western acorns (we-ah) from the black oak being preferred for the purpose when they could be had. Few acorns were gathered on this slope of the Sierras. A variety found on Oak Creek in Owens Valley and known as tse-ke-no, or che-ga-no, was less in demand.

Sugar substitute was secured from a common reed, either by scraping a parasitic covering from the stems and leaves and using it in crude form, or by cutting the plants, drying them in the sun, crushing the material and sifting out the finer product. This was ground into a gum-like mass and partially roasted. White men who saw it say that the crude sugar was filled with small green bugs, a detail not objectionable to the aboriginal user.

The county contains inexhaustible natural beds of salt, of more than 99 per cent purity, and the natives had but to gather up a commodity which in some other parts of the continent was much scarcer. Owens Valleyans probably made pilgrimages to stock up, but sometimes Indians of the Saline regions brought salt to trade for other goods. It has been stated that Indians in southern Mono obtained salt from salt grass, but Owens Valley natives tell us they never heard of that being done. Such recovery would be small, and more troublesome than a journey to where unlimited stores had but to be scraped up.

Salt was the principal article of commerce with the Yokuts of southern San Joaquin Valley, the Inyoites taking quantities of it to neutral trading ground on the mountain summit east of Kern River. The salt merchants appear to have been shrewd traders, giving little salt for much goods. Later, when a Yokut accompanied a party of white men to the east side and saw how easily the Piutes obtained their salt supply, he told a white friend that he felt like killing some of them. Bows and arrows were also bartered, those made by the Owens Valleyans being of superior quality. On such occasions, the Piutes received meal, acorns, deerskins and other articles. Armed and distrustful neutrality governed the trading occasions, the Yokuts admitting that they were afraid of the Piutes.

Deer and antelope were plentiful, and were usually caught by large hunting parties which stealthily surrounded the game; then wherever the hapless animal turned it found a club or an arrow, until a lucky shot brought it down.

There were but two species of native fish, chubs and suckers, besides tiny minnows, in native waters before the planting of trout by white men. There were some bone fishhooks. The spear, with a roughly barbed obsidian or bone point, was used in fishing, usually at night with a fire on the water's bank to attract victims. Periods of very low water were utilized for fish capture by making dams across the diminished stream, this method sometimes being accomplished by Indians standing in line across the channel to serve as backing against which to pile sods, brush and earth for the temporary purpose. As the channel below was drained, its fish were scooped out.

The Indian was not fastidious in his bill of fare; he could not afford to be. An occasional season of abundance might be followed by one of near starvation; there was little idea of looking out for the morrow by limitations on today. When food was hoarded it was because the immediate supply was too great for consumption.

Animals of all edible kinds and some insects helped the larder, and very little of each was wasted. In the early days of white occupation, the carcass of a cow, horse or other animal was soon cut up and taken away by non-paying customers who showed no curiosity as to the cause of the animal's death, so long as it had not occurred too far in the past.

A favorite food was a large caterpillar known as pe-ag-ge. This delicacy is the larva of the Pandora moth. Coloradia pandora. The moth is brownish gray, each wing bearing a small black spot. Its eggs are laid in early summer in tree bark; while the yellow pine is sometimes used for the purpose, forest men who have observed the point say that the Jeffrey pine is almost exclusively chosen, usually in a stand of its own species and not in a mixed collection of trees. Egg laying is on the sunny side of the tree, or on the side away from prevailing winds. Hatching occurs in August or September. The young caterpillars feed on leaves, moving upward until in October they gather in clusters like bees on the higher branches. Remaining dormant during cold weather, they continue to grow when spring comes, and move earthward. They are from 1½ to 3 inches long, and half an inch or more in diameter.

When not destined to become food for Indians, birds or animals, they reach the ground, burrow into it and there produce hard cocoons, and in the second year of the life cycle they become moths.

The Indians prepare to receive the caterpillars by surrounding each tree with a trench ten to sixteen inches deep and approximately two feet wide, with an almost vertical outer wall. The caterpillars collect in quantities and are scooped up, a single camp sometimes gathering a ton or more. The harvest was sometimes hastened by building a fire under the tree, the smoke causing the caterpillars to drop.

Fires were made and earth and peagges mixed with the coals in a mound. When the mass cooled off, the caterpillars were sifted out and stored in cool places for later use. When not eaten in this baked condition, they were mixed in stews and eaten with pinenuts and sunflower seeds.

Entomologists tells us that the Pandora moth is found along the Sierras as far north as southern Oregon and that its larva was eaten by other tribes. It is said that one of the wars between Indians east of the Sierras and those on the western slope arcse from an expedition made by Piutes to secure breeding stock from worm orchards across the summit. This credits them with a foresight unusual in their affairs.

Some of the inland lakes, notably Mono and formerly Owens, contain countless millions of the pupa of a fly, Ephydna hyans. The small shells cling to rocks under water until they loosen and are driven ashore in great windrows, where the women gathered them. They were dried in the sun and the shells rubbed off, leaving a small yellowish kernel of worm, which was used as food. This is termed "cozaby" by Indians with whom the author has talked. Scientists Wm. H. Brewer and J. M. Aldrich gave the insect some study, and Brewer spelled it "koo-tsabe," taking its pronunciation from Indian interviews.

Occasional invasions of the seventeen-year locust were not unwelcomed, for plenty of quick-lunch material was thus made available. Valley sloughs produced a species of mussel, which was gathered in such quantities that every camp had its large pile of shells shucked from the bivalves. The writer has seen many such.

While the lizard was probably legitimate game for all tribes of the Great Basin, the Panamints had a monopoly of the most meaty desert saurian, the chuckwalla. It is a fat-tailed vegetation-eating lizard, sometimes as long as eighteen inches. Preparing it for roasting was simple, being only to brush off any adhering soil or sand; the creature was cooked as it was when caught. White travelers who admitted having tried this diet said it was good eating.

Many things were eaten raw; others were dried. Cooking processes included roasting on sticks held over the fire, roasting in ashes, mixing with live coals in wicker baskets which were shaken to prevent burning, and boiling. There were no vessels which could be left on a fire, between the time of the ancient pottery makers—if any—and the white man with his utensils and his discarded tin cans. Boiling was done in pitch-lined watertight baskets, into which heated stones were dropped. Handling such stones necessitated the use of an implement made by twisting a willow withe into proper shape.

When food was plentiful, two daily meals was the rule; in scarcity it was a matter of eating when it could be had. Unlike civilized cooks, the Piute housewife was little troubled over selecting her menu; it was a question of what might be at hand, regardless of what meal it was. Too frequently there was little. Except on occasions of big gorges, the lady of the house dispensed the provender. Each tu-ah-mu-be, child, presented his wicker dish and received his allotment of food, so that a fairly even division was made all around.

One of the housewifely duties was to see that coals were left from the evening fire and kept alive so that a blaze could be started in the morning.

Smoking was practiced to a considerable extent. Pipes were made from the easily worked tufa, with stems of hollowed stalks of a mountain berry, or of cane. Mountain mahogany was also used for pipe bowls. Besides the "Indian tobacco" already mentioned, another plant, name to the writer unknown, was occasionally used, but because of a strong flavor it was less liked.

It cannot be learned that Owens Valley Indians made intoxicants of any kind, prior to the coming of the whites. A species of jimson weed, Datura meteloides, intensely narcotic, was used on rare occasions. It is a native of the eastern Inyo mountains as well as of some other parts of California, east to Texas and south to Mexico, and bears the name of tolguache in the Spanish-speaking regions, ton-ga-ne-ba among the Piutes. Elsewhere, it was made into a tea, a little of which causes delirium and too much causes death. Another plant, called mu-e-pa, produced delirium, or as the Indians tell us it made the user see visions. It was given as a special favor, in the form of a section of the stem to be chewed. Its evil effects were too manifest for even the untutored primitive mind to accept as popular; the wiser ones discouraged its use except when they thought it useful as medicine.

There was limited knowledge of poisons, and some use of them in hunting and probably in warfare. One is said to have been made from the contents of a gland found near the stomach of the deer or the mountain sheep. It was allowed to putrefy, and arrow points dipped in it. Another was made by taking blood from the deer's heart, mixing it with salt and ashes, and letting the mess rot. Putrefaction was the poisonous principle, with various ingredients probably added only to give consistency—though the manufacturers may have had a different belief. Roots of the wild parsnip contain a virulent poison, which the natives have been known to use for suicidal purposes; in one case, young Indians experimented on a white boy by inducing him to eat some of the roots, with almost fatal results.

A village consisted of a cluster of huts located regardless of any systematic arrangement. A better class to-ne (the Piute equivalent of wickiup) was built of tules (called si-ebu)—bulrushes for uninformed readers. They were bundled and bound into a wall several inches thick, and as weatherproof as a wooden structure. The base outline was circular, of whatever size the builder might prefer. The sides decreased in a rounded curve toward the top, making a dome-like shape. Smoke from the central fire escaped from a hole in the top; this, like the tunnel entrance through which the occupants crouched their way in or out, could be closed to make the place air and wind-tight. Ventilation was an unconsidered detail. Pallets of tree leaves and twigs or of grass lined the walls, on the ground. The individual went to bed by wrapping himself in his deerskin or whatever covering he might possess, and stretching out pillowless on the pallet.

The tribe was nomadic in only a very limited way. Migrations resulted from the gathering of pinenuts and peagges, when for brief seasons food supplies were not only harvested but also consumed in such quantities as human systems would accept. The harvest over, they sometimes returned to the valley, sometimes to former locations, to some other in the near vicinity. A death in a to-ne usually led to the burning of that structure and the building of another at another site.

Practical reasons governed selections or changes of camps. While proximity to water was desirable, so was nearness to a wood supply. Even though the Indian fireman got along with a fraction of the fuel that a white man would require, it was better that the women did not have too long a distance to move that little. If felling a tree became necessary, it was burned around at the ground level, there being no tools equal to the task.

Wickerwork cages show that the household sometimes had captive birds, which probably sooner or later went into the family stew. Indian authority tells us that there were no dogs in the camps, as there were on the plains and on the coast.

The Indian is a natural gambler, and undoubtedly the games played meant change of property ownership. The "stick game," called ny-ah-gwe, was a favorite. As in our youthful "Button, button, who's got the button?" a small bit of stick was passed from hand to hand along a line of players, and an opposing line won or lost according to ability to designate the hand having the stick. In the "ring game," called "pah-she," contestants sometimes tossed a woven willow ring endeavoring to hang it on a spear point set a little distance away; probably more often the effort was to throw the spear through a hoop as it was rolled. Contests of marksmen were frequent, as befitted a people depending on the bow and arrow. They played a form of football.

The big social occasions of the year were the tu-mah-ta or ne-ga-su-wit, ceremonial dances, to which the natives flocked from far and wide for a prolonged holiday. The people managing the dance sometimes accompanied the invitation to the pokonahbe of another camp with gifts. The custom sufficiently explains the term "Indian giver," for each gift was expected to be repaid. The more common dance, called na-nu-gah, was about the same as with other tribes—a shuffling circling by all comers, chanting words announced by a leader. There were no drums. War dances were accompanied by the rhythmic clacking of cleft sticks. Feasting and late-burning fires were part of the program. In more recent years, the young men and women have their own dances in regulation white style, and are said to be adept in the modern steps.

The ghost dances which agitated western America years ago received little attention from Inyo Piutes. Though the appearance of the "prophet" and the center of a disturbance that spread half way across the continent was but two hundred miles distant, the prophets and walking delegates found little response here.

Buying and selling was chiefly barter in kind, though strings of a form of bead, called pah-kah-de, served in some degree as a substitute for money.

There were no horses, and transportation was by woman power. Small articles were carried in pack baskets, funnel shaped affairs, kept on the bearer's back by a strap passed across her forehead.

Few to-nes or moo-zas are now to be found; one transplanted for exhibition at a fair in Bishop attracted much attention. Frame cabins are now the common habitation, and the housewives frequently keep them in a condition of which no white housekeeper would be ashamed. Sewing machines, rugs, carpets, occasionally a talking machine with well selected music, are not rare, and in at least one Indian home is a radio, owned by an Indian who has had some training as an electrician. There are Piutes whose education surpasses that of white men with whom they work. In an Inyo high school, when this is written, is a full-blooded Indian girl who ranks high in scholarship, and who won honors in an oratorical competition on the subject of the American government.

One must hunt long to find a rabbit robe, such as once garbed nearly every Indian woman. Men and women dress like white people, except that the older women usually wear handkerchief turbans. The young women have silk stockings and dresses such as their white sisters wear. The only paints on their faces are cosmetics, even to lipsticks now and then. Scores of descendants of those who fled at sight of the first wagons now drive their own automobiles.

The camp commissary is no longer repulsive in its viands, barring perhaps an occasional reversion to peagges. Groceries are chosen so fastidiously that the buyer insists on his preferred brand of flour or whatever commodity he purchases.

Those who know the Piutes will agree that there are differences in individual traits as in those of other races. Instances of gratitude and ingratitude, kindness and cruelty, loyalty and treachery, can be cited to a generous degree. A woman doing domestic work went about her tasks with tears streaming down her face for the loss of a white friend. One who was fed day after day when he appeared with the statement "Me hongry" did not hesitate to ask "How much?" each time he was asked to do some little chore after his free meal.

Perhaps the most illuminating evidence of the basic Indian character in general, however, is given by Mrs. Belle Dormer in a narrative of recollections of her childhood in Owens Valley:

Little Bean and Johnny Smith were Indian boys who worked on the ranch, doing all kinds of work and treated much as members of the family. Once a disturbance threatened Indian war. Mother asked the boys if they would help to protect the family that had given them a home and treated them so kindly. Bean, the smarter of the two, said: "Me, Johnny, Indians. We fight with our people; we no kill you. We kill other family; send other Indians kill you."

On Sundays the Indians went to town. One Sunday morning the wife of one of the Indians followed the boys for some distance begging him to come back with her. She had her year-old baby with her. Her husband refused to listen to her pleadings, and went away. The girl went back to her tent. In a short time Bean came over and told us the girl had eaten poison parsnip, drinking water to hasten its effects, and was dead. Mother asked Bean why he did not come and tell her when the girl ate the parsnip. "What for me tell you?" asked Bean; "she want to die."

One pinenut harvest time Johnny and Little Bean, beaming with happiness, joined their relatives and friends in the trip to the mountains for the great occasion. Afterward Johnny returned alone, coming in and sitting down at the table where he and Little Bean ate. "Where is Little Bean?" asked mother. He drank a portion of his coffee, and said: "I killed him." "You killed him?" mother exclaimed, not believing; "surely you would not kill your friend?" "Yes, he was a doctor; I had to kill him!" I cannot remember that anything was done about it.

There are skilled Piute tradesmen and capable musicians who are making their way in white surroundings. There is a degree of art talent; we have seen portraits drawn by an untaught Indian girl that were readily recognizable. Another placed some magazine covers with publishers. At the same time, such commendable native knowledge as basketry is becoming a lost art among them.

Old-time customs contrast sharply with present conditions. The Piute here has advanced more in his relatively short association with the whites than the latter advanced in twice the time in his own early civilization. The Piute fills an important economic place in eastern California industrial affairs. This evolution is partly the result of association with and imitation of the dominant race and recognition of the advantage of their ways, and partly due to the judicious labors of conscientious men and women who have been placed among them by the national government. The Indian is growing into full intelligent citizenship. He did his part in the Great War, and made an intelligent soldier. And here we note an occurrence of that struggle: Near a European battlefront it became necessary to send telephonic information to a distant point, with every probability that the Germans were listening in. No code and no European language was felt to be safe. An Inyo Piute, appreciating the situation, asked that he be allowed to talk to a friend in the other command. He took the phone and gave the message in his own language, and the enemy was completely baffled.

"Gradual" is hardly the fitting term to apply to the progress made by most of the Piutes of Inyo, since many of them now active were carried in the huvas on their mothers' backs. They are putting behind them many of the things of primitive days. Their future is a problem to be dealt with by those whom they know and who know them, and not by those whose theories (and sometimes self-serving schemes) do more harm than good.

The Piute of today is infinitely better off than his ancient progenitors, but his plight in Owens Valley deserves sympathetic attention. He has forsaken the ignorant benighted ways of his fathers, generally; but he has not reached a stage where he can, or is adapted to, go forth, as his white friends anticipating having to do, and battle with the world in other fields. The occupations he has learned are being taken from him by the depopulation of Owens Valley, and nothing comes to replace them. The national government has striven, after a fashion, to make him independent, but it still owes him the opportunity to live in the land his ancestors have occupied from time immemorial. It helps the more dependent of the tribe with barely enough to keep soul and body together, and it hedges that help about with most niggardly restrictions. The Indian Bureau of the United States should be, in common humanity, most liberal to the Piutes, whether now technically its wards or not. If it leaves them relatively helpless in the dark days that appear to be ahead for them, it will be an abandonment without justice or excuse.

CHAPTER VII

EARLY EXPLORATIONS

PADRES DID NOT REACH INYO—JEDEDIAH SMITH—GOLD FOUND AT
MONO LAKE—OGDEN, 1831—CAPTAIN JOE WALKER, 1833—CHILES
PARTY, 1842—WAGONS ABANDONED AT OWENS LAKE—FREMONT
EXPEDITIONS—NAMING OF OWENS RIVER

Franciscan missionaries, who played so large a part
in western and southern California affairs, did not cross
or even reach the Sierra Nevada range. Fr. Zephyrin
Engelhardt, authority on all historical matters connected
with his church on the coast, states that Hermenegildo
Garces journeyed from near Tucson, Arizona, across the
Mojave desert in 1775. His self-sacrificing wanderings are
part of the heroic history of the southwest, but they do
not appear to have touched Inyo except that he recorded
coming in contact with the Beneme Indians, whose habitat
extended into the present Inyo County.

Among the first visitors were travelers over the "old
Spanish trail," which cut across the southeastern tip of
this county, with a recuperation point at Resting Springs.
While that historic route appears to have been created by
missionary priests, probably about 1829, accounts indicate
that its greater use was ignoble, for over it traveled the
bands of thieves who, starting from Santa Fe and Tucson,
came to raid the bands of horses of the California missions and valleys. Fremont, following it in 1845, found
the bones of many animals, doubtless those which had
fallen by the wayside in their enforced migration eastward.

Historian Irving B. Richman's map of early California
routes gives that of Captain Joe Walker in 1833 as the
first through Owens Valley. Before him, Jedediah S.
Smith and his fellow trappers traversed eastern California,
and we credit evidence that their route was through Owens

Valley. During the last few years there has been much investigation of records concerning Smith, without settling disputed points. While Thompson & West's "History of Nevada" says that he came south along the east base of the Sierra, and entered the San Joaquin Valley through Walker's Pass in 1825, and Cronise, 1868, says the same, corroborative testimony on that is lacking. His return journey over the route is better confirmed, though some writers have him crossing the mountains at the headwaters of the Stanislaus River or even as far north as the American.

That his return journey was made northerly along the east base of the Sierras is the statement of Bancroft. A letter signed by Thomas Sprague and published in the San Francisco *Bulletin* and other coast papers in October, 1860, told of Smith's journeys. Of the return from his first visit to California it said:

He crossed the mountains near what is now known as Walker's Pass, and skirted the eastern slope of the mountains to near what is now known as Mono Lake, when he steered an east by north course for Salt Lake. On this portion of his route he found placer gold in quantities, and brought much of it with him to the encampment on Green River.

Thompson & West's "History of Nevada," 1881, quoted a letter from Captain Robert Lyon, of San Buenaventura, California, as follows:

His (Smith's) notes mention the discovery of Mono Lake, or dead sea, on his return trip in 1925. The upper end of Mono Gulch was very rich and shallow, and when the gulch was first prospected by Cord (Cord Norst), the discoverer, in 1859, gold could be seen lying on the granite rock where it had been washed in sight by the rains; and there is not a placer between Sacramento and Salt Lake where gold could be so easily obtained by inexperienced miners, with only a pan and knife, as in the upper end of Mono Gulch. Rocky Mountain Jack, or Uncle Jack as he was called, and Bill Reed both spent the summer of 1860 in Mono, and were well known at that time, and both of these old trappers declared they were with Smith in 1825, and that they spent a week prospecting and picking up gold in these foothills in 1825. . . . Bill Byrnes, well known in Carson City, always claimed that Jed Smith discovered the Mono mines in 1825, although he (Byrnes) was not of the party.

The author has seen a purported list of members of the Smith expedition, in which were the names of Reed and of several Johns, one of whom may have been Rocky Mountain Jack.

Thus there is testimony that Smith discovered gold in California over two score years before Marshall picked up at Coloma the nugget which started California's rush. But his find is merely to be noted as a historical fact; it had no other importance or result.

The year of Smith's coming is another argued point. The letters quoted make it 1825. Bancroft gives it as 1829. One early writer said it was 1824. Letters written by Smith and quoted by several authors go to prove that the first visit was made in 1826; that he with 15 hunters and trappers started from the fur company's post near Salt Lake, August 22, 1826. One of his letters dated in May, 1927, just before his second journey, said: "We were at the Mission San Gabriel in January last."

Peter Ogden, Hudson Bay trapper, worked on the San Joaquin and other California streams in 1829. Thompson & West say that he entered the central valley by the route they gave as Smith's—that is, through Walker's Pass; and Fletcher's "Early Nevada" mentions his travel over the same course.

Then came Captain Joe Walker—Joseph Ruddeford (sometimes given as Reddeford) Walker, to give him the full name appearing in the annals of the Missouri town of Independence. Walker's home was there, as were those of Smith, already mentioned, and Chiles, who was to lead the next expedition this way. It was the westernmost frontier settlement and the starting point of the sunset trails. In 1832 Walker left there as a lieutenant of Captain Bonneville, in the latter's company of 110 picked men, with exploration of the country around and beyond Great Salt Lake as their purpose. The party divided at that lake, and Walker with part of the company kept on westward. They finally reached Monterey. Richman marks his route as being through Owens Valley; another writer claims that he skirted the eastern base of the White Mountains and crossed Owens Valley southeast of Owens Lake. As his later guiding was unquestionably through the valley, it is probable that the earlier trip followed the same route.

Joseph B. Chiles organized a company of about fifty, including a few women and children, in Independence, Missouri, in 1843, and started for California. Wagons were substituted for pack trains in this expedition. Walker was met at Fort Laramie and Chiles employed him to guide the party through. The party divided at Fort Hall, Walker selecting the route through Owens Valley and taking all the families in his subdivision. He led them over his old course, via Walker Lake and southward. Infinite hardships, says one of their writers, attended their journey to Owens Valley. They traveled down the east side of Owens River to the lake. Their livestock was so jaded when that point was reached that it became necessary to abandon the cumbersome wagons. Some sawmill machinery had been brought, and this too was abandoned. The natives were terrorized at sight of the wagons and fled to the hills. They made trouble but once, when a night guard named Milton Little was wounded with an arrow fired in the darkness. A later search was made for the wagons and machinery, but everything had been carried away.

After abandoning the wagons, portable property was loaded on the animals able to carry it, and the company proceeded on foot to "the point of the mountain," Owens Peak and Walker's Pass—the former then unnamed, the latter, like the Nevada lake and river, named for the leader of this expedition. Their hardships increased as they passed through the mountains, past the later site of Visalia, and to the Gilroy ranch, which they reached in January, 1844. One of the families in this party was that of George Yount, whose ranch in Napa County became the site of Yountville.

This was the second wagon train to enter California from the east, though its vehicles did not cross the Sierras. The one before it was that of John Bidwell, traveling much farther north in 1841. The Chiles-Walker expedition, reaching the Mexican settlement, strengthened the Mexican authorities in their fear of American invasion across the plains.

The "old Spanish trail," which crossed the southeastern corner of the present Inyo County, became the route adopted by Mormon travelers to southern California, and was used until after the Mountain Meadows massacre. It was more used, however, as a way over which horses sometimes bought, sometimes stolen, in California were driven to Santa Fe. One of the watering places, which were far apart along its course, was known as the Archilette, later called Resting Springs from use as a place at which to recuperate livestock during journeys across the waste.

John C. Fremont, leaving California in the spring of 1844, laid his course to and along this trail. Eighty miles from the Archilette two Mexicans, a man named Andreas Fuentes and a boy of 11 named Pablo Hernandez, came to his camp. They had driven as far as the springs, in company with the wife of Fuentes, the father and mother of Pablo, and a man named Giacome, taking a band of thirty horses. A band of 100 Indians had attacked them. Fuentes and the boy were guarding the stock, and drove the animals through the attacking party. Knowing that possession of the horses was the aim of the Indians, they did not stop until they reached another spring 60 miles from their starting point. Leaving the horses at that place, Agua Tomaso, they hurried on to meet another caravan, and thus reached the Fremont camp.

Hurrying on to Agua Tomaso, Fremont found that the horses had been driven off by Indians. Kit Carson and Alex Godey, of Fremont's command, volunteered to pursue the marauders, and Fuentes went with them until the exhaustion of his horse compelled him to return to the main party.

Carson and Godey kept on the track of the Indians, and a day later came to their permanent camp. They charged the camp on foot, with warwhoops that convinced the Indians that a large party was at hand. Two Indians were killed and the rest fled. Large earthen vessels filled with horse meat were on the fires, and a boy whom they captured calmly began making his breakfast from a horse's head as soon as he found he was not to be killed. The scouts drove the fifteen remaining horses to the Fremont command, making a trip of 100 miles, vanquishing the foe-men and recovering what horses were living, in a period of 30 hours.

Fremont reached the Archilette on April 29th, and found the corpses of the two men; the women had been carried away captive. When the commander observed the pitiful lamentations of the orphaned boy, he recorded, all compunctions for the killing and scalping of the Indians by Carson and Godey ended. He renamed the springs Agua de Hernandez, in commemoration of its tragedy, but that designation did not last. An old sword, supposed to have been lost by one of his men, was found in that vicinity more than forty years later. Decay had destroyed its handle, and the blade was firmly rusted in the sheath; the pattern was that used in Fremont's day.

Again the name of Walker, whom some of his contem-poraries refer to as one of the best and bravest of moun-tain men, appears in the Inyo record, and with it that of Richard Owens. Fremont left Bent's Fort, on the Oregon trail, in the late summer of 1845, with sixty men. Some-where on the way he met Walker and Owens and added them to the party, "with great satisfaction," he notes.

As the Pathfinder gave the name of Owens to the Inyo County river, valley and lake, the tribute in his memoirs to that adventurer's capabilities and value is interesting. "He was a good mountaineer, good hunter and good shot; cool, brave and of good judgment." He was an officer of the later skirmishing in southern California. When Fre-mont was haled to Washington to account for some of his actions, Owens went as one of the principal witnesses. Owens did not see the valley, lake or river which bear his name. Fremont did the naming, after the expedition reached San Joaquin Valley.

The whole company traveled together until Walker Lake was reached, November 23, 1845. The Indians found there were not friendly, but made no hostile demonstration. A party of Piutes was met as Fremont rode near the lake, the two bands of men passing but a short distance apart. The Indians did not look up, and gave no sign of knowing that the white men were in the neighborhood. Fremont believed that his men were regarded as intruders, or else that the natives had received some recent injury.

Fremont, Owens, Kit Carson and twelve others went north to cross the Sierras along the Truckee, then called the Salmon Trout River. Theodore Talbot commanded the main party of about fifty, one of whom was Edward M. Kern, artist and topographer, whose name was given to our southwesterly neighbor county. This branch stayed at Walker Lake until December 8th, and reached "the head of Owens River," locality not definitely stated, on the 16th. They followed the river to the lake, near which they camped from the 19th to the 21st, then going on southerly and through Walker's Pass.

For many years a mound of stones some three or four feet high stood beside the road a short distance north of Independence. Popular tradition held that it marked the burial place of one of the Fremont-Talbot men who died in the valley. The belief is doubtless erroneous. Evidence indicates that the route of travel was closer to the river; and aside from this, the site of the cairn was on very stony ground, while ground much easier to dig was but a short distance away. An alternate explanation for the mound, which was there when white settlers first came but is now leveled, is that it marked an Indian subtribal boundary, it being in direct line between the Piute Monument on the White Mountains and a Sierra pinnacle which soldiers ascended but which stands no longer.

CHAPTER VIII

DEATH VALLEY PARTY OF 1849

A TRAIL MARKED BY GRAVES—START OF THE JAYHAWKERS—ADDITIONS TO EXPEDITION—BREAK-UP OF CARAVAN IN UTAH—GUIDE'S ADVICE REJECTED—INTO DEATH VALLEY—FORLORN HOPE SENT OUT—THE RETURN—FINAL ESCAPE

Next in Inyo annals comes the tragic story of the pioneers who, seeking a short route to California, marked their way across the deserts with abandoned equipages, lonely graves or unburied corpses, and found in Death Valley the culmination of their misfortunes and miseries.

A writer of the period said that the overland trail could be traced by the headboards and mounds above the bodies of its victims. Disease and hardships, the arrows of hostile Indians, and sometimes Mormondom's "destroying angels," all did their share toward justifying this assertion. Hundreds who set forth in hope were laid to rest by the wayside, their lonely graves more often visited by pariah coyotes or trampled by bison than seen by human beings. The full tale of those journeyings never has been told. Here and there some special tragedy found a place in the bloodstained annals of pioneering. None exceed in horror the truth about those who perished at the verge of the promised land, the Donner party famishing in Sierra snows and the Death Valley party starving in the desert. The record of the Death Valley party is found in the narratives of W. L. Manly, Mrs. Brier, J. B. Colton, Edward Coker, Thomas Shannon and L. Dow Stephens, who were among those entering the ill-reputed valley; of P. A. Chalfant, founder of the *Inyo Independent* and *Inyo Register,* who was with it part of the way but entered the State farther north; and of others having more or less information. There is not always agreement between the stories.

Since the first edition of this book, this subject has been set forth in the author's "Death Valley: the Facts." While it would be preferable not to repeat, this history of the county would be incomplete were it neglected here. Some material not available when "Death Valley" was written is added to the narrative of the first edition.

The nucleus of the expedition was a band of young men from Galesburg, Illinois, who organized to make the trip to the newly discovered land of gold. They were youths of buoyant spirits, and anticipated a journey of pleasure rather than hardships. The name of Jayhawkers was adopted, on the route. An impromptu initiation ceremony was used to test the fortitude of applicants for the undertaking. The candidate was first carried around the camp on the shoulders of four men. He then bared one leg to the knee and stood upright while he repeated a vow that he would stand by his comrades through all perils. Following this a small bit of flesh was nipped from his bare leg; this was done twice more, and if he showed a lack of fortitude on any of these tests he was deemed unworthy of membership. Little did those carefree young fellows dream the nature of the hardships they were to encounter. A few of them failed; most of them proved their worth.

Some additions to the train had been made by the time Salt Lake City was reached. All such travelers remained in the Mormon capital for some time, recruiting their livestock, securing supplies and otherwise preparing for the unknown journey ahead. The Jayhawkers reached there in July, 1849, and remained until toward the end of September. More emigrants joined the train in Salt Lake City, until when the caravan was finally complete, at a rendezvous 50 or 100 miles south, it comprised 105 to 112 wagons and about 500 head of stock. The original Jayhawkers numbered thirty-six. In the expedition as finally made up there were several times as many, with members from Illinois, Iowa, Missouri and other western States and Territories.

One of the subdivisions amalgamated into the great caravan was known as "the San Francisco party," which had started from Omaha with forty-five wagons June 6th. It was somewhat elaborately organized, with constitution and by-laws, and with some of the characteristics of a military expedition. John Brophy was its "colonel," Judge Haun bore the title of "major," and Rev. J. W. Brier was designated as "chaplain." One of its younger members was P. A. Chalfant, father of the compiler of this record.

It was decided to divide the consolidated expedition into seven different companies. Some of the units already had their organizations; the small companies and detached individuals were formed into new commands. The Jayhawkers, after long argument, decided against allowing any women or children in their division, and the families who had joined them made up a separate party. To this there was one exception, Rev. J. W. Brier preferring the Jayhawkers to the party with which he had come, and declaring that he and his wife and children would stay with the Illinois men in any case. From the fact that the Brier party traveled apart from the Jayhawkers during parts of the subsequent journey it is probable that his welcome to their camp was not cordial.

Here, through the kind assistance of Charles Kelley, of Salt Lake, author of "Salt Desert Trails," we introduce a new narrator: James S. Brown, who though then unable to read or write, was instructed by the Mormon church to proceed on a mission to the South Sea Islands. This was in September, and Brown and his companions were told to start as soon as possible, joining the emigrants. They did so, and as will be seen preferred to follow the judgment of the guide rather than to branch off as did the Jayhawkers and others. Brown's story of the Utah experiences of the entire caravan contains some inconsistencies, but it is the most complete known. During the later years he acquired some little education, and embodied his experiences in a book from which the following is taken:

The emigrants called a meeting before taking their departure. They had employed Captain Jefferson Hunt, of Company A, Mormon Battalion fame, to be their guide, as he had come through that route with pack animals. He was invited to tell them what they might expect. He described the route to them with the roughest side out, lest they might say he had misled them by making things more favorable than they really were. In concluding his remarks he said: "From Salt Springs we cross a sand desert, distance 75 miles to Bitter Springs, the water so bitter the devil would not drink it; and from thence away hellwards to California or some other place. Now, gentlemen, if you will stick together and follow me, I will lead you to California all right; but you will have to make your own road, for there is none save the old Spanish trail from Santa Fe to California, by the Cajon Pass through the Sierra Nevada mountains."

These men, with Alexander Williams, who joined them, were all Mormons, going on the island mission. At Provo there was an Indian scare.

The emigrant company consisted of about 500 souls and 100 wagons and teams, the latter in poor condition. Feeling in high spirits the company moved out between the first and eighth of October. C. C. Rich, Francis Pomeroy and I remained ⌄ follow on horseback in three or four days. Pratt and Blackwell, taking our team, started with the main body.

Through Brother Rich's influence the cause of the trouble was looked into, a conciliation effected and war averted. . . . We overtook the wagon train on Sevier River. We came up with the emigrants just as they were ready to move on, but did not find them so full of glee as they were on the start from the city. Still we rolled on very peaceably until we came to Beaver River, where the country began to look more forbidding. Then the ardor of the emigrants began to weaken.

At this place the company was joined by a man named Smith with a packtrain of about seventeen men; also James Fiske, with thirty Latter-Day Saints; besides there were William Farrar, John Dixon, H. W. Bigler (who had been in at the discovery of gold), George Q. Cannon and others whose names I do not now recall. Smith felt confident he could find Walker's Pass in the Sierra Nevada Mountains. This supposed pass had been spoken of often, but men had been disappointed so often in finding it. Smith's story excited our whole camp so that there was a general desire to try the new route, and go down through the canyon and out on the sandy desert. The whole company except a very few favored the idea of leaving the route they had hired a guide for, and they urged Captain Hunt to strike out and look for water. He said: "Gentlemen, I agreed to pilot you through to California on the old Spanish route by the Cajon Pass. I am ready to do so, and am not under any obligations to lead you any other way; and if you insist on my doing so you must be responsible, for I will not be responsible for anything. On this condition, if you insist on changing your route, I will do the best I can to find water, but I do not have any reason to hope for success when I leave the trail."

The company hurrahed for the Walker Pass, and Captain Hunt struck out a day ahead while the company shod and doctored their lame stock for one day. Then we moved out ten miles into the plain southwest of where Minersville, Utah, now stands, and camped.

Some time in the night Captain Hunt came into camp, so near choked from lack of water that his tongue was swollen till it protruded from his mouth; his eyes were so sunken in his head that he could scarcely be recognized. His horse, too, for the lack of water was blind and staggered as he was urged on. Their stay had been thirty-six hours on the sands without water. About 2 o'clock the next morning our stock stampeded from the guards and ran back to water. Two-thirds of the men went in pursuit, and animals and men did not return to camp until 2 o'clock in the afternoon.

By this time confusion and discontent abounded in camp. A committee was appointed to inquire into the condition of every team, and to ascertain the food supply, with the avowed intention of sendisg all back who failed to have what were considered requisites for the journey. I think that one-third of the company, our wagon included, was found wanting when weighed in that committee's balances. But when we were ordered to return, those who gave the command found they were without authority and no one would heed them. So the discontent was patched up for a time, and we proceeded on to the Little Salt Lake Valley, where we struck the old Spanish trail again. Then the company began to split up, some going after night and others stopping. . . .

As we passed along the Spanish trail, said to be 350 years old, on the great desert, we could follow the route by the bones of dead animals in many places.

When we reached what is called the Rim of the Basin, where the waters divide, part running into the Colorado River and on to the Pacific Ocean, and part into Salt Lake Valley, the company called meetings and several made speeches, saying there must be a nearer and better route than that on which the Mormon guide was leading them. One Methodist and one Campbellite preacher in the company (Rev. Brier was one) said they had started to California and not hellwards, as the Mormon guide had stated at the outset, quoting what Captain Hunt had said just before starting. Others claimed they had been on the mountains and upon looking west had seen something green, which they asserted was an indication of water. Some of them celebrated the proposed separation by boring holes in trees, then filling these with powder and firing them, exploded the trees in symbol of the break-up of the company.

Next morning all wagons save seven turned off to the right, toward the supposed Walker's Pass. We preferred to follow the guide. The company was thoroughly warned by Captain Hunt of the danger of dying from lack of water. In our party were eleven men, two women and three children. The main company expressed pity for us and tried to persuade us to go with them, but we felt confident that our course was the safest, notwithstanding their superior numbers. They seemed to rejoice at their conclusion, while we regretted it for their sakes. Thus we separated, the emigrant party headed for Walker's Pass and our small party continuing on the old Spanish trail to California.

Brown tells of the experiences of his party, including a snowstorm of which Manly speaks, finding some Indian places where the savages had raised corn, squash and wild wheat, and finding a note saying "Look out; we have killed two Indians here." Who left such a note is nowhere indicated. Several days later they found a cow with an Indian arrow in her body. This must have been left by an emigrant, though Hunt was supposed to be guiding the first emigrants and is quoted as saying there was no road. They camped on the Muddy River, in Nevada, and one of the party returned to camp with news that the emigrants had broken into factions and were demoralized. Some had abandoned their wagons and struck out afoot, their cattle dying. Brown and party reached the Las Vegas stream, and some days later came to water so strong with alkali they would not let their animals drink it. This may have been the Amargosa, which the trail touched. The Mormon party found gold, but for lack of water would not tarry to secure much of it. They crossed Cajon Pass, and were overtaken by half-starved deserters from the emigrant train, whom they fed. With Hunt and his party we have no further concern.

When, in Utah, the order was made excluding families from the Jayhawker train, two of the men who left it with their wives and children were Asabel Bennett and J. B. Arcane. W. L. Manly, whose story of the whole expedition west of the break-up point is the most complete, chose to go with Bennett, his close friend. This party traveled independent of the Jayhawkers, though taking the same general course and experiencing similar hardships. While the two bands were together at different times, their stories are separate.

Manly drove no team, but acted as a general scout. At the Utah camp he ascended the highest near point, and on returning to camp reported a belief that there was no water ahead for a hundred miles. Doty, the Jayhawker captain, admitted discouragement at this, but decided to go ahead on the same course. The next morning his men and their twenty wagons pulled out, leaving Bennett, Arcane, Manly and associates in camp with seven.

Doty traveled five days without finding water, and by then his party had used all that had been brought from a playa lake. A subdivision headed by a man named Martin struck out on a different route from the one followed by Doty the next day. The latter's plight, while sorry enough, was less desperate that it was to become. Toward morning of that night's camp, the sky clouded and a little snow fell. Enough of this was caught and melted to satisfy men and animals and to provide a little reserve.

No more water was found until the Amargosa (meaning bitter) river bed was reached. That stream is on rare occasions a torrent of large volume, but for part of its course is usually lost in the sands. The Doty men found a slight trickle of bitter fluid, and drank it freely. The water, heavily charged with minerals, made them ill, and they left the stream and struck out toward a pass ahead. They were near the eastern base of the Funeral range.

All the courage the party could muster was needed in reaching the summit. The way grew steeper. Debris and washouts filled the canyons, through which probably no human being, except possibly Indians, had ever passed. Men and oxen were weakened by the chemicals taken at the Amargosa. One of the oxen died on the way up, and its carcass was the last to be left without being utilized for food. Even that one was not wholly wasted, for a straggler of the expedition cut a steak from it. After two days of struggle the party stood on the summit and looked down into one of nature's freaks—Death Valley.

The train toiled down the pass, and on the third day reached some springs around which some coarse grass grew. Realizing that the oxen could not take the wagons farther, the party camped and prepared to finish the journey in the lightest possible marching order. Wagons were abandoned, and their woodwork was used to feed the fires over which the stringy flesh of the oxen was dried. Rice, tea and coffee were measured out by the spoonful, with an understanding that thereafter each individual must look out for himself and expect no help from anyone else. The canvas of the wagon covers was fashioned into knapsacks, and powder cans were set in slings to serve as canteens, none of the latter having been included in the equipment. Moccasins were made from the hides of slain animals, for the men and for the tender-footed among the surviving oxen.

The Martin party, which had branched off some days before, and the Bennett-Arcane subdivision both came into camp while these preparations were under way.

The Briers, traveling by themselves despite the father's objections, had reached Forty-Mile Canyon, in eastern Nevada, when the storm occurred that gave Doty water enough to enable him to reach the Amargosa. They remained there for a week to recuperate, though the oxen suffered much from the cold. On leaving, the oxen were laden with necessities and the wagons were burned, together with everything that was not considered necessary for traveling. Mrs. Brier, writing in later years, termed this action a fatal step. Somewhere between there and Death Valley the Briers fell in with the Bennett-Manly train. On the way they came upon a number of small squashes, cached by Indians, and took them. In view of the scarcity of provender among the Indians of that dreary region, it is not surprising that the natives sought vengeance, to the extent of a night attack on the camp. Arrows were shot into three oxen.

This party entered Death Valley by rounding the southern end of the Funerals, instead of toiling across as the Jayhawkers had. Mrs. Brier's account tells that her oldest boy, Kirk, aged nine years, gave out. She carried him on her back until he said he could walk. He made a manful effort, stumbling along for a while, then sank down and cried that he could go no farther. His heroic mother would then pick him up and carry him again. Though often falling to her knees from weakness, she got her little brood safely into the Death Valley camp.

The Martin party did not tarry. They were in marching order, and on leaving gave all their oxen to the Bennett-Brier camp, saying they could progress better without them. Martin struck out straight westward, his men carrying on their backs the things they deemed essential. While they were crossing one of the ranges, a man named Ischam, who had left the Doty party, as will be hereafter mentioned, struggled into their camp and died there. They crossed to the south of Saline Valley and reached Owens Lake. Hostile Indians were found at the lake and some skirmishing resulted, without harm to anyone. While they were there a snow fell and no fire could be made. Believing the lake to be of the playa kind, like so many with which they had become familiar on the desert, they were about to undertake to wade it, when one of the party found the old trail made by Walker's last party. A friendly Indian advised them to follow it, which they did, through Walker's Pass to safety.

From the accounts it appears clear that the Jayhawkers under Doty struck out from the Death Valley camp without encouraging Bennett and his party to accompany them. Brier again refused to accept dismissal, and forced himself and family in with them. Two days later Doty re-joined Bennett, and the two subdivisions were together at some camps, apart at others. The Jayhawkers' departure was, therefore, not a desertion but a following out of the plan of travel all the way.

Doty believed that the best way out was to the northward. On the way he found good water. He turned westerly from that spring and climbed the Panamint range.

They came upon the body of an ox, for which none of the stories account. They cut out what seemed to be the best of the meat, but after making a supper from it the remainder was thrown away. Darkness came on before they found a camping place, and to their astonishment they saw a fire ahead. They found at it a traveler who had wandered from one of the other parties.

They expected that the next day would reveal the valley of Los Angeles, west of the range they were climbing. Instead, on reaching the summit they beheld another lake, which they concluded to be another saline deposit. This was probably in Panamint Valley. The party divided, and each person made his own way across the valley. Some found good water; others found a supply of mesquite beans, in which unfortunately they saw no food value. On the west, or probably southwest, side the party reunited and toiled up a canyon. Near its head wet ground gave hope of finding water, but digging produced no results. Here one of the men, named Fish, died, and his body was left lying upon the ground.

A gentle grade sloped down from the next summit. A large lake was visible far to the left; from the descriptions given, this was probably Searles borax lake. Half way down the slope Ischam gave out, and was left. A little farther on one of the scattered men found a small spring of good water and called the others to it.

Here there is a contradiction in the accounts. The statement has been made that Ischam wandered into the Martin camp, and died there, and that this was at a point from which Owens Lake was reached. Colton's story is that from the spring mentioned in the last paragraph, certainly many miles south of Martin's course, a detachment went back to rescue Ischam. They found him alive, but with his tongue and throat so swollen that he could not swallow the water they gave him. While the rescuers were with him, says Colton, he died, and was buried in a shallow grave in the sand. Wherever this victim of the desert breathed his last, doubtless more than one of those with him wondered how soon his own turn would come to sink to rest in the desert and see, with scarcely comprehending eyes, his comrades pass on to escape a like fate.

An ox was killed at this spring, and the party was refreshed by the rest, good water and such sustenance as the carcass afforded. Proceeding, the party came upon a trail at a point south of Walker's Pass. Mindful of the Donner party's fate in the winter of 1846-7, Doty feared to undertake to cross the Sierras, the snow-crowned summits of which were visible ahead, so he turned south. At another spring some bunch grass was found, and the emaciated oxen were given a day's rest. One of them was slaughtered. Such were the straits of the men that hardly a part of the animal was wasted. The blood was saved for food. The intestines were cleansed with the fingers; the hair was singed from the hide, and all was roasted and eaten. One man softened the end of a horn in the fire and gnawed the softened part. Many bones of cattle were seen along the trail, evidence that others had come to grief in the same region. A man wandered from this camp, and was supposed to have perished until he was found in an Indian camp, years afterward.

The Brier family reached this camp before Doty left it, and were given portions of the slain ox. While Mrs. Brier was preparing a piece of liver for her children, a famishing Jayhawker took it from them while her attention was diverted. Such cases were few; the ordeals brought out more unselfishness than the reverse.

No other water supply was found for four or five days, while the worn travelers slowly made their way over the seemingly endless desert. The trail grew fainter and at last was wholly lost. Again small bands branched off to hunt for water. In one of these bands was Thomas Shannon. He started a jackrabbit from a bush and shot it. Drinking its blood he became delirious and was so found by a comrade who had come on a supply of water. A drink of water improved Shannon's condition, and the men made a meal from the first wholesome food they had had for days. All the others rallied to the spot except a man named

Robinson, who died before reaching it and was left in his blankets.

Another day's journey brought them to snow, and on February 4, 1850, they reached running streams and pleasant surroundings. Three wild mustangs were killed, supplying a hearty meal. Going on, the adventurers came to where many cattle ranged. Two animals soon fell before their guns. While they were feasting, two Mexicans approached, and proved friendly enough when they found that the marauders were not Indians as they had thought. From then on the Doty party members were cared for, and scattered to different parts of the State.

Having seen the Doty party to safety, we return to note the misfortunes of Bennett, Manly, Arcane and associates. Manly scouted far in advance, and while so doing he came on the carcass of an ox, from the thigh of which some meat had been cut. The sun had dried the flesh at the edge of the cut, and Manly made a meal of this raw dried beef. On Christmas Day he returned to the Brier camp, at that time distant from Doty's. He records that Brier was delivering a lecture on education, his family being his sole audience—a strange proceeding, Manly remarks, considering that the sole need at the time seemed to be something to sustain life.

Brier started on the next morning, and Manly found some scraps of bacon that had been thrown away at the camp. They seemed to him the best morsels he had ever tasted. Bennett's wagons were some miles back, and he rejoined them. Wild geese were heard overhead at night, and this was interpreted to mean that Owens Lake could not be far away. The next day he walked over the salt-crusted floor of Death Valley, and at dusk reached the campfire of the Doty party, then preparing to abandon their wagons. Meantime Bennett's gaunt oxen had dragged the wagons to Furnace Creek, to which he returned. The next stopping place was the "last camp," the location of which was much debated in after years. Manly's record indicates the spot as follows: Camped at a faint stream since named Furnace Creek; out of the canyon and into the valley; due south, distance not stated; across to the west side; the second night from Furnace Creek at a spring of good water coming from a high mountain which he says is now called Telescope Peak. This was the real "last camp." The party journeyed eight miles farther, reaching a sulphur spring on the top of a curious mound, from which return was made to the good water.

There was, however, more than one of the "last camps." The Jayhawkers burned their wagons a few miles from Furnace Creek, at a place called Lost Wagons. The Bennett camp, most prominent of all because of the long stay made there and the prolonged hardships of its occupants, was undoubtedly at Bennett's Wells, on the west side of Death Valley sink, and 260 feet below sea level. The water is brackish with salt and sulphate of soda, but is usable.

Four of the ox-team drivers concluded to strike out for themselves. Two of these were named Helmer and Abbott. It is probable that one of these was the individual whom the Jayhawkers picked up in the mountains. Two others later came into the Jayhawker camps, without having fared any better than those they had deserted.

After Bennett and party had gone back from the sulphur spring to Last Camp, a council decided that the only chance of getting any of the expedition through alive was to send out two of the strongest men as a forlorn hope, while the main party remained to await their return. W. L. Manly and John Rogers were selected for the undertaking. An ox which had given out was killed; so scanty was its flesh that seven-eighths of all of it was packed into the knapsacks of the two men. Two spoonfuls of rice and the same amount of tea was added to their stock, and after a parting which might prove to be the last they set out.

Those remaining in camp were Bennett, wife and three children; Arcane, wife and son; Captain Culverwell; two Earhart brothers; and four other grown persons, besides a Mr. and Mrs. Wade and their three children, who traveled the same course as the others but kept in a camp of their own. The Brier family were traveling in a free-lance

fashion, as has been set forth, not acceptable to the Jayhawkers and not choosing to join Bennett and Arcane.

The second day out Manly and Rogers found the body
of Fish on the trail, and saw the holes the Jayhawkers had
dug without finding water. Another range of mountains
was crossed before Rogers found a little sheet ice, which
they melted. The next night they overtook Doty and his
men and were supplied with meat and water to relieve their
immediate distress. They traveled on ahead, passing the
advanced members of the Jayhawkers and noting the skulls
of horses by the wayside.

One day after another the story was much the same
until they reached fresh water in the southern Sierra. A
crow, a hawk and a quail were the first fresh meat they
obtained; all three birds were stewed together. On the last
day of December, 1849, or the first day of January, 1850,
the men emerged from a barren valley into a meadow on
which cattle were grazing. A rifle shot soon supplied them
with food. A traveler named Springer, on his way to the
mines to the north, was met, and gave them further necessities. Reaching a ranch near San Fernando Mission they
obtained two horses, small sacks of beans, wheat, coarse
flour, and some dried meat. From another stockman they
bought a mule and a horse, and with this equipment took
the back track for Death Valley. The three horses gave
out one after another, the mule being the only animal able
to stand the hardships of the trip. The body of Captain
Culverwell was found as they neared Last Camp.

Seven wagons had been there when they left; only four
were seen as the anxious envoys looked from afar. The
canvas covers were gone. Had hostile Indians exterminated the unfortunates, or had they taken three of the
wagons and started in some other direction? Manly and
Rogers approached within a hundred years without seeing
a sign of life; then Manly fired a shot. All was quiet for
a few minutes, until a man crawled from under a wagon
and looked around. His shout, "The boys have come!"
electrified the camp, as well may be imagined. Bennett and
Arcane caught the returned men in their arms, and Mrs.

Bennett fell upon her knees and clung to Manly. Not a word was spoken, in the great emotion of all, until Mrs. Bennett exclaimed, "I know you have found some place, for you have a mule." It was some time before anyone could say anything without weeping. It had been twenty-six days since the forlorn hope had started out. All but the Bennett and Arcane families had abandoned the camp. Culverwell had set out with the last party before Manly and Rogers returned, but did not get far.

Wagons were abandoned, and the little procession set out for the land of running water and wholesome food. The children were slung in improvised "aparejos," made of stout shirts sewn together and thrown across the backs of oxen. The extreme emaciation of the animals did not prevent their bucking because of the unusual burden, and another camp had to be made to straighten out the tangle. The next day the party took its last view of the dreary surroundings, someone uttering: "Good-bye, Death Valley!" This appears to be the correct story of its naming.

The oxen became reconciled to their loads, and the women walked. In one place it became necessary to compel the beasts to jump off a precipice to a bed of sand the men piled up. Day by day the party moved along, with the important advantage over former experiences that they now had a better supply of food and some idea of their course. These facts did not, however, keep some of the weaker members from giving up hope, in spite of the assurances of Manly and Rogers, until discouragement finally ruled almost as it had before. Men, women and children were wasted, almost barefoot, and in tatters. The little ones cried for water that was not to be had. At last the melancholy procession passed through Red Rock Canyon and to a joyous resting place at springs not far from the southern end of that strangely sculptured defile. Strengthened and heartened, they pressed on, reaching snow in the Sierra nineteen days after leaving Death Valley. Toll was taken from the first herd of cattle found, and they were soon being cared for by the generous hospitality of the pioneer settlers.

This is a concentration of the most reliable accounts of that fearful experience. As stated earlier, there are contradictions without any sure indication of the true version; there are tales differing considerably from and doubtless less correct than this narration. Allowing for the differences mentioned, it is the story of the participants themselves, hence to be accepted beyond any of the distortions and variations which have crept into print at one time or another. J. B. Colton, of the Jayhawkers, wrote that four of his party perished in the Funeral Mountains, and that the range got its name from that fact. All other accounts agree that his detachment, commanded by Doty, reached the Panamint Range, west of Death Valley, before any of its members died, and that the death of Robinson, one of the four, occurred not far from the base of the Sierra. Colton stated that a dozen stragglers followed the expedition into Death Valley and that all perished from thirst and starvation; and that another train of thirty persons lowered their wagons into Death Valley by means of ropes and that all but two or three died while hunting for water. Having in mind the care with which Manly reviewed all details, his traveling back and forth between the parties, his having been over the ground after Colton and associates had gone on, and the fact that he makes no mention of these occurrences, the Colton account lacks confirmation and seems improbable.

While the foregoing travel details tell of but three of the seven companies, it is to be remembered that (according to Manly) the rest went southward with Hunt and reached Los Angeles safely. There may have been individuals who struck out independently on the Jayhawkers' trail and fared badly. Some names are mentioned more or less casually in one or another of the accounts without statement of what befell them. The Wade family is mentioned as being near Last Camp, without information as to what became of its members; likewise a Mr. Towne and family (hence Towne's Pass, in the Panamint Range) were connected with the expedition in some way not explained.

Different accounts say that eleven men left the Jayhawkers far east of Death Valley and that all but two perished. Manly explicitly states that these nine, the four Jayhawkers who died after leaving Death Valley, and Captain Culverwell summed up the death list. Whatever others may have died later, the evidence is that Culverwell was the only one of the expedition who died in Death Valley itself.

Every account pays tribute to Mrs. Brier. "She was a better man than her husband," wrote one. Manly says: "All agreed that she was the best man in the (Brier) party. She was the one who put the packs on the oxen in the morning. She it was who took them off at night, built the fires, helped the children, cooked the food, and did all sorts of work when the father of the family was too tired, which was almost all the time. It seemed almost impossible that one little woman could do so much. It was entirely due to her untiring devotion that her husband and children lived."

It is to be borne in mind that this grim tragedy occurred in midwinter, at the most favorable time of year for such a journey. The furnace-like heat that means death to travelers lost in that inferno was missing at that season; the dangers were in lack of water and sustenance. East of Death Valley lie hundreds of miles of desert, and every resource of the Forty-Niners was dangerously reduced. Had the expedition been undertaken in midsummer, probably few of the members would have survived to reach Death Valley, and none would have passed that formidable barrier.

Dr. S. G. George and party, visiting Death Valley in 1860, found unmistakable traces of the Death Valley party. Indians had drawn, on a smooth clay bed near one of the camps, a record of the occurrence. Men and women were shown with children slung in bags across the backs of oxen, in single file, headed in the direction taken by Bennett. No rain had destroyed the drawings in a decade. Numerous relics were found and given to different collections. Iron work of wagons, chains, cooking utensils and other articles were picked up by different visitors, many of the metal objects as free from rust as on the day they were discarded. Most of such finds went to the Society of California Pioneers, and like all else of interest in the society's museum were lost in the great fire of 1906.

Bones of animals indicated that earlier travelers had braved the same perils. Mexicans traveled the wastes, as "the old Spanish trail" goes to show, and probably they were the principal sufferers. There may have been other venturesome souls who, like many in later years on those deserts, simply dropped from human ken.

The George party found parts of skeletons near one of the springs. In one place a woman's skeleton, partly covered by a ragged calico garment, was found.

The Jayhawkers, though scattered to many different localities, held occasional reunions for many years. The last of these was at Mrs. Brier's home at Lodi, California, in 1911. Five of the party were living at that time, and three of them attended the reunion. Mrs. Brier died in 1913, at the age of 99 years. Manly died in San Jose in 1903, aged 83.

CHAPTER IX

A DECADE OF EXPLORATION

MORMONS SOUGHT SOUTHERN ROAD—AMARGOSA MINE FOUND—
SCHMIDT'S SURVEY 1855-1856—RESERVATION PROPOSED—PARTY
CROSSES KEARSARGE PASS—"WAKOPEE"—MONOVILLE A FACTOR IN
VALLEY HISTORY

After the Forty-Niners had walked in partnership with
tragedy through Death Valley, a new period of Inyo
history began. To call it a decade of exploration may seem
out of proportion, since we speak of but a single county;
but the term seems less inappropriate when it is recalled
that the county's borders include over ten thousand square
miles of diversified surface.

The Mormons, seeking to establish an outpost of their
faith at San Bernardino, wished to have a direct route
across the "leagues of cacti and sand and stars," through
southern Nevada, utilizing part of the "old Spanish trail,"
and entering California at the southeastern corner of the
Inyo of to-day. The springs which Fremont, in 1844,
named Agua de Hernandez were not far from the line of
travel, and afforded a place that in some degree helped to
break the long desert journey. They were renamed
Resting Springs, and still bear that fitting title. Years
later Philander Lee was to use the flow to irrigate a 200-
acre ranch; at that time the water nourished a goodly
meadow.

Mormon emigrants are said to have discovered, at a
point twenty-five miles south of the springs, the first gold
mine found in the desert. The year was 1854; the mine
was named the Amargosa. In later prospecting, the story
is, they discovered placer ground and worked it by hauling
the dirt three or four miles in wagons, to some salt springs.
`radition further has it that about 1858 Mormons found

silver ore in the Panamint Mountains, and produced some bullion from small furnaces at Anvil Springs and Furnace Creek. The gold discovery has the backing of this from Missionary Brown's book:

I had some specimens of the gold I had discovered near the southeastern boundary of California in 1849. . . . I showed the specimens to President Brigham Young, and in the spring of 1867, with a company which he authorized me to select, started for the California border. . . . We reached our destination in due course, and examined the gold prospect, which was quite rich. But there was no water within twenty-five miles, and it was not practicable to work the mines with the methods within our reach in those days.

There are serious discrepancies in the years, and hisorian Jensen, of the Mormon church, rather casts doubt on the whole story, Anvil Springs and all. The Mexicans worked the Amargosa mines about 1860, or before, and possibly built the little furnace in Death Valley. The finding of an old anvil in a Panamint canyon gave its name to Anvil Springs, but who left it there is indefinite.

Occasional adventurers were crossing the Sierra from the west. In 1853 Harry Edwards, an Indian agent, came into Owens Valley, if credence be placed in the headlines of San Francisco papers of that year; the printed text leaves the extent of his trip in doubt.

Earliest official attention to the eastern slope of the Sierras appears to have begun with a contract dated May 30, 1855, between Col. John C. Hays—Col. Jack Hays of Texas fame—who was then Surveyor of Public Lands in California, and A. W. Von Schmidt. The latter agreed to survey the public land east of the Sierras and south of Mono Lake. His work began that summer, and under a supplemental contract was continued and completed the following year. The survey extended from the Mount Diablo base line, a few miles south of Mono Lake, to a point south of Owens Lake, including the townships mapped as 1 to 12 south and 31 to 35 east. The party, as enumerated in Von Schmidt's field notes, included, besides himself, R. E. K. Whiting, compassman; Joseph Jefferson, E. Ross, E. Maginnis, J. W. Newton, chainmen; Henry Gardenier and E. S. Gersdorff, axmen.

Von Schmidt's field notes are liberal in comments on the region; his opinions are in many instances contradicted by the facts of present knowledge. Writing of Owens Valley he said:

Land entirely worthless with few exceptions. The only portion of any value is near the banks of the little streams of water coming from the Sierra Nevada mountains. This valley contains about 1000 Indians of the Mono tribe, and they are a fine looking set of men. They live principally on pine nuts, fish and hares, which are very plenty. On the western edge of this valley I found great quantities of grouse, other game very scarce. On a general average the country forming Owens Valley is worthless to the white man, both in soil and climate.

This note was dated July 15, 1855. The valley had, of course, no cultivation at that time, and except for natural meadows in lowland spots and occasional trees on the streams its stretches, generally sagebrush covered, were not inviting to one fresh from the springtime aspect of the grassy and flowered hills of western California.

Long Valley, with its miles of natural meadow and its delightful summer climate, impressed him much more favorably. "Splendid land for any purpose," he wrote; "soil first rate; fine grass, any quantity." However correct his estimate of the quality of that land may have been, he failed to take into account its 7,000 feet elevation and consequent winter severity.

He found many Indians in that region. Natural wonders received this mention:

Fine pine timber scattered over the township. There are also some of the most remarkable boiling springs and geysers that I have ever met with on the eastern slope of the Sierras. I have no doubt but what these springs will be of great value for medicinal purposes, as I found large deposits of sulphur, iron, soda and alum. In the south portion there is considerable fine grass, but its principal value is in its fine pine timber and mineral springs.

Another reference to the springs (those of Casa Diablo and Hot Creek) definitely asserts that they must have some connection with the orthodox infernal regions.

Von Schmidt found in Round Valley

land mostly level. Soil in general will average second rate, with fine grass, and also well watered, with but little pine timber on Indian

Creek. I found many Indians in this fractional township, who live in deep mountain ravines and come down here for grass to eat; also to dig roots called "sabouse" (taboose), which forms their principal article of food.

"Laid off today to fight Indians," remarks the surveyor in one place. There was little trouble with the natives, however, and as a rule the party conducted its observations in peace.

Now and then the field notes record that a township has fine streams of water, or that it is well covered with grass. With scarce an exception, however, the soil is classed as second or third rate.

The report of Thomas J. Henley, Superintendent of Indian Affairs in California, dated San Francisco, September 3, 1856, includes this reference:

A. W. Von Schmidt, Deputy United States Surveyor, relative to the Mono Indians living on the east side of the Sierra Nevada, in Mariposa and Tulare counties (the present Mono and Inyo) says: "They are a fine looking race, straight and of good height, and appear to be active. They live in families scattered through the entire valley, and get their living in various ways, such as it is. Game is very scarce; some few antelope are to be found in the valley, but the bow and arrow is not the proper instrument for game of that description, even if it were plenty. Hares are also found in some portions of the valley, which form their principal article of food in the meat line; but their principal article of food consists of clover and grass seeds, also of pine nuts, which I am told fail sometimes.

"They can also get fish, of a small size, in Owens River (the lakes Owens and Mono are both salt and have no fish.) But with all this they are in poor condition. The families being divided off and each having his own hunting ground causes some to go without food for days. One chief told me that sometimes he had nothing to eat for six days at a time. I estimated the number to be about 1000 in the entire valley. They are in a state of nudity, with the exception of a small cloth about their loins, and so far as I can see are in want of every article of clothing."

Though it is impossible to learn of all the white men who came to Owens Valley during the pre-settlement days, tarried briefly or not at all, and went on to other scenes, probably the total number was small. Two such visitors in 1857 were John Kispert and Charles Uhl, who had gone from Placerville, California, to the Nevada camp of

Johntown. Finding the placers there seemingly "played out," they started for Bear Valley, in southern California, to trap bears for the popular native Californian sport of bear-and-bull fighting. Whether that purpose was carried out we have no record, but their course was through Owens Valley. While not lingering, Kispert was so impressed by what he saw that in 1861 he returned and located at George's Creek, on ground to which he obtained government title years later. Necessity for building a log fortification during Indian hostilities did not prevent his tilling some acreage and raising crops of barley, much of which he marketed in Aurora at 36 cents a pound. The grain served human as well as equine life, the former parching it for use in lieu of coffee. Uhl's only other appearance in Inyo annals was as a member of Dr. Darwin French's expedition into southeastern Inyo in 1860.

Indian Agent J. R. Vineyard reported from Tejon Agency, California, August 20, 1858, as follows:

A delegation of Indians from the region of Owens Lake, east of the Sierra, visited the reservation a short time since. The people of that region, so far as I can learn, number about 1500. The delegation asked assistance to put in crops next season, also someone to instruct them in agriculture, etc. I would respectfully invite your attention to the subject, as they seem to be very sincere in their solicitations. I gave them presents of clothing and useful implements, and sent them back to their people, with the promise of transmitting their request to the great chief.

The Indian population of Owens Valley was augmented in 1859 by fugitive Indians from Tule River, in Tulare County. Deeds of violence had been going on in that region for several years, culminating in a campaign. The temporary advantage of the first fighting between the natives and settlers who sallied forth from Visalia was with the Indians. Old settlers, whites, asserted in later years that the white men were the ones at fault; the red warriors acted in a manner supporting this claim, for in their cabin-burnings and other depredations they attacked those who had taken the field against them. The war of a summer ended when soldiers from Fort Miller assisted the settlers in inflicting severe punishment, whether well

deserved or not, on the marauding reds. This has properly
a place in this history only because it sent into this county
numbers of Indians with a ready-made and burning hatred
of the white man and prepared to take part in keeping him
out of Owens Valley. It appears in fact that the worst
elements among the Owens Valley Indians throughout the
Indian war were renegades from other regions.

The events mentioned played a part in causing an order
by the national government, in February, 1859, suspending
from settlement township 13 south, range 35 east, Mount
Diablo base and meridian, this area extending from a point
west of Independence to the eastern foothills, and from
about three miles north of that point to an almost equal
distance south. The order of suspension, which stated that
the land was withdrawn pending decision as to making it
the location of an Indian reservation, was not revoked until
1864. As will be further disclosed, the idea of making
Owens Valley an Indian reservation persisted in official
circles almost up to the time of the revocation mentioned.
It was the purpose of several agents, and of a bill
introduced by Senator Latham in 1862.

During the summer of 1858 a Tulare man named J. H.
Johnson and five comrades were piloted across Kearsarge
Pass, west of Independence, by a Digger Indian named
Sampson—the latter a chief whose name was given to
Sampson's Flats, where many years later bandits Sontag
and Evans held the center of the stage very briefly. When
Johnson and his party reached this slope the Piutes were
found to be hostile, and two Indians were killed in a
skirmish. Their arms were bows and arrows and clubs.

After the secularization of the California missions,
many of the neophytes became renegades and joined the
Indians of the southern Sierras on the western slope. They
raided the scattered ranchos, driving away horses for food
purposes, until the designation of Horsethief Indians was
generally used as their tribal name. Owens Valley, known
but vaguely, was supposed to be one of their strongholds.
In July, 1859, a military expedition was organized at Fort
Tejon to explore the valley, investigate the character of its

inhabitants, and recover stolen stock. A correspondent accompanied the detachment, and an article from his pen was published in the Los Angeles *Star* of August 27, 1859, under the headlines, "Military Expedition to Owens Lake —No Stock in the Valley —Indians Peaceable and Reliable—Discovery of a New Route to Salt Lake." From it we learn that the expedition was commanded by Lieut. Col. Beall, who took a detachment of Co. K, First Dragoons, with Capt. Davidson and Lieut. Chapman as next in command. They started from Fort Tejon July 21, 1859, with rations for thirty days, a wagon, a howitzer and a pack train. Traveling via Walker's Basin, the Kern River mines, up the south fork of the Kern, and through Walker's Pass they came to Owens Lake. They found a fine meadow of 800 to 1,000 acres at the foot of the lake, and little or no meadow at any other one spot on its shores. The "emphatically saline" character of the lake water received comment; so also did "myriads of small flies over the water. The winds drive the larvae in large quantities upon the shore of the lake, where they are easily collected by the squaws."

The correspondent in speaking of Owens River says that the Indians call it "Wakopee." This is so similar in sound to "Waucoba" as to justify a surmise that the latter word may have had a more general application in the original naming of this region than has been commonly adopted or supposed.

The expedition found "beautiful streams of clear, cold water, irrigating beautiful and fertile sections of the valley for the following sixty-two miles from Pine Creek, principal among which are Clark's and Dragon forks, either of which supplies nearly as much water at this season of the year as does the Kern River." "One of the greatest aqueous curiosities of the trip," says the letter, "was a single spring, to which was given the name of Mammoth, from which runs a stream of water with a fair current fifteen of twenty feet wide and about two and one-half feet deep." Later residents know this as Black Rock Spring.

The correspondent writes:

Although for some distance below the lake we encountered temporary abodes of the Indians, yet in no instance were the troops enabled to get sight of a single one, they having fled before our approach (as we afterwards learned), they having been told they would be killed, until we reached Pine Creek, where the interpreter found a poor woman attempting to escape with her crippled child. She having been assured that the people would not be injured soon became the means of reassuring the Indians, after which there was but little difficulty in communicating with them.

To our surprise we saw but very few horses among them, and that, too, on the upper waters of Owens River, and these evidently were obtained from the Walker River Indians. They informed Captain Davidson that some four or five Indians, in years past, were in the habit of stealing horses for the purpose of eating them, but esteeming it wrong they some five years since punished some of the party with death and the rest had died from natural causes, since when none had been stolen by their people. They told us where we could find the bones of the animals they destroyed, and most certainly the appearance corroborated their statement, for there were no bones of more recent date than four or five years.

The Wakopee or Owens River Indians appear to be both morally and physically superior to any of their race in California, for in point of probity and honesty I certainly have never met their equal; and as to their physical condition, I saw none sick or infirm save the child already alluded to, although they will number 1200 or 1500 souls.

Whilst talking to their head men, who had assembled for that purpose, Captain Davidson informed them that so long as they were peaceful and honest the government would protect them in the enjoyment of their rights. Their reply was that such had always been their conduct and should ever be; that they had depended on their own unaided resources; that they had at all times treated the whites in a friendly manner, and intended to do so in the future. He further informed them that should they become dishonest and resort to murder and robbery, they would be pusished with the sword. The old captain or head man turned with a smile to the interpreter and said: "Tell him that we fear it not; that what I said, I have said. I have lain my heart at his feet; let him look at it."

When miner Cord Norst set out from the Mono camp of Dogtown, on July 4, 1859, to stroll over the hills, he made the first move in a train of consequences that materially affected Owens Valley. For Norst, wandering into Mono Gulch where Jedediah Smith had picked up gold

over thirty years before, accidentally found gold; not in
mere pinches, but in such quantity that Monoville came into
being within a week and within a few months was the
largest settlement between Salt Lake and the Sierras.
Savage tribes are credited with mysterious communicative
powers; like mysterious powers seem to account for the
spread of news of gold finds. From the camps of the
Mother Lode, from among the 11,000 people in the then
vast county of Los Angeles and the 4,000 within Tulare's
lines covering much of the southern San Joaquin Valley,
miners flocked to the new find, until it was claimed that
from 2,000 to 3,000 men were in or about the camp. Every
rod, said a report, of an eleven-mile ditch that was being
dug to bring water to the mines would pay from $3 to $150
per day per man. Lumber was needed by the ditchmakers,
and they whipsawed 40,000 feet before any of the five
sawmills that began business could get to producing lumber
that they sold at $125 per 1000 feet. Of the first thirty-one
buildings erected, twenty-two were liquor shops. By
January, 1860, there was talk of a new county east of the
Sierras, to govern a territory that a year earlier could not
muster more than a corporal's guard. Close on Monoville's
growth came the finding of Aurora, which was to reach
greater and more enduring importance. Owens Valley
became the thoroughfare for travel to those camps, and for
the stockmen who took their beeves from Tulare's plains.
Every issue of the Visalia paper, the *Delta,* told of parties
leaving for the mines, though it also noted such drawbacks
as five feet of snow in the mountains and living costs so
high that flour sold at the mines at $30 per hundred pounds.
In March it noted that our old friend, Captain Joe Walker,
was taking a party through. In May the paper expressed
the fear that there would not be men enough left in the
Visalia country to harvest the crops. All this travel had
much to do with creating knowledge of Owens Valley and
with starting an interest which suffered a setback when
the Indian war broke out. The Los Angeles *Star* remarked:

Within 60 or 80 miles of Owens Lake there is an immigration
of about 50 large wagons going to Aurora, loaded with valuable

goods and machinery, which can reach their destination by no other route than Owens Valley; besides which there are on the road a great many thousand head of cattle, sheep and hogs for the above destination.

Few records have been found showing the different parties that tarried in the valley during that period. One such was known as the Hill party, coming probably from Monoville. It established temporary headquarters where Lone Pine is, and prospected in the hills east and west. They named a Potosi district in the eastern range, but made no organization. Their travels included Mazourka Canyon, east of Independence, and there they located the Iowa and other claims.

Notes shown in Los Angeles in 1859 claimed that a deposit of coal existed in the southeastern part of the present Inyo, and Stephen G. Gregg, James Bell and —. Reynolds made a fruitless hunt for it.

Lewis Spitzer, in after years Assessor of Santa Clara County, California; Sam Kelsey, Charles and Jerome Smith and Charles Lumro stopped and prospected in Owens Valley early in 1860, but without finding anything to keep them from going on to Monoville, their original destination.

CHAPTER X

COSO AND THE DESERT CAMPS

DISCOVERIES THAT STARTED AN EXCITEMENT—FRENCH AND PARTY
LOCATE COSO—NARRATORS LIBERAL WITH FACTS—TELESCOPE DIS-
TRICT—ARGUS RANGE—MINING THE PUBLIC

If the Gunsight mine be not wholly a myth, that elusive bonanza was seen probably somewhere within the present borders of Inyo County, about 1849. There are stories, unverified, of Mormon mining in the Amargosa region within the next few years. Mineral-bearing rock had been found in the foothills east of Independence in 1859. But Inyo's mining day really dawned when Dr. Darwin French and his men, disdaining the lure of Monoville, set out to find the Gunsight, and instead discovered the ledges of Coso in March, 1860. During the next year Coso and its offshoot camps were the chief places of population south of Mono Lake; then their residents began to share Inyo history with adventurers who had gone into Owens Valley.

French, who appears to have started from Oroville, California, completed his party in Visalia, and started from there in late February or early March, 1860. With him were D. M. Harwood, Dennis Searles, Robert Bailey, James Hitchens, —. Walweber, Henry Siddons, Mont-gomery Smith, Sam Clinger, Zebe Lashley and Charles Uhl. Their Coso discoveries held them but briefly; they had not yet found the Gunsight. Going on, they found and named Darwin Canyon and Darwin Falls in honor of the leader.

On the return journey they gave more attention to Coso, and took samples and enthusiastic reports to Visalia. The find soon became the talk of that little town and of San Francisco as well. Tales of its richness, none too modest to begin with, soon matched the most extravagant that came from any find. M. H. Farley, soon on the ground, made further finds at what he named Silver Mountain, a few miles from Coso. He told in San Francisco, so that it was published in the *Alta California* July 24, that gold had been found going "fifty per cent to the pan." The same report said that "assays from samples from the Coso mines gave, in silver at $1.34 per ounce, $1,226.59, in gold $20.45" per ton of ore. He and those with him had not been backward in rewarding themselves for the arduous journey, having staked no less than ninety claims.

Farley described the country as sterile and waterless except for boiling springs, and further:

A few scattered Indians (the Coso tribe) live on herbs, roots and worms. They run swiftly away upon seeing the whites. About 20 miles to the southward of Silver Mountain the party visited an active volcano. On some of the cliffs in the neighborhood of the volcano were found sculptured and painted figures, the latter colored with some pigment, perhaps cinnabar. These were evidently the work of a former race, for the intelligence necessary to produce them does not exist among the squalid creatures now inhabiting that country.

He estimated that then, four months after the initial discovery, there were 500 men on the ground. His guess was probably as inaccurate as his reference to a volcano.

The Visalia *Delta* printed frequent references to Coso. Among those of July and August were the following;

Parties are leaving almost daily for the mines. There are now at the mines about 200 men, and about 100 prospectisg south and east of Owens Lake.

Excitement about the mines is still on the increase. A. H. Clarke took silver samples to San Francisco assaying $2000 to the ton.

Jacob Smith reports that ore from the Great Western, at Coso, assayed $2,750 to the ton, and from the Pioneer $2,552 to the ton.

Wm. Azbill reports the discovery of a cinnabar lead, traced seven miles. He dug down beside the ledge and could pan pure quicksilver.

Whether this remarkable cinnabar discovery was at Coso or nearer to Monoville is not made clear. Unfortunately the secret died with Azbill, for that ledge has never been heard of since. The mine boomer of to-day could teach those old-timers nothing of liberality of statements and economy of truthfulness.

The Oroville, Butte County, *Record* of July 21 reported, on the strength of statements by returned Orovillans, that eighty-two men were at the mines or in the vicinity, and that Oroville men had organized the Coso Mining Company, with Wm. McIntyre as president, W. C. Walden secretary, W. S. Finch treasurer, and with $78,000 capital stock, divided into 156 shares.

Practically all travel to and from the mines was via Visalia. The first wagons to try to get through Walker's Pass, en route to Monoville, had managed to make the journey in March, but almost all travel was by horseback over the trails. A letter in July told of the continuance of travel into Coso, and boasted that the camp would soon be within three and one-half days travel of Visalia.

French, having found and named the camp, organized a company to which he gave the same name, varying from that of the Oroville people by being the Coso Gold and Silver Mining Company.

Other prospecting parties had continued northward into Owens Valley, and detachments from them had gone in the desert northerly from Coso, into the Panamints and other ranges. Discoveries, at dates of which there is no record, had been made. W. T. Henderson had first climbed and named Telescope Peak, overlooking Death Valley, and a district bearing the name of Telescope was organized. W. B. Lilly was its recorder, E. McKinley his deputy, and adventurer Henderson was made superintendent of the Combination mines.

Henderson was a character of some notoriety. He had been a member of Harry Love's posse of manhunters who pursued and killed the outlaw Joaquin Murietta, of western California record. (Incidentally, accounts of Murietta's life show that during one of his flights from pursuit he holed up southeast of Mono Lake for a short time and made his way to Kern River through Owens Valley.) Many credited Henderson with having fired the shot that brought the redoubtable bandit low. Henderson himself denied this, and said that the robber was slain by J. A. White, who was also a member of the Telescope party and who was killed by Indians near those mines during the war. In later years Henderson became less averse to accepting the distinction, and when he died in Coarse Gold, Fresno County, in 1882, his reputed part in that affair was accepted by many as fact.

Some of the Telescope people went to San Francisco, taking several sacks of selected rich ore. An excitement of some consequence was skillfully worked up by those men, for whom a field had been prepared by the rich mines of the Comstock, Nevada, lode. Bailey, one of the Telescope locators, was a leader in working the financiers, and Jack Prouty was another who shared in the game of selling stock in companies formed to work claims or extensions. They picked up many thousands of dollars before they left the city "to develop the properties." Prouty got to Mazatlan, Mexico, where he was murdered—greatly to the satisfaction of Henderson, who wrote that "it was a timely end of a miserable humbug." Bailey disappeared also, so far as his dupes were concerned, with $25,000 of their money. Stephen G. Gregg, who had come across the Sierra with him, saw him afterward on a coast steamer, but was unable to find him when the boat reached San Francisco, or ever after.

Little work was done on the Telescope mines at that time. The following year Henderson and others started a 150-foot tunnel to tap the Christmas Gift ledge, found in 1860.

Argus district, nearer to Coso, was earlier than Telescope in being organized. Henry G. Hanks, in an address to the San Francisco Academy of Sciences, reported February 1, 1864, in the San Francisco *Bulletin,* gave its date as May 21, 1860. James E. Parker, in an address in Lone Pine on the Centennial Fourth of July, said it was July 23, 1860. These mines appear to have been found by a party independent of those heretofore mentioned, for neither the name of S. D. Hassey, chairman of the organization meeting, nor of M. Valentine, its secretary, appears on any of their rosters of membership.

The George party, of which Henderson was a member, made a trip into the Death Valley country the following December. This expedition thus avoided the heat which had been suffered on an earlier trip, succeeding so well that snow fell over the whole countryside before a start was made for home. Provisions began to give out, stated T. F. A. Connelly, another one of the party. The last baking of bread was cooked at Granite Springs, near old Coso. A mule and burro were turned loose to shift for themselves. The next morning the mule had frozen to death, and the burro was making a meal from the blanket which had been strapped on the mule to keep it warm. No more wood was available; sagebrush was not only scant but too wet to make a warming fire. The men kept from freezing by walking, jumping and dancing about the camp during the night. The next day the party reached Coso and its help, and from there went safely home.

Dr. French had heard of some place where the Indians shot golden bullets. Though he must have known that the savages had few guns for such uses, the story sounded so good that he organized another expedition. John and Dennis Searles, T. G. Beasley and T. F. A. Connelly, all well known in Inyo County in later years, were four of the nine men in the party. Though they spent eleven months in the desert, they failed to find any place where the yellow metal was so common, or where there was enough of it to tempt them to stay. They went back to Visalia satisfied that the story belonged in the same class as that of Ponce de Leon's fountain of eternal youth.

Coso continued to be the center of interest in the desert region, though occupying less newspaper space than in its first days. The Rough and Ready Mining Company, April, 1861, was one of the next organizations to bid for favor. A. H. Clarke was its president, H. U. Jennings secretary and Dennis Searles treasurer. It claimed 5400 feet of ledges, on a $540,000 capitalization.

That the camp took a fresh hold on public fancy toward the end of the year is evident from the fact that Captain George felt justified in starting an express between Visalia and the mines, making the horseback trip in four days. A company was formed to build a road to Owens Lake, and was granted a charter by the Legislature of 1862. This road was to run from the east side of Tulare Valley "between Deer Creek and Kings River, thence across the Sierra Nevada Mountains to a point between the north end of Owens Lake and the north end of Little Lake." This was intended to bring travel through Visalia for either Monoville or Coso. The promoters, having smoothed the legal path, found plenty of rivalry in willingness to share the prospective profits, the *Delta* noting that twenty-eight applications for the franchise had been filed. Nevertheless it does not appear that anything came of all this roadbuilding zeal.

While ambitious roadmakers were talking, John and William F. Jordan were going ahead with a trail project, under authority given by the Tulare Supervisors to "have made and declared open a pack trail or passway leading across the mountains from Tulare Valley to the south end of Big Owens Lake, running from Yokall" (Yokohl) Valley on the western side. Right of way for this trail was to be 33 feet wide, the trail to be completed within two years. While the petitioners did not mention wagon road, the Supervisors added the condition that a wagon road 16 feet wide should be completed within five years. John Jordan was drowned in Kern River in April, 1862, and this may have had something to do with the project being taken over by others. Henry Cowden, Lyman Martin and John B. Hockett reported to the Supervisors in December, 1863, that they had constructed the trail "to a point in the Owens River Valley at the foot of the Big Meadows and the Lone Pine Tree," at a cost of $1,000. The Supervisors thereupon set toll rates, 50 cents for a man and horse, 50 cents for a packed animal, 25 cents for each loose horse, mule or jack, 20 cents for each head of cattle, 5 cents for each hog, sheep or goat, 25 cents for each man on foot. Whether the builders ever got back their outlay, or even the one dollar per month they paid the county for the monopoly, no record shows. Their enterprise still exists as the well known Hockett trail.

Slate Range, not far from Coso, loomed up as a contender for attention. A district was organized there November 10, 1861, with Willet Dunn, P. Dean, W. S. Morrow and the ever active Searles brothers and A. H. Clarke as its chief citizens.

Sumner & Co., packing ore two and one-half miles from the Josephine mine in Coso district to small horse-driven arrastras, were taking out considerable gold. Hitchens & Munroe had built the first steam mill in the region, and were recovering $400 a ton from ore from the Winoshick mine.

But Indian warfare had been renewed in Owens Valley, and the scattered miners of the Coso country deemed it wise to seek safer climes for a while. Hitchens, in Visalia May 1, 1862, reported that the camp was deserted. He said a quantity of machinery was at Walker's Pass ready to go in when it was safe. Failing in an effort to secure military protection, 150 miners went back, finding that in their absence the Indians had demolished or carried off everything except the Hitchens & Munroe mill, the machinery of which may have awed them. An express was re-established, with T. G. Beasley as its courageous rider.

The Josephine mine was sold to Dr. J. B. Warfield and others that year. Coso was again on the wave of popularity, and prospects of heavy travel and consequent demand for feed for animals prompted San Franciscans who had branch houses in Visalia to wire instructions to buy up all the barley, it being anticipated that the price would reach twenty cents a pound before the following spring. The move was probably business, but it did not please the Visalians.

The Lotta mill at Granite Springs, driven by a 30-horsepower engine, started in August, and its performance delighted the owners. It was a custom concern, and its first contracts were on 25 tons from the Josephine and 50 tons from the Hyovee.

Slate Range was going ahead briskly. A mill there contracted to crush 3000 tons of rock from the Morrow, Albany and other leads for $35 a ton. The high price seemed relatively unimportant to the miners, for the Albany had been paying $150 per ton in gold when the ore was worked in a badly managed arrastra. Different companies, numerous by now, owned over three hundred claims. Other corporations were being organized; one of the more prominent was the Francis, incorporated for $1,000,000. Every report alleged that the ledges were immensely rich. A camp called Constitution, consisting of a dozen cabins, was started, but had a very brief existence. Ores from its mines were claimed to run $4000 a ton.

The Lotta mill, already mentioned, had cost $30,000, and included three four-stamp batteries, eight pans, etc., not to mention its reliance on the pioneer arrastra, of which it had four of 12-foot diameter, steam driven. Sagebrush was the only available fuel to use under its boiler.

Wadleigh & Holcomb, operating the Josephine, had forty men working, and had their shaft down 120 feet. One report published said that seven tons of the ore they were handling had paid $9,000, another that twenty-six pounds of gold had been received in Los Angeles from the mine. Other favorable reports of shipments were given out. But Indian troubles, again flaming out in Owens Valley, affected the enthusiasm, and one report said that only six companies were then operating, others closing down to wait for more peaceful times in the Coso country.

Slate Range developed other troubles as well. The readiness of the public to take up stock offerings and the lack of returns to investors caused the Visalia paper to observe that there was much feeling because of lack of development. More than one reference was made to this, the *Delta* saying that "Owners of Slate Range mines must quit trying to force their stock into the market, and develop their leads. Showing a piece of ore the size of a nut is played out." Floating companies seems to have been a popular proceeding, for in one issue alone of the *Delta* are particulars of the organization of seven new ones. The camp reached the stage of lawsuits, one injured individual bringing suit for $7,000 for trespass on his ground.

Slate Range answered the criticisms by reporting new "fabulous finds," and travel received fresh stimulus. Dennis Searles, coming out from the mines, met thirteen inbound packtrains in one day. Notwithstanding the complaints of fake stocks and lack of real work, shares of the Morrow company sold at $50, Albany at $40, others at nearly as good figures, in San Francisco. Dennis Searles sold an interest in six claims for $60,000 to men from Washoe (then a Nevada "excitement"), the Nevadans stating their conviction that Slate Range was rich as the soon-to-be famous Comstock lode.

The Lotta company, nearer Coso, saw opportunity for more than merely mining or mining promotion, and added land to their holdings. Their showing was so good that the *Pacific Mining Journal* advised its readers:

We have made a thorough investigation, and know of no other permanent investment so likely to pay a large and regular dividend to fortunate stockholders. The Lotta company owns the Wisconsin, Empire, Wadleigh and Abe Lincoln mines, showing assays of $400 to $600 per ton.

The Slate Range system of working the public rather than the ledges began to produce natural consequences. In one issue of the Visalia paper, August 7, 1863, were notices of assessments on eleven companies, in amounts ranging from $1.50 to $12 per share.

Farley, early comer into the Coso country, had as one of his ventures a mine called the Olancha, in the hills some eighteen miles southeast of Owens Lake. Ore was packed six miles and hauled twelve, to a mill which gave its name to the locality near which it was built. Having some trouble about what in these days would be termed labor turnover, Farley brought twenty-five freed negroes from Virginia, paying their transportation and promising ten dollars per month wages. The experiment was a failure; the colored men became dissatisfied with their job, and most of them failed to stay out the year they had agreed.

Large promises and small returns led to some investigation, and in 1865 the Visalia paper published charges of rascality against the management of the Josephine. The matter culminated in a Sheriff's sale at which the whole property went for $30,667. The mill, which T. F. A. Connelly had freighted in for 25 cents per pound, was naturally no larger than deemed necessary. While the batteries had shoes and dies of iron, wood served for the stems or long uprights by which the crushing mechanism was raised and dropped, and for every other possible part. The mill was burned during one of the periods of Indian-scare abandonment. Indians were claimed by the owners to have been responsible for the destruction, and an effort was made to collect $250,000 from the national government. Pioneers held very serious doubts as to the cause of the burning, believing that the mill had never paid, and was never worth the demanded price. Connelly's testimony on the freighting and his knowledge of the property helped to block the effort. The Searles mill in Slate Range was also burned, unquestionably by Indians.

The "fabulous finds" at Coso and Slate Range failed to last, and the American miners sought other fields. Mexicans succeeded them, in such numbers that by 1867 the locality bore the usual designation of "the Spanish mines." A record book of Coso district, now in the county museum, contains the minutes of a reorganization meeting held March 23, 1868. It is written in Spanish, and signed by eighteen Mexican names, with no other nationality represented. Mexicans continued to operate there on a small scale for a number of years. In more recent decades, some Americans have worked at Coso, but without restoring any degree of the excitement that once prevailed.

CHAPTER XI

COMING OF THE STOCKMEN

DISCOVERIES IN OWENS VALLEY—DERIVATION OF THE NAME INYO—
A THOROUGHFARE TO NORTHERN MINES—STOCKMEN BEGIN TO
DRIVE IN—FIRST BUILDINGS—"NO MAS KETCHUM SQUAW"—
BISHOP'S SAN FRANCIS RANCH—AN ELECTION FRAUD

Reference has been made to the George party of 1860.
In this company were Dr. S. G. George, Stephen G. Gregg,
adventurer Henderson, Moses Thayer, and others. This
expedition, leaving Visalia, got as far as Walker's Pass
before meeting another, which bore the ambitious name of
New World Mining and Exploration Company. This
latter company, formed in San Francisco and led by Col.
H. P. Russ, included T. H. Goodman, afterward captain of
a military company at Camp Independence and in his
closing years a high official of the Southern Pacific
Railroad Company; O. L. Mathews, who was to become
Inyo's first County Judge; and other men who later
figured prominently in affairs. The two companies joined,
and entered Owens Valley together. Henderson and hi
associates branched off at the foot of Owens Lake, to head
for the Telescope region.

The north-traveling section established a camp on
Owens River, a few miles southeast of the later site of
Independence. Dr. George observed, through a field glass,
bold outcroppings which he and Russ located, after
examination, as the Union lode. Because of the
encouraging outlook camp was moved to that vicinity, and
the men proceeded to organize Russ district, the first
semblance of any form of government in the territory now
included in Inyo County. Russ was chairman of the
meeting and George its secretary. Hanks, in his address,
gave the date as April 20, 1860. Among the claims located

at this time were the Union, Eclipse and Ida, as well as a
number which, unlike these, received little attention
afterward. Thayer was appointed superintendent, but was
soon succeeded by Gregg. Two years later the district was
reorganized, at a meeting which elected Lyman Tuttle
recorder and named Moses Thayer, J. R. Bell and R. S.
Whigham as a committee to revise its laws.

Indians began to visit the camp in a friendly way, and
were well treated. The whites sought to learn from them
the names of surrounding objects. Chief George (who
became a leader in the Indian war) told them the name of
the mountain range to the eastward was "Inyo," meaning,
as near as could be ascertained, "the dwelling place of a
great spirit." This was the origin of the county's name,
and the occasion was the first time it had come to the white
men's attention.

Prospecting had been the main purpose of immigrants
from across the Sierra prior to 1861, but a new factor,
the stockmen, was about to enter into Owens Valley
affairs. Some livestock had been driven through on the
way to the mining camps to the north, and the drovers
noted the fine grazing possibilities.

Mr. and Mrs. Alney T. McGee, their sons Alney, John
and Barton, Mr. and Mrs. J. N. Summers and Taylor
McGee gathered a herd of beef cattle in Tulare Valley in
the spring of 1861 and started for Monoville via Walker's
Pass. Barton McGee's account relates that from Roberts'
ranch on the south fork of Kern River to Adobe Meadows
in Mono County, considerably more than 100 miles, not a
white person or white settlement was seen. They
estimated that Owens Valley contained 1000 Indians, who
were not friendly to the whites and considered that
every one who came through their territory should pay
tribute. Their demands on the McGee party were refused.
No violence was offered, though efforts were made to
stampede the cattle, until threats of death if there were
further attempts in that direction put an end to such
interference. The journey was finished without further
molestation.

The first stockman to come this way to remain was Henry Vansickle, of Carson (then called Eagle) Valley, Nevada. A. Van Fleet came with him. W. S. Bailey drove his herds into Long Valley, just north of Inyo line, about the same time.

Van Fleet was accompanied by men named Coverdale and Ethridge. The three went south as far as Lone Pine Creek, seeing no white men except a few scattered prospectors in the White Mountain foothills. Returning to the northern end of the valley, Van Fleet made camp at the river bend near the present site of Laws, and prepared for permanent residence. He put up a cabin of sod and stone, completing it in August, 1861—the first white man's habitation in Owens Valley. He cut some wild hay that summer, the first harvest of any kind.

While Van Fleet was building, a rough stone cabin was begun by Charles Putnam, at Little Pine, later Independence, a stone's throw westerly from where the county jail now stands. The building was torn down in 1876. During the war period it was as much fortress as residence, and was used as house of refuge, home station and hospital. The neighborhood took the name of Putnam's, and was so known for some years. Once during the war, when the whites abandoned the valley, they prepared a surprise for any marauding natives who might undertake to destroy the cabin. A trench was dug around it and a quantity of blasting powder was poured into the trench, with a train leading to the wooden roof. The expectation was that one of the first acts of wreckage would be to burn the roof, and while the red men stood around enjoying the spectacle more or less of them would be blown into the happy hunting ground. But the close watch kept by the Indians defeated the plan. They carefully dug out the powder, and set a squaw at work with a stone mortar to reduce the grains to size suitable for rifle use. While this was being done, a spark was struck in the mortar. The consequences were laconically explained by an Indian some years afterward; he told of gathering up the powder and putting some of it into the mortar, with the rest piled up close by, then "No mas (no more) ketchum squaw!"

Soon after Putnam put up his house, Fred Uhlmeyer and J. F. Wilson came from Visalia and "squatted" on land near Independence.

Samuel A. Bishop and his retinue started from Fort Tejon July 3, 1861, for the Owens River country, which had been examined by his scouts. Mrs. Bishop, the first white woman to tarry in the valley, came with her husband; in the party were also Mrs. Bishop's brother, named Sam Young, E. P. ("Stock") Robinson, Pat Gallagher and several Indian herders. They drove between 500 and 600 head of cattle and 50 horses. On August 22 they reached Bishop Creek, and established a camp at what Bishop named the San Francis Ranch, at a point where the stream leaves the higher sandy bench lands and gravel foothill slopes and enters the lower level of the valley, about three miles south of west of the present town of Bishop.

Pines growing near by were felled, and from them slabs were hewn for the construction of the first wooden structures, two small cabins.

While Bishop's residence in this valley was brief, as his name was given to the stream and later to the town we note some details of his career. Samuel Addison Bishop was born in Albemarle County, Virginia, September 2, 1825. He started for California April 15, 1849, and after an adventurous journey reached Los Angeles October 8th. We next hear of him as an officer in a war with the Mariposa Indians in 1851. By 1853, he was virtually in charge of the Indian reservation at Fort Tejon. That year he and General Beale, later prominent in Kern County affairs, formed a partnership in stockraising and land ownership. During the period he was the sole judge of what courts there were in the region, and appears to have filled his trust with credit. In 1854 he and Alex Godey, one of Fremont's scouts, contracted to furnish provisions for the troops at Fort Tejon. The government decided to build a military road from Fort Smith, Arkansas, to Fort Tejon, and Bishop and Beale took a contract for its construction. While Beale began at the Fort Smith end, Bishop started to build easterly from Tejon. The partners were allowed the use of camels which the government had imported for desert work. The undertaking was full of adventures with which this record has no special concern.

Bishop's next venture was into this valley, after he and Beale had dissolved partnership. Following his stay in Inyo, he took a prominent part in affairs in Kern, and became one of that county's first Supervisors when its government was created in 1866. Two years later he and others secured a franchise for constructing a car line in San Jose, and that city was thereafter his home up to his death, June 3, 1893.

In the fall of 1861 J. S. Broder, Col. L. F. Cralley, Dan Wyman (hence Wyman Creek), Graves brothers and others came from Aurora to seek placer mines said to exist on the east side of the White Mountains. They spent the winter on Cottonwood Creek. Early the following year Indians from farther eastward ordered them to leave, when Chief Joe Bowers interfered, saying it was his territory. He later warned the whites, however, that they had better go, as he might not be able to protect them though he wished to do so. They took his advice, after giving him such provisions as they did not need and caching their mining goods. After the first hostilities of the war had ended, the party went back, accompanied by T. F. A. Connelly. Joe helped them to find the cached goods, which had been raided. One item in the stock was a flask of quicksilver. A hole had been broken in the iron flask, and the metal spilled. In explaining the occurrence, Joe demonstrated by making motions of picking up something, then showing his empty fingers, with the remark: "Heap no ketchum." Joe was friendly to the whites throughout the Indian troubles; and as will later appear, one of the men he specially befriended had less of decency and justice in his makeup than did the aboriginal chief.

The brief tenancy of prospectors in "White Mountain District" in the fall of 1861 served as a basis for an attempted election fraud which attracted much attention

in California legislative affairs in 1862 and 1863. That
section, now in Inyo County, was then under Mono's
jurisdiction. The latter county was joined in a legislative
district with Tuolumne, for election of State Senator and
Assemblyman.

"Big Springs Precinct" was established by Mono
Supervisors, August 26, 1861, with its polling place at
what is now known as Deep Springs. This was done by
the Mono board on a request bearing one or two
signatures. The election was held September 4th, so the
precinct was created less than two weeks in advance.

The candidates for the State Senate from the district
were Leander Quint, Union Democrat, and Joseph M.
Cavis, Union; for the Assembly, B. K. Davis, Brecken-
ridge Democrat, and Nelson M. Orr, Republican. Election
returns as submitted by the County Clerk gave the vote as
follows: For Senator: Cavis 372 in Mono, 1,664 in
Tuolumne; total 2,036; Quint 741 in Mono, 1,467 in
Tuolumne, total 2,208. For Assemblyman: Orr 1,728 in
Tuolumne, 344 in Mono, total 2,072; Davis 1,563 in
Tuolumne, 657 in Mono, total 2,220. On the face of the
returns, therefore, Quint and Davis were elected.

Orr, of Tuolumne, was convinced that there was
something wrong with the figures, so he came over to Mono
and made a personal investigation. The returns of that
county showed that Big Springs precinct had cast a total
of 521 votes. McConnell, for Governor, had received 406
of these. Quint had been given 510, and Davis 298. Not
a single Republican vote was noted, and another singular
disclosure was that while a full State ticket was being
elected no votes were returned for any office except
Governor, Senator and Assemblyman. Orr visited Big
Springs precinct, and was able to find only a handful of
men in the region.

Orr and Cavis applied to the respective Houses of the
Legislature to be seated in place of Davis and Quint. The
Assembly Committee on Elections held a lengthy hearing,
calling many witnesses from Mono County. Orr,
petitioner, alleged that no election was held in the so-called

Big Springs precinct, and produced evidence that there was virtually no population in the precinct. Davis's witnesses (none of whom were from the precinct) testified that they had sold goods to be taken to Big Springs to an amount indicating a large population, and that they believed there were at least 500 voters there. They also testified that one of Orr's witnesses had been paid $250 for his testimony. R. M. Wilson, County Clerk of Mono, when called on to produce the ballots and poll list, said he had mailed them to Sacramento, but singularly they failed to reach that city.

A witness testified that he saw the alleged poll list and election returns prepared in a cabin near Mono Lake; that they were written on torn fractional sheets of blue foolscap paper. Others were unable to identify more than two or three names on the alleged poll list, when it had been presented to the Supervisors, as being those of persons known to be in Mono County. A citizen who looked over the list was struck with the familiar appearance of some of the names, and finally ascertained that they had been copied from the passenger list of the steamer on which he had come from Panama to San Francisco.

Notwithstanding the palpable fraud, a few in each House were found to support its beneficiaries. Orr was declared to have been elected, by vote of the Assembly February 13, 1862, forty-eight for Orr, four for Davis. The Senate, like the Assembly, had a Democratic majority in that session, but proved to be less ready to right the wrong; and it was not until March 28, 1863, well into the session of a year later, that Cavis was seated by a three-fourths Union Senate.

CHAPTER XII

BEGINNING OF INDIAN WAR

CATTLEMEN WINTER IN VALLEY—SEVEREST SEASON IN INYO ANNALS
—SETTLERS MENACED AT SAN FRANCIS—TREATY SIGNED—A SCRAP
OF PAPER—MARAUDING COMMENCED—INDIANS KILLED AT PUT-
NAM'S—MURDER OF WHITE MEN—ALABAMA HILLS FIGHT

As the winter of 1861-62 approached, some of the cattlemen who had driven into Owens Valley saw no reason for leaving its abundant grazing. As late as the first week in November Barton and Alney McGee got together a drove of 1,500 head of cattle, and came this way. While they were at Lone Pine, on November 12th, snow fell to a depth of four inches. They went on to George's Creek, then concluded to winter in the valley. Barton McGee reported that there were then settlers on Little Pine Creek (Independence), Bishop Creek and in Round Valley. He went to Aurora for supplies, where he found eight feet of snow. Returning with provender, the party went to Lone Pine and put up a cabin. Fine weather favored them until Christmas Eve, when there came the real beginning of probably the hardest winter that white men ever saw in Inyo. McGee noted that there was not a day of the next fifty-four without a downpour of either rain or snow; "not continuous," he wrote, "but at no time did it quit for a whole day, snowing to a depth of two feet or more and then raining it off. The whole country was soaked through and all the hills were deeply covered. All the streams became impassable, while the river was from one-fourth to one mile in width, about half ice and half water, and sweeping on to the lake, paying no respect to the crooks and curves of the old channel in its course to the lake, which it raised twelve feet." These reports of severe weather in Inyo are corroborated by official records for other parts of

California, for during that January the rainfall at Sacramento was over fifteen inches. A book published two years later refers to the floods of that winter as "the most overwhelming and disastrous that have visited this State since its occupation by Americans." The first flood submerged the Sacramento Valley about December 10th, the water rising higher than in either of the memorable floods of 1851 and 1852. For six weeks thereafter an unusual amount of rain descended. On the 24th of January the second flood attained its greatest height, and the Sacramento and San Joaquin valleys were transformed into a broad inland sea stretching from the foothills of the Sierra to the Coast Range, and somewhat similar in extent and shape to Lake Michigan. In that same month of January, a rain of three days' duration fell on the accumulated snow around Aurora, many of the adobe and stone buildings of the camp fell, and loss of life was occasioned by a flood in Bodie Creek. The McGee account indicates that Owens Valley shared fully in the great downpour.

The few white men in the valley had nothing on which to subsist except beef, and much of the time they were without salt to make their monotonous fare more palatable. What must have been the plight of the Indians? Life was a hard struggle for them at the best; and under the conditions of that severe winter the herds of the whites offered the only means of preventing starvation. Besides, the Piute held that the white men were intruders. That the natives began to gather food from the ranges was only what might have been expected; it was what most white men would have done under such circumstances. The whites submitted to the loss of many animals before beginning retaliation.

The first act of revenge by the white men occurred when Al Thompson, a herder in Vansickle's employ, saw an Indian driving away an animal and promptly shot him. This occurred not far southeast of Bishop. A man named Crossen, better known as Yank, was then captured and killed by the Indians. He had come from Aurora and had stayed for a few days with Van Fleet. He crossed the river to the west side and was taken not far from where Thompson had done his killing. All that was ever seen of him again was part of his scalp, found at Big Pine, and some of his clothing worn by Indians.

It appears to be true, however, that scalping was not a usual practice of the Owens Valley Indians. Instances of that kind were very few. During the Indian war, a collection of a dozen scalps of white men were found in a cave near Haiwai (now Haiwee). The supposition was that they were evidence of a massacre by some other tribe.

The principal Indian settlement of the northern part of the valley was on Bishop Creek, within a short distance of Bishop's camp. Indians from all parts of the valley, and beyond, gathered there in the fall of 1861 and held a big fandango. Among those who were mixing war medicine were the usual sorcerers, who claimed that their magic would make the white men's guns so they could not be fired. The anxious stockmen kept their weakness concealed as well as they could, until reinforcements happened to arrive. A storm had wet the guns in camp, and to insure their reliability when needed they were taken outside and fired. This, disclosing to the tribesmen that the sorcerers' guarantees were not wholly dependable, helped to prevent the threatened assault, and the gathered Indians moved away.

The situation caused great alarm among the scattered settlers, and they gladly agreed to a pow-wow with the Indian chieftains. This conference was held at the San Francis ranch on the last day of January, 1862. Chief George defined the Indian view by marking two lines on the ground to show that the score was then even, referring to the Indian killed by Thompson, and the killing of Crossen. A treaty was drawn up and signed, as follows:

We the undersigned, citizens of Owens Valley, with Indian chiefs representing the different tribes and rancherias of said valley, having met together at San Francis ranch, and after talking over all past grievances, have agreed to let what is past be buried in oblivion; and as evidence of all things that have transpired having been amicably settled between both Indians and whites, each one of the chiefs and whites present have voluntarily signed their names to this instrument of writing.

And it is further agreed that the Indians are not to be molested in their daily avocations by which they gain an honest living.

And it is further agreed upon the part of the Indians that they are not to molest the property of the whites, nor to drive off or kill cattle that are running in the valley, and for both parties to live in peace and strive to promote amicably the general interests of both whites and Indians.

Given under our hands at San Francis ranch this 31st day of January, 1862.

Signed for the Indians by Chief George, Chief Dick and Little Chief Dick, each of whom made his mark; for the whites by Samuel A. Bishop, L. J. Cralley, A. Van Fleet, S. E. Graves, W. A. Greenly, T. Everlett, John Welch, J. S. Howell, Daniel Wyman, A. Thomson and E. P. Robinson.

One of the chiefs missing from the conference was Joaquin Jim, leader of the tribe in southern Mono, which then included the valley as far south as Big Pine Creek. It was probably Joaquin Jim's braves who began renewed depredations. At any rate, the treaty proved to be merely a passing incident. Within two months war was on in earnest.

During February Jesse Summers came from Aurora for beef for that market. He gathered a few in the southern end of the valley and went back to Aurora, leaving Bart and Alney McGee to drive the band. They got as far as Big Pine Creek, where Jim's camp happened to be at the time. Jim and a few of his men visited the McGee camp, and acted so unfriendly that the brothers concluded to move. Alney went to get the horses, and Jim demanded something to eat. Bart poured him a cup of coffee, which he threw, cup and all, into the fire. McGee jumped toward the guns, which the Indians had set to one side. McGee took the precaution to discharge the weapons, then told Jim to take them and go, which he did. The brothers moved on and spent the night safely though uncomfortably in a wet meadow, with their horses close at hand. Alney went on the next day with Summers, whom he met at Van

Fleet's. Bart went to the San Francis ranch. The next day he rode back to Putnam's and reported that the northern settlers wanted help. On his way down the speed of his horse got him safely past a band of Indians at Fish Springs, untouched by the many shots they fired at him.

Fifteen men came with McGee from Putnam's to help to move the cattle from Bishop Creek. The night they reached the San Francis ranch the Piutes provided a striking exhibition of fireworks, running about and waving burning pitchpine torches secured to long poles. The Indians surrounded the cabin and sent in a delegation. Though they claimed to be friendly, they held a war dance around the building, and told the whites that the Piutes had charmed lives and could spit out the bullets that might enter their bodies. The night passed without violence.

The next morning the drive of stock began, reaching what is now Keough's Hot Springs the first night. Though pickets were put out, Indians succeeded in driving off 200 or more head of cattle. The next morning three of the men went after the stock, and were met by a line of forty or fifty Indians who ordered them back—an order with which they could do nothing but comply. Indians hovered about the flanks of the drive down the valley, but did not molest it further.

A few days later Barton and John McGee, Taylor McGee, Allen Van Fleet, James Harness, Tom Hubbard, Tom Passmore, Pete Wilson and Charley Tyler ("Nigger Charley") were near Putnam's when they saw four Indians going toward the cattle. Bart and Taylor McGee, Van Fleet, Harness and Tyler went out to where they were. The Indians when interrogated said they were going after their horses. They were told they could go on, but must leave their weapons until they came back. This they refused to do. The controversy continued for some time. One account is that Van Fleet made the first threatening move by leveling his gun at an Indian; his own story, and that of other whites, was that the Indian first pointed an arrow at him. Whatever the facts of this, Van Fleet turned his body and got the first wound, an arrow in his

side, where its obsidian head remained until his death fifty
years later. Harness was also wounded before the whites
shot. In the melee which ensued all the Indians, one of
whom was Chief Shondow, were slain. Hubbard was shot
through the arm with an arrow.

It is fully possible that the whites were to blame in this
affair. An account reaching Aurora held them responsible,
and Barton McGee in writing of it, said: "This occurrence
created a little trouble in our ranks, some thinking we were
not justified in firing on them and others saying we did
exactly right. Be that as it may, it was done." This does
not well accord with the narration of the fight as above
printed on the statements of McGee and Van Fleet.

A few more than forty white men were gathered at
Putnam's, and they began to strengthen their fortification.
Rocks, old wagons, boxes and other materials were used to
pile up a barricade. Charles Anderson was elected captain,
and a constant guard was maintained while the company
remained there. Sheriff Scott, of Mono, was among the
men, and in a letter said: "The Indians appear warlike
here, and we expect a battle before many days—possibly
tonight. There are forty-two of us, armed with rifles,
shotguns and sixshooters. We have fortified ourselves the
best we could with wagons, oxbows, yokes, rawhides, etc.
I can escape easily, but to do so would be to weaken the
force in the fort, and so enable the redskins to wipe out
those who would be obliged to remain."

A band of natives had gone to Van Fleet's cabin on
the river, previous to this gathering at Putnam's, and had
demanded admission. After some parley he gave them
provisions. They set out toward Benton, then known as
Hot Springs. Prospector E. S. Taylor lived alone in a
stone cabin at a place still called Taylor Springs, a mile or
more northeast of Hot Springs. A Benton Indian known
as Butcher Fred, at last accounts still living though blind
and decrepit, was a boy with the attacking party, and in
later years told white acquaintances of the affair. He said
the Indians surrounded the cabin and besieged it for two
days before succeeding in setting its thatched roof afire.

That forced Taylor to come out, and he was pierced by many arrows. During the siege he killed ten Indians. Taylor, known as "Black," had been a companion of W. S. Bodey when the latter discovered the famous mines to which his name was given. Until recently, at least, traces of Taylor's cabin were still to be seen at the scene of this killing.

Whatever of division there may have been in the Putnam camp over the killing of Shondow, there was no dissent when it was proposed to strike a blow that would discourage raids on the cattle. Preparations for a campaign were made, and twenty-three men, led by Anderson, left Putnam's after dusk masked their movements. Cralley was chosen lieutenant. Scott Broder, the McGees, Tyler, Harness and Shea were among those in the column, which went that night to the sod cabin of Ault and Sadler, not far from the Alabama hills.

As soon as the east began to gray, three men were left with the horses at the cabin and the others set out in two equal squads. Anderson's detachment went to where the light of campfires could be seen over the Alabama hills; the others went up the stream. The sun was just rising as Anderson came up to where the Indians were breakfasting. Firing commenced at once, a number of Indians being killed at the first volley. They ran to shelter in the rocks, "and a good shelter it was," wrote Bart McGee, "cavities where they were out of sight in less than thirty seconds. We could not follow them in, so we did the best we could from the outside, shooting into the mouths of their dens, while the Indians threw arrows among us in showers. It seemed the air was full of arrows all the time. They did not have any guns or they would have made it a hard fight for us. We fought there for about an hour before the other boys, hearing our firing and coming across the rough hill, could reach us. We fought until about 1 o'clock, hitting some 30 or 40 of them, destroying about a ton of dried meat and some of their camp outfits." The white casualties included another arrow hole in Hubbard's arm, a wound in Harness's forehead made by an arrow which shattered against the skull without penetrating, and an arrow wound in Scott Broder's shoulder. The last mentioned injury was so troublesome that the citizens withdrew to the fort, leaving the natives in their stronghold. While McGee mentions that 30 or 40 Indians were hit, and another account said that Negro Charley Tyler himself shot four Indians, a report sent to Los Angeles gave the total Indian strength in the fight as 40 and said that their dead numbered eleven.

CHAPTER XIII

WHITES DEFEATED AT BISHOP CREEK

INDIANS SEEK OUTSIDE HELP—INDIAN ELOQUENCE—RENEGADE RED
MEN GATHER IN OWENS VALLEY—MERCHANTS SUPPLY THEIR
AMMUNITION—KELLOGG AND MAYFIELD COMMANDS—DEATHS OF
SCOTT, MORRISON AND PLEASANT—FIELD ABANDONED

During this time Owens Valley Indians had appealed to their people elsewhere for aid. Nevada Piutes had suffered severely in a recent war of their own, and the majority were not inclined to hunt further trouble. They had realized the truth of predictions attributed to Numaga, one of their leaders. As was observed in an earlier chapter, authenticity of reports of Indian eloquence is not above question; however, Numaga, endeavoring to keep his people from the warpath, is alleged to have spoken thus:

You would make war upon the whites. I ask you to pause and reflect. The white men are like the stars over your heads. You have wrongs, great wrongs, that rise up like these mountains before you; but can you from the mountain tops reach up and blot out those stars? Your enemies are like the sands in the beds of your rivers; when taken away they only give place for more to come and settle here. Could you defeat the whites, from over the mountains in California would come to help them an army of white men that would cover your country like a blanket. What hope is there for the Piute? From where is to come your guns, your powder, your lead, your dried meats to live upon, and hay to feed your ponies while you carry on this war? Your enemies have all these things, more than they can use. They will come like the sand in a whirlwind, and drive you from your homes. You will be forced among the barren rocks of the north, where your ponies will die, where you will see the women and old men starve, and listen to the cries of your children for food. I love my people; let them live; and when their spirit shall be called to the great camp in the southern sky, let their bones rest where their fathers were buried.

But in spite of their wiser leaders, many Nevada warriors came to Owens Valley. More came from the west, from the Tulare and Kern bands that had been but recently defeated, and from southern California. Indian Agent Wasson, of Nevada, asserted in the Carson *Silver Age,* April 18, 1862, that the combatants were mostly California Diggers, and that the Piutes were averse to hostilities. The Visalia *Delta* of that May disputed this, declaring that the Indians of Tule River, at least, were not hostile; they had given up their arms, and said that if they were furnished with food they would agree that every Indian in the district would be on the reserve and would answer roll call every morning. They were anxious to stay and work, but would not stay and starve. The same paper at different times referred to alleged misuse of Indian supply funds, so that it is not hard to credit that some of the western recruits in the valley came because of thieving white men.

An important ally came in the person of Joaquin Jim, a Fresno renegade who had been outlawed by his own people, a man of unusual courage and determination, and one who never became reconciled to white dominance. By the time the warriors had congregated in Owens Valley, it was estimated that they numbered from 1,500 to 2,000 fighting men.

The red men also found assistance in Aurora, where merchants Wingate and Cohn were said to do a thriving traffic in ammunition for what guns the Indians had. The same Wingate refused to sell ammunition to a messenger from the settlers, asserting his belief that all the white people in Owens Valley should be killed. A Visalia storekeeper was mentioned by the paper there as furnishing ammunition intended for the Indians.

Al Thompson and a companion were sent to Aurora for help for the white men, and secured the coming of a party of eighteen, commanded by Captain John J. Kellogg, a former army officer. One of the volunteers was Alney L. McGee.

After the Lone Pine battle the citizens at Putnam's had elected Mayfield their captain. Accounts of the expedition next starting from there do not agree, ranging from twenty-two to thirty-five; the best supported estimate seems to be thirty-three. This force moved northerly to attack the Indians. At Big Pine they found the bodies of R. Hanson and Tallman (or Townsend), who had been killed by the Indians a few days before. Both corpses had been torn and mutilated by coyotes, and that of Hanson (a brother of A. C. Hanson, one of the expedition, in later years County Judge) was identified by the teeth.

Kellogg came down east of the river, the same day. He believed the Mayfield command, which could be seen across the valley, to be hostiles. The mistake was straightened out and the two commands united. All night long the hostiles occupied the rock strewn hillsides near by, and kept up a continuous howling. The next day, as the force moved northward, an Indian scout was killed by Tex Berry. Dr. A. H. Mitchell, who proved to be an abject coward in the later fight, acted consistently with that character by scalping the Indian and tying the bloody trophy to his saddle. He afterward lost horse, saddle and all. About noon of April 6th camp was made at a ditch or ravine about two miles southwest of the present town of Bishop.

The Indians held a line extending from a small black butte in the valley across Bishop Creek and to the foothills south. Their numbers were variously estimated at from 500 to 1,500. Opposing them was a white force of from fifty to sixty-three men.

The Piutes were defiant in their demonstrations, and the white men waited only long enough to eat a meal before going into action. Kellogg's force moved up along the creek; Mayfield took his men more southerly. A deep wash was encountered, and the pack animals were left there with a man in charge. Mayfield, Morrison and Van Fleet were at the head of the line when the Indians opened fire. Van Fleet dismounted and handed his bridle to Mayfield. A bullet penetrated Morrison's body, and Mayfield, not seeing his men coming up, became panic-stricken and would have fled leaving Van Fleet afoot if he had not been threatened with summary vengeance.

Kellogg saw that the Indians were about to move around and either cut off the line of retreat or separate the two parties of whites. In response to his call for a volunteer to warn Mayfield, Alney McGee made the ride, during which his horse was killed.

The white men then retreated to the shelter of the ditch. Morrison was put in front of Bart McGee, on the latter's horse, and with Alney McGee steadying him was taken to the trench. "Cage," or James Pleasant, a dairy-man who had come from Visalia, was in front of them. They happened to be looking directly at him when a bullet hole appeared in the light gum coat he wore. He did not reply to a question asked, but rose in his stirrups and fell from his horse, dead. The situation was so pressing that for the time the body was left where it fell.

Anderson collected some of the men at a small hill and kept the foe back until Morrison could be taken to a safer place. As the men went back, an Indian wearing only some feathers in his hair was seen going toward the pack train. It was suggested to Hanson that there was his chance to get revenge for his brother's death, and Hanson and Tyler rode out and killed the too venturesome red man. The latter's costume was similar to what a great many of the warriors were wearing at the time. "The uniforms they wore was nawthin' much before, an' rawther less than 'arf o' that be'ind."

The whites reached the ditch entrenchment without further casualties, and from there maintained a defensive battle. One veteran of the fight stated that "Stock" Robin-son killed an Indian who was crawling through the ditch to get at close quarters with the defenders. One Indian had a point of vantage behind a pile of grass from which he fired several shots. He was killed by Van Fleet, who watched for his rising to shoot. Mitchell, who had dis-tinguished himself by scalping the Indian scout killed on the way up the valley, proposed that all made a run for safety. Anderson, knowing that if that were done the whole party would be exterminated, said he would shoot the first man who left them to run. Mitchell then bravely proclaimed his own intention of taking a shot at any one who would exhibit such miserable cowardice.

The whites had spread out some of their powder to have it handy for loading purposes. Some one struck a match which fell into it, and one man was severely burned in the explosion which followed.

Darkness came on, and firing from the Indian lines almost ceased. N. F. Scott, Sheriff of Mono, who had come from Putnam's with the Mayfield party, raised his head above the ditch rim as he undertook to light his pipe. As he did an Indian bullet struck him in the temple, causing instant death. He had come into the valley on official business a short time before.

The beleaguered whites waited until the moon went down, well along in the night, before making a move. Then they retreated to Big Pine, unmolested. Morrison was taken with them, but died soon after reaching Big Pine Creek. This brought the white dead up to three. The number of Indians who fell was unknown, but was variously estimated at from five to fifteen or more. A report published soon afterward said that eleven Indians were killed. The fatalities in this affair, as in nearly every case during the fighting, resulted from bullet wounds. Indian arrows did little harm except at close quarters. Fortunately for their opponents the Indians had but few guns, and were too ignorant of their care and use to make them very effective. Had Piutes possessed any marked degree of courage they could have wiped out the little company of white men, though of course it would have been at a heavy cost to themselves.

The men, who were in this fight, so far as ascertained from different records, included Harrison Morrison, "Cage" Pleasant and N. F. Scott, who were killed; Captain Mayfield, Charles Anderson, Alney McGee, Barton McGee, A Van Fleet, A. C. Hanson, Thos. G. Beasley, R. E. Phelps, E. P. Robinson, John Welch, Thomas Hubbard, Thomas Passmore, William L. Moore, A. Graves, James Harness, John Shea, —. Boland, Pete Wilson, L. F. Cralley, Tex Berry, James Palmer, A. H. Mitchell,

"Negro" Charley Tyler, a Tejon Indian and others unrecorded.

No two of the several accounts of this fight, as obtained many years later by the author from participants, agree in all respects; the versions having the most corroboration of fact or probability have been accepted. White evidence did not agree as to where their men made a stand; the statement by one of them that it was at the west side of what is now the Barlow ranch, about two miles west of Bishop, agrees with what Indians have said about it.

CHAPTER XIV

WHITES AGAIN BEATEN

INDIAN AGENT WASSON COMES TO MAKE PEACE—APPEAL FOR TROOPS
—A CAUTIOUS GOVERNOR—WASSON ENTERS VALLEY AT HOUR OF
BATTLE—EVANS' TROOPERS ARRIVE FROM SOUTH—SOLDIERS AND
CITIZENS RETREAT FROM ROUND VALLEY—MAYFIELD KILLED

Enters now into these chronicles the nation's soldiery, also one Warren Wasson, acting Indian Agent for the Territory of Nevada.

Through news reaching Carson by way of Aurora, Wasson learned of the beginning of trouble in Owens Valley. Under date of March 25, 1862, he telegraphed to James W. Nye, Governor of Nevada, who was then in San Francisco:

Indian difficulties on Owens River confirmed. Hostiles advancing this way. I desire to go and if possible prevent the war from reaching this territory. If a few men poorly armed go against those Indians defeat will follow and a long and bloody war will ensue. If the whites on Owens River had prompt and adequate assistance it could be checked there. I have just returned from Walker River. Piutes alarmed. I await reply.

Governor Nye promptly conferred with General Wright, commanding the Department of the Pacific, and on the same day notified Wasson to the following effect:

General Wright will order 50 men to go with you to the scene of action. You may take 50 of my muskets at the fort, and some ammunition with you, and bring them back. Confer with Captais Rowe.

It will be observed that the Governor was careful of the property under his charge. Presumably the guns were for the arming of settlers in the valley.

Captain E. A. Rowe, of Company A, Second California Cavalry, was ranking officer and commander at Fort Churchill, Nevada. Wasson immediately visited him, and the result was an order to Lieutenant Herman Noble to take fifty men to "Aurora and vicinity." "You will be governed by circumstances, in a great measure," his instructions read, "but upon all occasions it is desirable that you consult the Indian Agent, Mr. W. Wasson, who accompanies the expedition for the purpose of restraining the Indians from hostilities. Upon no consideration will you allow your men to engage the Indians without his sanction."

Wasson came on ahead of the troops. He found the Walker River Indians greatly excited, and apprehensive of general war with the whites. He sent messengers to the different bands of Piutes in that region, with instructions to keep quiet until his return. The mass of the natives were anxious to keep out of trouble, and he found all quiet when he went back.

A Piute named Robert accompanied him to Mono Lake, where the Indians congregated and preparing for a war they feared. They were much pleased with his mission, and sent with him one of their number who could speak the Owens River Piute dialect.

Wasson and his interpreters joined Noble's column at Adobe Meadows on the night of April 4th. The next day he traveled eight or ten miles ahead of the soldiers, and about noon passed the boundary of the Owens River Piute territory. On the night of the 6th camp was made at the northerly crossing of Owens River. At that very hour the Mayfield and Kellogg companies were defending themselves in the trench near Bishop Creek. Wasson saw no Indians, but plenty of fresh signs. On the following morning the Mono Indian said that he knew the Indians were to the right and up the valley. He was sent to interview them, with a message that the purpose of the mission was to inquire into the cause of the difficulties and to arrange a fair settlement.

Wasson and the Walker River Indian went on south. After going twelve miles down the river they saw a body of men at the foot of the Sierras and waited until Noble came up. Lieutenant Noble and Wasson then left the cavalry and went across the valley to learn who the men were. They found the citizens who had retreated from Bishop Creek, together with troopers of the Second California Cavalry under Lieutenant-Colonel George S. Evans. Evans had left Los Angeles March 19th, and shortened the trip to Owens Valley by keeping to the east of the Sierra instead of going into the San Joaquin Valley and crossing Walker's Pass, as seems to have been the invariable route before then. This appears to have been the first travel on the route now used south of Walker's Pass. He arrived at Owens Lake April 2nd. He found a dozen men and a few women and children at Putnam's "fort." Leaving Captain Winne and seven soldiers there, Evans moved on up the valley with seventy-three men and met the Mayfield-Kellogg men near Big Pine.

Wasson made his mission known, but found little encouragement for peaceful hopes. The larger force wished only to exterminate the hostiles. When Mayfield met the cavalry, Evans had induced forty-five of the citizens to turn northward with his company, the rest being sent on to Putnam's.

The meeting with the contingent from Nevada occurred about six miles south of Bishop Creek. Evans, being the ranking officer, directed Noble to bring up his company. When this was done the force moved to and camped at the scene of the previous day's fighting. The body of Pleasant, left in the flight of the citizens, was found, shockingly mutilated. All his clothing had been taken for Indian use. The body, wrapped in a blanket, was buried. It may be noted that when circumstances favored the Piutes again dug up the remains and took therefrom the blanket shrouding them. Once more the whites made a grave for Pleasant, at a point a little east of the San Francis ranch. Search in later years failed to discover the place of its final interment. Pleasant Valley, a small subdivision of Owens Valley, was named for this victim of the war. The body of Scott, buried in the trench the night of the retreat, was undisturbed.

Evans started scouting parties in different directions at daylight of the 8th. Eight or ten men who had gone north-westerly returned about noon and reported having found the enemy in force twelve miles to the northwest, in what is now called Round Valley. A rapid movement in that direction was ordered, and in two hours the soldiers and citizens reached the mouth of the canyon in which the Indians were believed to be. A heavy snowstorm had be-gun there, and a strong gale swept down from the summits. Evans ordered an advance, sending Lieutenants Noble and Oliver up one ridge with forty men while he and Lieutenant French, with an equal number, took the opposite wall of the canyon. Wasson criticizes the wisdom of this plan, as the gale, all in favor of the Indians, would have given them a strong advantage. The pursued foes had gone on, how-ever, and no Indians were found. The troops returned to the valley below.

The storm abating somewhat, Wasson did some inves-tigating for himself, and discovered Indian signs in a can-yon a mile to the north of the camp. Following it, he came upon a fresh trail leading northerly. At a point over two miles from the command he turned back. As he started back, he heard a call from rocks a few hundred years away. He replied, in English, Spanish and Piute, but got no re-sponse. This performance was repeated several times as he rode toward camp; he believed it to be an effort to decoy him. That night campfires were visible in the canyon.

The next morning Evans ordered Lieutenant Noble and nine of his men to reconnoiter the canyon, while the whole command moved in that direction. The detail was fired upon after it had advanced some 300 yards into the canyon. Trooper Christopher Gillespie mas instantly killed and Cor-poral John Harries was wounded in the left arm. Gilles-pie's body was left behind in the retreat, but was after-ward recovered. A published report mentioned the killing of a Sergeant McKenzie, but this is not confirmed by the military report.

The main command was half a mile below the mouth of the canyon. The cavalrymen were dismounted, and Noble and his company were sent to occupy the mountain side at the left, or south, side, Mayfield and four other citizens accompanying them. Evans was to take the north side of the canyon, and the citizens not with Noble were to remain at its mouth. Noble reached his designated position, and drew a brisk fire from two directions. Mayfield was wounded, and Noble, seeing that to hold his position would probably mean heavy loss, ordered a retreat. Mayfield was being carried back when a bullet passed between the legs of citizen John Welch and inflicted a fatal wound on the already injured citizen captain. John A. Hubinger, bugler, later a physician in Pasadena, was surrounded by Indians, and a bullet grazed his ear, but he made good his escape.

Evans found that the mountain side was too rugged and steep to permit the advance he had planned for his company, and he also ordered a retreat, not only from the immediate vicinity but back into Owens Valley. Before the soldiers had gone a mile and a half the camp ground they had occupied was dotted with Indian campfires.

Wasson's report, dated April 20, 1862, gives little credit to Evans for his management of the affair. He wrote:

During the engagement I selected a high rock at about the center of the operations, where I could observe all parties, and I am satisfied there were not over 25 Indians who had been left behind as a decoy to the whites and to protect the main body and families, who had gone on into the mountains to the north to avoid a collision with the troops. . . . Lieutenant Noble conferred with men and we agreed as to the course to be pursued, until we met Col. Evans, who then took command. This reinforcement ruined all our plans. We might have done better; we certainly could not have done worse. Lieutenant Noble and his men behaved gallantly on the field.

In referring to the Bishop Creek fight of April 6th, Wasson says the citizens had been "shamefully defeated." That is, after starting a campaign against from ten to thirty times their number, the white command had been forced to retreat. If to abandon that undertaking were "shameful," what shall be said of the result in Round Valley? Evans had under him a force of more than 150 men, of whom more than 100 were soldiers. After a skirmish, he abandoned the whole attempt, without discovering anything about how many or how few foes he had engaged. The sole result of his campaigning was to increase the confidence of the Indians, as Wasson had foretold, and to add to the probability of other outbreaks.

Evans camped that night on the Bishop Creek battleground. He had no provisions except what he procured in the valley—a singular condition which he attributed to his having distributed supplies to needy settlers—and was compelled to return to Camp Drum. A newspaper comment alleged that Evans had taken only enough supplies to last forty days. Lieutenant Noble acompanied him as far as Putnam's, to escort the settlers from the valley with their herds and flocks. The latter included 4,000 head of cattle and 2,500 sheep. Among the men who left at that time were the McGees, who met Indians, but were not molested. A general exodus took place.

Wasson appears to have had not only much sympathy with the Indians in their pathetic resistance to the inevitable white domination, but a bias that led to occasional overstatement. He assured Governor Nye that they "had dug ditches and irrigated nearly all the arable land in that section of the country, and live by its products." The products were the native plants, irrigated to a limited extent and not cultivated at all. We quote him further:

They have been repeatedly told by officers of the government that they should have exclusive possession of these lands, and they are now fighting to obtain that possession. . . . Having taken up their abode along Owens River as a place of last resort, they will fight to the last extremity in defense of their homes.

CHAPTER XV

TEMPORARY PEACE

INDIANS IN FULL POSSESSION—MILITARY EXPEDITION—CAMP INDE-
PENDENCE ESTABLISHED—PEACE ARRANGED—SAN CARLOS MINES
FOUND—BILL TO ESTABLISH RESERVATION CREATES CONTROVERSY
AND IS FINALLY FORGOTTEN

By the first of May, 1862, the Indians were in almost undisputed possession of the whole Owens Valley. Occasional venturesome travelers fared badly. Harvey C. Ladd had left San Bernardino two months earlier with his family, wagons and stock, and lost all his possessions, the persons being fortunate enough to escape. Alex Godey, ex-scout and at that time Indian agent, reported that a man named Pete Abel and thirteen others had been massacred, only one man escaping to tell the tale. The party had four wagons loaded with provisions, and 45 horses. They were besieged in a corral which they formed with their wagons, and in an attempt to escape all but one lost their lives. The truth of this report was disputed, however, by the Visalia paper. Another party of six all fell victims. Information reaching Los Angeles was that the Indians had acquired a hundred rifles; that there were 1,000 to 1,200 warriors in the valley; that they had killed or stolen 1,000 head of cattle, and that practically every white habitation east of the Sierra and north of Walker's Pass had been destroyed.

General Andres Pico, in Los Angeles, sought permission to organize an independent expedition against the Indians. Volunteers for his proposed forces were numerous enough, but Governor Stanford refused the desired permission.

A letter purporting to come from "citizens residing in the vicinity of Owens River" reached the authorities asking that no steps be taken for the establishment of a military

post; that if the soldiers would come and clear out the valley, giving the whites possession, the latter would take care
of themselves. The communication was believed to have
originated with designing plunderers. A Los Angeles
paper said that to send out the expedition for only 60 days
would cost $100,000, and called for a public meeting to
urge the establishment of a military post in Owens Valley.

Whatever the motive for the alleged protest, it was un-
heeded, and General Wright directed Colonel Evans to
prepare for the "Mono and Owens River Military Expedition."

During May, Captain Rowe, from Fort Churchill, Nevada, had a conference with the Indians at Mono Lake,
after an interpreter had induced them to hold a parley.
None of the fighting had been in that area, but their sympathy with their tribal brethren was apparent in their sul-
lenness. They did not care whether peace was made or not,
they said; as many whites as Indians had been killed, and
while they were satisfied to quit, they were equally willing
to have the war go on.

As ordered by General Wright, Col. Evans started from
Fort Latham, between Los Angeles and Santa Monica,
June 12th, with 157 men, including Company G and detachments from Companies D and I of his regiment, the
Second California Cavalry. Captain Winne, who had
commanded G Company on the first trip into Owens Valley, had committed suicide in a Los Angeles hotel while
temporarily deranged, and T. H. Goodman had replaced
him in command. The cavalrymen made camp on Oak
Creek July 4, 1862; erected a 50-foot flagstaff, raised the
flag, fired salutes, gave three times three cheers, and
otherwise departed from the daily routine. Because of the
day, the site selected by Col. Evans was named Camp Independence. The soldiers immediately began to provide shelters for themselves, some building rude cabins and some
digging out caves in the walls of a large ravine near by.

A note from a soldier to the Visalia *Delta* told of the
arrival at Camp Independence, and said the Indians were
showing signs of hostility. Bands of warriors, one of 300,

one of 200 and one of 40, had been seen and pursued on the way north, but fled to the mountains, losing two of their number. It was found that much of the scanty property in the valley had been destroyed, and the quartz mill of Cralley and Graves brothers had been burned.

John C. Willett, for many years a resident near Independence, was a saddler with Company G. In a letter written in 1903 he stated that when the soldiers reached the foot of Owens Lake they were instructed to kill all the Indians they saw. One Indian was slain at the lake.

A man named Cox was caught away from the fort and surrounded by Indians. Instead of killing him, they sent him to Col. Evans with a message that they wanted peace. They had not wanted to fight, they said; it was the tribesmen farther north who had made the trouble. This claim was supported by Indian Agent Wasson, who had had a talk with Chief George and sent him to meet the troops at the Alabama Hills with a flag of truce. George delivered a letter from Wasson directing a cessation of hostilities, and saying that he believed peace could be arranged.

Captain Rowe's command had come into the valley from Fort Churchill and made camp east of the river opposite Camp Independence. He held a pow-wow with the native leaders on July 5th and made temporary peace. During that month, Wasson was called to confer with Governor Stanford, General Wright and J. H. P. Wentworth, Indian Agent for the Southern District of California, regarding the Owens Valley situation. He was directed to collect the Indians at Camp Independence, to which point Wentworth was to come with presents and to make a treaty.

No friction was reported during the summer, though a letter written at the time said: "The Indians feign friendship, but show what they would do but for the troops."

Wentworth left San Francisco by steamer for San Pedro in September. He went on to Fort Tejon and secured the aid of Alex Godey as guide and interpreter. They brought a quantity of provisions and presents. Responding to messages by runners, many Piutes from the rancherias and bands gathered for a council at Camp Independence. They asked only that they be given protection and means of support. They were assured of the folly of war, and were told that while good conduct would be rewarded, rebellion would insure punishment. A treaty was made October 6th, and the natives celebrated it with a fandango. Chief George remained at the fort as a hostage. While this was transpiring, other factors were brewing renewed trouble; but on the surface at this time, Owens Valley, or at least its southern part, had passed to the control of the whites within a few months of the time they had been driven from it.

During the summer "Lake City" was laid out near Owens Lake by T. F. A. Connelly and W. B. Lilly. A few small shanties proved to be the final extent of the "city." Other occurrences of those months included the beginning of work at the Eclipse mine, under R. S. Whigham, and the bringing to Coso of quartz mill machinery, at a freight rate of 25 cents per pound.

A prospecting soldier found free gold in the range east of Independence. It was sent to San Francisco, and immediately caused the organization of the San Carlos Mining and Exploration Company. On September 24th Henry G. Hanks, later State Mineralogist, James Hutchings of Yosemite Valley note and Captain Corcoran left the city as representatives of the company to investigate the ledge from which the specimens had come. They outfitted in Stockton, and crossed the Sierra at Bloody Canyon, near Mono Lake. In passing through Yosemite they gave to Cathedral Spires the name now borne by that bit of scenic grandeur. Their route was via Monoville and Aurora, and at the latter place they were joined by George K. Phillips. Coming southward, they passed Bodie, where some prospecting was going on. At Hot Springs they saw the riddled cabin in which Taylor had been killed by the Indians some months before. On October 24th, a month from the day of starting, they made camp three miles northeast of Camp Independence.

A rich galena vein was found the following day, within a mile of the camp, and the Romelia claim was located on it.

Hanks, assayer for the party, tested the ore under difficulties. When the work was nearly done, he related, a dog
upset the balances and spilled the small buttons of metal.
A long search failed to bring the missing buttons to light,
and the prospect was that the laborious process would have
to be repeated, when some one suggested that the missing
material might have fallen into the dog's fur. The canine
was given a combing, the buttons were found, and ascertained to show a richness of ore that highly encouraged
the men.

News of the find created strong interest in San Francisco. Companies and stocks were plentiful, and parties of
prospectors headed for the new bonanza. San Carlos camp
became a busy little place the following year.

While these happenings forecasted the ultimate occupation of Owens Valley by white people, officialdom had, just
before, remembered the earlier intention of establishing an
Indian reservation. Senator Latham introduced his bill to
sell the reservation lands in the southern part of the State
and move their populations to Owens Valley. Agent Wentworth made strong objections; that his objections served
the purpose is sufficient without quibbling at these reasons
he set forth in a report dated August 30, 1862:

> The scheme is utterly impracticable. In my department there
> are 16,000 Indians, and Owens River Valley, cultivated in the most
> skillful manner, with all the modern improvements, by intelligent
> white labor, would not support that population. How then would it
> be possible for the numerous tribes, strangers to each other and com-
> paratively ignorant of the first principles of agricultural pursuits, to
> sustain themselves on such a reservation? The narrow valley of
> Owens River is only, at this time, sufficient for the very small num-
> ber of Indians, 1500 by census, who at present occupy and inhabit
> it, and the cause of the war now waged there is the desperation of
> the Indians because of the fact that the emigration to the mines has
> destroyed the grass seed upon which they, in a large measure, had
> been accustomed to subsist. . . . The war there has already cost the
> Government more than $90,000. If the Committee on Indian Affairs
> had responded promptly to the estimate which I made last winter for
> funds, viz., $59,300, I sincerely believe the whole difficulty would
> have been avoided.

Wentworth had, however, laid off a reservation for the Piutes, embracing six townships, extending from foothill to foothill and from Big Pine Creek on the north to George's Creek on the south. He reported that while it seemed large for the number of Indians, about 2,000 (disagreeing with the alleged census of 1,500), "it must be remember that it is only in small spots that it is susceptible of cultivation, the balance being scarcely fit for grazing purposes, and none of it attractive to settlers." This reservation was recognized and respected by the whites during the brief peace of that summer.

The agent further reported:

Should the Department agree with me, as I trust it will for I see no other way of keeping these Indians quiet, I hope it will recommend to Congress the immediate appropriation of $30,000 for the purpose of enabling me to establish this reservation. That sum, judiciously expended in the purchase of seed, stock cattle, mules, wagons, ploughs, etc., would place these wretched people beyond the necessity of stealing for a livelihood, and would relieve the Government from any further expense for their support, as well as dispense with the necessity of maintaining an expensive military post in a country where everything has to be hauled a distance of 300 miles over a sandy road, with water only at long intervals, and every obstacle to surmount which is objectionable for a military depot. Already the Government has expended many thousands of dollars in sending and keeping troops there to suppress difficulties that would never have occurred had Congress appropriated, a year ago, for this reservation.

The discovery of gold and silver mines in the ranges of the mountains on the borders of the Great Basin make what was three years ago an unknown region at this time a great thoroughfare; and the importance of averting at this time such a calamity as an Indian war is more pressing, as it would prevent travel and deprive the country of valuable resources made known by the energy of our hardy pioneers.

It would be impossible to remove the Indians of the more southerly portion of my district to this proposed reservation, because the rigor of the climate is such that it would be difficult to keep them during the inclement portion of the year, when snow covers the ground, even if the expense of moving them were not an insurmountable objection to such a proposition. The importance of prompt action by Congress in this matter cannot be presented more strongly than in the fact that it can, by a small appropriation, if made at once, secure permanent peace with a people who have shown themselves formidable in war, and save the Government the enormous expense attendant upon an interminable Indian difficulty which will inevitably occur.

Aside from this view of the matter, every principle of justice and humanity demands that a portion of what really belongs to them by inheritance should be secured to them, and that a nation as noble as ours should lend a helping hand to these people to raise them from their degradation.

Wentworth's recommendations went to Wm. P. Dole, Commissioner of Indian Affairs. Dole passed them on to J. P. Usher, Secretary of the Interior, but with a letter of disapproval. He favored finding some other location, large enough to accommodate all the Indians of the District of Southern California.

Nothing came of either Latham's bill or of Wentworth's recommendations. Congressman Aaron A. Sargent successfully opposed the latter, claiming that the amount asked was too much, and unnecessary, as there were not 500 Indians in the whole Owens River country. Wentworth came back in a later report with evidence that Sargent did not know what he was talking about, and that the original claim of Indian population was correct, but no further action was taken.

The year closed peacefully in Owens Valley, though isolated localities remained dangerous for white men.

CHAPTER XVI

FRESH OUTBREAKS

WAR MEDICINE MADE—LONE TRAVELERS MURDERED—MC DONALD
KILLED AT BIG PINE—CABINS BROKEN OPEN AND PILLAGED—WEAK
MILITARY DEMONSTRATIONS—MC GEE PARTY'S NOTABLE ESCAPE—
TYLER CAPTURED BY INDIANS TO SUFFER UNKNOWN FATE

After the ostensible pacification of the Piutes, part of
the military force at Camp Independence returned to Camp
Babbitt, near Visalia, Captain McLaughlin and 57 men and
Captain Jones and 20 men being transferred. Captain
Goodman and Company G remained at Camp Independence. Goodman resigned the following January, and the
command devolved upon James Ropes, promoted to a captaincy.

Wentworth and Wasson believed they had made progress in their philanthropic efforts to better conditions for
the Owens Valley natives, and Captain George seemed to
be sincere in wanting peace. But Joaquin Jim and his followers north of Big Pine Creek were not in sympathy with
George's pacific attitude, and remained hostile. The outlaw element of Kern River, Tehachapi and the eastern desert region were equally unreconciled. They held a great
powwow in September 1862, on an island in the south fork
of Kern River, and agreed on a campaign in Owens Valley
the following winter and spring. One of them told rancher
Weldon, of that vicinity, that they intended to keep the
Mormons out of Owens Valley.

John Lee and Jose Grijalva, packing goods to Coso,
were murdered at Canebrake, in Walker's Pass, in September. Two teamsters met a like fate not far from Weldon's.
Five men bringing freight from Los Angeles were fired on
from ambush by a band of about 40 Tehachapis. Martin
Hart was killed by a shot in the head. Oliver Burke was

shot in the arm before he fired twice at the assailants, killing one. Teamster Dawson took him in his arms and was carrying him to greater safety when Burke was again shot, in the side. He asked Dawson to put him down as he was dying. He still had strength enough to shoot again, and died in preparing to try a fourth shot. Dawson and his companions Hertz and Twitty then escaped. The Indians overhauled the goods, dressed themselves in the clothing that formed part of the load, and took two cases of pistols as a portion of their plunder.

Lone white men were killed, in the region south of the lake mostly, whenever safe opportunity offered itself to the red men. Prospectors Hall, Shepherd, Turner and White (the latter of the Murietta pursuit party) were among the victims. Five woodchoppers in the hills northeast of Lone Pine went the same way. Men named Morrison, McGuire, Taylor, Cowles and Hall were besieged in a camp near Coso, and escaped by abandoning their horses and camp.

During the forenoon of March 3, 1863, a meeting was being held at San Carlos to organize a district. While it was in session, men named Walker, Bellows, Crohn and Badger came in with a young man named Ayres, just escaped from an adventure in which a companion had lost his life at Big Pine. The meeting hastily adjourned, after deciding that until the valley reached a more peaceful state all development work might be suspended without prejudice to the validity of locations already made.

Three Ayres brothers, Hiram, aged 35, Albert, 25, and William, 21, and Hiram McDonald were camped at Big Pine Creek March 2, 1862. Hiram Ayres had gone to the hills to cut some stakes. Returning toward camp, he saw an Indian loading horses with camp property, while none of the white men were in sight. He hid until towards morning, when the moon went down, then started for Camp Independence, where he arrived the following midnight.

William Ayres was the one who was brought in by Walker and associates. He said he was in camp at dusk when he heard McDonald exclaim: "Look out, Bill! They're going to shoot!" Then a gun was fired; he saw an

Indian running toward him with an arrow fixed. He ran
and was shot as he did so. He got into thick brush and
under a bank washed out by high water. Though the Indians hunted and even poked his body with sticks they did
not find him. When all was quiet he stole out and escaped,
carrying an arrow in his body. He was taken to Camp Independence, where after long treatment by the post sur-
geon, Horn, he recovered.

Hanks, William Wallace, Oscar Bacon and ..... McNa-
mara set out to seek Albert Ayres, whom they found strug-
gling toward camp. He had been with McDonald until
the latter had been struck by four arrows and had given up
all hope of escape. Ayres pulled out the arrows and urged
McDonald to try to get away, but the victim insisted on
Ayres leaving him and going to warn the miners to the
southward. When McDonald was last seen the Indians
were pelting him with stones.

Word came from Captain Ropes that Chief George had
disappeared from the fort after receiving his rations on
March 1st, and trouble was expected. Several hundred
Indians were seen March 2nd, passing along the valley
across the river from the mining camp. Their women and
children were with them, which the miners afterward concluded was the reason they did not then attack the camp.
Ten well-armed men were in the camp, and believed they
could have put up a good battle.

Hanks and partners had returned to their claims and
were working when they were told that their cabin had
been broken into and ransacked. On going to it they found
everything except the laboratory table in a state of wreckage. Superstitious fears probably accounted for the table
and apparatus being undisturbed. All clothing, guns, ammunition, knives, looking glasses and portable stuff for
which the marauders had a fancy had been taken. Mat-
tresses had been cut, emptied and their cloth taken. The
door had been broken open with the camp ax. Hanks
wrote, following this:

I am beginning to change my mind about Indians. I used to
think they were a much-abused race and that the whites were gen-

erally to blame in troubles like this, but now I know to the contrary. Those very Indians who had been entertained at our house were the ones to attack it, and would have murdered us had we been at home.

Again he wrote:

I want you to use all your influence to have the Indian reservation done away with, and to prevent a treaty until the Indians are punished severely. The citizens of this valley are exasperated to the extent that they will not respect any treaty until the Indians are completely conquered and punished. The Indians are a cruel, cowardly, treacherous race. The whites have treated them well, paid them faithfully for all services performed by them, and have used the reservation only after gaining the consent of Captain George, their chief. After living on the charity of whites all winter, having gambled away the blankets and beads given them by the Government, they now, without giving us the slightest warning, pounce down like vultures, rob those who have treated them best, and murdered where they could without danger to themselves. They rush upon their prey in great numbers, like a pack of wolves, and not satisfied in filling the bodies of their victims with glass-pointed arrows, beat them into a pumice with stones. Can we be expected to give such inhuman wretches a chance at us again? We call upon you, the people of California, State and Federal authorities, to have this reservation and this set of wild savages removed to some other point. This valley is the natural thoroughfare through the mountains, and destined by nature to be the seat of a large population.

A lone cabin owned by a miner named Ladd, a mile from the San Carlos camp, was broken open and robbed March 6th. That same day, not far from Ida camp, east of the present Manzanar, Curtis Bellows fell a victim to lurking Indians. The natives, seeking lead which to make bullets for their guns, had destroyed the lead pipe supplying their place with water, making it necessary for Bellows and his partner, Milton Lambert, to carry water from a spring half a mile distant. Bellows was returning from such a journey when an arrow from ambush entered his body. He pulled it out and broke it. Another and more fatal shot struck him, and he sank dead upon the trail. Lambert, seeing Bellows fall, ran to their cabin. The Indians pursued, but by shouting orders Lambert made them believe that several men were inside, and they decamped. As soon as he dared to venture out, Lambert took from Bellows' body a money belt containing $150 and made his way to Camp Independence. A detail of fifteen soldiers went back with him and recovered the body, which they brought and buried in a ravine near the site of Independence. A marble tombstone, later erected, long marked the spot but in after years an unsentimental owner of the land filled the ravine and buried tombstone and grave from sight.

A letter from San Carlos said:

There is every probability that the Indians will want another treaty very soon, when they find nothing can be gained by fighting. They have been treated well, many of them fed by the United States, and their persons and those of their women protected by stringent military orders. I have yet to hear of the first act of injustice toward them since the treaty.

Said the *Delta,* March 11, 1863:

There has not been the slightest cause or provocation for this outbreak except that the Government has laid off a reserve and settlers are locating farms. The presumption is that they want another treaty with plenty of blankets. Capt. Ropes sent to Camp Babbitt for assistance, and 45 men under Lieutenant Davis left March 1st.

Captain Ropes sent Lieutenant Doughty and six men to Black Rocks, where the Indians were known to be in force. No statement of the purpose of this weak expedition is found in any military or other record. Near Black Rock Springs they were attacked by a band of Indians estimated at 200, armed with guns as well as with bows and arrows. Private Jabez T. Lovejoy was shot through the body and died that evening. Privates George W. Hazen, John W. Armstrong and George Sourwine were wounded, and Lieutenant Doughty was shot in the hand with an arrow. Sourwine's horse was killed; he took Lovejoy's and carried the mortally wounded man in front of him to Camp Independence.

An account written at the time gives the name of Henry Bosworth as one of the wounded men, but no such name appears on the company roll.

Three days later Ropes took twenty-seven soldiers, accompanied by Charles Anderson, Dr. Burnham and other citizens, to the Black Rocks. As they neared the tumbled

lava masses, a few Indians were seen, throwing sand in the
air and yelling like fiends. They opened fire on the whites,
but without doing any damage. Hanks wrote: "Ropes
retreated slowly to draw the Indians from the rocks, but
they were too wary to be trapped, and stayed in the natural
stronghold of the Black Rocks. After a few vain shots the
soldiers went back to camp." Local stories alleged that
Ropes made a disgraceful retreat. John C. Willett, writing
of it, said the soldiers were short of ammunition.

One of the most noted events of the war was the escape
of the McGee party from the Indians, on March 7, 1863.
This story has been printed in different journals, generally
with errors and embellishments designed to add to its
readability. The following is the account given to the
author by Alney L. McGee, for many years a citizen of
Inyo and with a record of uprightness in keeping with his
personal bravery:

A party composed of Mr. and Mrs. Jesse Summers,
Alney L. McGee, his mother, a little girl (his niece) and
Negro Charley Tyler camped at the soon-to-be site of
Owensville on the night of March 6th, during a journey
from Aurora to Visalia. Near Big Pine they came upon
the body of McDonald, whose murder has been narrated.
The corpse had been stripped of every shred of clothing.
This discovery spurred them to a hasty flight down the
valley. Signal smokes were seen as they neared the hills
below Fish Springs. As the party moved east of that low
range, a band of Indians estimated at 150 was seen
blocking the way ahead. The party left the poorly marked
road to cross the river. The wagons stuck in the soft mud
in the bottom of the stream, then at a low stage, and the
horses were cut loose. By the time the whites had crossed
the Piutes were at the western bank, sending arrows and
bullets among them. This was near a mound ever since
known as Charley's Butte, a short distance from the
present intake of the Los Angeles aqueduct.

On reaching the east bank Summers and McGee put the
women and little girl on the horses' backs, and ran
alongside, holding to the manes, and thus drew beyond the

Indians' reach. The yelling Indians pursued, but their inferior ponies were unable to overtake the fugitives, who reached Camp Independence that night. Negro Charley was less fortunate. He tried to catch one of the band of loose horses which were being driven with the party, but did not succeed. When last seen he was running and fighting, and without doubt some of the assailants paid with their lives. He had taken part in the valley's Indian fighting, and had accounted for several of the enemy. His fate was never definitely known. Captain George claimed that he was taken alive and was tortured to death on Big Pine Creek. A pioneer told of the finding of a skull and vertebræ of a man, later that year, on a stream west of Charley's Butte. The skull had been so crushed that its race could not be determined. It appeared that the victim must have been dead before his body was triced up with withes over a fire. Mr. McGee did not believe that Charley was taken alive.

When the escapes reached the fort they were halted by John C. Willett, doing sentry duty. When Mrs. McGee was lifted from her horse she was unable to stand. At their request Willett hunted up citizen acquaintances in the camp, and the matter was reported to Captain Ropes. The latter's reception of them was not to his credit; however, they remained at the post until May, when they went back to Aurora.

The party lost twenty-two horses and their wagon with its load of personal property, including $640 in money. Unlike many other cases of Indian depredations, this loss was never made good by the Government.

A San Carlos report said that Captain Ropes was to send men northward to prevent similar attacks on other travelers.

CHAPTER XVII

CONTINUATION OF THE WAR

SETTLERS ON DEFENSIVE—MORE TROOPS ARRIVE—A SUCCESSFUL MUTINY—FIGHTING ON BIG PINE CREEK—WARRIORS FOLLOWED BY CITIZENS TO BATTLEGROUND ON WEST SHORE OF OWENS LAKE —INDIAN BAND ALMOST EXTERMINATED.

Assayer Hanks, reporting to the president of the San Carlos company in San Francisco on March 8th, wrote that Capt. (Chas.) Anderson and himself had taken six carbines and a lot of cartridges to the Union mill, probably eight miles south of San Carlos. "I look on the magnificent landscape," he writes, "and thought that such a valley was well worth fighting for." At Rodebank's (an error for Coburn's, according to some old residents) on George's Creek, everybody was armed and expecting an attack. Putnam's stone cabin on Little Pine Creek sheltered a number of men, prepared to defy any Indian force. Lone Pine had two camps wherein citizens had gathered for defense. Four men were fortified at Clayton's house (locality not stated). Everywhere all hands were burning off brush, moving hay, cleaning guns, cutting portholes in cabin walls, and otherwise preparing for battle. Two nights earlier Indians had fired the haystack near the Union mill, and the camp was burned at the same time. Hanks remained to help defend the Union mill; he notes that he considered the preservation of the mill to be of great importance.

Troopers Johnson and Potter had left Camp Independence early in March for Aurora, for a purpose not explained but probably to warn intending travelers. When they reached Black Rocks, March 12th, on their return trip, they found 300 Indians along the road, with 50 guns. Chief George gave them a pressing invitation to come to his camp, but they preferred not to be the central fignres in an Indian holiday. Riding close to him, they put spurs to their horses and dashed through the line, escaping with nothing more serious than a wound in Johnson's hand and a bullet crease across the neck of his horse.

Hanks' manuscript, March 10th:

Today 14 soldiers under Lieut. Doty (Doughty) crossed at the ferry and went up to the ford to put up a notice of warning to any party who may be on the way down, to come down and cross at San Carlos. Last night Indians were all around the mill, as we could see their tracks this morning.

March 11.—Today Mr. Summers, one of the men who escaped from the Indians, came down to the mill. He tells a thrilling story. He says the Indians did not go up the river yesterday. They found the ferry boat had been cut loose. Party left the Union mill this morning and went up as far as San Carlos. Found the rope cut and boat gone, and window and door smashed at the house. No other damage was done.

Hanks' notes of March 12th relate the Johnson-Potter incident, with the remark that a large party of soldiers had gone to see if they could find the Indians.

No record of events of the latter half of March is available, though it was in the middle of the busiest season of trouble. On the 4th of April the military force at Camp Independence was augmented by the arrival of Company E, Second California Cavalry, under Captain Herman Noble—the same who as Lieutenant of Company A had accompanied Wasson in his wasted peace mission the year before.

Company E had the unique record of being the only successful mutineers in the United States army. While the incident is aside from the purpose of this history, it is worth preservation as well as being a temporary change from the narration of the guerrilla warfare then prevailing. It was told by Chauncey L. Canfield, a private in the company: Company E was made up of Tuolumne County volunteers, and was allowed to choose its own officers. The choice for captain fell upon D. B. Akey, a Mexican War veteran, hard-working miner and good citizen. Like other California volunteers, the members expected to be sent to the battlefields of the Civil War; and like others, the company was held in the West. This started the discontent; a march to Fort Humboldt during a hard winter increased it; and the climax was reached in Akey's proving to be a veritable tyrant. The company fought Indians in northern California until midsummer of 1862. It was then agreed among the men that on a specified date no man should obey any order given by Akey, though expressing a willingness to act under any other officer. Though under the Articles of War each was liable to death for mutiny, it was felt that the circumstances justified desperate measures. Akey got wind of the situation, and went to San Francisco. During his absence the company was moved to Red Bluff, but any hope that some other officer would be sent in his place was shattered by his arrival there. At Akey's direction the orderly sergeant had the company drawn up in line. He then said: "All those who intend to refuse to obey my commands as their superior officer step two paces to the front." That command, at least, they obeyed, for every man, except two who had joined subsequent to the compact, took the two steps forward. The captain glanced up and down the line, said nothing, and turned and walked to the ferry, passing from his company forever. The company remained there four months, while the War Department was considering its case. The decision was to muster it out of service, without pay, and it was marched to Benicia Barracks for that purpose; but through the intervention of Governor Stanford the sentence was revoked. Noble was appointed its captain November 21, 1862, and in December the march for Owens Valley began. Akey was transferred to Noble's former company, A, and resigned eleven days later. He went to Nevada, and in after years visited Inyo.

The two companies at Camp Independence left there April 9, Ropes in command. A member of the expedition, writing to the author from Massachusetts, stated that the white force included 120 soldiers and 35 citizens. The following day a band of 200 Indians was found strongly posted on a spur of the Sierra north of Big Pine Creek.

Firing lasted all afternoon, and toward evening the Indians withdrew into the mountains. A number (not definitely stated) of Indians were killed or wounded; white casualties, Private Thomas Spratt, of G Company, dangerously shot in the head, and Private John Burden, of E Company, slightly wounded.

Sergeant Huntington and a small body of soldiers and citizens were taking the wounded men to Camp Independence when, among the Black Rocks, they saw a few Indians, whom them immediately attacked. The Indians retreated, and Captain George, leading them, made good his escape though several shots were fired at him. The troopers found that they had been drawn into an ambush, a hundred Indians surrounding them. They took position on a hill and kept the Indians busy until the wagon with the wounded had passed a danger point of the road, then followed with the Indians in pursuit. A courier rode to the fort for help, and on his report there the soldiers mounted without waiting for orders and rode to the rescue. As they neared the wagon and its attackers the latter "scattered like a flock of quail," said the account, and were seen no more. It was considered unsafe to leave the fort with only the few men then there, and some of the men who were in the field were sent back to garrison it. The night of the attack on the wagon, Indians got among the horses of the cavalrymen at Bishop Creek and killed eight animals.

The chief Indian headquarters of the southern part of the valley was at Chief George's rancheria on the creek which still bears his name, west of the present Manzanar townsite. The natives had a feast there, having slain a work ox belonging to the whites. The next morning J. L. Bodle, with a small ranch not far from that dangerous location, saw them leaving in a southerly direction, and with his companions counted thirty-seven strung out in single file. Word was at once taken to Camp Independence, and Captain Ropes, guessing that they would probably intercept mail rider James White, from Visalia, started Lieut. Doughty and twenty soldiers in pursuit. The command was joined by almost as many citizens. The correct date of this, according to published reports, was March 19, 1863.

The trail was followed west of the Alabama Hills, to a point two miles or so north of Cottonwood Creek, when a bullet through a man's hat gave warning of the nearness of the foe. The Indians were found strongly posted in a ravine about five miles south of the head of Owens Lake. They were dislodged, and a running fight ensued, the whole action taking about four hours before they made a last stand on the lake shore, not far from the mouth of Cottonwood Creek. Their guns were so foul that bullets could be put into the barrels only by pounding the ramrods with stones. Lieutenant Doughty was dismounted by accidentally shooting his own horse through the head. Corporal McKenna received a load of buckshot in his foot from another accidental shot and an Indian arrow in his chest. When he fell, a Piute known as Chief Butcherknife ran up to finish him, but was slain. More casualties to the whites resulted from bad handling of their own weapons than from those of the foe.

With sixteen dead on the field, the remaining Indians sought refuge in the waters of the lake. A strong wind blowing from the east interfered with their escape by swimming, and one after another was killed in the light of a full moon rising over the eastern mountains. The soldiers established a cordon along the shore, and remained until the bodies began to wash in. A pioneer participant alleged that the next morning a pair of water-soaked moccasins was found near the lake, indicating that an Indian had survived the rain of lead and had emerged when opportunity offered. One Indian fled westward during the fight; he headed up the mountain, with derisive signs, and thereafter made his home with the Kern Indians. Taking the count made at George's Creek, thirty-five or thirty-six Indians were killed in that affair. Milo Page, a pioneer, asserted that he passed the spot afterward and saw thirty-three skulls from which coyotes or other wild life had stripped the flesh, piled up in one place. Bancroft's Handbook, 1864, said sixteen Indians were killed in the fight; evidence is that this was much understated, and possibly referred to those slain on the field. A. L. McGee, John Kispert, W. A. Greenly and others well known in later Indian affairs were among the citizen combatants.

From the body of one of the dead Indians was taken the Colt's powder and ball pistol which Negro Charley Tyler had carried, and this weapon was in the possession of Alney McGee at the time of his death some years ago. Mr. McGee stated that it was the only property of the Summers-McGee party recovered from the marauding Indians.

CHAPTER XVIII

RUTHLESS SLAUGHTERINGS

SOLDIERS MASSACRE INDIANS OF KERN RIVER—PRISONERS TAKEN
BY TROOPS—DESTRUCTION OF INDIAN STORES—POWWOW WITH
CHIEF GEORGE—MANY INDIANS SURRENDER—TAKEN ACROSS
SIERRA—MURDERS BY WHITES—MERRIAM'S THRILLING ESCAPE.

Company L, Second California Cavalry, Captain Albert
Brown commanding, arrived at Bishop Creek in April,
1863, and remained for a few weeks before going on to
Camp Independence. Its stay in the valley was short, the
company returning to Fort Churchill in June.

Company D of the same regiment became more
prominent in Owens Valley affairs. With Captain Moses
A. McLaughlin in command, it left Camp Babbitt April 12
and reached Keyesville, on Kern River, six days later. The
official report says:

Heard that a large party of Indians were camped a few miles
above, and at 2 o'clock in the morning of the next day surrounded
their camp and killed 35 of them. Not a soldier injured.

Pioneers of both Inyo and Kern counties speak of this
affair as a cold-blooded massacre. While the Visalia *Delta*
asserted that Owens Valley bands were being provided for
by Tulare Valley Indians who stole cattle to keep them
supplied, the Kern Indians were generally disposed to be
peaceable. Hearing of the coming of the soldiers, they were
much alarmed, but were advised by white acquaintances to
give up their arms and stay close to the settlements. They
delivered eighteen guns to the white settlers, and camped
near Kernville (then called Whisky Flat) about eight miles
from Keyesville. The soldiers surrounded the camp and
told two Kern petty chiefs to pick out the members of their
own bands. The thirty five remaining Indians from outside
camps were then herded to one side and shot down. This
was the account given by J. W. Sumner, a resident there at

the time.   He said further that no evidence existed to
implicate the victims in the Owens Valley troubles a
hundred miles away.   The superintendent of the Tule
River Reservation, the nearest, mentions in a report that
year that the Indians under his charge had frequently given
information in regard to the movements of their more
hostile neighbors in Owens Valley, and when solicited to
join against the whites had absolutely refused.   There were
renegades among them, however, who had participated in
the Kern River war council that had decided on a spring
campaign.

McLaughlin's command reached Camp Independence
April 24, and he, as senior captain, became ranking officer
at the post.   The next day Company D started on an
unsuccessful two day scout after Indians.   On the arrival
of this reinforcement the Summers-McGee party, which
had remained at the fort ever since their escape early in
March, asked for a military escort to accompany them back
to Aurora, but the request was refused.   During May a
strong party of citizens was organized for the dangerous
journey, and the refugees went with them.   On the way out
Alney McGee and H. Hurley encountered and killed three
Indians on Owens River.

During May the cavalrymen were active.   Lieutenant
George D. French, of Company D, and twenty men made a
scouting trip, during which French and seven of his men
attacked an Indian band, killing one and mortally
wounding three.   About the 10th or 12th twenty-five or
thirty Indian prisoners were taken at Big Pine and sent to
the fort, by a detachment of Company E.   Four men of
Company L, under Sergeant Henry C. Church, came on a
party of fourteen Indians on the headwaters of Owens
River and killed four, the rest retreating into the rocks.
This company was out almost continuously, and by its
destruction of many caches of Indian stores inflicted more
serious punishment than the killing of a few braves.
During the month it destroyed about 300 bushels of "seed"
(pine nuts and taboose) found cached in the vicinity of
Bishop Creek.   Captain McLaughlin himself was in the

field with a detachment, seeking Joaquin Jim, leader of the southern Mono Piutes. Jim's camp was found and destroyed, its residents escaping. A report published in June alleged that the cavalrymen were not only destroying provisions but were guarding the springs so closely that Indians were actually dying of thirst—a tale which those acquainted with Owens Valley's numerous and bountiful streams probably doubted.

Sergeant McLaughlin (not the captain) succeeded in getting a conference with Captain George, and induced him to visit the fort in peace, arriving there May 22. Subchief Dick came also. The Indians were fed and treated well, and said they had no further wish to fight the white man. Other Indians began coming in, "clad in native costume, a head of hair," remarked an unidentified correspondent of a San Francisco paper of that year. Captain or Chief George is described as second to Joaquin Jim alone in influence over his people. He was about 36 years old, of medium height, wily and shrewd, and manly in bearing. His face, normally round and full, was wan and pinched from privation when he was brought to the post. As has been noted in an earlier chapter, getting enough to eat, under normal conditions, was an ever-present problem with the Owens Valley Indians, and for some the situation was aggravated by the strict enforcement of native boundaries on hunting grounds. At this time the persistent destruction of their food stores and their constant flights had brought them to dire want.

The soldiers themselves were ready for a rest. Company D's report for May said:

The company during the month has performed several severe marches in the mountains, suffering much for want of water and rations. These marches have been performed on foot, it being impossible to use horses; but their labors, combined with that of other troops in the valley, have been crowned with success, resulting as they have in the subjugation of the Indians, and terminating thus speedily a war which promised to be of much longer duration.

While such congratulatory reflections seemed justified at the moment, they proved to be premature.

Four hundred Indians surrendered at Camp Independence June 4. Runners to outlying bands met with fair success, but their work was largely nullified by the acts of a few white men. Captain Ropes, in a letter published in the Esmeralda *Star,* of Aurora, July 30, bitterly criticized citizens who had lacked the courage to bear their share of fighting and danger.

As soon as a cessation of hostilities was proclaimed by the commanding officers these stay-at-home fellows grew wondrous brave, and boldly declared their animosity to the whole red race. Two Indian messengers that were sent from the post to the White Mountain district to gather these Indians were fired upon by some chivalrous miners, though the messengers were unarmed and bore a white flag. Of course they never returned, and today prospectors are in danger of their lives. Then, again, a Tehachapi Indian who had been for three months in irons was released and sent home to induce his tribe to cease hostilities and come in. With what would have been considered astonishing good faith in even a white man, he seems to have worked faithfully to accomplish his mission, and was returning with a number of his people, men, women and children, when they were fired upon in a most cowardly way while they were sitting in their camp only 15 miles from the post. Two men and one little girl were killed, and all were scalped by these brave and chivalrous gentlemen, who rode off and exhibited their bloody trophies of the war. At the Big Lake the recollection of their glorious deeds so stirred their noble souls that they became slightly oblivious, and in that state one of the noble trio, Frank Whitson, was arrested by Lieutenant French, who had been sent for him. The gentleman is now in our guard house in irons, and awaits an order for trial. Of the Indians who escaped from this attack, most of them made their way to the mountains, where they now are and where they will remain for all that anyone can do to drive them out. Never again can any of them be induced to place any faith in the promises of white men, and if another outbreak occurs it will be far the most desperate we have ever seen.

I should have mentioned that the last party of Indians mentioned also bore a white flag, traveled openly in the road in daylight, and that their purpose was known to everyone. But for such ruffians as those who fired upon them, unarmed as they were, there would not today be a hostile Indian in the entire country; and those who may hereafter suffer will have Mr. Whitson and others of like ilk to thank for it.

Milo Page, writing many years later, gave a version of this affair quite different in details, but not changing the appearance of murderous treachery. His statement was that an Indian known as Thieving Charley was given a white flag by Captain McLaughlin, with a note stating to whoever read it that Charley was on his way to bring the Panamint Indians to Camp Independence to surrender. This note fell into the hands of W. T. Henderson, in the Panamint region. Charley rounded up eleven Indians, and on his return to Owens Valley he was followed by Henderson, Lyman Martin, John Shipe, Frank Whitson and —— Ringgold. At Charley Johnson's, at Lone Pine, Ringgold got drunk and was not in the subsequent affair— a procedure which Henderson claimed resulted from cowardice and intention. The Indians camped near the Alabama hills. Henderson and fellow murderers attacked them early the next morning and killed nine of the twelve. The three survivors went on to Camp Independence and reported to Captain McLaughlin. A detachment of soldiers was sent to bring in the culprits. At Olancha the commander asked loudly if anyone there had been killing Indians. Answered in the negative, he told his men they could go in and get a drink. Henderson, Martin and Shipe were visible as they crawled into the brush from their blankets. Whitson ran to catch his mule, and a corporal went, under instructions, to ask if he had been killing Indians. If Whitson had said no (says Page's story) there would have been a report that no guilty men could be found; instead, Whitson said, "Yes; what are you going to do about it?" He was arrested and taken to Camp Independence, where he was kept under guard. Finally word was sent by Page that they were tired of guarding him, and if he would try to escape the soldiers would shoot at him but not try to hit. Still Whitson refused to escape, and was taken to Fort Tejon, where he was kept for a few months and finally released.

The Visalia *Delta,* deploring this murderous affair, said that the excuse for it was that some of the Indians had on clothing that had belonged to whites who had been killed. "The result came near undoing the labors of troops for the last three months. The Indians at Camp Independence made instant preparations to leave for the mountains, and

but for the promptness and energy of McLaughlin there
would have been a stampede with all its deplorable
consequences."

With such happenings as this and the Kern River
massacre in mind, it was not surprising that many of the
Indians remained utterly unreconciled, and that as
opportunity offered they resorted to every primitive method
of revenge and reprisal. They could not be more vicious
than some whites had proved to be. However, at that time
they were completely beaten in the valley of which they had
been so recently the complete masters. Chiefs George and
Dick knew that resuming the warpath meant hunger, if not
starvation, for their families and people. At the post they
were safe and were being fed.

Indian Agent Wentworth was requested by General
Wright, commanding the California department, to receive
the Owens Valley Indians at San Sebastian Reservation,
near Fort Tejon. Pursuant to instructions, McLaughlin
left Camp Independence July 11, 1863, with a few more
than 900 Indian men, women and children. The escort
comprised 70 men of companies D, E and G, and 22 men of
the Fourth California Infantry. The *Alta California*
correspondent (J. M. Hutchings, later of Yosemite fame)
wrote:

Yesterday 908 Indians were started from Owens Valley. Some
squaws were fortunate enough to get to ride in wagons with the
children and other valuables, consisting of baskets, old clothing,
etc., and looked as pleased as children over their first ride in a
carriage. The men and remaining women trudged on afoot, and
looked, generally, pretty serious. Captain George rode his horse,
as dignifiedly as could be imagined; he didn't seem to like it very
much. It appears that Capt. McLaughlin had assembled all the
Indians, men, women and children, on the south side of the stable,
and then and there informed them that he had orders to take them
to the Tejon Reservation, where they would all be taken care of;
but he had also received his orders that in case they refused to go
that every one refusing would be killed. All this was given through
an interpreter, Chico. Bows and arrows and some forty guns were
taken from them. Perhaps I ought to say that the rifle and shotgun,
on my application to Captain George, which had been taken from
our cabin at the commencement of the difficulties, were returned
to Captain McLaughlin, he saying "He (Hutchings) want 'em."

The band of Piute captives arrived at Fort Tejon July 22. Many Indians had escaped along the way, to return to Owens Valley, but Wentworth reported the delivery of 850 at the reservation, and said that twice as many were yet in the valley. When the settlers learned that stragglers were returning from their unusual journey they made a virtue of necessity and sent an invitation to the exiles to return and live in peace.

Wentworth, in a report dated September 1, 1863, referred to a $30,000 appropriation for which he had asked for the benefit of the Inyo natives. Had Congress granted it, he said,

no Indian war would have been waged, and the country would have been saved more than $250,000 in its treasury, the lives of many of its valuable citizens, and many of the poor misguided Indians, to whom the Government has promised protection, would today, instead of being dead, be living and tilling the soil of their native valley, and through their own willing hands obtaining an honest and well-earned livelihood. . . .Owing to recent and extensive mines discovered in the Owens River Valley, and the consequent rush of miners and settlers there, I deem that locality for an Indian reserve entirely impracticable, and the present war fully demonstrates that the Indian and white race can never live peacefully in close proximity to each other. I have therefore to recommend the abandonment of this valley for an Indian reservation. The mines, which are of unsurpassed riches, will cause thousands to permanently settle there during the coming year, and as heretofore throughout all California, the rights of the Indian will be disregarded, and constant turmoil and war will be a natural result.

Even while McLaughlin was convoying his captives to Tejon, the valley north of Big Pine Creek was as dangerous as ever to isolated men. While Joaquin Jim's chief stronghold was in Long Valley, he constituted himself the overlord of northern Owens Valley as well. Two of his warriors were killed in the White Mountains by prospectors, who after this amicable preliminary left a white flag as a bid for peace. Jim himself gave the answer, as the next visit of the whites to that locality disclosed, by carrying away the flag, and putting in its place his own war banner, a scarlet cloth bordered with raven feathers—said to have been a handsome piece of work.

About the first of August nine prospectors ventured into Little Round Valley, at the threshold of Jim's stronghold. Part of them warily prospected while the others remained as a camp guard. No Indians were seen until the following evening, when the camp was attacked in force. Two Indians were killed. The whites were unhurt, but made their way to Fish Slough that night, and to Owens River the next morning.

W. L. Moore and Mark Cornish, coming from Aurora, battled with Indians, killing two near Adobe Meadows.

In the early part of July there came to the valley a company known as the Church party. Its members, named Parker, Long, Ericson, Chase, Evans, Miller and one more, were from San Francisco. They believed that Indian friendship would result from an attitude of generosity and good will. This party made its camp near where Laws now is. Nothing is narrated of the doings of these men prior to the arrival, late in August, of Ezra D. Merriam, a young man who brought letters of introduction from mutual friends in San Francisco. During the weeks reports and warnings of Indian dangers had come to their camp, but nothing of those facts was told to Merriam; it would appear that he did not take strongly to the olive-branch idea.

On the invitation of Silas Parker, Edmund Long and Edward Ericson, Merriam started with them to locate timber on the mountains northwest of the valley. This trip resulted in the deaths of the first three, and gave Merriam an experience that ranks among the notable incidents of the period. We narrate it in his own words, as found in the Hanks collection of manuscripts:

We left camp in the Keyes district, Owens River Valley, September 2d, to locate some timber on the headwaters of Owens River. We camped at night twenty miles from the starting point, being unable to reach water. Resumed our journey at daylight on the third. Saw signs of Indians five miles further on. Five miles more brought us to the timber, where the Indians had been gathering pine nuts. We were unable to get a road and concluded to cross the river. We found an Indian trail to the river, half a mile from the top of the bank down the trail, and 600 feet perpendicular. Breakfasted at the river at noon—the first water we had for twenty-three hours. We saddled our horses and started up the other bank, after one and one-half hours rest, with Parker in lead, Long second, Ericson third and myself last.

When we were twenty-five yards from the top, which was covered with large rocks, eight rifle shots were fired. Parker fell, pierced by two balls through the breast, exclaiming "My God, I'm shot!"

Long and Ericson left their horses and jumped behind rocks, rifles in hand. Not seeing an enemy I took refuge behind a rock ten feet from Ericson, who had laid down his rifle and was exposing himself, calling to Parker. I saw the crumbling of a rock from the top of the hill, and dodged my head down as a ball whizzed past, a few inches above.

The Indians were in front and on both flanks. About the same time a shot was fired from the right. I asked Ericson if he was hit. He said he was. He was clasping his thigh, and raised his hand, from which blood was streaming. I saw nothing of Long after he went behind his rock.

I then attempted to get to another rock, but missed my footing and slid down the bank for twenty feet. Indians on the left started down the trail. I reached the bank at a different point from the trail, could not cross, and hid in the chaparral. Heard two more rifle shots, but saw no Indians for two hours; then I saw seven Indians on the opposite bank, motioning to others on my side of the river and pointing to where I was concealed. I worked through the chaparral, and saw ten Indians coming there, so I rose and ran down the canyon. They whooped and gave chase.

I outran them for a time, then found that they were gaining on me. I jumped into the river, but found that I could not cross it on account of the rapid current. Half a mile below I came to a fall fifteen feet high. Tried to reach the bank but could not, and was carried over. The current had carried me faster than the Indians could pursue. I struck bottom and caught between two rocks, and had almost lost breath when a final struggle extricated me. Came to the surface, caught my breath, then dove and came up under chaparral on the bank, hiding me from view. A small rock projected twelve inches from the bank and three inches above the water. I sank my body and raised my nose under the rock.

In a few minutes I heard Indians on the bank and just above my head, and saw two on the opposite bank with rifles, scanning the bank under which I was. Some of the Indians on my side moved part of the chaparral that covered me. My hat had washed ashore, and an Indian took it. I remained there three hours before the Indians left. Half an hour later all was silent; and I floated down stream until I struck a large rock on which I climbed. Jumped for shore, caught a bush, and finally got out. I hid in a canebrake until dark, completely chilled and scarcely able to move. Could see no signs of Indians. Finally I managed to get up motion, reached the top of the hill and ran through the timber. I went to the camp we had left on the 2d, traveling all night and until 10:00 the next morning without water, until I reached the valley. On my way down I saw several Indian camp-fires.

Word was sent to San Carlos, Bend City and the Union mill, and from each came men to take a hand in punishing the Indians. George K. Phillips was elected captain of the company of thirty well armed men. A letter of the time comments that it was a strangely assorted band, though a determined one. There were Texas rangers and frontiersmen, and there were those but recently from clerkships or to whom for other reasons outdoor life was a novelty and who were scarcely browned by exposure. The party rode up Bishop Creek to the foothills, and along the latter to "Greenly's Valley," (Round Valley). Camp was made, and to insure intent alertness pickets were changed hourly. One of the pickets created an alarm by firing, harmlessly, at one of his fellows. The next morning Merriam guided the party to the scene of the ambush. Long's body was found, pierced by nine bullets. Ericson had been shot through the head. Both bodies had been dragged along the trail, that of Ericson by a willow withe around his neck. The body of Parker was not found, nor was it accounted for, except by the supposition that he had been captured alive. The following paragraphs are from a letter written by one of the men of the expedition:

On finding the bodies of Ericson and Long, we dug graves, covered the bodies with pine branches, piled in rocks and earth. One man said: "Come, boys, let's go; we can do no more for the poor fellows;" then in a lower and tremulous voice added: "God give his soul a better show than this." I have listened to long prayers in grand cathedrals, where the sunlight poured in through stained glass windows asd fell on pews of carved oak, but I never heard so fervent, so touching a prayer as this, far away in this mountain land, among the pines, under the shadow of the giant Sierras, where the river, deep in the wild and rocky canyon below, murmured the requiem of the dead; where the blue sky, widespread, extends from mountain range to mountain range, over mile upon mile of valley land and wooded hills. We left them, sadly and silently, and went up to our comrades on the hill.

We examined where the men fell, and saw where the rocks were drenched with their blood. We saw where Mr. Merriam ran down the hill, and wondered how it was possible for a man to accomplish so much. We came to the conclusion that this was not a war party, although we think Joaquin Jim was among them. . . . . . Joaquin Jim has never been conquered. He has said frequently that he would not let the whites occupy his domain. ,

After we had buried the dead and returned to our horses we commenced a search about the Indian camp. We found baskets, great quantities of pinons cached, the bridle of Mr. Merriam's horse, a pair of shoes which belonged to Mr. Ericson, and his hat with a bullet hole through it, covered with blood. We each took as many pinons as we could carry. One or two stayed behind and destroyed all that remained by burning them.

Unless something is done for us we shall have much trouble. We cannot prospect and watch Indians at the same time. We cannot prospect with a rifle. There is no need of a military force near San Carlos—we can defend it ourselves; but we want stations along the valley so that people may safely pass, and prospectors find a refuge from the savage, who is peaceful today and warlike tomorrow.

The chase seeming to be hopeless, return was made to San Carlos. On the way down, the party met two men named Bell and Slocum at Big Pine, where they had gone with the idea of starting a sawmill. Indians had warned them to leave, and after talking with the Phillips company they concluded that it would be wise to comply.

Henderson and associates, mining in the southeastern Inyo ranges, had been driven out in March by Indian dangers. They then went back after an absence of not more than a month. On reaching the Josephine mill they learned that Chief Bigfoot had the better of a fight with the miners the day before and had gone across to the Panamint Mountains. Henderson waited until the arrival of Ringgold from Owens Lake, and the two followed the trail to their mines in the Panamints. After traveling seventy miles camp was found at Mesquite Springs. Going on, Indians were seen in pursuit. Henderson and Ringgold waited until they came near enough to parley. The Indian spokesman said in Spanish that the men were up in the mountains. The whites, seeing that a battle was intended, opened fire and killed two of the leaders. A fifteen-mile running fight ensued; its casualties were the killing of three

Indians and Ringgold's being left afoot by the killing of his horse. Henderson visited the neighborhood in 1870, and found parts of the skeletons of three men and some bones of a woman in the ruins of a cabin which had been burned at Combination Camp. He gives the date of the killing of his companions as April 13, 1863.

Ten or twelve skulls of white men, and other human bones, were found under a shelving pile of rocks near Anvil Springs in 1874. Nothing was known of the identity of the victims or of the time of their deaths. The supposition was that they had there taken refuge from Indians and had all been killed. For this discovery there had been found but one authority. It is certain, however, that an unknown number perished on the lonesome trails of that region.

CHAPTER XIX

PIONEER SETTLEMENTS

MILLS AND HOUSES PUT UP—SAN CARLOS, BEND CITY, OWENSVILLE
—PLACES THE SITES OF WHICH ARE UNKNOWN—A FOURTH OF
JULY CELEBRATION IN 1864—A SMELTER THAT SMELTED ITSELF
—SAWMILL BUILT—FARMING IN ROUND VALLEY AND ELSEWHERE.

Confidence in restoration of peace started a stream of immigration into Owens Valley. While there was some travel from the north, most came from the south through the natural entrance at Little Lake. Merchants Hobart & Reed had established a store there, carrying "everything in the line of general merchandise" in their little structure, and claiming to do $50,000 worth of business annually. A petition for a mail service between Visalia and Lakeville, or Lake City, was well signed, and a Congressional resolution three months later put the route on paper. It may have been the reason for some of the intermittent service referred to as "express," but no record of actual establishment of the route has been found. Passage of a resolution the following year, 1863, by the California Legislature, asking for establishment of a mail route from Keyesville to Owens River, indicates that the Lakeville plan was never put into effect.

That travel came into Owens Valley at a lively rate during the summer and autumn of 1863 and into 1864 is evidenced by published items in nearly every issue of the Visalia paper beginning with July, and in frequent mentions in other publications. The following extracts, used without special attention to sequence, are from papers of that period:

Owens Valley is filling up rapidly with permanent settlers. San Carlos, Centerville and Bend City are projected.

A new town called Black Rock, 15 miles above the Ida mill, has been launched.

In two years Owens Valley will be the most densely populated of any east of the Sierras in California. On the west side of the valley is a belt of agricultural land not surpassed by any land in the State. . . . If the boulders in the river were removed the river would be navigable all the way to the upper valley. It is a country for pleasure seekers and hunters—bear in abundance, deer, antelope, sagehen, grouse, etc., and fish innumerable.

In view of the general scramble for land in Owens Valley, locators are advised to comply with laws to avoid being ousted. A steady stream of immigration is pouring into Owens Valley. The farming land is being rapidly taken up and a population of thousands is predicted in less than a year.

San Carlos and Bend City are going ahead at railroad speed. Houses and mills are going up. Prospectors and families are flocking in. Large numbers of beef cattle are being driven across the mountains via Owens River to Aurora and Carson.

There are 200 Union votes on Owens River, and if the influx continues as in the past thirty days I would not be surprised if there would be 400.

The Union men held a meeting to name delegates to a county convention in Visalia, and if an item in the *Delta* of July 2, 1863, is a statement of fact and not pleasantry they took an action most surprising for that time and place:

The Union men on Owens River instructed their delegates to the county convention to vote for no man who drank whisky or played cards.

Social matters were not altogether overlooked:

San Carlos, August 27.—Yesterday a fellow named Johnson took a pop at Mr. Lentell, but the bullet striking his rotund corporosity glanced off, inflicting a flesh wound. The fellow came into Lentell's shop, and on being escorted out he acknowledged the courtesy by blazing away. The bystanders interfered and wrested the pistol from him. This was the first shooting affray in San Carlos.

Nor were mining interests neglected, according to sundry items of different dates:

The half has not been told. Richness of the ledges is fabulous —Jefferson over $7,000, Chrysopolis as high as $1,200, Oro Fino $1,500, etc. Captain McLaughlin has prohibited all attempts to locate land upon the proposed Indian reservation. This comprises all the good land.

Dr. George, here from Owens River, brings mineral which only wants the impress of the eagle upon it to make it the pure spelter.

San Francisco quotations on stock of the Owens River mine have advanced from $40 to $75, and on Santa Rita from $10 to $25.

R. S. Whigham is in Visalia, bringing with him $10,000 worth of amalgam from rock worked in the Union mill.

The Ida company is now working ten men at its mine. Its mill is completed. Mr. Whiteman says he has a mill in transit to be erected on the Santa Rita mine in Mazourka Canyon.

El Paso mining district has been organized.

Bell, Fox & Co. have machinery for a sawmill on Big Pine Creek.

Mills are going up and houses are being built at San Carlos and elsewhere. The San Carlos company have finished 2,700 feet of their ditch and are rapidly progressing with their mill. The Center company are running three tunnels. The Nelson mining company are about to commence work, their teams, with provisions, tools, etc., having arrived. The Monster Hill Tunnel company, Regina Tunsel company and Clara company are about to commence. The Inyo G. & S. M. Co. have commenced running a tunnel on the Lucerne and Granada. From Chrysopolis the most flattering reports and rock full of gold are sent down. In Russ district several companies are at work. The Eclipse is turning out very rich ore and is of great extent. If it is not the richest mine in all California we are much mistaken. . . . It would be impossible to name or notice all the numerous leads which have been recorded in the various districts. . . . Our miners, who are generally men of education, vie with each other in selecting refined names for their mines. Silver Cloud, Norma, Olympic, Golden Era, Welcome, Chrysopolis, Gem, Green Monster, Blue Bird, Red Bird, Evadne, Fleta, Bonnie Blossom, Calliope, Romelia, Lucerne, Pluto's Pot, Birousa, Proserpine, Altahualpa and Ida are among the mines here. . . . San Carlos is progressing rapidly. It now boasts of two stores, two butcher shops, two assay offices, an express office, a saloon, and mechanics of all kinds.

Our population is about 200. Yesterday we polled 106 votes, 58 of which were Union. Many of our citizens went down to the Union mill to vote, as it was feared there might be a dispute, it not being certain yet whether we are in Mono or Tulare county. Others who claim a residence in Mono went up to Van Fleet's to vote.

There is a new express started from San Carlos to Aurora. Perhaps when we grow a little Messrs. Wells, Fargo & Co. will honor us with an office. We are quite as worthy of it as Fresno City, yet I saw their sign on a house there which was, at the time, deserted.

There is quite a competition between the rival citizens of Bend City and San Carlos. They are but three miles apart. We predict that within one year they will jointly have a larger population than Visalia. Pre-emption claims and homesteads have been tendered for over 15,000 acres of land in the Owens River Valley.

December 30.—Bend City is three months old. It has 25 or 30 good houses. The bridge question created an excitement. The question is whether to put the bridge at the upper or the lower end of the city. A vote was carried by the down-towners, whereupon the uptowners decided to build a bridge of their own. Parties across the river fired the dry grass, and eight or ten horses were burned to death or had to be shot.

The bridge mentioned was constructed by Thomas Passmore at a cost of $2,000, which the uptowners, chiefly, contributed. This enterprise resulted from objections to paying tolls on a primitive ferry, consisting of a raft hauled back and forth by ropes. San Carlos was first with the ferry idea, and gave free service, while the Bend City ferryman charged his passengers. The election to settle the bridge location, but which seems to have failed in that purpose, called out sixty votes, according to clerk Will Hicks Graham.

At Owens River, the Union mill is at work; eight stamps; steam used here and at Ida mill, a mile above.

At Bend City now (December 17, 1863) about 30 houses, adobes. This city has been regularly surveyed. A grand ball is on the tapis for Christmas Eve.

The most work has been done by the Clara company. Mt. St. George, in the first range of hills at the foot of the Inyo Range, adjoining town, appears to be a complete network of leads of the richest mineral. The Clara company has fourteen claims.

With regard to the Indians, all has been quiet on Owens River for months past, and there is no prospect for a renewal of hostilities.

Bend City, January 28, 1864.—We now have five mercantile houses, two eating houses, two blacksmith shops, shoe shop, saddle and harness maker, tailor shop, and a laundry conducted by Chung Ah Ting and lady. There is an abundance of everything to eat and wear. Biled shirts and blacked boots have become common.

Owens Valley must be getting populous. No less than 65 teams have passed through Visalia within the last thirty days, besides horsemen, and still they come.

Traveling time from San Francisco to San Carlos is now six days. The trip costs for fare, via Visalia, $2 on railroad to San Jose, $24 on stage to Visalia, $25 for use of horse to San Carlos; via Aurora, boat to Sacramento $5, stage to Carson $25, stage to Aurora $15, horseback to San Carlos $15.

March 3, 1864.—The road across Greenhorn is finished. It is one of the finest mountain roads in the State.

A San Carlos letter mentions the first death in the camp, except those from Indian warfare, as that of a man named Warner, February 11, 1864, his demise resulting from an accidental wound in the arm. The marriage of Mr. Woolsey to Miss Warner (no relative of the deceased) is mentioned in the same epistle, doubtless the first marriage in the valley; no information as to what civil or religious authority happened to be there to tie the knot. This letter predicted great things for Keyes district and the Rubicon mine, somewhere in the later Poleta neighborhood.

Bend City appears to have outgrown its rival settlement. One of its residents was authority for the statement that it reached a maximum of sixty to seventy buildings, nearly all adobe. It had two hotels, the Morrow House being the "swell" place. A circulating library was a public convenience. Even a stock exchange was listed among the institutions, though a notation of a trade in which a burro paid for a block of stock does not indicate brisk transactions

I. N. Buckwalter and A. C. Robinson, running a tunnel not far from the mouth of Mazourka Canyon, twice lost their stores of provisions through Indian raids, during the more unsettled period, but escaped personal harm. Mr. Buckwalter came from Pennsylvania, his later home, in 1915 to revisit those old scenes, and unearthed a number of mining tools which he had cached when he left his claims in that earlier period. During his visit he told of having paid the Bend City cobbler $2.50 for nailing on a bootheel, the cobbler using three sixpenny nails and three minutes of time.

Among the many who drifted into Bend City were two brothers, William and Al Graves, and a comrade named Riley. They traveled on into Deep Springs Valley, east of the White Mountains, and there at their campfire in late March, 1864, one of the brothers shot and killed Riley. Pioneers charged William with the killing; the Visalia news report laid it to Al. The latter had a hard name. He was a secessionist, and Riley a Union man. Politics and bad whisky were given as the cause of the homicide. News of the occurrence led to formation of a vigilance committee in Bend City, but nothing was done. There were no peace officers in the region, and the Tulare Supervisors then named John Beveridge as Justice of the Peace at Bend City, with one Kendall as his Constable.

The vigilantes and the officers soon had business to do, when on April 20th John Mitchell shot and killed a man named Cuddy, as given by pioneers, or Cudangly, as printed in Visalia. Cuddy had vowed to kill Mitchell, following a dispute. Knife in hand he crossed the street in San Carlos to Lentell's store. Mitchell did not wait to be carved, but shot from within the store and instantly killed his antagonist. Mitchell was taken into custody. T. F. A. Connelly acted as prosecutor and Campbell, correspondent of the San Francisco *Alta California,* defended the accused. The vigilantes demanded the privilege of being present, otherwise they would take the prisoner and dispose of the case themselves. At the close of the hearing they took a vote and decided the case to be one of justifiable self-defense. Judge Beveridge took a different view, and directed Constable Kendall to take Mitchell to Visalia for trial. The vigilantes did not interfere, until Kendall got ready to make Mitchell walk the whole distance, guarded by himself on horseback. That plan was effectively vetoed. Mitchell was turned loose after remaining in jail a few months.

No such inconvenience attended the next crime, in which T. J. Hazlett shot and killed I. T. Dimitt a few miles from Haiwai on April 24th. The succinct report reads: "Murderer left; corpse buried."

Russ district, oldest in the region, was divided, Inyo district being created to include the area north of a line westerly from the Piute Monument. Claims were limited to a length of 300 feet and a width of 15 feet on each side of the vein. In case of trouble with Indians, the district laws provided, each claim would hold good until danger was over; otherwise one day's work must be done within thirty days, and that would hold the claim for one year. Any person destroying or changing any mining notice was liable to a fine of $50 and the confiscation of any claim he might have in the district—though there was no legal method of collecting the fine, or of enforcing confiscation. Soldiers were permitted to locate free of labor or expense until 90 days after expiration of their terms of enlistment. Labor to the extent of $50 conferred perpetual title.

The San Carlos company completed its mill in time to startle the inhabitants of the camp of the same name on July 4, 1864, with blasts of its steam whistle The struc ture stood "at the corner of Romelia and Silver streets." First operated by steam, the intention was to substitute water power when a suitable conduit from the river was completed. Five 750-pound stamps and a separator was the modest equipment, but the building was planned for additions within its walls of stone set in lime mortar. Besides listening to the ambitious tooting from the whistle, the inhabitants celebrated the nation's birthday by "horse racing and a ball at Hughes," wherever Hughes was.

One of the companies sent out a Dr. Wellings and party to explore east of Owens Valley. They reported having penetrated the desert for 150 miles. During the journey they found an old wagon track, which they followed for 80 miles, possibly realizing that they were traversing country through which the Death Valley expeditions of 1849 had passed.

Arrival of expressman Bostwick in the camps with San Francisco papers only four days old was a "feat unprecedented in the annals of Owens Valley expressing." The Visalia editor made the horseback trip, and his account says that the return took seven days of long and hard travel. While the account does not say so, it is inferred that he made two trips—his first and his last—on that occasion. He thought well enough of the mineral showings, but denounced the practice of putting the property in the hands of superintendents wholly ignorant of mining. He saw only one mine operated on correct principles, he wrote; and he found the beginnings of agriculture to be as unsystematic.

The saloonkeepers of Owens Valley found themselves under the operation of a law that made them liable for all expenses of trials of parties committing crimes while under influence of liquor, the costs to be levied by the county Supervisors and assessed pro-rata on the saloons.

Some further newspaper notes:

Expressman Bostwick cut his time in half by reaching San Carlos from Visalia in two days, (in July, 1864). Surely the world does move!

A very rich ledge was struck in the foothills of the Sierra near Lone Pine; over $600 silver per ton.

The new sawmill at Bishop Creek will be ready to run next week. The sawmill at Big Pine is turning out a fine quality of lumber.

Vegetables throughout the valley look fine, and we have all we can pay for.

This is the first season farming has been attempted in Owens Valley. Much hay has been cut, 300 or 400 tons in this vicinity. Barley is a success; so are corn, potatoes, sweet potatoes, cabbage, onions, tomatoes and melons. Fire clay has been found near here.

San Carlos, August 31, 1864.—Hard times. With ores all around us we never see a dollar. Many are leaving, frozen out though the mercury is 100 in the shade. The ranches are luxuriant with all the vegetables of the season, but no one has money to buy. One man has threshed out 150 bushels of barley. All that is needed is capital and population to make this the richest valley in California, if not in the world.

The camps had passed their peak. Bend City was proposed as the county seat of a new county, by a law passed in 1864, as will be taken up later. The plan failed, and for the next two years there was so little energy in the region that Bend City and San Carlos were very rarely mentioned in print. With the founding of Independence, in 1865, their day closed. The projected towns of Black Rock and Centerville seem to have gotten into print only the once. Recurrence of Indian troubles had some part in checking the ambitions of the settlers.

A San Francisco *Alta* correspondent had written in September 1863:

A small post is needed in the vicinity of Round Valley or Bishop Creek. The Indians are numerous there, and decidedly hostile. It is the finest part of the valley. It is reported that troops will return this winter; no need of them here, but actual necessity for them above. Either that part of the valley and the adjacent mines must be abandoned or else protected by the Government until like this it is able to protect itself.

A letter in the *Alta* in the winter of 1863 said:

A few months ago scarce a house would be seen throughout the extent of this valley, but now animation, life and activity greet the eye wherever you look. A fine settlement has been formed at Lone Pine, near the mouth of Owens River. Bend City is a town of sixty or seventy houses, San Carlos is about the same size, and both rapidly improving; while further up the river Chrysopolis, Galena, Riverside (alias Graham City) and Owensville are raising their voices for recognition.

Still farther north, Benton, Partzwick, Yellow Jacket, Camp Enterprise and Montgomery were bidding for places on the map. Galena, Riverside or Graham City and Camp Enterprise are so completely buried in oblivion that even their sites can no longer be learned.

Owensville fared better, and for several years was a place of some size, the only real settlement in the valley north of Big Pine Creek, in the section long mapped as Bishop Creek Valley. It began some time in the latter part of 1863, for in December a letter to the *Alta California* bore an Owensville date. It read:

I have just arrived with a party of 56 men, one family, 82 yoke of oxen and saddle horses innumerable. The valley contains 52 claims of 160 acres each, and Wm. McBride and the Hutchison boys have surveyed the Bishop Creek Valley at the risk of their lives. Just heard of 40 men, all farmers, and twelve ox teams, who have arrived.

Owensville was on the east bank of Owens River, near the present Laws. A circular corral, standing within its townsite, is built of stones that once served as foundations for Owensville buildings. A little to the northeast, a rough slab of stone marked the grave of Mrs. T. H. Soper, who died there. No other trace of habitation remains; the old-time streets are part of the river bottom's level and unbroken meadow.

John H. Soper, a resident of the place when his mother died, later went to Hawaii and was commander in chief of the military forces of Hawaii's provisional government which dethroned Queen Liliuokalani preceding the islands becoming American. In correspondence General Soper narrated the shooting of two members of a gang of ruffians from Montana by "Pap" Russell. Russell's offense, according to a printed report, consisted in his being a "black Republican." One of his assailants was killed, the other badly wounded. Another of the General's stories was of an unsuccessful attempt by a disreputable Owensville resident to organize a punitive expedition against two old squaws who had given him a thrashing, doubtless deservedly.

John E. and Thomas E. Jones, pioneer settlers in Round Valley, came to Owensville in 1864. Notes by T. E. Jones enumerate many of its residents, among them the father and mother of Rev. Andrew Clark, the valley's pioneer minister; their son Thomas; the Soper, Gill and Hightower families; J. L. Garretson, H. Caleff, J. F. and Thomas K. Hutchison, A. Thomson, W. P. George, William Horton, W. S. Bailey, Reuben Merryman, Frank Powers, William and John McBride, nearly all of whom were well known in Inyo in later years, and most of whom ended their days here. George Hightower and wife were residents, and their daughter Ada was the first white child born in the northern part of the valley so far as known evidence shows. John B. White, who was murdered at Big Pine twenty-odd years later, had a saloon. John W. McMurry was storekeeper, restaurant man and postmaster. He chanced to become the victim of an accidental shot, getting a bullet from his burning house from which he was saving personal property. He recovered, to become a leading citizen of Big Pine. Andy Ault and Jesse Spray and their wives were among the arrivals from Bridgeport. Ault took the liberty, at Adobe Meadows during one of his trips, to kill an Indian whom he suspected of having stolen his pistol. Whether or not he felt mortified over his act when he later found the gun hanging on a wall under a garment is not recorded.

Milo Page, a participant in many of the happenings of the period, told of a Fourth of July celebration in Owensville in 1864. Will Hicks Graham, a capable lawyer who was said to have been Pat Reddy's instructor, was master of ceremonies and orator. A newspaper account names J. E. Goodall, later prominent in Bodie, as reader of the Declaration; John Evans, superintendent of the Great Eastern mining company, chaplain; W. P. George, author of an original poem. Music and singing by the seven ladies present was much appreciated by the 150 men who thronged "C. B. Seat's commodious stone building" in which the affair was held. The instrument used was a portable melodeon belonging to and played by Thomas Soper. There were many southerners among the men, but all joined in the commemoration regardless of the great war then waging between the States, and presumably raised their voices in "America, of Thee" and "Star Spangled Banner," the songs on the program. A sumptuous banquet at the Owensville Hotel concluded the holiday. Earlier than this, on May 1, had occurred probably the first social event of any kind in the northern part of the valley, a dance in a ten by twelve adobe cabin. One of the institutions of the place was a lodge of the Sons of Temperance, of which C. C. Scott was the head.

Aurora was the nearest source of supplies. Communication was difficult, and stores ran low at times. During such a period, McMurry refused an offer of $20 for a sack of flour, saying that he would not sell it for $40, as he would need it for his family. A pony mail service was started by Daniel Wellington, with W. J. Gill as the rider. This service connected at Benton with a semi-weekly pony express to Aurora. Each letter had to bear the proper postage and to be accompanied by a 25-cent payment as recompense to the mail carrier.

Owensville looked to mines in the White Mountains for its upbuilding. The Golden Wedge mine, many years later still bearing that name and included in a group known as the Southern Belle, was the first find. Its discoverers were Charles Nunn and Robert Morrison, who was later killed at Convict Lake. Another mine not wholly forgotten was the Yellow Jacket, belonging to a company organized in Gilroy, California. A reduction plant was built on Swansea Flat

(Fish Slough) by an Owensville company with T. H. Soper, president; H. Caleff, metallurgist; John Soper, H. Chambers, G. Thomas, Dawson, Snooks, the Round Valley Jones brothers and another Jones as members. An arrastra was built to pulverize supposedly fireproof material transported to the scene by horse and ox-teams. Even barren quartz was crushed and brick molded from it. Alleged fireproof stone was hauled from Aurora. Almost daily specimens were brought in by prospectors, and Tom Jones records that Judge Caleff usually pronounced them "very fine conglomerations of argentiferous galena." The furnace was completed, and melted down as quickly as the ore with which it had been charged. Undaunted, the amateur smelters obtained different materials and built another plant. It was crammed full of wood, charcoal, ore and flux, and fired—and in a few hours was, like its predecessor, a seething, plastic pile of ruins. It may be noted that a precisely similar experience befell a furnace undertaking by Greenly, Edwards and others that same year at a site a little east of the present court house at Independence.

Demands for lumber were met by the erection of a sawmill in the Sierras near Bishop, by John Pugh and Joe Spear, with T. D. Lewis as its manager either from the first or soon after. Machinery for it was hauled by wagon from Stockton by John Clarke at a freight rate of twenty-five cents a pound. After the decline of Owensville this lumber was taken from its buildings and rafted down the river by A. A. Riddle, to be used in Independence and Lone Pine, and to a less extent in Big Pine. The latter settlement, when it started, had a mill nearer, Bell and partner having returned in 1864 to the project they had abandoned under protest the year before.

Owensville's career was brief. Its corner lots were held at $1,000 and even $1,500 each for a short time, but before the end of 1864 some of its buildings were torn down. One of them, the blacksmith shop of the Consort mining company, was bought by Clarke and moved, becoming the first structure of any kind on the present Bishop townsite.

It stood a little distance to the south of West Line street and near Main. It was put up late in 1864.

During the quieter portion of 1863 a beginning on farm work was made not far from Bishop. W. P. George and associates put in a truck patch a little to the west. Andrew Thomson broke ground in West Bishop, and also established G. W. Norton on a place a mile north of the present townsite. Tom Evans located in Pleasant Valley. It is probable that similar undertakings were begun at Lone Pine that year, though no confirmation of that is available. A little patch of corn was planted at Independence.

One of the companies operating in the White Mountains bore the name of the San Francisco. A "town," called Graham City, after D. S. Graham, the superintendent, was started "at the foot of Keyes district, opposite Bishop Creek Valley," says a letter of the time. No other identification is obtainable, though its prospects were supposed to be so promising that a correspondent of the *Alta* wrote: "Should the mines (and of this there appears to be no doubt) turn out all right, this town will rival Aurora or Virginia City itself for population." If there were other aspiring settlements, not herein named, in the valley north of Chrysopolis, no record of them has been left.

John E. and Thomas E. Jones decided to undertake ranching in Round Valley, and sowed the first wheat there in the spring of 1865. They had been preceded by a man named William Frank, who had built a small stone cabin. John E. Jones's own story of experience during those early years gives but an inkling of the hardships undergone by the pioneers of this valley, rich as it was in all but man-made necessities. They had found the poor roads so badly washed that it took a week to move their team the last five miles into Aurora from the north. At Aurora they had to pay $25 for enough hay to feed their five oxen over night. It was necessary to lighten the load by storing half of it, including tools, stoves and heavy goods, for later recovery; this jettisoning was because of encountering a depth of more than five feet of snow to be broken through. The stored goods were never again seen by the owners. They finally reached Round Valley; then one of the oxen died, and another was stolen. By borrowing from others, enough of a team was made up to laboriously break up 4½ acres of the heavy sod. In this soil the first wheat in the valley was sowed. Five thousand head of livestock were being pastured in the valley, and in mid June the herds invaded the little ranch and destroyed the crop. Jones replanted his tract, made a shelter of willow boughs and a wagon sheet and alone watched day and night until his wheat ripened. His food was taboose, pinenuts, and occasionally beef. Thomas Jones was mining at Hot Springs, as Benton was called, and took his brother's place while the latter went to Carson for his family. Thomas cut and stacked the grain. The family arrived in September, 1865. Their flour was made by grinding it through a hand mill (now in the museum at Independence) until Jones rigged up a water power to drive the little machine. He made the family footwear, and built a little cabin with slabs obtained from the sawmill then running. This mere touching upon pioneering experience suggests endless details of hardships under such circumstances, drawbacks that in our pampered days would seem almost insuperable, but such as were uncomplainingly borne by pioneer men and pioneer women in bringing this fair valley to the homeland it was to become.

White Mountain City and Roachville were settlements just over the White Mountain summit from Owens Valley, in that White Mountain District which had been used for fraudulent election purposes in 1861. A writer visiting there in 1864 tells all that we know of those would-be mining centers. The "city" from which he wrote was on Wyman Creek, on the Deep Spring slope; its rival, Roachville, was on Cottonwood Creek, and was named by its proprietor, William Roach, hailing from Santa Cruz. Both places had regularly surveyed town plats. S. (no doubt Scott) Broder was the District Recorder.

CHAPTER XX

MORE INDIAN TROUBLES

COSO COUNTY AUTHORIZED—POLITICAL CONVENTION—PIUTES START
NEW DEPREDATIONS—AFFAIR AT CINDERELLA MINE—MRS.
MCGUIRE AND SON KILLED AT HAIWAI—VENGEANCE OF CITIZENS
—INTERMITTENT HOSTILITIES AND UNREST.

Formation of new counties in California is now
dependent on large populations, all sections being as well
supplied with local government as appears to be consistent
with both efficient administration and judicious economy.
Railroads, telegraph and telephone lines, highways a￼ little
foreseen by the pioneers as were the automobiles that share
in the annihilation of isolation and distance, have brought
all sections comparatively close together. Not so in the
'60's; thinly settled communities, separated by many miles,
were days apart in communication; horseflesh provided the
chief motive power for travel; telegraph lines were few;
and the whole West was lawless. Only a liberal policy of
county government could provide any civil control over
tens of thousands of square miles of territory. Maps of
that period show counties duly outlined, but containing no
place of more than crossroads dignity.

Agitation for a county east of the Sierras in 1860,
following the discovery of Aurora, had led to the official
establishment of Mono county in 1861. When resurvey of
the State line showed that Aurora, the chief reason for
Mono's creation, was outside of that county's borders, the
population of Mono was found to be but 430, Indians
included. With this and other examples before them,
Owens Valleyans did not hesitate to petition the
Legislature, in February, 1864, to create a county on the
eastern Sierra slope south of Mono. It was proposed to
name the county Monache, to make San Carlos its county

seat, and to establish the northern boundary near Mono Lake. But when the bill went into the Legislature, it had been materially changed. The name was to be Coso, Bend City the provisional county seat, and Big Pine Creek, thence east to the State line, the northern boundary. E. S. Sayles, G. J. Slocum, D. C. Owen, John R. Hughes and John Lentell were named as commissioners to designate precincts, name election officers, canvass returns, and co-operate with a County Judge, to be named by the Governor, in getting the new machinery into working shape. Dr. S. G. George was offered the judgeship, but declined. Owens Valleyans wanted Oscar L. Matthews appointed, but no appointment was made.

As a full corps of county officers was to be elected, the Republicans held a convention in San Carlos May 20th. Any one who stated himself to be a Republican was allowed full voice in the proceedings. The result of an orderly and harmonious session was the nomination of W. A. Greenly for Sheriff, John Thorn for Clerk, Abraham Parker for Treasurer and W. S. Morrow for District Attorney.

June 6, 1864, was set by the enactment as the date for the election. But legal notice of their appointments and authority to proceed failed to reach the commissioners in time; and as no provision was made for changing the election day the whole matter went by default.

A law passed by that legislative session chartered the Owens River Canal Company, to construct canals for transporting passengers and freight and for irrigation and water power. It was to improve Owens River canyon, and was to collect tolls for fifteen years, unless Mono County should exercise its privilege of taking over the enterprise after ten years. Mono Supervisors were to set tolls that would yield 2 per cent per month on the investment. R. S. Whigham, Speer Riddle, Wm. Fleming, Wm. P. Pratt and Isaac Swain were named as trustees of the company, of which no more was heard.

These gropings toward local self-government and permanency were broken into by further threats of Indian troubles. Abandonment of Camp Independence the year before had been highly unwelcome to the settlers. Particularly after the Merriam affair the white people avoided the neighborhoods which Joaquin Jim, most dreaded among the Indian leaders, claimed as his own. During the latter part of 1864 depredations began once more. The Piutes moved their women and children into the mountains, a move taken to be in anticipation of a new campaign. Lone white men were killed where it could be done safely. One such instance was that of a man named Watkins, who had brought a band of horses into the valley and located not far from Black Rock Springs. In his isolated position he fell an easy prey. This event and other signs of a coming outbreak led to the sending of petitions to General McDowell, then commanding at the San Francisco Presidio. McDowell could not, or at least did not, spare any troops for Owens Valley at that time. Learning this, many of the residents struck out for safer climes; those remaining determined to fight the issue to a finish. At Owensville, considered the most dangerously situated point, the citizens organized with Will Hicks Graham as captain; and at Bend City W. L. ("Dad") Moore and W. A. Greenly were selected as leaders of the volunteer forces.

Among the miners who had ventured into the lone places believing that hostilities were over were three named Crow, Mathews and Byrnes. They located a claim which they named the Cinderella, about four miles from the Gilbert ranch in Deep Springs Valley. On November 21, 1864, Mathews was cooking dinner while his partners were at the claim. An Indian and his squaw came to the camp and asked for something to eat. As Mathews turned to get something for them the Indian shot him through the jaw. About the same time a shot from another Indian ended the life of Crow, working at the mine windlass. His body either fell into the shaft or was thrown in by the Indians. Byrnes, 60 or 70 feet below, was kept busy dodging rocks with which the attackers tried to kill him, but by dextrous use of his shovel he managed to fend off the missiles.

Mathews had been wounded, but not enough to prevent his fighting. When he opened fire the two who had attacked him ran away. He was sure his partners had been killed, and determined to strike out for Owens Valley. He had a rifle, a shotgun and a revolver, but soon threw away both of the large weapons. It took him two agonizing days to get over the mountains, his sufferings being intensified by lack of water. Reaching Owens River, he fell into shallow water while trying to get a drink. This loosened the clotted blood in his mouth and throat—a relief on which he dwelt in narrating the circumstances. The attention of a horseman was attracted, and Mathews was taken to a ranch where Big Pine now is. For many days he was fed through a cowhorn, and at last he recovered his general health. He was never afterward free from some effects of his wound, however; to the day of his death, in Round Valley twenty-four years later, his speech was intelligible to only a few. He had been in California since 1831.

While Mathews was escaping, Byrnes was prisoned in the shaft with the body of Crow for company. The Indians had taken away the windlass rope. Joe Bowers, Indian chieftain, came to the place soon afterward and found means of lowering water to Byrnes, then came across the mountains and told the whites what had occurred. S. G. Gregg went as far as Lone Pine and gathered a party of thirty men to rescue Byrnes. The latter had been in the shaft five days when he was hauled out. The body of Crow was buried there.

Now mark the ingratitude of the man whose life Joe had saved. The Piute leader had his home camp at a place called Antelope Springs. A few years subsequently Byrnes decided that he needed the land and water more than Joe Bowers did, so he drove the latter away. Joe went to Independence and told his loyal white friends, who formed a posse and forced Byrnes to vacate. Fourteen also joined in an agreement to support Joe, as a reward for his friendship and services during the Indian troubles, and thenceforward he was quarterly supplied with provisions and clothing. Capt. MacGowan, a later commandant at Camp Independence, employed him as a scout. The departure of the soldiers from Owens Valley, when the post was finally abandoned, dropped Joe from the payroll, but left him with a claim to a six dollar pension. This was regularly collected by S. G. Gregg and used for the old Piute's welfare. Signing the receipt for this (with an X) was an important ceremony for the beneficiary. He was taken to San Francisco in 1871 to see the wondrous achievements of the white man, and attracted no little attention. During the early '70's, a reception given to a land officer who had engineered a land steal caused a burlesque of the affair to be given in Joe's honor, at which he was presented with a hat, a pipe and tobacco, and made a spech admitting his own merits. He died early in this century in Deep Spring Valley.

It is not to be inferred that Joe was a second Uncas in virtues. He had many of the failings of his people, and one of the chief cares of his white friends was to see that he did not gamble away what they provided for his welfare. He took a moral view of things, and his condemnations of intemperance and other vices were more picturesque and forcible than adapted for polite ears. He had foreseen more clearly than his fellows the ultimate success of the whites, and appreciated the advantages they possessed. He was always their friend, sometimes at his own peril, and was respected by his own people as well.

The murder of Mrs. McGuire and her little son at Haiwai, and the settlers' retribution in Indian lives, were with very few exceptions the last items of Indian warfare.

The waters of Haiwee reservoir of the Los Angeles aqueduct system now cover lands known in pioneer days, and for years later, as Haiwai Meadows. (Haiwee is the Indian word for dove.) To those meadows, 25 miles south of Owens Lake, came in 1864 a man named McGuire, with his wife and six-year-old son. They established a little way station, which received the patronage of the scant travel between Visalia and Owens Valley. The hostess endeared herself to all who came, and her bright little son was a favorite.

On the last day of 1864 two men were at the place. Their names as given by H. T. Reed, whose letter written a few days later is principally followed in the details of which he professed to be well informed, were Newman and Flanigan. Another account calls them O'Dale and Kittridge—which may be remarked to somewhat resemble the names Coverdale and Ethridge, of earlier Inyo record. McGuire had occasion to go to Big Pine for a plow, and asked them to remain until he returned. Before daylight of the following morning, January 1, 1865, the occupants of the house were awakened by fire, and found that the roof was blazing. The men ran out, but on being fired on ran back into the house. They commenced knocking off shingles from the inside, and by using what water was at hand and the brine from several barrels of corned beef had nearly extinguished the fire when the attack was renewed with firebrands, stones and shots. The heat became so intense that to remain inside was impossible. The men urged Mrs. McGuire to run with them and endeavor to escape; she refused, saying that nothing could save them and it would be no use. Flanigan and Newman, unwilling to share her peril, ran, escaping with a wound in the forehead of one and a shot through the hat of the other. Says Reed's letter: "They arrived here (at Little Lake, 17 miles) at 11 a. m., Newman weak from loss of blood and both nearly exhausted."

Walter James and John Harmon, southbound, reached Haiwai that forenoon. Smoke was still rising from the embers of the burned dwelling. Mrs. McGuire was a hundred feet or more from it. She was mercifully unconscious; fourteen arrows were in her body, and her neck was marked with fingerprints. An ax was by her side. But a few moments of life remained to her after the men arrived. The little boy was dead; his arm was broken, and a wound showed in his forehead. His tiny hand clasped a stone, indicating a spirit of defense to the last. Six

arrows had pierced his body, and had been pulled out by his
mother. Both were in their night clothing. Quoting Reed
again:

Both Mr. and Mrs. McGuire had done more for the Indians
than they were able, often denying themselves to feed them. Her
loss is deeply felt by all, and no one who ever stopped there will fail
to remember the hearty welcome and the happy face of bright little
Johnny and his noble mother.

The bodies of the victims were placed in a wagon box
and James remained to guard them while Harmon hurried
back to Owens Lake. A messenger was sent to Lone Pine,
where the bodies were brought that day for burial.

Some pioneers who were implacable foes of the Indians
acquitted the latter of guilt for this atrocity, maintaining
that it was the deed of the two white men. Reed's letter
indicates no such doubt, however, nor does any other
account or reference at the time nor the later story of it
written in a letter by W. L. Moore. The arrows found and
the trail followed by the avengers supported the white
fugitives' story. The unmanly and selfish cowardice of
those men received ample comment in the accounts at that
time.

A dozen or more men, headed by W. L. Moore and W.
A. Greenly, immediately started for Haiwai, camping near
Olancha that night. The next day they went to Haiwai
and took up the trail of a party of fifteen or sixteen Indians
until it divided among the sand hills east of the meadows.
Some of the natives had started southerly to the Kern
River trail, the rest going northerly and east of Owens
Lake. From the dividing point the citizens returned to
Haiwai, and Moore and Thos. Passmore (each of whom
later became Sheriff and each of whom was killed in the
discharge of official duty) took up the trail of Newman
and Flanigan. On the way they picked up a loaded rifle, a
little further on a loaded pistol, and still further along a
shotgun with one barrel loaded. The trail was followed
to Little Lake where the two men were found. They told
the story as here written. They were told to leave the
country at once and not to return, under penalty of death.

When Moore and Passmore returned to Haiwai the party went to Coso, reaching that settlement January 3d. The Mexican miners who composed its population showed no disposition to aid in any way or to accommodate the Americans. The latter wasted scant ceremony in supplying the needs of themselves and their animals. Returning toward the valley, the Indian trail was again picked up, and followed directly to an Indian camp near the lake shore east of the river's mouth. The party rode on past the camp to Lone Pine.

Four Piute prisoners were being held in that settlement. Some of the citizens advocated slaughtering them forthwith; others objected. A letter written that evening said they had Indians under guard, "who will hardly see the sun rise." This forecast was borne out by the narrative afterward written by a pioneer:

During the discussion one of the Indians saw a chance to run, and did so, escaping at least a score of shots until Dick Mead jumped on a horse and overtook and killed the fugitive. Thos May and John Tilly took the remaining prisoners to Tilly's house for safe-keeping during the night. One, outside with May, made a break for liberty and was shot. Those in the house, hearing the shot, also undertook to escape, when Tilly killed one with a blow from a six-shooter and May shot the other.

A correspondent wrote:

The cry now is for extermination. For some time we have been compelled to let the Indians do as they pleased. Only last week an Indian drew his knife on my wife because she would not let him take possession of the kitchen and give him sugar in his coffee. "Poor Indian" is played out with this settler.

A general council of whites held at Lone Pine determined to inflict a crushing blow on the natives by destroying their settlement near the mouth of Owens River. A day or two was spent in gathering a force, which left Lone Pine during the night of January 5th to reach the lake camp by daylight of the 6th. Greenly and Moore commanded; with them were Passmore, Tilly, Chas. D. Begole, Thos. May, T. F. A. Connelly, Dick Mead, R. M. Shuey, H. Meyer, John Kispert, F. W. Fickert (later a prominent rancher of the Tehachapi region), James Heffner, Haslem, McGuire (husband of the murdered woman), Rogers (whose shocking ending will be presently recorded), Green Hitchcock and three or four of his brothers, Charles Robinson, Hugh P. Edwards, and others to a total strength of thirty-two.

The plan was for Greenly's detachment to cross the river and guard against escape to the eastward, while Moore's party was to attack the camp. Snow covered the ground. The Indians, unsuspicious of danger, had no sentries, and were awakened by the blazing guns of the horsemen who rode among the wickiups. Greenly's three-mile detour was not allowed for, and Moore and his men had practically concluded the bloody work before Greenly appeared.

According to the judgment of those who had trailed the Indians from Haiwai, eight or ten of the perpetrators of that atrocity were in the lake camp. For their guilt the whole village population, of whom at least three-fourths were innocent of any possible participation in the Haiwai deed, were ruthlessly slaughtered—as the whites would have been had circumstances been reversed. Neither age nor sex were spared among the forty-one who died there. Six Indians had taken to the icy waters of the lake. The account by Fickert said that two squaws and two little boys were permitted to come out alive; that of T. F. A. Connelly said that three, a boy and his two sisters, were spared. McGuire shot two bucks in the water. The boy, aged about fourteen, was shot at, and asked in English why they wanted to kill him. He said he had not hurt any one. Heffner told him that if he would come out he would not be hurt. The boy also said his two sisters were in the lake, and was bidden to tell them to come out.

By this time the Greenly subdivision had come up. Some in each party were anxious to do away with the young captives. Heffner asked how many would stand with him in protecting them, and about half declared in his favor. The wrangle threatened to result in bloodshed among the citizens, when Mead requested all who favored sparing the children to stand with him. Two-thirds of the company moved to his side, after which there was no further argument. The girls were taken as far as the foot of the lake and there released. Heffner adopted the boy.

This version faithfully follows accounts given to the author, personally or by letter, by several of the men who were present, and narratives written by others within a few years of the occurrence. This fact is mentioned because this affair, more than any other occurrence of the Indian war, was distorted and garbled in California papers at the time. Some of the reports then published contradict themselves, when read by any one who knows the country. Some other statements they contain may or may not have been true, no other light having been obtained. One was that an Indian had Mrs. McGuire's purse, with a few dollars in money; this is probably false, as the McGuire house was not believed to have been raided. Another was that one of the slain Indians had a rifle which had belonged to William Jones, a miner, said to have been killed in the White Mountains two weeks before. Large quantities of freshly painted arrows were said to have been found in the camp. No account given to the writer mentioned such a find; it may have been made, though painting arrows was unusual.

Apparently a little earlier than the Owens Lake affair, a sortie by a white expedition resulted in the killing of seventeen Indians near the stream now known as Division Creek, north of Independence. Two prisoners at Camp Independence were shot by a man named McVickers, who said they were attempting to escape.

January 3d a white force of seventeen men went to the Black Rocks and found that the Piutes had burned the camps and fled to the mountains, killing cattle as they went.

Earlier, probably in the fall of 1864, an Indian Agent had visited the valley, accompanied by a Lieutenant Daley, who reported:

The Indian supplies are not good, and most of the Indians have left for the mountains. The Indian Agent invited them to come in; sixteen came, who said they had been maltreated. Said the whites would not pay the Indians who worked for them. I learned from Mr. Maloney, one of the present proprietors of Camp Independence, that settlers would go to Tule River reservation for Indians to come and work, and when they got through would decline paying them and drive them away. The Indians said they would retaliate and drive the whites out.

Reed, heretofore quoted, wrote that Daley's report was not founded on fact, and that he knew of no single instance where the Indians had been treated wrongfully. Nor does it look reasonable, in view of all the trouble that had occurred, that any settler would go as far as Tule River to bring back more Indians with whom he planned to have further difficulty.

During January, 1865, Company C, 94 men, arrived at Bishop Creek and remained until April, when under peremptory orders the company went on to Independence. Its commander was Captain Kelley, who was not without western experience. He had been one of the daring pony express riders, in which capacity he had some thrilling adventures. His military commission, it was said, was won from Nevada's Governor in a poker game.

In February, Rogers, the only man except one employee then remaining at Owens Lake, was attacked by Indians while proceeding to Little Lake. Six arrows fired from ambush struck him, none inflicting a disabling wound. Occasional shots from his revolver kept the foes at bay, in a running fight, until he reached Little Lake. He went back to his lone situation and fortified his quarters.

The Union mill southeast of Independence was burned by Indians June 25th.

If peace did not prevail during the spring and summer, at least there are few mentions of encounters. A German at a mill at Owens Lake was shot in July, receiving wounds from four arrows and from a bullet. Almarin B. Paul, writing from Kearsarge in September, said: "The Indians have made a rule: 'Indian no go in valley, white man no go in mountain.' I never saw such inveterate haters of Indians."

A November note said:

There are occasional depredations by roving Indians under a subchief known as "Old Hungry." Lieut. Hardenburg and 30 men have left Visalia, part of the soldiers to be stationed at the lower end of Owens Lake, part at Camp Indepesdence.

Another note that month stated that Captain Noble and Company E had been sent to Camp Independence, and the Nevada company under Kelley would be mustered out.

January 3, 1866: San Carlos and Bend City are entirely abandoned. Soldiers are stationed there to protect buildings from fire by Indians, who are still hostile. Indians wishing to travel through the valley are furnished escorts to protect them from worthless white men.

The guards were not sufficient, however, for on the night of March 11th four houses in San Carlos were burned, the two soldiers there shooting at the red incendiaries without effect.

A Kearsarge letter of January 18th said:

The Indians still make small raids on the settlers in the lower part of the valley. The Indians have no interest in being honest, having secure retreats which are never visited by citizens or soldiers. The citizens will not permit the Indians to come around, but declare war against them and kill them on sight. Property in the upper portion of the valley is perfectly secure, the settlers there giving work to Indians, many of them cultivating their grass seed ground or having little patches of corn, or live securely on their fishing grounds without fear of white men.

Notwithstanding the reported security in the upper end of the valley, Captain Noble and part of his command traveled to Round Valley in March. Chieftains met them, and offered Noble "all the wealth of their nation—four ponies, eleven buckskins, a rusty dinner bell, 25 dimes and $10 gold—if he would leave Round Valley and take away his banner of stars." But while he was cultivating amity in that locality, Indians killed stock within a mile of Fort Independence, and stole part of the beef that had been killed for the troops. The correspondent reporting this believed that if the peaceably inclined Indians were let alone and the renegades hunted down the trouble would soon end.

In the meantime the natives had entered deserted Bend City, at a favorable opportunity, and nearly destroyed the place.

Soldiers from Camp Independence had a fight with Indians on the east side of Owens Lake in August, 1866, killing several and taking five prisoners. While crossing the river on their way to camp three of the prisoners plunged into the stream and attempted to escape. Two were shot and the third retaken. The commandant at Camp Independence used the prisoners as a means of communicating with the hostiles in an effort to obtain some arrangement or treaty.

No further record of valley hostilities has been found. The desert Indians were still unsatisfied, however, and on March 4, 1867, raided "the Spanish mines" at Coso. One miner was killed, and everything portable was taken away. Cattle and horses had been killed at Owens Lake just before. A detachment of twelve cavalrymen, under Sergeant F. R. Neil, was sent from Camp Independence, March 7, to pursue and if possible chastise the offenders. Owing to heavy snow on the eastern mountains the pursuit to the desert could not be made, and the soldiers returned to Thomas Franklin's ranch near Owens Lake. Franklin volunteered as guide, and 3 o'clock on the morning of March 12th the start was made. It was expected that the Indians would be found at Coso Hot Springs, but they were not there. The route was then to "Rainy Springs Canyon," twenty miles distant, where "sign" was found. The rancheria, on a slope surrounded by large pine trees, was reached about 4:30 in the afternoon. The troopers dismounted and took a trail made by squaws in carrying water to their camp. As they reached the summit each party saw the other and firing began. The white men charged while the reds ran to positions behind rocks. The chief, Barbe, handled his men skillfully and exposed himself too bravely, for he was shot and killed. The troopers, veterans who had served under Sheridan, drove the enemy from rock to rock, killing four warriors besides the chief and wounding others. At the rancheria, which was the best appointed the men had seen, they found a pistol known to have been taken the preceding fall in an attack on a mine, and other articles stolen from whites. After destroying the camp, the expedition started for Owens Lake, where it arrived after a continuous ride of 90 miles. Thomas Franklin, whose account is here given, wrote that although he was a heavy loser from depredations he felt that he had satisfaction.

This appears to have been the final clash of the war. Soldiers were sent out once more, in 1870, when the situation in Round Valley was considered threatening. Again in 1871 there were fears of an outbreak, which were quieted largely through the influence of Joe Bowers. He told his people the white men would mow them down like grass if they resumed fighting. Though the trouble makers called him the white man's captain, they were wise enough to heed his advice.

The Indian attitude was sullen and defiant for a long time, and disquieting rumors were circulated at different times for several years. White efforts to prevent murders of medicine men were the most frequent cause of friction.

It has been noted that one Indian chief never submitted to white domination. Joaquin Jim, while he ceased marauding, remained aloof to the end of his days. The Indian story was that he came to his death after the war, from overeating some special tribal delicacy; the white version was that he was killed by one of his own warriors. Another so-called Joaquin Jim appeared at Tule River Reservation in 1863 to be treated for wounds received in Owens Valley. A squad of soldiers from Camp Babbitt went to arrest him, but he saw them coming, fled, and was pursued and killed. "The body was found with a number of fresh wounds and many scars. Joaquin Jim was known to have murdered two white men in cold blood, and had fought desperately in several battles," said a published report. Nevertheless, that Indian was not the noted southern Mono leader, who was leading his band on this slope at a later date.

Residents of Owensville estimated the total death list of the war, so far as they knew it, at 60 whites and about 200 Indians.

Perhaps it is not the business of a record of this character to philosophize on the Indian war subject. The facts have been set down as fully and impartially as they have been learned. That the Indian should resist trespass on his hereditary domain was but natural. Some white men proved themselves as savage and ruthless as those they fought. But the white domination, and its ability to make use of resources which to the Indian meant far less than the comparative comfort the conquerors have brought to him, were as inevitable here as they have been elsewhere as civilization advanced.

CHAPTER XXI

WHITES IN POSSESSION

TRAVEL IN VALLEY CONSIDERED SAFE—LAND ENTRIES—KEARSARGE
MINE DISCOVERED—A REVOLTING CRIME—HARD TIMES—AVA-
LANCHE SWEEPS AWAY PART OF KEARSARGE CAMP—SOME OF THE
RECORD OF THE MINE.

Re-establishment of a garrison at Camp Independence, together with the severe lessons given to warring Indians on every provocation, justified white settlers in believing their supremacy in Owens Valley would not again be seriously disputed. Though the record, doubtless incomplete, given in the last preceding chapter proves that danger still existed, Almarin B. Paul, writing from Kearsarge May 5, 1866, said:

It is now fully as safe to travel up and down the valley, so far as Indians go, as it is in the streets of Sacramento or San Francisco. The worst class of Indians who formerly made this valley their hunting ground have moved farther eastward. Those who are in the valley prefer peace and to work, which they do for fifty cents a day and hogadie (food).

Many of the settlers who shared in the first rush for Owens Valley lands had made locations. Renewed Indian troubles sent many of them out as fast as they had come, and few of them ever perfected their claims. Search of land office records shows that the earliest locations were abandoned, including those of Jacob Nash and E. D. French at Olancha, March 9, 1863; John M. George, Lone Pine, April 2, 1863; James A. Brewer, George's Creek, May 21, 1863; J. C. White, Independence, June 5, 1863.

The oldest patent of which record is found was issued to Thomas Edwards, December 5, 1866, for land on which he had already laid out the townsite of Independence. A later addition to that townsite was made when Paul W. Bennett, who did not receive his patent until 1874, began selling lots in the south end of the present townsite. W. L. Moore, who with Chas. D. Begole had held squatter title in the vicinity of Lone Pine since 1863, probably, did not make legal filing until July 17, 1867, and his patent was dated June 1, 1868. It was the last few months of 1869 before the first claims in the vicinity of Big Pine were taken up by Duncan Campbell, Fred Reinhakel, W. F. Uhlmeyer and S. G. Gregg. The earliest patents there were issued to Duncan Campbell and David Naylor, April 20, 1874. The earliest patent in the vicinity of Bishop was for land that had been filed on by Robert Bowne, who appears to have utilized a special privilege arising from his having served as a second lieutenant in the Black Hawk war. This claim was transferred to William Hyer, to whom patent was issued February 1, 1868. The description shows that this first location included part of the south end of the present town. Land within the townsite was patented to John Clarke, Dorcas Clark (widow of Wm. Clark), Thomas Clark, Milton S. Clark and Minerva Powers, all in 1874 or later. A record of irrigation in 1870 shows that 34 farm claimants were then drawing water supplies from Bishop Creek.

An optimistic resident wrote, September 7, 1865:

It is not unreasonable to predict that within seven years this valley will have a population of a hundred thousand. The proposed Atlantic and Pacific railroad is expected to come this way. The question is no longer what can be raised, but what is there that will not do well. This season's crops include 100 acres of potatoes, 100 acres of corn, a few of wheat and barley, and several acres of different kinds of vegetables.

The San Francisco *Alta California,* of September 30, 1865, told of plans for a railroad via Stockton, Visalia, Owens River and Austin, Nevada, to connect with the Great Pacific road projected from the East.

"Very heavy immigration," said a letter from Little Pine (soon to be Independence), June 14, 1865, "has created demand for a town which is being built on Thomas Edwards's land and has been named Independence." A September letter said the place consisted of twenty houses "of an original style of architecture." In the following

January, report was made that it had "four (whisky) mills, two stores, hay yard, hotel, blacksmith shop and one dwelling house." With true American spirit, the inhabitants built a schoolhouse which cost $1000. Talk of a new county had been revived, and Independence and Kearsarge were mentioned as candidates for county seat honors. Edwards had his townsite survey completed February 13, 1866, though it was not recorded until May 12, 1867. In the meantime, according to a letter dated July 29, 1865, "An attempt has been made to build a town half way between Little Pine and Oak Creek. So far only one small house and a lonely proprietor afford any evidence of the city of Oakdale."

Bishop property, long unsurveyed, was bought and sold by measured metes and bounds for years; in some instances its lot descriptions began with such impermanent starting points as "a willow tree," "the center of a ditch," etc., to make trouble later when exact boundaries became important.

Laws, originally Bishop Station, was surveyed on the building of the railroad, some of its lots being where the primitive cabins of Owensville had stood. Keeler also was laid out when the railroad was built; whether its name should be Keeler or Hawley was an unsettled question for some time. Darwin was also one of the earlier surveyed townsites.

On the founding of Independence, Bend City residents promptly moved there, leaving their adobe habitations to become crumbling piles under the combined ravages of Indians and weather. San Carlos faded as rapidly, though a masonry smokestack long stood to mark its site. Owensville, by that name, lost its last inhabitant in 1871. Most of its residents had moved to Bishop Creek, the name of which was changed to Bishop in 1889.

After this digression, we return to 1865. J. N. Rogers has been mentioned, as one of those attacking the Indian camp at Owens Lake, and as escaping from pursuing Indians. His ranch near the lake became the scene of a unique and revolting crime, of which he was the victim.

Some details of the account as heretofore published have been corrected in accordance with facts developed at the trial of King, the murderer.

"Hog" Rogers, so dubbed because of his having been in the hog raising business in Tulare, fed and lodged travelers at his lake place as occasion might require. One E. M. King, who claimed to have been a preacher, came to the place in the spring of 1865, and remained there for two or three months. Rogers was missed by passers-by in June, and King gave some explanation of his absence, also exhibiting a paper purporting to be a deed from Rogers for half of the latter's property. He also said Rogers had told him if he did not return from his journey King was to fall heir to the remainder. Travelers Snow and Dearborn, tarrying at the place, partook heartily of a meal served to them by King, who finally asked them if they know what kind of meat they had been eating. They said they supposed it was pork. "Well, that's some of old Rogers," was their startling enlightenment. They reported to Thomas Franklin, to whom King accounted for the human remains scattered about the place by saying that he had killed an Indian. Search disclosed parts of a body, and finally the head and face of the victim. It developed that King had killed Rogers, made a razor strop from a strip of his skin, fed some of the flesh to hogs and chickens, and had lived for days amid the decaying fragments around the premises. Franklin arrested the murderer and took him to Independence, where Justice Beveridge averted a lynching by putting him into custody of the soldiers. He managed to escape in August, and made his way into the Sierra. In September his zeal to vote caused him to enter Woodville, in Tulare county, where he gave the name of Butterfield. He was recognized and arrested, and the following month was convicted of murder in the first degree, after a trial in Visalia in which sickening details of brutality were disclosed. He was hanged in that town December 12.

Before the establishment of the sawmills at Big Pine and Bishop Creek, and a third mill northwest of Independence, lumber was cut by the slow process of whipsawing. Among those who had been cutting in the primitive way were Thomas W. Hill, G. W. Cornell and A. Kittleson, camped at what was long known as Todd's, now Gray's Meadows, west of Independence. Hardships of the period were graphically related by Mr. Hill to the author during the course of a day's railroad journey together. The need for haste in gathering the reminiscences of the old-timers was singularly illustrated in his case, for the old pioneer died of heart failure before he left the car that evening.

Cattle ranged all over the valley, Mr. Hill said. Owners knowing that Indians would take the stock as opportunity offered, gave settlers permission to do the same. There being no local agriculture of any consequence, and outside communication being uncertain or worse, the roving cattle were often the sole reliance for food. Even if farming had been seriously undertaken, that was a specially discouraging season, for it is said that the year 1864 was so dry that in midsummer Little Pine Creek's flow did not get down as far as Independence.

Hill and his partners had raised a little corn in their mountain nook, and from it ground four sacks of meal, using a coffee mill. It was agreed among them that because of the improbability of getting other supplies none of the meal should be sold. One day while Hill was alone in camp, a man came from Bend City and said his wife and children had nothing to eat and he did not know where to get food for them. Finally Hill said: "We agreed not to sell any of this meal, and I'm not going to do it. I'm going to the creek after some water, and if there happens to be a sack missing when I get back I won't do much hunting for it." His back was scarcely turned when he heard his visitor's wagon clattering away, and that evening Hill had to account for the meal.

The men prospected from their camp. In the fall of 1864 they with Thomas May and C. McCormack discovered promising croppings. Shortly before, sympathizers with the South in the Civil War had named the Alabama Hills, near Lone Pine, in evidence of their gratification at the destructive career of the Confederate privateer Alabama. Having the ending of that career by the Kearsarge fresh in mind, Hill and his partner, staunch Unionists, evened it up by calling their claim after the Union battleship.

Other discoveries, including the Silver Sprout and Virginia, were made on the slopes of the great peak which took the name of its first mine. Kearsarge mining district was organized September 19, 1864, at a meeting with J. B. Rowley as chairman and G. W. Cornell as secretary. Its boundaries were extensive—Owens River on the east, the Sierra summit on the west, Big Pine Creek on the north, the Alabama Hills on the south.

Four tons of Kearsarge ore were sent to Rall's mill, near Ophir, Nevada, and netted $900 a ton. The phenomenal find attracted attention, and a controlling interest was sold to Charles Tozier, Almarin B. Paul, D. L. Bliss, Chas. Vangorder, I. L. Requa and John Gillig— all men of prominence then and later in coast mining and financial circles. Systematic development of the claims began in the spring of 1865. A letter in June said:

Surface rock upon Little Pine silver ledges is the richest ever discovered on the Pacific Coast. It is calculated that the bulk of the ledge will average $5000 a ton by working process.

Work progressed on the mines through 1865 and 1866, or rather during such periods as permitted by heavy snows in that elevated situation. Quite a camp grew in the canyon at the western base of the peak's highest rise. Almarin B. Paul, appointed superintendent, put up a $40,000 ten-stamp mill which began operations in July, 1866. A report from it said the first run produced 300 to 400 pounds of bullion worth from $3.50 to $12 per ounce. Lodes were selling at $100 per foot. Silver Sprout ore had worked out $720 to the ton.

Some of the miners stayed in their camp two miles above the sea through the winter of 1866-7. February came, with storms of great violence. Snow, driven by gales whirled in clouds, and still more violently around Kearsarge Peak and the cabins under its shoulder. New-fallen snow massed on the surface of the winter's earlier coatings, and began to shoot down the declivities. The camp escaped damage until the afternoon of March 1, 1867, when an avalanche swept away eleven cabins, buried others, and took a life.

Messengers went at once from the houses which were undamaged, making hard-won progress to Hill's, Camp Independence and Bend City. Every available man answered the summons, Hill, Kittleson and Cornell being the first to reach the scene. Occupants of destroyed cabins were accounted for until that occupied by mine foreman C. W. Mills and his wife was reached. The house had been crushed until no trace of it could be seen above the snow. After some digging a part of the rough stone wall was found. Hill was the first to grasp a bit of cloth, part of the dress enclosing the lifeless form of Mrs. Mills. Death had come with so little warning that her stiffened fingers still grasped a needle and the thread that she was about to place in it. Search for the body of Mills was about to be abandoned when a man known as "Crazy" insisted on keeping up the hunt. Mills was finally found, barely alive, and with a broken leg. He recovered. E. Chaquette and wife occupied a house in the edge of the slide's path. A dog's barking caused him to look out in time to see the avalanche coming. He caught up his wife and ran, and escaped so narrowly that the edge of the slide caught him and broke his leg.

The population of Kearsarge moved that night to Hill's, and preparations for safer stopping places were made the next day. Development of the mine went on unchecked. To follow to a conclusion the fortunes of the property: The bullion produced was sent to Gold Hill, with an escort of soldiers. When it was found to net but 12½ cents an ounce Paul quit in disgust, and I. L. Requa became superintendent, with D. P. Pierce in direct charge. Pierce's first working produced $60 per ton of ore. He had found the company $15,000 in debt when he took hold. After a month's smooth running, and when he began to be hopeful of success, creditors demanded that the bullion be turned over to them. Pierce, intending to use the proceeds to settle affairs in his own way, hid it. The matter got into the courts and a receivership was ordered. Finally the property passed to other owners, with George Stead as manager. One of the first acts was to sell to the miners the ore that was then on the dump and at the mill. Some of this was sorted and sent to San Francisco, where it yielded over $700 a ton. Stead soon left, and his successor, D. P. Low, bought from the creditors what ore remained, paying them $40 a ton. Some of it, specially selected, brought $700 a ton, and the average was $140 a ton. Another change in the scrambled affairs of the company occurred in 1869. The ore continued to prove its value, fifty tons of it averaging $165, while the average of all that was worked from the mine was $60. Managements came and went for a number of years; and for all the rich returns that were reported the old mine showed a balance on the wrong side of the ledger and was virtually abandoned by the company, passing to other hands.

CHAPTER XXII

INYO COUNTY ESTABLISHED

MORMON EFFORTS TO SECURE TERRITORY EAST OF SIERRAS—INYO COUNTY CREATED—TOTAL VOTE NINETY-ONE AT FIRST ELECTION —FIRST OFFICERS—HUGE SCHOOL DISTRICTS—FIRST CHURCH ORGANIZATION—BOUNDARY CHANGES.

Records show that for a little time the Mormons had hopes of ruling the Great Basin as far westward as the summit of the Sierra Nevada Mountains, including the area now comprised in Inyo County. In March, 1849, they held a convention in Salt Lake City and (so far as they could) organized the "State of Deseret." It included the present Utah, Arizona, some of Colorado, some of Oregon, southern California south of Santa Monica, eastward and northward through half of the present Kern and Tulare counties, and across the Sierras. This took in our present county as well as others to the north. This liberal claim of territory was ignored, so far as California was concerned, by the Act admitting this State into the Union and ratification of its constitution prescribing the boundaries as they now exist. That the Mormons meant business in their claim was indicated by an invitation "to the inhabitants of that portion of Upper California lying east of the Sierra Nevada Mountains" to participate in their convention. Needless to say there was no response from any of the country south of Lake Tahoe, at least.

How the eastern line of California, which later became also the eastern line of this county, was set as it is was part of the history of the anti-slavery and pro-slavery factions in the State constitutional convention. Angling the line southeasterly through hundreds of miles of utterly unknown desert can be attributed to nothing better than a compromise between contending views.

When people of western Nevada held a mass meeting at Genoa August 8, 1857, and prepared a petition asking Congress to organize a new Territory, separate from Utah, they looked on the Sierras as the natural boundary, and suggested that the range be made the western line of their soon-to-be Nevada. This too was disregarded in defining the lines in the Nevada enabling act.

The great part of the present Inyo County was within the lines set in 1852 for Tulare, and up to 1866 that county exercised a shadowy jurisdiction over Owens Valley south of Big Pine Creek. Owens Valley north of that stream had been allotted to Mono when in 1861 it was created from "those portions of Calaveras, Mariposa and Fresno Counties lying east of the summit of the Sierra Nevada Mountains." In the original laying out of county lines, all this region was included in Mariposa; part of it was put into Fresno in 1856, then into Mono.

The unsuccessful effort to establish Coso County has been set forth. Owens Valley's scattered settlers memorialized the next Legislature, and on February 17, 1866, Assemblyman J. E. Goodall introduced a bill to establish Inyo County. It passed without opposition, Tulare parting with the valley willingly, according to the press, because of fear of expense. Boundaries of the new county were the same as had been set for Coso County— the Sierra summit and the State line on the west and east, Tulare's southern boundary and "down the middle of Big Pine Creek to its mouth, thence due east to the State line" for the other limits. While Kearsarge was the most populous place in the territory, its claim for county seat honors were wisely set aside and Independence was named until the citizens should decide otherwise. Thos. J. Goodale, Lyman Tuttle, L. F. Cooper, W. A. Greenly and W. A. Baker were appointed commissioners to manage proceedings. The date for the election was set for March 3, but as the bill did not become law until March 22 the whole matter would have fallen through again but for a saving provision, suggested by the Coso County failure, that in case the election was not held at the time set it might be held at such time, within one year, as the commissioners might designate.

Salaries of the officers and their official bonds were set as follows: County Judge, salary $1,000; District Attorney, salary $500, bond $2,000; Supervisors, salary $300 each, bond $1,000. The Sheriff, whose bond was $7,000; Clerk, bond $3,000; Treasurer, bond $10,000; Assessor, bond $1,000; Coroner, bond $2,000, and Surveyor, bond $2,000, were to be paid according to a general State law enacted in 1855. The Assessor's pay was $8 per day while at work, and the Superintendent of Schools drew $150 per year. Though money was more valuable in those times than it is now, the salary list was certainly modest.

Inyo was attached to Mono County for Assembly district purposes, and to that and several other counties in a judicial district.

A provision of the act required the appointment of commissioners to confer with appointees from Tulare to decide the proportion of Tulare County's debt to be taken over by Inyo. The Clerk of Tulare was instructed in July to correspond with the Clerk in Inyo on this matter. In August, Tulare named Pleasant Byrd and S. C. Brown as its representatives, and in September Inyo designated W. A. Greenly and L. F. Cooper to act for it. A subsequent record of the Inyo Supervisors notes that the commissioners presented their report, without giving an inkling of its tenor or the action taken on it. Tulare's records are equally incomplete, not only regarding the settlement with Inyo but also in like cases of territory settlements with Los Angeles, Kern and Fresno. So far as shown by books of Clerk or Treasurer, the matter came to nothing whatever.

Inyo Republicans met in Independence April 18, 1866, with Lieutenant David Love as chairman and O. L. Matthews (who had been appointed County Judge) as secretary. Its ticket was W. A. Greenly for Sheriff; Thomas Passmore, Clerk; J. Harris, Treasurer; A. J. Close, District Attorney; R. D. Blaney, Coroner; J. H.

Gibbs, Assessor; Lyman Tuttle, Surveyor; Josiah Earl, Superintendent of Schools; J. Westervelt, R. Hilton and C. D. Begole, Supervisors.

A Democratic ticket was put up, but no information about its convention is available. After the election, which was held on some May date not disclosed by county records, the Democrats claimed that the influence of soldiers of Company E, at Camp Independence, defeated them. They were generous enough to say that their opponents had put up good men, however. First returns, published in Visalia, showed a close finish in some cases, with Close leading his opponent by only 7 and Gibbs but 2 ahead. The official record shows the election of John T. Ryan, Assessor; John Beveridge, District Attorney; John Lentell, Treasurer; J. R. Hughes defeating Hilton for Supervisor—presumably Democratic nominees, and of Republican nominees for the other offices. Beveridge failed to qualify as District Attorney and Thomas P. Slade was appointed.

The Supervisors convened in Independence May 31st, and elected Hughes chairman. An election for township officers was called, to be held June 16th. The townships then established, polling places designated and the smaller vote cast indicate the new county's limitations of population:

First township: Polling places, George Shedd's house at Fish Springs, Oro Fino Co.'s office at Chrysopolis; election officers, J. S. Gill, E. M. Goodale and M. Stewart, and R. S. Whigham, Wm. Pedlar and Wm. Fleming respectively at the two places. In a total vote of 15, Fleming was elected Justice and Jack Shepherd and P. Green, Constables.

The Second township also had two polling places; at Kearsarge, where votes were counted at M. J. Byrne's house and the election officers were M. Meagher, Samuel McGee and W. J. Lake; and the Independence school-house, with S. P. Moffatt, R. Hilton and J. G. Payne as officers. The total vote of the township was 56, and the officers elected were J. J. Mankin and S. L. McGee Justices and Wm. J. Lake and Wm. Wallace Constables.

In the Third township voters cast their ballots at Moore and Begole's house, with A. C. Stevens, Lyman Tuttle and Robert Law as election officers. Four of the twenty voters were put into official positions—R. M. Shuey and J. J. Moore as Justices and N. F. Coburn and Peter Peerson as Constables.

Appointment of George Shedd, J. G. Payne and Reuben Van Dyke as Road Overseers completed the governmental machinery of Inyo County.

While the salary of the County Judge was small, his duties generally corresponded, having jurisdiction between the Justice of the Peace and the District Court. The latter resembled the present Superior Court except that it embraced several counties. Judge Matthews took office too late to deal with the first shooting affray in Independence, in which the exchange of ten shots between disputants had no result more serious than to clip a finger from one of the poor marksmen. His first case was more serious, a dispute over water on George's Creek leading to E. H. Rogers "laying for" Theodore Bayer and using a revolver and a shotgun in slaying him. Rogers saved county expense by escaping from the guardhouse wherein he was confined, and not being caught. Matthews next had two "civil" cases to decide, then a bankruptcy proceeding. He had no occasion to impose a sentence during his term, the first commitment to San Quentin being made by Judge A. C. Hanson in 1869, when a grand larcenist "went below" for three years.

Three school districts were established. One included all the county north of Independence; Independence and vicinity was the second, and the southernmost included all territory "south of the first section line south of J. W. Symmes." It would appear than the Supervisors looked on Mr. Symmes as a landmark.

Such looseness of wording was common in the early records of this county, as of probably many others. A small morocco-covered book in the courthouse contains the early minutes of the Board; a critical reader will find it very incomplete in details. Three of the public roads were described as "running from Bend City to Kearsarge," "from Independence to the northern line of the county," "from Cerro Gordo to the summit of the Sierra Nevada Mountains." The descriptions doubtless sufficed and were as well understood by laymen as if they had been sprinkled with survey figures and "thences."

In the winter of 1866-7 A. N. Bell built a flouring mill on Oak Creek, north of west of Independence. It was burned April 12, 1870. John E. Jones, in Round Valley, had already rigged up a primitive mill, and Joel H. Smith and A. A. Cashbaugh early, but at a date of which no record is available, built on Bishop Creek the mill which served until its power was sold to the Bishop Light and Power Company many years later.

When the election of 1867 came, Chrysopolis was as dead as Bend City, and Kearsarge had been swept out of existence. Cerro Gordo had started and was given a precinct. Fish Springs cast 31 votes, Independence 115, Lone Pine 53 and Cerro Gordo 7. The county was almost even in national party voting, 102 Republican, 104 Democratic. The county officers were on party tickets, but then as generally ever since voters chose as between individuals rather than according to party label.

Changes in the official corps were frequent during the first few years. It appears to have been considered courteous for the Sheriff whose term was about to end to resign in order than his elected successor might acquire a little experience. Greenly resigned in November, 1867, and W. L. ("Dad") Moore, who had been elected, was appointed for the month before the beginning of his own term. Two years later, he resigned to make way for A. B. Elder, just elected. The District Attorney's office was hard to keep filled. Beveridge, first elected, failed to qualify, and Thos. Slade was appointed. Slade was re-elected, and resigned. Pat Reddy was appointed, and failed to qualify. Paul W. Bennett served out the term. Beveridge, again elected in 1869, again failed to qualify, and Bennett was again appointed. Passmore gave up the Clerkship after a year's trial, and S. P. Moffatt was appointed. A. C. Stevens, elected Assessor in 1867, quit a year later, and was succeeded by L. A. Talcott. A. Farnsworth had defeated John A. Lank, 104 to 102, for Coroner, but was hardly more than sworn in before he resigned, and Lank was appointed. The old-timers were soon satisfied with office-holding and the slender emoluments; it was no more than an even chance whether any one elected would complete his set term.

A report of conditions in 1867 said that 2,000 acres of land had been enclosed in the county—that is, south of Big Pine Creek; half of the enclosed area was in cultivation. Barley was the principal crop. Independence had a population of 100. Fourteen quartz mills, of which ten were steam driven, were operating, dropping 130 stamps and representing a $350,000 investment. The San Carlos canal, discussed for several years, was again proposed, to be 15 miles long and to cost $30,000. It was estimated that there were 500 voters in the county. A road across Kearsage Pass to Visalia was advocated. One of the facts mentioned in argument for it was that Thomas Passmore had made the trip on foot in 48 hours. While nothing ever came of the discussion, the idea lasted so well that in 1870 a survey was made and some money subscribed to a company with which to finance the undertaking, which had been authorized by a legislative act of 1867.

Nothing has been unearthed from county records to show who first served as teachers of the children of Inyo's huge districts. Independence had a schoolhouse, and presumably a teacher. The first school in northern Owens Valley, then belonging to Mono County, was supported by subscription, in 1866. In the early months of the year but one white child of school age was in the territory, until the arrival of Mr. and Mrs. Joel Smith and six children in March, one of the first large families. Other families came, and Mrs. Smith began her school. The first public school teacher north of Independence was Milton S. Clark, at Bishop.

Mr. and Mrs. Thomas Clark have been named among the Owensville inhabitants. Their sons came soon afterward; one was Rev. Andrew Clark, and his young family. That pioneer minister and his brothers had served in the Union army, at Shiloh and other battlefields during the Civil War; and with the coming of peace they looked to the far West. Sincere in convictions, Mr. Clark arranged for a church organization; and on January 1, 1869, he and six others established the Baptist church at Bishop Creek, as the settlement was then called. This was the first religious society in eastern California. The Methodists sent their first resident minister, Rev. E. H. Orne, to Independence as the central point of "the Owens River Charge" two years later. These pioneer laborers in the cause of Christianity underwent virtually all the hardships of the circuit-riders of the mid-West, holding services regularly all the way from Benton to Cerro Gordo, well over a hundred miles, and in Deep Springs Valley, to the eastward.

Temperance societies were first among fraternities in the field. Existence of the Sons of Temperance at Owensville has been noted; the lodge's career was brief. Next in secret society pioneering was St. Orme's Lodge of Good Templars in Round Valley in 1869, soon reinforced by Oasis Lodge of the same order at Bishop. The first of the greater fraternities to come was the Masonic order, Inyo Lodge of which, meeting at Independence, was chartered in 1872.

Placer gold was found on Big Pine Creek in 1869, the first discovery being a two-ounce nugget. Some placer mining was done there and in the foothills west of Bishop during later years.

During the season of 1869 the valley's estimated grain production was 250 tons; lands cultivated amounted to 5,000 acres. Home mills were producing flour and lumber for all needs. Seven steam and two waterpower quartz mills were dropping 100 stamps steadily, and four furnaces and twenty arrastras were helping to swell mineral production. Freights, coming from Los Angeles as chance offered, cost 10 to 12 cents a pound.

A bill was introduced in the Legislature, passed, and approved by Governor Haight March 28, 1870, changing the northern boundary of Inyo County from Big Pine Creek to the line between townships five and six south of Mt. Diablo base line. In consideration of the transfer of territory, provision was made for payment of $12,000 by Inyo to Mono. This was payable $3,000 annually, beginning January, 1871. The last of the debt was paid in 1875.

The precise location of the boundary between the two counties was in dispute until a survey was made by J. G. Thompson, of Mono, in 1876. Prior to that the neighbor county had laid claim to a large part of Round Valley, and finding that the claim was incorrect caused much resentment, particularly in Benton, then a camp of considerable importance and liveliness.

Another boundary change was made in 1872. The southern line, as inherited from Tulare, ran northeasterly from the Sierra Nevadas to the State line. The new code description changed it to a straight east and west line. While the old boundary had never been surveyed, it intersected the Nevada boundary almost directly east of Independence, excluding from Inyo part of Panamint Valley and all of Death Valley south of Stovepipe Wells, which territory was added to this county by the change.

While these were the last changes, that fact is not due to lack of agitation. In 1864 the Nevadans returned to their original idea of jurisdiction to the summit of the Sierra, and memoralized the California Legislature asking that all California territory east of the Sierra be transferred to the Silver State. If the whole could not be so transferred, the petitioners urged that Mono and Alpine, at least, should be. John R. Dudleston, then a prominent Monoite, urged that the line be run from Mt. Dana to Mt. McBride, "where the State line crosses the White Mountains." The effort had no result. Passage by the Nevada Legislature in 1870 of a resolution asking for the proposed cession was as fruitless. The same proposal, covering all the Inyo-Mono area, was brought forward at intervals during the next twenty years, and at times had considerable support in the area affected.

In 1872 residents of the northern part of the county, disgruntled at some county matter, started a movement to have the county line re-established at Big Pine Creek, throwing the Bishop vicinity back into Mono. Three years later the subject was seriously renewed, and grew to such proportions that the Supervisors took official notice. A protest against any change was adopted by the votes of Curtis, of Independence, and Meysan, of Lone Pine, Garretson, of Bishop Creek, voting against it. Next came Assemblyman Griswold, of Mono, with a bill to create Monache County, to include Olancha, the booming camps of Darwin and Panamint, and the desert region generally. The bill died on the files.

A resolution adopted by the Nevada Legislature in March, 1907, asked that the California Legislature submit to vote of the people of Inyo, Mono, Alpine, Lassen and Modoc counties the question of ceding those counties to Nevada. At that time, Inyo, in particular, might have been more ready than it had been to forego its loyalty to California, in the hope that a different State line would prevent its resources being plundered for the benefit of Los Angeles. The latter would have been equally ready to oppose, doubtless successfully, any such interference as a change of jurisdiction would cause.

A step forward for the county was made when in July, 1870, a newspaper, the *Inyo Independent,* was established at Independence by Chalfant & Parker. Among its items were statements that a petition was in circulation to secure a tri-weekly mail between Independence and Aurora. Mines at Fish Springs were paying well. That camp was headquarters for a tough crowd known as "Morgan Courtney's gang"—characters who later contributed to the criminal records of some of the Nevada towns. Discussion of the wagon road between Independence and Visalia was going on. Inyo County's debt was $33,525.52. Bullion to the amount of 1,419,387 pounds had gone out from the

Cerro Gordo furnaces. It gave pleasure to announce that two regular mails a week had been arranged for, the government paying for one and the stage company carrying one of its own accord. Henry G. Hanks had refused $30,000 for the Monte Diablo (later Mount Diablo) mine at Candelaria. Isaac Friedlander was making application for a patent on the Eclipse mine southeast of Independence —one of those found by the Russ party years earlier.

The election year of 1871 developed some of the hottest politics the county ever experienced. A feature was a campaign journal called the *Inyo Lancet,* of which Thomas J. Goodale was the editor. The fact that the *Lancet* unsparingly scored the *Independent* and its candidates, and that the *Independent* poured abundant vitriol on the *Lancet* and its editor and ticket, did not interfere with the *Lancet's* mechanical work being done by the *Independent.* The issues involved were of but temporary interest. Precincts in the territory acquired from Mono County cast votes as follows: Deep Springs 18, Round Valley 40, Bishop Creek 92. Other Inyo precincts cast 77 votes at Fish Springs, 111 at Independence, 95 at Lone Pine, 29 at Swansea, 124 at Cerro Gordo.

CHAPTER XXIII

TWO AFFAIRS OF 1871

CONVICTS ESCAPING FROM CARSON HEAD TOWARD INYO—THEIR TRAIL TO LONG VALLEY—MORRISON KILLED AT CONVICT LAKE—SLAYERS CAPTURED, TRIED AND EXECUTED—UNEXPLAINED DISAPPEARANCE OF GUIDES EGAN AND HAHN, WITH WHEELER EXPEDITION.

The most desperate prison break in the history of the West occurred at the Nevada penitentiary at Carson on the evening of Sunday, September 17, 1871. Twenty-nine convicts, murderers, train robbers, horse thieves and others of like ilk, gained temporary liberty after killing one man and wounding half a dozen more. The bravery of the handful of prison guards, the action of a life prisoner in opposing the escape and fighting the convicts, and other details make an interesting story, but one outside the field of this history. Inyo's interest in the affair became direct when one of the gangs of desperadoes started with intent to recuperate in Owens and Fish Lake valleys, as a preliminary to raiding a store at Silver Peak and escaping with their loot to seek refuge among the renegades, Indians and whites, who had established themselves in the far deserts.

Billy Poor, a mail rider, was met by the convicts, who murdered him in cold blood, took his horse and clothing and dressed the corpse in discarded prison garb. When news of the occurrence reached Aurora, the boy's home, a posse set out in pursuit of the escapers. The trail was found at Adobe Meadows, in southern Mono, and word was sent to Deputy Sheriff George Hightower, at Benton. Hightower and ten others from Benton trailed the fugitives into Long Valley. Robert Morrison, who came to Owensville in 1863 and was at this time a Benton merchant, first sighted the men, in the evening of Friday the 23d. The pursuers went to the McGee place, in southern Long Valley, and spent the night, and the following morning went up the stream then known as Monte Diablo Creek, but now called Convict.

As the posse neared the narrow at the eastern end of the deep cup in which Convict Lake is situated, a man was seen running down a hill a hundred yards ahead. The pursuers spurred up their horses and soon found themselves within forty feet of the convicts' camp. Three convicts took shelter behind a large pine tree on the south side of the stream, and began firing. Two of the horses of the posse were killed and two others wounded, and one of the posse was shot through the hand. Morrison dismounted, began crawling down the hillside to get nearer, and was shot in the side. The rest of the posse fled. Black, convict, went after Morrison, passing him until Morrison snapped his gun without its being discharged; Black then shot him through the head.

The convicts went up the canyon to where an Indian known as Mono Jim was keeping some of the citizens' horses. Thinking that the approaching men belonged to the posse, Jim announced that he had seen three men down the canyon. As he saw his mistake Black shot him. Jim returned the fire, wounding two of the horses the convicts had, and was then killed. Morrison's body remained where it fell until Alney McGee went from the house in the valley that evening and recovered it. The convicts had left. Morrison's body was taken to Benton and buried by the Masonic fraternity.

"Convict" was thenceforward adopted as the name of the beautiful lake and stream near the scene. A mighty peak that towers over the lake bears the name of Mount Morrison.

Word had been sent from Benton to Bishop, and a posse headed by John Crough and John Clarke left the latter place, after some delay due to failure of the messenger to deliver his letter. The trail was picked up in Round Valley, which the convicts had crossed. The latter had made their way into Pine Creek Canyon, and were so hard pressed that they abandoned one of their horses and lost another over a precipice. News that the men were located, and the fact that they were armed with Henry rifles, superior to the weapons of the citizens, was taken to Independence by I. P. Yaney. The military post was at that time commanded by Major Harry C. Egbert, who afterward became General Egbert and lost his life as a brave soldier in the Philippines. Major Egbert selected five men to accompany him in the hunt, and also provided a supply of arms for any citizens who might wish to use them for the main purpose. They made the trip to Bishop in seven hours, which was rapid traveling in those days.

Convicts Morton and Black were captured in the sandhills five miles southeast of Round Valley, on Wednesday night, ten days after their escape. They were taken by J. L. C. Sherwin, Hubbard, Armstead, McLeod and two Indians. A few shots were exchanged before the fugitives threw up their hands in token of surrender. An Indian mistook the motion and fired, the shot striking Black in the temple and passing through his head, but strangely not killing him. The two were taken to Birchim's place in Round Valley. Black was able to talk, and laid the killing of Morrison on Roberts, a nineteen-year old boy. After hearing his story a posse resumed the hunt for Roberts in Pine Creek Canyon.

This posse was eating lunch in the canyon on Friday when they observed a movement in a clump of willows within twenty yards of them. The place was surrounded and Roberts was ordered to come out and surrender. He did so, saying that if they intended to kill him he was ready if he could have a cup of coffee. He had been five and one-half days without food. When he confronted Black at Birchim's, the conduct of the older villain satisfied all that he and not Roberts had slain Morrison.

The three prisoners were placed in a spring wagon Sunday evening, October 1st, and with a guard of horsemen started from Round Valley for Carson. Near Pinchower's store, where the northern road through West Bishop intersected the main drive of that vicinity, the escort and wagon were surrounded by a large body of armed citizens. "Who is the captain of this guard?" was asked. "I am; turn to the left and go on." But the mob did not turn to the left nor was there any resistance. Morton, who sat with the driver, said: "Give me the reins and I'll drive after them; I'm a pretty good driver myself." Roberts, who had been shot in the shoulder and in the foot in the encounter in Long Valley, was lying in the bottom of the wagon. He offered objections to going with the citizens, but without effect, and with Morton driving to his own hanging, the wagon and its escort moved across the unfenced meadow to a vacant cabin about a mile northeasterly. On arrival there, Black and Roberts were carried into the house, both being wounded. Morton got down from the wagon with little assistance and went in with them.

Lights were procured, and all present except the guards over the prisoners formed a jury. The convicts were questioned for two hours before votes were taken, separately on each prisoner. It was decreed that Black and Morton should be hanged at once. The vote on Roberts was equally divided for and against execution, and his life was saved by that fact.

A scaffold was hastily set up at the end of the house, one end of its beam resting on the top of its low chimney, the other supported by a tripod of timbers. Morton heard the preparations going on, and asked: "Black, are you ready to die?" "No, this is not the crowd that will hang us," replied Black. "Yes, it is," said Morton; "don't you hear them building the scaffold?" Morton was asked if he wished to stand nearer the fire which had been made to modify the chill of the late autumn night. "No, it isn't worth while warming now," he answered; and turning to Roberts he said: "We are to swing, and I mean to have you swing with us if we can; we want company." Black was carried out and lifted into a wagon which had been driven under the scaffold; after being raised to his feet he stood unsupported. Morton walked out and looked over the arrangements calmly, climbed into the wagon, and placed the noose over his own head. He asked that his hands be made fast so that he could not jump up and catch the rope. Black asked for water; Morton asked him what he wanted with water then. When asked if they had anything to say, Black said no. Morton said that it wasn't well for a man to be taken off without some religious ceremony, and if there was a minister present he would like to have a prayer. Whether it seems strange or otherwise, there was a minister present by request. He spoke a few words, after which Morton said: "I am prepared to meet my God—but I don't know that there is any God." He shook hands with the men on the wagon, and then the minister prayed. Only his voice and a sigh from Black broke the stillness. As "Amen" was pronounced the wagon moved slowly away. Black was a large and heavy man and died without a struggle. Morton, a very small man, sprang into the air as the wagon started, and did not move a muscle after his weight rested on the rope.

Young Roberts was taken to the county jail at Independence, and after partial recovery from his wounds was returned to the Carson prison. Others among the escapes were believed to have come this way, and hard search was made for them through the mountains. That one named Charley Jones had come to Bishop Creek and had probably received some assistance was a general belief, but what became of him was never known unless to a select circle. Four of the escapes were captured on Walker River while they were feasting on baked coyote. Eighteen of the twenty-nine were captured or killed within two months of the prison break.

One of the Government's parties of exploration sent into the Great Basin during the 1870 decade was the Wheeler expedition. Its visit to Inyo in 1871 would be worthy of but passing note in this record but for two desert tragedies connected with it, to wit: the disappearance of guides Egan and Hahn.

The expedition comprised sixty men, including soldiers, geologists, botanists, photographers, meteorologists, naturalists, and representatives of other branches of knowledge within the field of government investigation. With them as press correspondent came Fred W. Loring, a talented young Bostonian, whose promising career as a writer was cut short soon afterward by Arizona Apaches. The force was divided into two detachments, with Lieutenant George M. Wheeler as commander of one and Lieutenant D. A. Lyle as chief of the other.

The party left the Central Pacific Railroad at Carlin, Nevada, and traversed the deserts southwesterly, arriving at Independence in July, 1871. Their investigations had proved very satisfactory; the country had been mapped, and each scientist had discoveries in his special line later incorporated in the reports that may be found in official repositories.

Lyle's detachment left Camp Independence July 21st to cross the eastern range. The guide for his party was C. F. R. Hahn, one of the county's pioneers, discoverer of some of the mines of Cerro Gordo, an accomplished linguist and educated man as well as miner and mountaineer.

According to the story later told by Lyle and John Koehler, naturalist with this detachment, Hahn left camp two days out from Owens Valley, to go ahead and prospect for water. He did not return, and no Inyo acquaintances ever saw him again. The detachment took no time to hunt for him. The belief was general in the county at that time that he had been basely deserted by the company— equivalent to murder, in that region in midsummer. It was established that Koehler had said that he would make Hahn find water or kill him. A. J. Close, a sometime resident of Independence, wrote from Colorado in 1875 that he had seen a man who claimed to have known Hahn in Arizona afterward. This man said that the missing man had been killed in that wild territory, but that previous to his death he had told of leaving the Lyle party. He had been unable to find water and was afraid to go back. He stripped the saddle from his mule, and left it, with other personal effects and papers to create the belief that he had perished, and had then ridden horseback across the desert into Arizona. Hahn's belongings, or some of them, were found in a canyon near the head of Death Valley a short time afterward. A pair of field glasses, believed to have been Hahn's, were found at another place, by an Indian. They came into P. A. Chalfant's possession, and were destroyed in the burning of his home many years later. They had special value because of their associations, and further because of a curious phenomenon in their appearance. The cement uniting the prisms of the object lenses had been formed into miniature representations of sage bushes, though whether this was actually a picturing of those within the lenses' range or merely a form taken by the cement under action of the excessive heat of the desert was only surmise. Notwithstanding, the serviceability of the glasses was unimpaired.

Lyle finished his journey at Gold Mountain, Nevada, and returned to Camp Independence and on August 12 set out again, with orders to meet Wheeler at a point to the eastward. He took a more southerly route, under guidance of William Egan, a scholarly gentleman well known in many parts of the intermountain region. He consented to guide the soldiers as far as the Amargosa, knowing the country that far. Not even a rumor of his ever being seen again ever came back to his friends in Inyo. Lyle's official report accounted for him by saying that he had gone with two men to meet Wheeler at a designated point (Cottonwood Canyon, on the west side of upper Death Valley). He left the men, Lyle said, and went on ahead. They did not see him again. Lyle said he left a note and rations at the point where Egan had left the company; he supposed the guide had lost himself in Death Valley. "He did not come back—he never will come back," wrote Loring, a correspondent for *Appleton's Journal.*

Lyle commanded both expeditions. While Wheeler and Lyle were both characterized as brutal and overbearing, acting on the belief that their military commissions were ample warrant for any attitude they chose to take toward civilians in their employ, the blame in both cases was Lyle's. A blacksmith who accompanied the expedition from Eureka, Nevada, said no inquiries were ever made in the camp concerning Egan's whereabouts. His pack animal and prospecting outfit were taken and used as government property. Lyle gave this blacksmith to understand that Lyle had deserted, and that if time permitted he would return and shoot him.

Putting the best possible construction on such circumstances as were known, the two guides were virtually abandoned in the desert. Harsh inferences were corroborated by authenticated incidents of the journey. Near Belmont, Nevada, one of the outfit's mules strayed. Men hunting the animal came upon a boy herding cattle. He professed to know nothing of the mule, but was brought into camp. Wheeler had him tied up by the thumbs in an effort to extort knowledge that the boy did not have. Again, at Ash Meadows, Wheeler tried to get an Indian to take a note to his brother at a point 70 miles distant. The Indian asked for five dollars, a shirt and a pair of pants as pay. This was refused and he left camp. The next morning he returned, with four others. All were seized and tied up. One broke away, started to run, and was shot and killed. The rest of them set out, under guard, with the note; the corporal reported that they had run away, with shots flying after them. In this dilemma Wheeler concluded to go himself, with an orderly. He was surrounded, somewhere during his trip, by a dozen Indians, and would have been killed had it not been for the interposition of a Salt Lake Indian with the crowd.

The comparative prominence of the missing guides, and the curt information given to those who would have made the hunt the military men failed to make, caused much adverse comment and feeling in Owens Valley. That two men familiar with the country should disappear while the expeditions they guided went through without marked difficulty, was a singular fact. The abandonment of the men, the lack of effort to locate them, and the indifference of the commanders to any inquiries, added to a desert mystery that, at least in the case of Egan, was never solved in any way whatsoever.

CHAPTER XXIV

EL TEMBLOR

THE GREAT EARTHQUAKE OF 1872—ALMOST SIMULTANEOUS DIS-
TURBANCES IN MANY LANDS—SOME FACTS AND INCIDENTS OF
THE TIME—PROF. WHITNEY'S OBSERVATIONS—REBUILDING—
MONEY BORROWED AT EXPENSIVE RATES—OPPORTUNE LEGISLA-
TION.

The great earthquake of March 26, 1872, stands alone in its awe-inspiring magnitude as an item of Inyo County history. Other earthquakes have been known here, but beside them it was as a cyclone to a summer breeze. It was Mother Earth's time for readjustment somewhere in the region—such an occurrence as different parts of the New World and the Old have had, as at New Madrid, Charleston, San Francisco, and in many foreign lands. That the seismic disturbance originated somewhere near Owens Valley was evident; it appears to have been an affair in which we had original and proprietary interest, though the effects were felt nearly simultaneously from Mexico to British Columbia and eastward to Utah.

The shake came at 2:30 on the morning of March 26th. Premonitory symptoms, if such they were, had appeared during many months. A shock of some severity was reported at Lone Pine March 17th. The main event came unheralded save by a mighty rumble. The shock was reported by Camp Independence observers to have lasted three minutes; its worst effects occurred in the first minute. Next in severity, but still much milder, was one at 6:30 the same morning. The Camp Independence record noted 200 shocks or tremors from the hour of the big shake up to 5:00 the following afternoon. In its issue of April 6, 1872, the Inyo Independent observed that the earth was quieting down, as shocks were from twelve to twenty hours apart.

One can read, in publications of the time, many tales of the earthquake, nearly all written by non-residents with able imaginations and a belief that the remoteness of the region would permit any sort of story to be accepted. The facts were startling enough, without gratuitous additions.

Fissures opened at different points, generally but not in all cases paralleling the valley axis. In a few instances there were changes in the level of the ground bordering such breaks. The chief of these was at Lone Pine, where a twelve-mile crack opened. Whether the land on the east was lowered or that on the west was raised no scientist ever took the trouble to announce, but a difference of from four to twelve feet was made. Also, the land on the east side was moved northward, or that on the west was moved southward, several feet, as broken fences across the fissure proved. Another large fissure appeared near Big Pine.

Twenty-four persons were killed at Lone Pine, and about the same number escaped with severe or minor injuries. One person was killed and one injured at Eclipse, on the river southeast of Independence; one killed at Camp Independence, and several injured; one hurt at Bishop. The property loss was never accurately determined, but was estimated at from $150,000 to $200,000.

Every instance of personal harm was due to the character of buildings which had until then been in use. The population of Lone Pine was largely composed of Mexicans, who had exercised their preference for sun-dried bricks, or adobes, as building material. While such construction was more in use there than in other parts of the valley, the scarcity and high cost of lumber helped in making the use of adobes quite general in the small settlements. Three-fourths of Lone Pine's buildings were thus made, and about sixty of them toppled down in the shake like piles of children's blocks. The buildings at Eclipse, all adobe, and some others elsewhere shared the same fate. The courthouse at Independence was of burned bricks, and collapsed. Only one frame building in the valley was leveled, and that was an unsubstantial and cheap shed. Many, however, were racked, and all plastering was shattered. Adobes were promptly stricken from the list of favored building materials; probably there was never a more instantaneous and general change of opinion regarding construction methods.

Some of the curiosities of the earthquake are worth noting. At George's Creek water burst from the ground up into a floorless cabin, in such volume as to flood out the occupants if they had awaited further notice to vacate. Not far off, a horse's hoof protruding from the ground, where a crack had opened and then closed, gave reasonable inference as to where the rest of the animal might be found. Similarly, at Fish Springs a crack swallowed an ox, only his tail being left out in the air as a card indicating that he had not strayed. Near by, another ox was dead on the ground, with not a sign of injury. Of two adobe huts a mile apart, one crumbled, the other was not damaged at all.

In an Independence law office, two adjoining rooms contained shelves of books on the north and south walls. In one, the north shelves were completely emptied, every book being thrown to the floor, while those on the opposite shelves remained undisturbed. In the adjoining room, next west, exactly the reverse occurred; the south shelves were emptied while the ones on the north stood as usual.

At Bishop, a stone chimney fell across a bed which two young ladies would have been occupying had they not been away at a dance at the time.

The course of Owens River was changed east of Independence, and the site of Bend City was left neighboring an empty ravine instead of the river bank.

Dust hung over the Sierra for two days after the earthquake, while the White Mountains were obscured by haze and dust for a shorter period. The rolling of stones and the sparks struck in their descents were vividly described by beholders.

In spite of widespread interest and veritable volumes of printed matter, opportunity for scientific investigation was neglected. Prof. J. D. Whitney and Clarence King, two of the most noted scientists of the West, made flying trips into the valley, tarrying but briefly. Professor Whitney afterward published two articles on the Inyo earthquake, one of which excited local derision because of its inaccuracy as to facts. The other was a general dissertation on the subject of earthquakes, and probably entitled to more serious consideration than his hastily gathered Owens Valley notes.

He mentioned a tradition of the Piutes that a similar shake had occurred eighty years earlier—that is, about 1790. He concluded that an earthquake is a passage of an elastic wave of motion through a portion of the crust of the earth, and that unusual seismic manifestations in one part of the earth are likely to be followed by like disturbances elsewhere. He figured that the Inyo earthquake was one of a chain, extending through the winter and spring of that year. He enumerated a long list of shocks, during the months of January, February, March and April, in Asia, Australia, Europe, Minnesota, Illinois, Germany, Japan, Mexico, Kentucky, Africa, Ireland, and the Philippine Islands. Our little agitation was of small consequence— except to ourselves—by comparison with the leveling of a Persian city and death of 30,000 of its inhabitants that January; destruction of cities near the Caucasus Mountains and in Japan; the killing of a thousand or fifteen hundred persons at historic Antioch; the greatest eruption of Vesuvius since 1632, and other notable events of that season.

Whitney concluded that the focus of the Owens Valley earthquake was somewhere beneath the Sierra, in the belt between Owens Lake and Independence, at a depth of at least fifty miles, and extending for probably 100 miles in length. The wave motion traveled, he decided, at a velocity of probably thirty-five miles a minute. Its greatest velocity effects were manifested where changes in geological formations were found; for instance, fissures usually occurred where the sandy slope joined alluvial soil, dry abutting against wet material. At such points the rate of motion is changed and a disturbance ensues. He decided that the force was about uniform from Olancha to Big

Pine. In all cases observers said that the shock seemed to come from the Sierran region mentioned. At Lone Pine it came from the west; farther north, from the southwest.

Professor Whitney explained further that the earth's crust is, or rather must be, in a condition of tension in places, of compression in others. Sooner or later the material gives way, a fissure forms, and a powerful impulse is communicated to the mass above. This starts the wave of action which when it reaches the surface we know as an earthquake.

He was undecided as to attributing the widespread disturbances of March 26th to the Inyo earthquake. A terrific volcanic eruption occurred in Mexico that day, which he believed might be a wholly separate and detached occurrence.

Rebuilding began promptly. The national Government set aside $30,000 for reconstructing Camp Independence; most of it was used in putting up substantial frame buildings. The county was still speedier in its action. The destroyed courthouse, a two-story brick, accepted February 1, 1869, had cost $9,832. It had never been satisfactory, and a providential bill had passed the Legislature only two weeks before the earthquake authorizing the county to issue $40,000 bonds for building a new courthouse and new bridges across the river. The latter were to be at Lone Pine, Bend City, and at either Big Pine or Bishop as the Supervisors might decide. So when the earthquake wrecked the old building more expeditiously than a contractor would have done, no time was lost in moving for its replacement. The bonds were issued, and though bearing 10 per cent interest they were sold for 80 cents on the dollar, besides which the county paid something over $2,000 for the expense of making the sale; consequently the $40,000 issue put a little less than $30,000 into the treasury. "The remains of the late courthouse," as the advertisement put it, were offered for sale, and brought $120. Bids for a new building were not opened until September, when a contract was let to E. Chaquette to erect the building for $15,900. Work was under way when an epidemic of the horse disease known as the epizootic swept the country. Animals died by hundreds, and teaming systems were practically put out of business. Most of the lumber in the new building was being "imported," and Chaquette was unavoidably given an extension of time on his contract. The building was accepted July 3, 1873, and on the following day was used for exercises of the greatest celebration the county had ever had. The structure was a far better building than the one which afterward replaced it, as well as an improvement on its predecessor.

Business buildings and residences were also begun, and in most cases were completed with rather more expedition than attended the county's reconstructive work.

CHAPTER XXV

YEARS OF RAMPANT CRIME

INYO A REFUGE FOR BAD MEN—LAW EXISTENT BUT INEFFECTIVE—
CERRO GORDO'S STAINED RECORD—JUDGE REED, A MAN FOR THE
PERIOD—VASQUEZ, MASTER ROAD AGENT—CAUGHT THE WRONG
MAN—DEATHS OF SHERIFFS PASSMORE AND MOORE.

Inyo County was, in those days, essentially and thoroughly a frontier of "the old West." Many substantial and law-respecting citizens had come, laying the foundation for the later communities; but at that period untamed tendencies had the upper hand in many respects. The forms of law were available, but were not appreciated by a large percentage of the inhabitants. Villains from other parts found in this out-of-the-way region a comparatively safe refuge, or tarried here on their way to the still more inaccessible isolation of the southern Nevada deserts. To the new-sprung mining camps came hard characters from everywhere, and Colt and Bowie were the authorities usually called in when disputes arose. Railroads and telegraphs were hundreds of miles distant. To reach any place where conditions were materially different involved an arduous journey. San Francisco was distant three days and three nights of staging—and $60 fare. Arrival of papers four days old from Los Angeles were mentioned by the local paper as a notable event, and as being faster service than the mails. Going to any outside point was as costly, and more inconvenient, than is a journey half way across the continent at the present time. And moreover, hard as conditions were from a moral standpoint, they were not greatly worse than those generally prevalent west of the Rockies at that time.

Judge Hannah thus charged one of his grand juries:

Crime has been exceedingly prevalent, and seems to have run rampant in certain sections of the county, especially at Cerro Gordo.

. . . So far as I am informed the guilty parties have never been brought to justice to answer for their misdeeds. . . . It is your duty that you exhaust, if necessary, every means known to the law to protect the peaceful citizen from these lawless ruffians.

In another charge, to one of the first grand juries called by Judge Hannah, he called attention to the commission of eighty serious and unpunished crimes in the few years the county had then been in existence. This was before the notable prominence of Cerro Gordo, with its still bloodier record. Crimes then became of almost weekly frequency, largely committed "up on the hill"—that is, Cerro Gordo. It is safe to say that between the county's organization and the advent of the railroad, in the early '80's, more men had been killed or wounded in self-defense or in cold blood than the total of white victims of the Indian war.

Comments in the *Inyo Independent* reflected a prevalent sentiment when, after a Cerro Gordo affair in which two toughs were wounded and sent to the county hospital, it remarked:

In those rows where the principals are killed outright we have a sort of morbid satisfaction in so reporting it; but when they are only maimed and become expensive public charges it is a bad go. But frequently innocent parties are the victims; and if there is law to do it these affrays should be stopped on that account, if no other.

Tribal orgies among the Indians supplied with liquor by unprincipled whites were frequent, and a slit Piute throat was not an unusual result. Once in a while the initial crime would bring its own punishment, as when a keeper of a portable dive at George's Creek, sharing a grand drunk with his Indian customers, took occasion to shoot two of them and was himself neatly and properly slain.

It is not to be supposed that the machinery of the law was wholly idle. Officers made arrests for crimes, but where there was not real ground of defense others of the criminal's own stripe supplied evidence that a jury, however conscientious, had to accept as justification. The public prosecutor of those days was usually a very weak sister; and the defender of most of the major cases was Pat Reddy, a specialist in criminal defense, an expert in jury selection, and a lawyer of ability. It was said that he was

the means of freeing more than one hundred men charged
with murder in this county, Mono County, and adjacent
counties in Nevada.

In probably three cases out of four, the hard cases
operated on each other, and society was somewhat
improved by the net result.

Such serious offenses as murder came within the
jurisdiction of the District Court, at that time presided
over by Theron Y. Reed, a man whose mettle fitted the
times. Serving his circuit, Kern, Inyo, Mono and Alpine
counties, involved a degree of personal hardship. To reach
his different county seats, Judge Reed journeyed from
Havilah to Millerton (now forgotten), thence via
Sacramento and Sonora across the Sierra to Bridgeport
and Markleeville, thence to Independence via Aurora and
Benton, on horseback or by the sometimes but weekly
stages.

An illustrative occurrence was stated to the writer by
Paul W. Bennett, an attorney in Independence when the
incident happened. Judge Reed was holding court at
Independence when a man from Fish Springs was brought
in, whether for rebellion against the Morgan Courtney
gang of roughs then dominating that neighborhood or for
some other reason there is no evidence. Pat Reddy, then
new in his career, Lucius Cooper and Thomas Slade were
the attorneys. Each was there to win his case. Abuse
and disputing ruled the court the first day, despite Judge
Reed's admonitions and threats of fines. When court
opened the next morning Judge Reed entered the room
with a double barreled shotgun on his arm. He cocked both
barrels of the gun and set it by his chair, and remarked:
"Gentlemen, there will be order in this court today." Mr.
Bennett, who witnessed the occurrence, said that the
judge's prediction was correct; there was order.

In another court in the county, an attorney protested a
ruling until the irate magistrate roared: "Sit down or I'll
knock you down!" The same judge, after a protesting
attorney suggested that he refer to his books, gathered up
his meager library and threw it at the offender; striking a

belligerent attitude and patting the swelling muscle of his right arm, he declared: "I don't know nothing about book law, but here's a law no lawyer can dispute!" No exception was taken to the ruling. A Mexican, objecting to the conduct of his wife, consulted the Justice. The latter found printed authority for performing marriage ceremonies and nothing forbidding his granting a divorce, so for a $20 fee he unmarried the aggrieved Mexican. Ere long, learning that his official conduct was to be made the subject of legal inquiry, he resigned.

As a help in picturing conditions, we turn to the local columns of the *Inyo Independent*. All the following items are from the same issue of that paper. Other issues might show more or less notes of similar nature; this one was not selected, but was the first one examined in this particular respect. This issue is dated July 13, 1872, and mentions these occurrences:

A desperado named White appeared at Benton on the 4th with a horse to put in the races. A bystander recognized the horse as one stolen from him, whereupon White drew a pistol and would have done some murdering but for interference. . . . He was arrested and taken to Bridgeport on three charges of horse stealing. *As he didn't actually murder anybody* his prospect of spending a few summers at the seaside is exceedingly flattering.

"At the seaside" means San Quentin prison. Note the inference, which we italicize, that he would probably have escaped punishment if his offense had been so petty as murder, instead of horse stealing. Again:

Some six-shooters got on a drunk in Lida Valley on the night of the 4th, and one of them going off accidentally inflicted a slight wound in Guadalupe Ochar's arm. On the same day Len Martin gave some sheep-herder's delight to two men he met; a free fight ensued, from which Martin, by the free use of a pick-handle, came off first best. A great future for Lida is now considered certain.

Justice Pearson's court at Lone Pine is examining George Lee for shooting George Bircham, because of difficulties growing out of alleged horse-stealing on the part of Lee.

Pearce, arrested on a charge of horse-stealing, was discharged from custody. After an interesting interview the accuser was willinig to swear that Pearce wasn't much of a horse-thief after all.

R. Van Dyke lost forty tons of hay near Lone Pine through the cussedness of a Piute who attempted to test its dryness with a match.

This contribution is from another issue of the same paper:

Cerro Gordo is a prolific source of the "man for breakfast" order of items. . . . Four Americans, including Johnny Stewart, who recently had occasion to shoot a Mexican, in Lone Pine (and who was later hanged at Columbus, Nevada), undertook to run the "Waterfall" place. A Mexican stepped up and put a pistol almost in contact with Walker's head, and fired, but the bullet did not kill him. The firing became general, during which Clark got a dose of lead that knocked him hors du combat. During the same night, at another dance house, a Mexican received a shot through the abdomen. The night following the Waterfall affray another shooting match took place between two Mexicans, in which one of them got a ball through his leg and the other through his arm. If such poor shooting as this is unfortunately to be the rule, active measures will have to be adopted by citizens who have a morbid desire to attend funerals. . . . Last week two Mexicans from Cerro Gordo lifted three horses and riding gear from Lone Pine, and are missing, despite a warrant. . . . At Lida on the night of the 6th Abram Altamarino received a severe knife wound.

But the greatest reign of terror experienced by the county's people, after the close of the Indian war, was not caused by the miscellaneous roughs and their festive handling of weapons. It was during the months that the bandit Vasquez and his gang ruled the southern stage road and the highways of southern Inyo, early in 1874, with a return engagement in the spring of 1875. Most of the Vasquez deviltry was committed in other fields than Inyo, but during his sojourn on the eastern slope of the Sierras there were few weeks without their tales of the operations of the "road agents."

Tiburcio Vasquez was second only to Joaquin Murietta in notoriety as a California bandit. He was prominent in highwaymen circles from 1852 to 1875. His own story was that he was hounded by Americans until at the age of seventeen he decided to become a robber. He began his career near Salinas, Cal., and soon gathered a band of subordinates of his own lawless kind. In 1857 he was caught and was in San Quentin penitentiary until his discharge in 1863. He then took up with other noted bandits of the time, and the combination did a flourishing business until the killing of one of his partners, Soto, some years later. Vasquez became the leader of his own gang of cutthroats about 1871, and for three years they committed crime after crime. Their escape from capture was probably due in part to the existence of confederates in different places, as well as to the readiness with which the outlaws picked up the best horseflesh whenever it was needed. After robbing a store and killing two men at Tres Pinos, Monterey County, they moved into Fresno County, then as thinly populated as Owens Valley. One daring crime after another caused the Legislature to authorize Governor Booth to spend $15,000 in capturing or exterminating the gang. In November 12th Vasquez and fourteen of his men went to the little town of Kingston, and after tying up thirty-five men robbed the place to their hearts' content. They were "hotly pursued," and as usual escaped. The gang appears to have scattered for a short time, but in February Vasquez called his forces together in Tejon Canyon, twenty men appearing. Inyo County and the highway leading to it were selected as promising abundant loot, and operations on this slope began two weeks later. Their first appearance in the new field was at Coyote Holes, on the southern stage road, February 25, 1874.

A traveler, who had stayed all night at the station, set out on foot to find a stray horse. A mile from the station he met two Mexicans, one of whom said he was Vasquez. They made the luckless traveler return to the station with them, and on the way met Raymond, the station keeper. Both men were tied up and left on a hillside. The Mexicans went on toward the house, announcing their coming by firing fifteen shots through its walls. Six persons were inside, but had no weapons except a Henry rifle with no cartridges and an unloaded shotgun, and did not think it wise to argue about the irregularity of the proceedings. Under orders, they filed out, Vasquez finding it necessary to stimulate the lagging steps of a man known (as probably some thousands have been) as "Tex." All were escorted off to one side and made to sit down. Tex had imbibed too freely to display first-class judgment and proved

themselves in the box of a wagon that was being driven to the house. The officers jumped out, and Vasquez, seeing them, went through a narrow window and ran for his horse. Bullets flew around him so thickly that he saw it was hopeless, and gave up. Chaves had also been in the house, but was not then captured. Vasquez was taken to San Jose, tried for murder, and hanged March 19, 1875. Before his execution he said that he had never killed any one. He said that at Coyote Holes he tied up twenty men; that one shot at and wounded him, but was not punished by being killed as he might have been.

With the leader gone, the capture or killing of the rest of the gang was an easier matter. Chavez was killed by a citizen of Monterey County, and a reward which had grown to $5,000 was collected for him. Such, at least, was a report of the time. Recently a published story said that in reality Chavez fled to Arizona and that while he was working on an irrigation ditch in that then lawless region he was slain by a fellow countryman. The breaking up of the outlaw band was a relief to all the southern part of the State, and was particularly welcome in southern Inyo.

Minor organizations of criminals did some business in the county at one time or another, but all finally came to grief. One of these was a band of horsethieves, operating from Nevada through this county and far southward. At another time, this in 1875, three men, one aged twenty-five, the others each under twenty, and a girl about the latter age, came over the Sierra to go adventuring as bandits in this apparently promising field. Their most important enterprise was in "sticking up" T. J. Graves and family at their little mountain ranch on the south fork of Oak Creek, westerly from Independence. Graves and his wife and little son were tied up for several hours, while the robbers cooked supper and pillaged their meagerly supplied home. Late that night the gang struck out across the mountains with all they chose to take from the place. Graves, barefooted because the bandits had taken his boots, got loose and made his way into Independence. The next morning a posse took the trail, and after traveling thirty miles into the Sierra found a bit of paper bearing Mrs. Graves's name on an address label. With this assurance, the posse kept on. The next morning Tom Hill (heretofore mentioned in this record) happened onto the bandit camp, while the inmates were at breakfast. He pretended to be diligently hunting grouse until out of sight of the camp. The rest of the posse was notified, and the crowd was captured without resistance. The men in due time went to the penitentiary, and the woman was discharged by over-gallant officers.

That was a crime-stained decade in the history of Inyo County. This sketchy outline of it may fittingly conclude, without enumerating other sinister occurrences, with mention of the death of two officers who lost their lives in the discharge of their official duty. These men, Thomas Passmore and William L. Moore, had been among the earliest residents of the valley; had taken part in the Indian war, and each was a citizen held in high esteem.

Passmore was elected Sheriff in 1875, and again in 1877. He was in Lone Pine on the night of February 12, 1878. That night an Indian was murdered by a hardened criminal named Palacio. The murderer took refuge in a deadfall run by Frank Dabeeny, another individual of the same stripe, and refused to surrender to local citizens. Passmore, being somewhat ill, had gone to bed early in the evening. He was called, and went to the place and demanded admission. The door did not open, the demand was repeated, and Passmore attempted to force an entrance. Shots were fired inside of the house; the Sheriff exclaimed "Boys, I'm shot!" handed his pistol to a bystander, and fell dead.

Wild excitement ensued. A fusillade of lead riddled the building. As those within seemed disposed to hold the fort, its destruction by either fire or dynamite was proposed. A messenger was sent to Independence, and the siege was still in progress when citizens from there, eighteen miles away, reached Lone Pine. Dabeeny and Palacio both ran out, and both fell, pierced by many bullets.

Then others were allowed to come out and surrender. Some of them, of previous good character and guilty of no offense except being in bad company, were released. Two were told to leave Lone Pine and never to return. They left, and the next day their bodies were found beside the road leading southerly.

W. L. (Dad) Moore was appointed to the office made vacant by Passmore's death. He was said to have received his nickname by reason of having been the "dad" of the town of Lone Pine, having been one of its first residents. He had filled the Sheriff's office before.

The town of Independence prepared to celebrate the Fourth of July, 1879, in fitting style, but the celebration was not to occur. Late on the afternoon of the 3d a drunken row started between men named Welch and Tessier, in what was known as the Aldine saloon on the site more recently occupied by a bank. Moore, hearing the disturbance, went in and stepped between them to keep the peace. Welch had his pistol drawn and brought it down opposite the Sheriff's body, and it was discharged immediately. The bullet passed through Moore's watch, then through his body, and he died in a few minutes. Welch was promptly put into jail. Tessier fled, and a frenzied hunt for him began. Some hours later he was found under a house. Though he was wholly innocent of the Sheriff's murder, popular excitement was inflamed, and while Welch reposed in the safety of a cell Tessier would probably have been lynched but for the counsels of Pat Reddy. Welch, who fired the fatal shot, played insanity and "went up" for ten years; Tessier, who was guilty of nothing worse than brawling, was given a three-year sentence.

CHAPTER XXVI

CERRO GORDO

INYO'S GREATEST PRODUCER OF MINERAL WEALTH—DISCOVERY—A BOOMING CAMP—TRANSPORTATION—LIBERAL MINING CLAIMS— SAN FELIPE—UNION LAWSUIT—THROWING GOLD OVER WASTE DUMP—CAMP STAGES A COMEBACK.

Cerro Gordo stands undisputedly as the Inyo County camp of greatest production, notwithstanding that no one knows, within some millions, what the total was. About $13,000,000 was the estimate at the close of its first period of life. The boom spirit of mining writers some twenty years ago raised the statement to $28,000,000, apparently just for the sound of it. The best available information is that the actual gross production of the camp's best days was approximately $17,000,000.

Tradition long current in Inyo, and supported by pioneers of the old camp, has it that the first discovery was made by one Pablo Flores and two other Mexicans in 1865; that the companions of Flores were killed by Indians and that he was allowed to go after promising never to return. A letter written from the camp in 1868 said only that Flores had found some very rich float while traveling from the eastward with an Indian guide.

Another version was current and believed in Virginia City, Nevada, at the time of Cerro Gordo's prosperity. It ran that a packer named Savariano, employed by a Comstock Mexican mine owner, ran away with a packtrain of forty mules laden with very rich ore. This he was supposed to take to Placerville for reduction, and he started according to program. When out of sight of his employer he headed south with the whole cavalcade. On this trip he was said to have found the Cerro Gordo mines. A Virginia paper said the absconding of Savariano was a matter of common knowledge. Be that as it may, the

Flores version was accepted by Inyoites, including those who knew the old Mexican up to the time of his death near Owens Lake.

Flores and a few companions were on the ground later in 1865 and located the Ygnacio, San Felipe and San Francisco claims. A small amount of ore was worked in the vesos, or crude furnaces. Their success brought a few Americans to the camp; the latter people made some locations, but did little or no work.

The first sincere effort at development was made by a Mexican named Ochoa, who began work on a claim known as the San Lucas. He employed a few of his countrymen, and had the ore worked at the Silver Sprout mill, west of Independence. An increased number of miners came, and on April 5, 1866, Lone Pine district, including the new camp, was organized, with J. J. Moore as its Recorder. The first claim offered for record was the Jesus Maria. On January 1, 1870, 999 locations had been filed for record in the district.

Among the early arrivals were M. W. Belshaw and A. B. Elder. After examination they left, but soon returned to begin development. Elder was succeeded by Victor Beaudry. Belshaw & Beaudry remained the bonanza firm of the hill; with them were associated Egbert Judson and others as parties in interest.

To supply the water required for the camp Belshaw & Beaudry laid a pipe line, which froze and bursted the following winter, and was then replaced by a better system. The firm began acquiring control of "the hill," as the camp was generally called throughout the region. Among their purchases was a group of four claims for which they paid John B. White and P. Williams $20,000. Important ground adjoining the Union, one of their chief properties, remained independent, however, and under the same ownership as the Owens Lake Silver-Lead Company later became the basis of the suit which helped to check operations.

C. F. R. Hahn, the mystery of whose loss has been mentioned in this record, was one of the discoverers of wholly new ground to the eastward of the main camp. W. L. Hunter, John Beveridge and others of honored Inyo memory were also among the owners in the eastern section.

Two slagging furnaces, two blast furnaces, crusher, blower and other equipment were in use in the camp by 1870, all operated by steam and all well housed. In 1871 the use of slagging furnaces was done away with, decreasing expenses $50 a day at each furnace. Another improvement was the application of the water jacket, first devised and used by Belshaw.

One of the first undertakings was a tollroad up from Owens Valley, a few miles distant. The road was held by Belshaw & Beaudry, though others assisted in its building for the benefit of their own properties. Those others found themselves on the same footing as strangers when it came to paying tolls. Their objections ended with complaints until 1871, when citizen John Simpson was arrested for misdemeanor in passing the tollgate without paying. To secure a jury used up venires amounting to ninety men; the Justice trial filled two days, and ended in a verdict of not guilty. A popular subscription was immediately raised and a free road was built to Cerro Gordo. The toll road went out of commission.

Two stage companies ran daily conveyances from Lone Pine, every vehicle carrying full loads. A through-service line ran between Aurora, Nevada, and Cerro Gordo, charging $39 for the trip.

When the not always dependable pipe lines were out of order, water was brought in on pack mules and sold at 10 cents per gallon for the small buyer and from 5 to 8¾ cents for the wholesale consumer. The water bill of the American Hotel was $300 a month, and each furnace and the Union hoist ran at a daily expense of $120 for water. Ffty pack mules were busy in the water service.

In 1872 Beaudry bought the San Lucia (or San Lucas) and added it to the syndicate's list. Eleven producing mines were being operated. In addition to the furnaces at the camp, ore was being smelted at the Owens Lake Silver-Lead company's plant at Swansea, at the lake.

While the bulk of production came from ores of more moderate grade, values up to $800 or more per ton were too common to attract much attention. One of the mines counted rock carrying 180 ounces of silver as its second-class grade. Beaudry reported in 1872 that "the mine" (probably the Union) was sending up 70 tons of ore each ten hours. He was about to increase his furnace capacity to ten tons of bullion daily. Each furnace was then turning out 100 to 150 83-pound bars each twenty-four hours.

Transportation of the bullion was a problem, and it was not unusual for the furnaces to shut down because of being too far ahead of the teams. For a while hauling contracts were made with any and all comers, but this proved unsatisfactory, and the mine owners organized the Cerro Gordo Freighting Company. They associated R. Nadeau, a teamster, with them; he took active charge, and made a fortune from the service. The corporation became the dominant factor in Inyo transportation, and so remained up to the advent of the railroad. The line was equipped with huge wagons, each hauled by sixteen to twenty animals. Fifty-six of these outfits were on the road, and still could not move the bullion to tidewater half as fast as it rolled from the furnaces. Some relief was given by the building of the small steamer Bessie Brady, a craft of 85 feet length and 16 feet beam. This vessel plying between Swansea, at the northeastern corner of the lake, Ferguson's Landing, at the northwestern, and Cartago, at the southwestern, took eight days out of the round trips of the teams, yet the increased number of trips of the wagons could not move the bullion fast enough. To see the bullion piled up like cordwood at different points was quite the usual thing. Piled up bars were sometimes used for constructing temporary shelters, by those without other resources. While the bullion was not high grade, those shacks were often worth more money than their occupants ever dreamed of possessing.

A contemporary estimate stated the bullion output in tons as follows: 1869, 1,000; 1870, 1,500; 1871, 2,500; 1872, 4,000; 1873, 5,000; 1874, 6,000. An authentic record of at least part of the output is afforded by the records of the Los Angeles and San Pedro Railroad, opened November 1, 1869. From that date to the end of 1870 the road carried 21,704 bars, 1,589,000 pounds of Cerro Gordo bullion; 1871, 51,100 bars, 4,491,000 pounds; 1872, 62,390 bars, 5,303,150 pounds; 1873, 58,056 bars, 4,826,741 pounds; during January, 1874, 9,570 bars, 789,961 pounds. During some of the period of greatest production a large part of the bullion did not go over that road.

Large mining locations were permitted. The Santa Maria, for example, was 3,000 feet in length, though but 150 feet wide. It was 1872 before any change was made in the district; it was then reorganized under the name of Cerro Gordo and regulations were adopted conforming to the newly made Federal requirements.

The San Felipe claim was one that Belshaw & Beaudry were unable to secure. Inspection of a map of the district shows that its boundaries crossed Belshaw's ground, outlining an area to which both ownerships laid claim. Ore had been coming up through the Union shaft, near the doubly-claimed ground, for five years, however, before the inevitable litigation began. Suit was started in January, 1873, by the San Felipe company, Galen M. Fisher, Chas. H. Wheeler and Alfred Wheeler, plaintiffs, against Belshaw & Beaudry, to recover possession of 2,100 feet of the San Felipe mine—another illustration of the generous manner in which the locators had helped themselves. The plaintiffs also asked for $20,000 damages, and rents and profits amounting to $1,000,000; also for possession of the San Felipe tunnel and $15,000 damages on that account. The suit was tried in Independence in June 1873, and occupied nine days. Judge Belden of San Jose, presiding, instructed the jury that if it found that the San Felipe and Union veins were separate its verdict should be for the latter company. Experts Goodyear, Price and Hensch swore to the distinct character of the two properties. Reports of the case may have been somewhat prejudiced, but rather favored the Union contention; nevertheless the San Felipe people were given possession of the disputed ground. The demands for damages seem to have been dropped, for they do not appear in the judgment. The suit dragged through the courts until in 1876 the warring interests united in forming the Union Consolidated Company, with representatives of each side on the directorate. Belshaw was one of the directors, but did not thereafter participate in the management. The Union works were burned August 14, 1877; the furnaces closed down the following February.

Other properties, notably the Ygnacio, had been contributing to the camp's production during all this period; but the stoppage of work on the Union marked the end of that era of Cerro Gordo's activity. The verdict that the mines were worked out was of course commonly accepted; the fallacy of this belief was to be amply demonstrated later.

From December 1, 1873, to November 1, 1874, the Union produced 12,171 tons of ore averaging 87 ounces silver and 47 per cent lead per ton. With silver worth $1.29 per ounce and lead worth 5 cents per pound, conditions were more favorable than those which came along later. On the other hand, other conditions were much less favorable. The daily cost of water, already mentioned, was but a small item in the total. Transportation for machinery and supplies in, and bullion out, cost from $55.50 to $120 per ton. Wood had been abundant when the first work was done, but the hillsides near at hand were soon swept bare, and fuel rose to $10 a cord for wood and 32½ cents a bushel for charcoal, the only fuels available for the furnaces. Belshaw stated in 1876 that it cost $19.62 a ton to mine and work the ore. In the earlier days, average recovery of metal was from 50 to 65 per cent of the lead and 90 per cent of the silver.

An incident of the camp was the discovery that much quartz richly laden with gold had gone over the dump as waste. Its value had been hidden by peculiar discoloration. Thousands of dollars of it were stolen by men who became informed sooner than did the mine management.

One company or lessee after another undertook to work the old mines after the Union Consolidated people quit, but for three decades the record was one of failure. Then in 1911 Louis D. Gordon took hold, after discovering that quantities of zinc ores had been thrown away or disregarded by former managements. He proceeded with development along original lines, under discouraging circumstances, with such results that Cerro Gordo once more made Inyo the leading California county in lead and silver as well as zinc production.

CHAPTER XXVII

PANAMINT

RICH ORES START A NEW RUSH—SENATORS JONES AND STEWART DROP TWO MILLIONS IN VENTURE—MINE OWNERS OF DOUBTFUL RECORDS—PROCESS OF OPENING NEW SALOON—NEWS AS PRESENTED BY CAMP PAPER—SOME OTHER DISTRICTS.

Cerro Gordo having passed through the preliminary stages of a mining-camp stampede, and being an established and producing camp, the "excitement" followers were ready for a new field. It soon appeared, in Panamint—a name which divers fiction writers use even to this day as a place for locating some of their imaginings.

The first discoveries were made in April, 1873, by R. C. Jacobs, R. B. Stewart and W. L. Kennedy. By June eighty or more locations had been made. Some of the ore samples showed values running into the thousands of dollars. E. P. Raines, a man of daring character but limited attainments, secured a bond on the principal claims, and undertook to finance the camp. No success met his first efforts, and he had to return to Panamint for samples of the ore as verification of his highly colored statements. He selected half a ton of rich samples, and sent it to Los Angeles. In the barroom of one of the principals hotels there he made a display that was the talk of the town. He made no effort to do business, but gained the confidence of prominent citizens and induced a commercial body to take up the building of a road to the mines. His efforts resulted in much newspaper publicity, which stood him in good stead when he proceeded to San Francisco, his chosen field. "Colonel" Raines, as he was soon dubbed, went to the metropolis and his display of ores made as much of a furore there as it had in Los Angeles. He approached Senator John P. Jones and secured a loan of $1,000, which vanished in a huge celebration that night. The next morning Raines was in jail and Senator Jones was on his way to Washington. The "Colonel" found a friend who provided bail and loaned him money enough with which to go to Washington. There he presented the cause of the Panamint mines so plausibly that Jones advanced more money, to the total of $15,000. Then Senators Jones and Stewart organized the Panamint Mining Company, with $2,000,000 capital stock—and it is said that the camp cost those gentlemen just about that much.

The road to the camp at that time was by way of Little Lake, or Lagunita, as it was then called. The first rush went that way, but ere long a more convenient way was opened and Panamint was brought into closer touch with Owens Valley.

Senators Jones and Stewart had paid $350,000 for some of the more prominent claims. Many other sales were made. Some of the early locators bore unsavory reputations, and perforce had to do business through trusted middlemen. In one instance, a sale was made and the owners went to San Francisco to get their money. At this juncture representatives of Wells, Fargo & Co. stepped in and demanded $12,000 to cover losses due to former depredations on the express company's treasure box by some of the parties who were selling the mines. The party chiefly concerned was given his choice to making that payment or submitting to arrest. He paid and coolly asked for a receipt in full.

Many companies were organized, nearly all finally either flickering out or being united in the Surprise Valley Mill & Mining Company. Some of the ore was worked in England; that it could be mined, shipped hundreds of miles over the desert, then to England, and finally worked and return a substantial profit to the mine owners is sufficient evidence of its value.

The first mill was built on the Jacob's Wonder mine. The "big mill" of twenty stamp was built by the company and began running June 29, 1875.

In March, 1874, an enthusiastic Panaminter claimed that there were 125 men in the camp. In November the most conservative estimate of population put it at 1,000. The maximum population was probably 1,500, though a San Francisco writer in January, 1875, said there were 2,000 to 2,500 in camp. As late as 1876 the camp was still "going strong," for there were 963 votes cast at an election for Recorder.

The main camp was laid out—or more properly speaking, laid itself out, along the bottom of a narrow canyon high up on the western slope of the Panamint Mountains, which form the western rim of Death Valley. For a while it consisted of a mile of tent-lined street; then stone and frame buildings began to rise. This was after the transportation had been improved by the building of a road, a process requiring, in some places, the blasting of a way out of solid rock.

A pioneer resident of the camp writes that few wagons were used after reaching the town, because the canyon and hillsides were so steep that wheels were useless. Nearly all transportation at that period was on the backs of mules and burros. But one wagon was in use in the camp, and it was used by the butcher to move meats from the slaughter house to the market. This outfit served many purposes, including service as a hearse when it was needed.

Undoubtedly Panamint contained an assortment of the worst desperadoes on the coast outside of the penitentiaries. There was as much violence, in proportion, as in any of the earlier camps. The disappearance of a well-known denizen of the resorts might be explained to an inquirer by the terse statement: "Oh, he's planted in Sour Dough," the latter being a little canyon in which the burial ground was situated.

Senator Stewart's reminiscences tell of his arranging for amnesty for the robbers from whom he had bought the mines, as related earlier in this chapter. The original locators still remained in the camp, and were so interested in knowing when bullion shipments would begin, Stewart says, that he realized they had sold, not with the intention of giving up the profits, but of collecting them after some one else had done the development and milling.

Facing this prospect, Stewart asked Wells, Fargo & Co. to establish an express office in Panamint, as was customary in nearly all mining camps. But Wells-Fargo had had enough experience with the known bandits to satisfy them, and that company "guessed not." The new owners were stumped. Plenty of ore was being taken out, but there was reasonable certainty that as soon as its precious metals were run into bullion the property would change hands. Then Stewart had some big moulds made in which the bullion would be cast into 750-pound balls.

When the road agents saw what was being done, continued Stewart, they remonstrated and acted as though they were being cheated. He was the meanest man that had ever showed up in that locality. "Those fellows fairly sweated themselves trying to lug one of those silver cannon balls off, but they couldn't budge it. They rode off on their horses as mad as hornets, and by and by they came back and cussed me out, and said I'd be sorry for being such a mean ungenerous skunk. And then they rode away, and came back again. It seemed they just couldn't stay away. Half a dozen of them pried and tugged and strained and grunted, trying to hoist one of them on a mule; but that made the mule mad and he took a hand in the proceedings and made those outlaws feel pretty sick. After that they gave it up, and while we were loading five of the cannon balls into a freight wagon they sat around disconsolate and solemn like pall-bearers at a funeral. We hauled that silver out of there like ordinary freight, without a guard. There wasn't any place where the outlaws could have driven the wagon except to the settlements, or I suppose they would have stolen the whole thing."

Senator Stewart and Trenor W. Park, his confidential agent and assistant, visited Panamint to look over their properties during the summer of 1875. As they were preparing to take their seats in the stage, on the morning of their departure, one of their employees, a man named McKinley, had a dispute with one Jim Bruce. With but a few preliminaries the disputants pulled guns and began firing. The Senator and his comrade hastily took refuge behind a stone wall until the bombardment was over. Both gunners were laid out and ready for the stretchers kept in the office of the Justice of the Peace for such uses. Bruce recovered with a crippled arm, but McKinley died three days later. The local paper casually remarked:

An Unfortunate Affair.—We are pained to record that during an unfortunate affair which occurred at the express office, previous to the departure of the stage three days ago, one of our esteemed fellow citizens was compelled to resort to violent measures to protect his person. His opponent will be buried tomorrow in the little cemetery in Sour Dough.

The matter was too inconsequential to justify publishing the victim's name.

Bruce was put to the inconvenience of arrest and examination by the Justice of the Peace, but was discharged on the usual ground of self-defense.

In all mining camps of that period saloons were among the first establishments to open, and were the most numerous in the business census. The only absolute requisites for beginning were a barrel or two of alcoholic compound and utensils for dishing it up for customers. Profits soon led to expansion. Panamint had not only this class of deadfalls but also "gin mills" of much more pretensions. One of these, fitted up at a cost of $10,000, was the property of Dave Nagle, the man who same years later shot and killed Judge Terry, of early California notoriety. The opening of a better class saloon in Panamint is thus described by one who saw much of the camp's life:

The representative men in camp were duly notified and invited to be present; they always were duly expected to be there and they always were, if not prevented by a previous drunk or ill luck in a shooting scrape. The leading mining superintendent, who represented companies expending a million or more, was counted on for an expenditure of at least $500, and he never disappointed the boys. The festivities usually opened early and mildly, with free drinks to any and all visitors, who were cordially invited to partake often and stay all night. The latter request was usually put in such liberal spirit as to impress all with its honesty, for later on when the fun grew furious each head counted in the score for a drink, which were ordered by men amply able to pay in cash, or by check "good as wheat" on presentation at the company's office.

As the night grew on and the fun increased there was no limit to the number except as the common guzzlers fell by the wayside. The "tony crowd" were left to indulge in champagne in quantities unlimited. It often resulted in a rivalry of wild pandemonium, for as the barkeeper drank often he became very tired and would expedite his labors in filling an order for a basket of champagne by placing it on the floor, removing the lid and directing the revelers to help themselves. This generally occurred during the early morning hours. Often the roisterers had divested themselves of most of their clothing, and, whooping like Indians, would march around the open basket, each with a bottle in his hand, drinking, and firing their revolvers into the floor or up into the ceiling. Then was the time to look for bad blood, and hostilities opened between rival "bad men," who were in numbers sufficient to rule the camp, and who took such opportunities to even up old scores. On such occasions very often a man would be killed, when the crowd would scatter and the festivities stop. The slayer would be duly arrested, taken to his cabin by a constable and allowed to take a nap. Later in the day he would be taken before the Justice, who after hearing evidence would invariably, out of deference to the ruling element, discharge the defendant on the ground of self-defense.

Gambling there, as in other camps, was on a scale corresponding to the general wide-openness. Fortunes changed hands on trivial hazards; a sample poker game opened with an initial bet of $1,000, which was "seen" and "raised" $4,000 more, so that a "pot" of $10,000 was ready for the winner when he "showed down" a pair of aces and a pair of sixes. And there were other games of much larger proportions.

Mention has been made of the local paper. This was a sheet containing four pages, each measuring a little less than seven by fourteen inches, including generous margins. Its first copy was dated November 26, 1874, and bore the names of D. P. Carr as editor and T. S. Harris as manager. Issue No. 2, on the 28th, notified the public that Carr was no longer connected with the paper; issue No. 3, December 1st, denounced the late partner as an unprincipled deadbeat who had collected ahead for work in sight and left for other climes.

The Panamint *News*, tri-weekly, cost its subscribers 50 cents a week, $2 a month by carrier, $1.50 a month by mail. Advertising in it cost $4 a month for four lines, or 75 cents per line per issue.

Some quotations from its columns will help to depict conditions:

The town of Panamint now consists of twenty-six frame and board buildings besides a large number of stockades and tents. Within the next month, if lumber can be had, at least one hundred dwellings will be erected.

Meals can be had for 75 cents at one restaurant and $1 at others. Market prices: Flour per 100 lbs., $8.50 and $9; bacon per lb., 28c; ham, 30c; meats, 20c and 30c; potatoes, 10c; sugar, 20c and 25c; butter, 75c and $1; apples, 25c; barley, 8c and 10c; hay, 6c to 10c; eggs, per dozen, $1 to $2.

There are now over 600 locations in the district. The ores are mainly copper-silver glance and chloride of silver. Assays and working tests show values of from $100 to $4,000, the average being about $400.

The Cerro Gordo Freighting Company is running a line of teams from Cerro Gordo to Panamint; freight 5 cents per pound.

The Fourth of July, 1875, was duly celebrated in Panamint. The same little butcher's cart which had been used impartially for hauling carcasses of beeves and of roughs who had died with their boots on was on this occasion made to do service as a car of state. It was preceded by the "band," consisting (an eye witness states) of a tuba and a bass drum. When the procession reached the point for turning to countermarch, the canyon was so narrow that the outfit had to be lifted around by man-power. In the vehicle was a young lady, representing the Goddess of Liberty, and three little girls, all there were in camp. This is the way editor Harris described it:

The Car of State was decorated by Grand Marshal Paris and Mr. Stebbins, and reflected much credit on those gentlemen for its gorgeous beauty. It was brought into the procession at the proper time, filled with the young ladies and children of Panamint.

He avoided contradicting the inferences of his flowery account by "being unable to obtain for publication the names of the children."

An incident of the place was the adoption by a miners' meeting of a resolution excluding Chinese.

The rich ores were there, but in most cases in such metallurgical combinations as to defy the working processes in vogue. While some money was recovered from them, the yield was not commensurate with the cost of recovery.

Stewart and Jones tired of spending huge sums in trying to overcome the drawbacks. They persisted, however, for more than two years, but in May, 1877, the end of that regime came in the shutting down of the Surprise Valley mill.

CHAPTER XXVIII

OTHER MINING DISCOVERIES

OPTIMISM OF THE PROSPECTOR—WAUCOBA, LUCKY JIM, UBEHEBE, BEVERIDGE, POLETA—DARWIN LIVELY—GREENWATER, WHERE MILLIONS WERE SPENT—SKIDOO—JUDGE LYNCH'S DICTUM— TUNGSTEN, MARBLE, SODA, SALT, BORAX.

Most of the Inyo mining districts now known were discovered within a few years of the rise of Cerro Gordo. Some attracting much attention at the time are unknown to the Inyoite of today; others are still on the producing list.

A fact that impresses the investigator in connection with those discoveries was the invariable belief of the finder that he had come upon one of the greatest bonanzas on record. "The biggest mine in the world," "the most important mining discovery ever made in the county," "a find that will surpass Cerro Gordo," "a perfect Comstock," are bona fide sample phrases from descriptions of prospects which long since have been abandoned. Truly the prospector is ever optimistic. Had every find measured up to the claim made for it, gold and silver would have become but common metals.

Waucoba was one of the first of the new districts. Its discovery date is unknown. Col. James Brady was actively at work there in 1872, and the Waucoba Mining and Smelting Company built, in 1873, a road which is still in use for reaching latter-day producing properties in that general vicinity.

The district was so promising that in July, 1872, the *Inyo Independent* anticipated that "ere the half of another decade passes away a majority of the citizens of Inyo county will demand the location of its courthouse on the eastern side of the Inyo range. Already Waucoba district bids fair to have the largest population within a year of any in the county. The very first railroad to touch any part of this county will be on that side; at least such is the present indication."

Pigeon Springs and Log Springs were among the bidders for favor in 1873. Another district of that year was Sylvania, organized June 14th, and situated on the Nevada border line. W. S. Kincaid was its discoverer. Two later revivals and the expenditure of much money are in its record.

One of the other locations of the period was the Lucky Jim property in 1875, which was sold that year by James Ferguson, who afterward organized the New Coso Mining Company. Ubehebe, for some time known as Rose Springs district, was found by W. L. Hunter, J. B. Hunter, J. L. Porter and Thomas McDonough in 1875. They sold to M. W. Belshaw, who talked of building reduction works, probably in Saline Valley, but did not carry out the plan. Beveridge district, named for pioneer John Beveridge, was discovered by W. L. Hunter and others in 1877. Poleta provided the mining excitement of 1881. Prospecting had gone on in the White Mountains east of Bishop from the earliest coming of white settlers, with such results that more than one ambitious "city" had been staked out, only to be forgotten. In all probability some of the claims which changed hands for thousands during the days of Poleta were on the same ground that made Keyes District the hope of prospectors in the middle '60's.

These were all discoveries that could be matched many times over, in the matter of real results. The finding of the mines at Darwin, in November 1874, was of more consequence. It became the successor of Panamint in public interest, and had a boom ranking next to that camp and to Cerra Gordo. Furnaces were built to smelt its rich ores. Water was piped several miles into the camp. Harris moved his printing office from Panamint and produced a typographically handsome weekly paper. Hundreds of men were employed in the mines and mills. The usual detail of assisted mortality developed; a peace officer there declared that of 124 graves in the cemetery 122 were filled by the work of bullet or knife—a statement not wholly accepted. An outstanding incident was a labor strike in 1878, in which a handful of courageous officers defied a large organization and put an end to a threatened reign of anarchy and terrorism.

Two booming camps that were products of later years were Greenwater and Skidoo. The record of Greenwater has few parallels in its sudden rise, great outlays, small returns and quick decline. Locations had been made there as early as 1884, and others were made in 1894 by Doctor Trotter, for gold and silver values. Inaccessibility caused all these claims to be abandoned—though that quality seems to contribute to the success of "excitements," once they are fairly launched. It was high grade copper ore that caused the final rush, twenty years later than the locations for more precious metals.

The camp was situated on the sunrise side of the Black Mountains, but a short distance across the crest from where the slope into Death Valley begins. It looked out easterly over hundreds of miles of barren wastes. The Amargosa's bitter flow, twenty-four miles away, was the most easily reached water when the camp began. Obtaining supplies involved hauling for many miles over roads so trying that the portion traversed in approaching the claims was fittingly named Dead Horse Gulch.

Contemporary newspaper records credit the first copper discoveries to men named McAllister and Cook, with whom Arthur Kunze soon became associated. The Copper Blue ledge was found in February, 1905, by Fred Birney and Phil Creaser, who took samples of the outcrop to Independence when they went there to record their claims. While at the county seat they sent specimens of the ore to Patsy Clark, prominent in the copper mining world. Clark was so impressed that he sent engineer Joseph P. Harvey to investigate. Harvey, leaving the railroad at Daggett, Cal., lost his outfit in a cloudburst at Cave Springs, and had to go back for a fresh start. On his second trip he reached the right locality, but owing to faulty directions was unable to find the claims. Birney and Creaser afterward went there and did some development work, and again sought to enlist Clark's interest. This time Clark came to Rhyolite, Nevada, and from there sent Cleary, another of his engineers, to make the examination. The report was so favorable that Clark immediately bought the Birney and Creaser holdings. Dennis Clark, brother of Patsy, visited the prospects and confirmed previous reports, as well as sending in men and supplies for real development. Cleary also sent men on his own account, and became the owner of some of the most prominent locations in the district. Others who promptly invested were Chas. Schwab, Augustus Heinze, T. L. Oddie, F. M. (Borax) Smith and others hardly less prominent in financial affairs.

Within a month the population grew from 70 to over 1,000, with at least a hundred newcomers over the desert roads every day. The copper kings who had taken hold began hiring all applicants, with the purpose of the speediest possible development. An early estimate of the amount paid for claims was $4,125,000. In four months and twelve days from the camp's start 2,500 claims had been recorded. Stakes and monuments made a practically continuous string for thirty miles along the range, ground good, bad and indifferent being freely located. The first 50,000 shares of one of the companies were sold at Rhyolite, the nearest settlement. The records of easy and quick fortunes made in Tonopah and Goldfield stocks made marketing of shares easy. Prospectors in many cases wisely sold their claims, for ten, twenty or more thousands of dollars—whatever "pocket money" they could get. And in many instances it was only pocket money, for it was used to "feed the tiger" in the gambling room and for other cash-reducing purposes.

In one case, an engineer grubstaked a prospector, who located a claim and sold it for $5,000, of which the engineer got his part. The buyer asked the same engineer the next morning to visit and report on the property, and was told it was worthless. To be a party to locating a claim, share in the proceeds of its sale, and then get a fee for condemning it was something unique, at least. It was said, however, that the engineer did not know that he was reporting on his own claim.

Greenwater was a camp "without a lid," but not without law of a kind. It was without peace officers for months, but made its own codes. An instance: One night an elderly man was robbed of $80. The four robbers were found by a select committee, and were instructed to be on the main street at 9 o'clock the next morning. Nearly the whole town was out at that hour to observe proceedings. In brief and pointed remarks the culprits were informed that they had thirty minutes in which to adjust their affairs before leaving. One of the accused thought it would take him an hour to get things settled so he could leave, but after further remarks by the committee he found that he could finish his business and get away very handily within the time set.

The barren hills afforded little fuel. During a storm flurry coal sold at $100 a ton and wood at $60 a cord. Water sold, at first, at $15 a barrel, later at half that figure —and small wonder at either figure since it had to be hauled from twenty-eight to thirty-five miles. Lumber cost $165 for 1,000 feet. A frame store 35 by 60 feet, unshingled, cost $5,400. Hay was $6 and $7 a bale; grain $5 and $6 a sack; gasoline a dollar a gallon or $10 a case; potatoes and onions 10 to 12½ cents a pound; ice, brought from Las Vegas, Nevada, the last fifty-five miles by auto, cost $10 for 100 pounds. Wages in the mines were $5 to $7; carpenters got $8 and $10; musicians were paid $8, and such skilled labor as faro dealers drew $8 a shift.

The postoffice was run on economical lines. The Nasby in charge paid his clerks $5 for eight hours, which was more than his own return from the Government. Mail went into a box, and each individual fished out his own letters.

On one occasion there was a water famine in camp. An enterprising resident borrowed a team and drove to Furnace Creek, twenty-eight miles, returning with two barrels of water. One was given to the owner of the team; the other, dished out to pails and canteens, netted about $30.

Though in the heart of the wilds, Greenwater had two newspapers, a small magazine, a $100,000 bank, express and telephone service, professional men of all kinds, and of course ordinary lines of business.

When the camp began to show signs of depression, a man named McCarty walked into a neighboring saloon and remarked to the owner: "Nichols, two saloons on this side of the street are too many; I'll shake you the dice to see whether you take mine or I take yours." Nichols, without a word, reached back and picked up a dice box, and threw five sixes. McCarty shook and threw five aces. Nichols picked up his hat and started out. "Hold on," said McCarty; "take a drink." The transaction was complete.

The stage to Greenwater burned one afternoon, and with it the mailbags containing $30,000. The driver's first knowledge of the fire was when a bale of hay on the vehicle blazed up. The team was cut loose; the rest of the outfit was a total loss.

It was from that locality somewhere that a cheerful wag wrote that he was employed on the "graveyard shift in the Coffin mine, Tombstone Mountains, Funeral Range, overlooking Death Valley." The graveyard shift, it may be remarked for the benefit of readers unacquainted with mining slang, is the one which includes midnight, when sepulchers traditionally yawn.

The owning corporations spent much money in trying to prove their mines. The ledges "went down," but values of encouraging degree ended at about 200 feet depth. Workings were continued far underground, while various Greenwater stocks held a place in eastern exchanges, until finally abandonment was necessary. Some of the location monuments were made of high grade ore and were included in the shipments made to smelters. The last watchman on the ground, it was said, was a rancher whose home was at Ash Meadows, on the Amargosa. He had teams and wagons and time to spare, so more or less of the decadent city may still serve a useful purpose in a changed situation.

Greenwater's nearest neighbor was Skidoo, on the mountain summit on the western edge of Death Valley.

That camp did not reach Greenwater's height of fame, nor did it fall as rapidly, for it was a producer for some years after the copper camp had become as deserted as when the Death Valley party of '49 had toiled along within sight of its location. The Skidoovians numbered 700 or more, at the camp's maximum. A bank and a newspaper were among its institutions. Gold and silver ores were its sources of production. One of its contributions to the records was a lynching affair, the only such instance in Inyo county except the summary vengeance taken on the convicts in 1871. The Skidoo affair happened April 22, 1908. The desperado whose career was cut short was named Joe Simpson. Three days earlier he had entered the bank and demanded twenty dollars. Being refused and disarmed, he had gone away and "heeled himself," returned and shot a clerk. As he had previously declared an intention of killing four other citizens, Skidoo sentiment fully coincided with the paper's page-wide headline "Murdered Lynched with General Approval," and its comment that "the removal of this pest by a feeling so excellent has caused a feeling of relief throughout the camp." There was certainly no great squeamishness about it, for when a resident wanted a photograph of the suspended Simpson's appearance the corpse was again connected with the rope and put into the position occupied in his final moments. The noose was treasured as a souvenir by a morbid-minded bartender. An inquest was held, at which one witness testified to having been awakened twenty-three times during the day to hear the news, and he had been greatly surprised each time. Another said Joe "was a true Bohemian—he hung around all night."

The camp was, however, above the average in law observance, and little crime occurred in it.

The finest of mountain water was piped many miles from high up on Telescope Peak. Skidoo's mining settled to a one-company basis, and in time its deposits were, apparently, worked out.

A new mineral was added to Inyo's known list (already pronounced by authorities to be more comprehensive than that of any other county), when in August, 1913, James Powning picked up tungsten float in the hills west of Bishop, at a spot where he had gone to pick up a rabbit he had shot. The claim then located was named the Jackrabbit. A. W. Nobles and C. C. Cooper were in partnership with him in the find. It was not until the spring of 1916 that sufficient money for developing the claims became available, when F. M. Townsend, A. J. Clark and others bought the original and subsequent locations. Mills were built, one of them the largest tungsten concentrating plant in the world. Production continued to be important until the fall of prices following the Great War made it impossible to work those and other large properties of the same nature, in that general locality, at a profit.

During the middle '80's large marble quarries were opened near Keeler, producing a material which tests proved to be stronger in crushing resistance than any other known. Much marble was taken out during succeeding years, more or less of it being used for finishing some of the coast's large buildings.

The growth of another mineral industry is also to be noted, in the reclamation of soda and other salts from the heavily mineralized waters of Owens Lake. Locations on the shore of Owens Lake were made in the early months of 1885, by L. F. J. Wrinkle, for the purpose of constructing vats in which to evaporate the water in order to recover the saline contents. Names of 839 persons were on the original notice, which serves to indicate the large area claimed. The Inyo Development Company was formed by Nevada capitalists, and for years it continued to gather the residue from those vats. Noah Wrinkle, son of the original locator, worked out a chemical process by which a wider range of products was obtained, and less dependent on the density of the water used. This was the basis of the Natural Soda Products Company, which Watterson Brothers took up at a critical stage of the company's career, and which became an enterprise as great in magnitude as it was unique in its processes. Others of similar nature have also been established to reclaim the lake's mineral wealth.

Saline Valley, containing vast beds of salt, of a grade purer in its natural state than any other known, has been the scene of some development operation, and in time its resources may come to be of extensive importance. Another yield of the burning deserts is borax, which has been to some extent recovered in Saline Valley, but principally mined in the far eastern region of the county as more fully mentioned in a later chapter.

Ballarat, a central point for miners in the Panamints, and Modock, Ubehebe, Bishop Creek, Bunker Hill and other camps which as a rule have been or are single-mine enterprises appear in the county's mining record; however, the purpose of these chapters is not to review details but to note the outstanding facts of mining progress.

CHAPTER XXIX

LATER DEATH VALLEY HISTORY

MEXICANS THE PIONEERS IN THAT REGION—EARLY AMERICAN
VISITORS—A REFUGE FOR THE LAWLESS—"BELLERIN'" TECK—
DISCOVERY OF BORAX—A DESERT HOME—"SHE BURNS GREEN!"—
PACIFIC COAST BORAX COMPANY.

The best evidence as to early comers in the Death Valley region awards priority to Mexicans. There were Mormon explorers and miners who penetrated those wastes; but their tenancy was short in comparison with that of the Spanish-speaking people. It appears that the naming of Furnace Creek was due to a small reduction plant found there by Americans; and that plant doubtless owed its existence to Mexicans.

The first visit to the valley by scientific observers was by a Dr. Owen and other members of the State boundary commission in 1861. Dr. Darwin French and associates had been in the valley the year before.

W. T. Henderson, heretofore mentioned in these chronicles, went there and climbed the highest point of the Panamints. To the west he saw the Slate, Argus and other ranges, and beyond them the Sierra. To the south rose the Calico range, Pilot Butte, and the far-off San Bernardinos. Northward were the White Mountains; to the east, the Funerals, and one unnamed range after another. Two miles below were beds of salt, soda, borax; the black dots of lava buttes, mesquite trees made specks of dark green; apparent stream channels showed where cloudbursts had ripped open the earth's surface. Telescope Peak he named the commanding mountain, a name so fitting that Telescope Peak it is today.

Dr. S. G. George and others, including Henderson, made their visits in 1860, and saw many relics of the emigrants of '49, as well as of other travelers. The latter were accounted for by the finding of skeletons, some of them in the vicinity of the springs. One of George's finds was a slab of marble about an inch thick, about the size of a common washboard, and perfectly grooved in a similar manner.

Those who went to Death Valley between 1849 and the discovery of borax included all elements of society. There were men of education seeking scientific information; there were honest prospectors with no reason for avoiding the haunts of men; and, particularly during the early 70's, there were some about whom it was well not to be too inquisitive. Undue curiosity in such matters was an infraction of the social code that sometimes brought serious, if not fatal, results. It was said that the region contained deserters from Civil War armies, draft dodgers, and men who "had no use for sheriffs nohow." It is certain that when even the free and easy atmosphere of early Nevada and Inyo proved too dangerous for certain individuals they headed for the deep desert. There was a resident Indian population of reasonable repute, and there were Indian as well as white renegades.

In 1870 one "Bellerin'" Teck appeared upon the scene. "Bellerin's" characteristics are unrecorded, beyond the fact that he was a "bad man." Furnace Creek was the site he chose for a location, and there he was said to have raised "alfalfa, barley and quails." One of his visitors was a Mormon named Jackson, who traded him a yoke of oxen in exchange for part of the ranch. The partnership was of brief duration, for "Bellerin'" and a shotgun ran the Saint out of the valley within a week. Teck, together with the voice from which it is presumed he derived his soubriquet, passes from our record.

The general average improved considerably when borax operations began, and forces of workingmen were taken in. About forty men were employed at the works when they were busiest. Later, Greenwater lived its feverish hour just over the summit to the east of Death Valley, and Skidoo's population could look down into the noted spot. A townsite, christened Midway, was staked out on the Death

Valley slope of the Black Mountains during the Greenwater excitement, but it is not recorded that anyone, even the stakers, lived there.

The industrial history of Death Valley began with the discovery of borax in 1880.

Some time in those lonely years one Aaron Winters and his frail Spanish-American wife, Rosie, located at Ash Meadows, a place eastward across the Funerals from Death Valley, and 200 miles from the then nearest railroad station or settlement. A visitor to their home thus described it:

Close against the hill, one side half hewn out of rock, stood a low stone building with tule thatched roof. The single room was about 15 feet square. In front was a canvas-covered addition about the same size. The earth served as a floor for both rooms. One side was the lady's boudoir. There was a window with a deep ledge, in the center of which was a starch box supporting a small looking-glass. On each side of the mirror hung old brushes, badly worn bits of ribbon, and some other fixings for the hair. Handy by was a lamp mat, covered with bottles of magnolia balm, complexion powders and Florida water—all, alas, empty, but still cherished by the wife. In place of a library there were a number of copies of the Police Gazette. The sugar, tea and coffee were kept under the bed. The water of the spring ran down the hill and formed a pool in front of the house, and here a number of ducks and chickens, with a pig and a big dog, formed a happy group, a group that wandered about in the house as well as romped beside the waters of the spring.

One night a strolling prospector tarried at the Winters home. He told about the Nevada borax deposits, and what a great fortune was ready for whoever could find more borax beds. Winters, careful not to indicate any special reason for seeking knowledge, asked many questions in a casual way. Among other things he learned that supposed borax could be tested by pouring certain chemicals over it and firing the mixture. If it burned green, borax was present.

When the guest left, Winters made haste to get chemicals from some remote supply point. He had seen stuff in Death Valley answering the general description of the Nevada borax. Equipped with testing supplies, Winters and his wife journeyed across the Funeral summit to Furnace Creek and made camp, then went to the marsh and got samples of the deposit. At night, they mixed their powdered samples, as they had been told, poured alcohol over it, and struck the match that was to tell the story.

How would it burn? For years they had lived as the Piutes of the desert. Mesquite beans and chuckwalla had served them for food when flour and bacon were missing. The wife had felt the utter loneliness of their situation and the absence of everything dear to the feminine heart. The color of the flame would tell them whether better things were ahead, or if the same dreary existence must continue.

Winters held a match to the mixture with a trembling hand. After an instant's pause he shouted at the top of his voice: "She burns green, Rosie! We're rich!"

When the news reached San Francisco W. T. Coleman and F. M. Smith sent agents to the rude habitation in Ash Meadows. When the purpose of the visit was made known, Rosie fished out a bag of pine nuts, and as the party munched them around the campfire the bargain was made. Winters and Rosie received $20,000 for their find.

Before following the development of the borax fields, let us give a farewell word to Winters. On getting his money he bought out the Pahrump ranch, giving $15,000 cash and $5,000 in a mortgage. For a little while life held new charms for the couple but desert hardships had sapped the wife's slender vitality and she died ere long.

It is told that one fall Winters had to go to Belmont, hundreds of miles away, to pay his taxes and do other business. Those were the days of "road agents," and he prepared for emergencies. On the dash of his buckboard was a holster into which he put a worthless pistol; a serviceable "navy" was concealed under the cushion on the seat. Nearing Belmont, two men invited him to dismount and turn over his money. Argument was useless and he had to comply. One of the bandits discovered the useless pistol in its holster, and it and the old man's demeanor served to throw the pair completely off their guard. Winters took a favorable opportunity to take the pistol from the seat and shoot one robber, and then to compel the other to put the corpse on the buckboard and go into Belmont with him. Through Winters' intercession the captured man was released and taken by him to the Pahrump ranch to do honest toil.

The earliest borax corporation in Death Valley was the Eagle company, with a plant near Bennett's Wells. The Pacific Coast borax company, producing "Twenty Mule Team" borax, extensively advertised, took the lead in interest and in development, and conferred on F. M. Smith the newspaper title of "Borax King." Securing title necessitated sending a survey party to the scene. This party, headed by Engineer McGillivray, found that the earlier Government surveys were absolutely unreliable. None of the work of staking out the townships had actually been done, while descriptions were so inaccurate that tracts appearing on field notes as level were really 8,000 feet above sea level and stood at a forty-five-degree angle.

There were no roads worth the name, yet as every item of material had to be hauled great distances, across a little-known desert, that lack had to be supplied. A road more than 160 miles long was made, with watering places more then fifty miles apart in some cases. One section of it crossed the valley on a foundation of solid salt. In many places the surface is only a crust over underlying mud; in others there are solid ridges. On one of these the borax people laid out their route, when it became necessary to cross from the east side, on which the works were built. The marsh was eight miles wide where the crossing was made; level, as a whole, but so pitted and uneven that it is said a man could not stand flat-footed in a single spot on the course. The grading tools were sledgehammers. Day after day the workmen pounded off the little hillocks and finally completed one of the most singular stretches of road in the country.

How to move the bulky output to the railroad was a problem that had to be met. It was solved by the construction of wagons each of which carried ten tons or more. The beds measured sixteen feet in length, six in depth and four in width. They rested on solid steel axles over six inches in diameter, and allowing for a six-foot tread. The rear wheels were seven feet in diameter, and were covered with tires an inch thick and eight inches wide. The woodwork was in proportion.

As the "twenty mule teams" traveled only about twenty miles a day, and water holes or springs were sometimes fifty miles apart, plans had to be made for hauling water. This was done by building tank wagons, which hauled water to the dry camps among the ten stopping places established as part of the system. Springs were dug out and improved, and water pipes laid.

In the hottest weather, mid-day travel was impossible. Hauling was done at night, or the road was temporarily abandoned. Five teams were kept on the road, each taking twenty days for the round trip to and from the railroad.

One of the details of recovering borax is cooking the crude material in huge vats. Maintaining the fires strips the surrounding country of the sagebrush, which is most convenient for fuel. In Death Valley the fuel problem was of rather more seriousness than in some other places. The drug, once selling by the ounce, lowered in price with the increased supply provided by that and other discoveries. Other deposits more economical in working were found by "Borax" Smith's and Coleman interests. All these things contributed to the closing down of those works.

Death Valley has yet a large part to play in affairs, and large contributions to make for the world's welfare. When this is written, the region is taking a large place as an objective for travelers; and within sight of spots where lost unfortunates perished in the lonely waste, modern hotels offer metropolitan accommodations.

CHAPTER XXX

TRANSPORTATION

RAILROAD TALK ALWAYS WITH US—AN EARLY-DAY SURVEY—HIGH
FREIGHTS—CERRO GORDO FREIGHTING COMPANY—STEAMERS ON
OWENS LAKE—ADVENT OF CARSON & COLORADO RAILROAD—OTHER
RAILROAD NOTES—EL CAMINO SIERRA, OF STATE HIGHWAY
SYSTEM.

Almost as early as the beginning of settlement in
Owens Valley t- k of a railroad connection started. When
the first transcontinental railroad was launched, the paper
at Visalia informed its readers that the road was expected
to come through Owens Valley and to Visalia; this in 1865.
In December 1870, a company was incorporated to build a
road from Wilmington, Los Angeles County, to Wicken-
burg, Arizona, with a branch into Owens Valley; it was
to be of 30-inch gauge. That project ended, as have several others, in talk.

With the growth of Cerro Gordo, the people of Los
Angeles began to appreciate that Inyo might become a
valuable factor in their affairs. Completion of the railroad
between that city and San Pedro, in 1869, opened a route
which, though distant, was utilized for Inyo freights to
and from San Francisco for several years. Ores and supplies were hauled by teams between Los Angeles and
Owens Valley, and the volume of business done was pleas-
ing to the southern pueblo as well as a matter of some envy
to Visalia. The Los Angeles and Independence railroad
was promoted by Senator John P. Jones, ex-Governor
Downey and others. A franchise bill was introduced in
the Assembly by James E. Parker, of Inyo, and became law
in the spring of 1873. It granted to the company the right
to collect eight cents per mile for fare and ten cents per
ton mile for freight. At least $20,000 was to be expended
on the project within twelve months. Subscription books

were opened in Los Angeles, and half of the $2,200,000 capital stock was subscribed at once.

The chief engineer of the project made two preliminary surveys. One was via San Bernardino, and was the more favorable of the two in grades and expense. Its grading was figured to cost $321,400. The San Fernando route was the shorter. Estimated cost of a standard gauge road, laid with 45-pound iron, complete, was put at $11,400 a mile; 3-foot gauge, 35-pound iron, $10,000 a mile; strap rail, $5,400 a mile; wooden stringers, no rails, $4,233 a mile. Narrow gauge railroads were then coming into favor and that suggestion met no opposition. As may rightly be guessed, the idea of strapiron rails did not commend itself, particularly to those acquainted with the fashion in which "snakeheads" on early railroads sometimes rose up to punch through car bottoms. The wooden rail idea was the touch that forecasted the project's finish. Eighteen miles of track was laid from Los Angeles, but in another direction, and in time became part of the Southern Pacifiic system. The company continued to exist and to make occasional reports of investigations for several years before its final demise.

The limited agriculture of Owens Valley fell short of ability to supply demands, and in consequence prices were high for all such produce. This was some offset for the enormous freight rates that prevailed; for while every importation paid a freight tariff of five to seven cents a pound—even ten to twelve cents in the late '60's—the producer who contracted his barley in the field at four cents a pound and his hay in the field sometimes as high as $50 a ton, got some return from the freighters, which had to buy produce to feed the hundreds of animals used in the service.

None of the old-time freight bills are now available, but an indication of them is given by a contract made between the freighters and Camp Independence authorities for delivery of freight from San Francisco at $5.96 per one hundred pounds during the summer months and $6.96 during the winter.

While some teaming was done from Wadsworth, Nevada, on the Central Pacific, the bulk of Inyo shipments came and went the southern way. Ventura, Santa Barbara and Bakersfield all made bids to become the county's shipping point, but Los Angeles secured most of the trade.

The most important factor in pioneer transportation, and in fact the first regular and dependable service, was the Cerro Gordo Freighting Company, organized in 1873 primarily to transport Cerro Gordo bullion and supplies. Nadeau, its chief promoter, had been a freighter in a small way, as had a number of others. He secured backing from Belshaw & Beaudry with a three-year contract for transporting Cerro Gordo bullion on a systematic basis. Eighty wagons were specially built, and 56 of them were in regular service. Stations, watering places and camps were provided along the route. Each outfit had from sixteen to twenty animals as motive power, and the teams were scheduled almost to the hour, on a basis of twenty-one or twenty-two days for the round trip. The wagons were huge affairs, each holding almost as much load as a narrowgauge boxcar.

The company acquired the Bessie Brady, a little steamer that had been launched on Owens Lake June 17, 1872, to help in moving bullion. The boat, 85 feet long and 16 feet beam, was propellor-driven by a 20-horsepower engine. It had cost about $10,000, when built by D. H. Ferguson and James Brady, superintendent of the smelting company operating at Swansea. Bessie Brady, the superintendent's daughter, broke the traditional bottle of wine on the ship's bow at an elaboraate launching ceremony. This appears to have been the first boat launched for commercial purposes on western inland lakes. Making a round trip daily from Swansea (three miles north of the present site of Keeler) to Cartago, at the foot of the lake, and carrying 70 tons of freight, the steamer performed service cheaper than had previously been given in hauling one-tenth of the weight between the same terminals in five days by teams. A 300-foot wharf was built at Swansea. Bullion formed the bulk of the freight taken southward, and supplies for the mines and for Owens Valley provided return cargoes. Valley freights were discharged at Ferguson's Landing, at the northwest corner of the lake. The steamer bore an honorable part in the business of the time. She was burned near Keeler some years after retirement from service. An old tree has long stood near the site of Ferguson's Landing; but the old wharves and other marks of that service have disappeared as completely as the little vessel and her path above the beds of mineral salts where once rolled miles of blue water.

Another steamer, the Mollie Stevens, was launched in 1877 for transporting lumber, wood and charcoal across the lake for Cerro Gordo. Her engine was one that had been used in the United States vessel Pensacola. Her part in general transportation matters was small.

The Cerro Gordo Freighting Company abandoned the field in 1881. Nadeau, its chief owner, became a Los Angeles hotel man. In that year the Carson & Colorado railroad was completed to Belleville, Nevada, which point became the transshipping headquarters for Inyo freight. It so continued until the road was built across the White Mountains to Benton and into Owens Valley in 1883. D. O. Mills was the money power behind this road. In the belief that its shipping advantages would stimulate ore shipments from the many claims along the White Mountains, the base of which it skirted to the terminus at Keeler, the management resisted all inducements to lay its track through the more settled western side of Owens Valley, touching the established towns. It is probable that anticipated greater cost of construction and maintenance on the west side had some effect in shaping the company's determination.

Candelaria had then become a Nevada mining camp of importance and drew on Owens Valley for much of its supplies. The railroad brought the Candelaria region nearer, but whether the valley materially gained from its building, so far as the Nevada markets were concerned, is debatable. Previously teams had found occupation in hauling to the camps, and Owens Valley had practically a monopoly of the business of furnishing many kinds of supplies. The railroads eliminated the teaming, and at the same time bridged the gap between the camps and other producing regions.

But against that disadvantage were to be set some gains. Nevada capital came to Inyo with the railroad, and forthwith began different steps toward developing resources that had been latent or unknown. Among them was the opening of the Inyo marble quarries. There were contributions to land development. At Owens Lake, where locations had been made as early as 1865 for the "salt, soda and borax" contained in that water, the soda reclamation industry began on an extensive scale. The isolation of this region was to a large extent ended.

A little more than ten years later the Southern Pacific took over the Carson & Colorado. The ever-present hope of a southern railroad was encouraged. Collis P. Huntington, head of the greater company, decided to complete the line through this valley, connecting the transcontinental systems to the south and the north. Before he proceeded with that plan, death claimed him, and his successors held a different view. When the Los Angeles aqueduct required large quantities of freight, the long-wanted road was built, and its last spike was driven at Owenyo October 18, 1910. It gave the valley a southern rail connection, though the narrowgauge traversing Owens Valley as far as Owenyo has never been standardized.

There were other surveys. A company went to the extent of securing rights of way from Bishop south through the valley, and graded a roadbed between Bishop and a connection with the Southern Pacific at Laws. There have been repeated and fruitless endeavors to secure the location of a line of rails that would better serve the valley towns. There was a promise, implied if not actual, in the course of a gigantic suit by the Government to "unscramble" the Central Pacific and Southern Pacific systems, that when certain other large improvements had been made the "Slim Princess," as the narrowgauge was locally dubbed, would be made a part of a through north-and-south interior system. But those improvements have been completed, and there still remains 134 miles of the narrow-gauge which Mills said had been "built 300 miles too long and 300 years too soon."

The most revolutionary change in Inyo transportation affairs has been made by the splendid State highway system. Twenty years ago, when the first timid steps toward such a system were made, there was formed in Bishop an organization called the Inyo Good Road Club. In season and out, it neglected no opportunity to impress on State authorities the need of a first-class highway east of the Sierras. That club was never strong in numbers, but under the persistent efforts principally of W. Gillette Scott, its executive secretary, it impressed its ideas, and secured attention which has at all times since given to this slope a consideration of importance. The State Highway Commissions have supported the idea, and there now exists between Owens Valley and the general systems of the State an unbroken mileage of thoroughfare second to none. That excellent thoroughfare is being completed to the northward as well. Gasoline-driven vehicles now cover the distances in the same number of hours that it took in days in the time of the early pioneers.

CHAPTER XXXI

SUNDRY WAYMARKS OF HISTORY

ATTEMPT TO GRAB OWENS VALLEY AS SWAMP LAND—LATER PLAN TO
MAKE MUCH OF IT STOCK RANGE—NO-FENCE ISSUE—MT. WHIT-
NEY DISPUTE—SLACK REQUIREMENTS FOR TEACHING—SOCIETY OF
PIONEERS—RETURNS THROWN OUT—LOCAL OPTION IN '74—CAMP
INDEPENDENCE ABANDONED

A land-grabbing scheme of the first magnitude
threatened to dispossess Owens Valley homesteaders in
1873.

California was then having a run of what were termed
"swamp land steals." Congress had passed a law providing
for the survey and segregation of swamp and overflowed
lands. Each State was permitted to make its own
regulations as to the disposition of such lands within its
borders. Claimants were unrestricted as to the area they
could obtain on a suitable showing as to its physical
condition. California was a field ripe for harvesting by
monopolists, and history shows that the opportunity was
not neglected. Spanish land grants had provided the
original confusion, and railroad subsidies and unwise
legislation made matters worse. Legislatures and officers
were named in corporation headquarters in many cases.
The great central valleys were hardly better than stock
ranges. Concentrated wealth, besides being in close touch
with opportunities, was able to lay claim to great domains
and wait for future returns, while the settlers the State
needed could not afford to court starvation on the available
tracts. An example of how the situation worked out was
in Kern County, where the holdings of thirteen persons
amounted to 488,000 acres, and seven others held 65,000
acres or more.

The United States Land Office was moved from
Aurora, Nevada, to Independence in June, 1873. Josiah

Earl was nominated to be Register, and P. A. Chalfant was named as Receiver. The latter appointment was unsought, and when its beneficiary learned that he had been suggested by political elements with which he was not in accord he promptly resigned. Earl took full charge of the office, though his appointment had not been confirmed by the Senate.

In July, 1873, several persons, prominent among them Mr. Earl and W. S. Powell, a Tulare County surveyor, filed numerous applications for the survey and purchase of all or parts of 221 sections of land in Owens Valley, extending from Round Valley to Owens Lake, and involving 133,000 acres. Without going into minor details of description, suffice it to state that practically every township in the valley was touched in some degree or as a whole by the claim. Applicants made oath that the lands were swamp or overflowed, though most of the land so claimed was covered with sagebrush, and much of it would not come under even the liberal General Land Office ruling that "land too wet for irrigation at the usual seeding time, though later requiring irrigation" should be subject to sale as swamp.

Applicants further certified that lands sought were unoccupied, while the fact was that on at least ninety-four of the claimed sections homes had been established and the beginnings of farming made. It is probable that the occupants ultimately would have legally withstood any attempts at their eviction; at the time they would have done it by force of arms. Yet with the examples they could cite in which aggregated wealth had overborne justice, some of them were none too sanguine on that point. At the best, the claims promised wearisome litigation and expense which none could afford.

Proceedings had been so well masked that three months elapsed between the filing of the swamp land claims and knowledge of them reaching the people of the valley. The *Inyo Independent*, of which Mr. Chalfant, who had refused to serve as Land Office Receiver, was editor, ascertained and revealed the facts. Indignation swept the valley.

Public meetings were held, and every citizen who had any outside acquaintanceship exerted himself to the utmost to upset the sinister plan. The law required that action on such applications should be suspended for six months, during which time protests might be filed with the land authorities. Half of the period had passed, but three months still remained to the people. The vigorous campaign made caused suspension of action pending further investigation, and two months later, in March, 1874, the applications were rejected.

An effort was made to secure the conviction of Powell on a charge of perjury but it did not succeed. A petition for Earl's removal was generally signed throughout the valley. His appointment had not been confirmed by the Senate, though he continued to discharge the duties of the Registership. Senators Sargent, of California, and Jones, of Nevada, Governor Newton Booth, of California, and others of less prominence took an active part in opposing Earl's confirmation. The matter had not come to a Senate vote when in May, 1874, he settled it by resigning.

Let us anticipate the passage of nearly a decade to refer to another plan for monopolizing a large part of Owens Valley, though in the later case open purchase was proposed. There would have been, naturally, the accompaniment of many sales forced by circumstances. This was in 1882, when multimillionaires W. S. Hobart and Alvinza Hayward conceived the idea of securing the area noted on maps as Bishop Creek Valley and making it into a stock range. James Cross, a mining man long connected with Nevada and California affairs, was their representative. George M. Gill, afterward Superior Judge of this county, was their attorney. Theodore T. Cook, a Bishop bookkeeper, was sent to Independence to list the assessed value of all properties in the area desired, and to investigate titles. Hobart and Hayward planned to offer twenty-five per cent above assessed values, and believed that while many residents would be unwilling to sell they would be virtually compelled to if a sufficient proportion of their neighbors sold. Cook's investigations of different kinds showed that the probable cost of carrying out the enterprise would be $1,500,000. Whether this was larger than the projectors were willing to stand, or whatever the reason, no further steps were taken.

An important issue of the early '70's was the "no-fence law." As in most agricultural communities, and particularly those as new as Owens Valley then was, many settlers were without means with which to fence their holdings. Barbed wire, now in common use, was new to this market, and its cost was twenty-five cents a pound, and rough lumber sold at $55 or more per thousand feet. While the ranchers were starting their crops, grazing was also a leading industry. An item of 1873 said that there were 200,000 head of cattle, horses and sheep in the mountains around Mount Whitney, and many of them wintered in Owens Valley. The driving of herds through the valley to their summer ranges often meant the destruction of growing crops along the route, where the tracts were usually unfenced. Considerable agitation attended the passage of a law that placed responsibility for destruction of crops on the stockmen, whether the land was or was not fenced. Nevertheless, a special act of that kind was passed for Inyo County, and a few other counties received the same consideration.

Columns of newspaper space were used in a controversy over the identity of the real Mount Whitney. Scientists were in error until 1873, as the uninformed person would be now if while in Lone Pine, nearest to the peak, he were asked to point it out. Clarence King climbed "old" Mount Whitney in 1871, and later came all the way from New York to make another ascent, ascertaining that he had been mistaken. John Muir and others of note took a hand in the debate. The first ascent of the real Mount Whitney was made August 18, 1873, by A. H. Johnson, J. J. Lucas and C. D. Begole, who built a monument on it. Prof. Brewer had discovered and named the mountain in 1864, and King at that time had climbed to within 300 feet of the top. Afterward he and others gave the name to a peak several miles southeast, believing it to be the one he had ascended from the west. "Old" Mount Whitney bore the name for three or four years, while there were attempts to give the higher summit some other name. "Fisherman's Peak," "Dome of the Continent," and "Dome of Inyo" all had supporters. An Inyo Assemblyman introduced a bill in 1878 to fix the name of "Fisherman's Peak" on the mountain, and it passed the Assembly. The Senate changed it to read "Fowler's Peak." Fortunately the bill did not become law.

The out-of-the-wayness of Inyo and Mono Counties in those days was illustrated by the enactment of a law permitting, in these counties, the employment of public school teachers regardless of their possessing certificates of qualification. Being sometimes unable to secure certified teachers, the districts were permitted to enlist anyone whom they believed to be able to instruct the rising generation. The law was repealed in 1876.

In more modern days, "the big earthquake" seems to mark almost the beginning of history in Inyo. Such an idea would have been scorned by the Benevolent Society of Owens Valley Pioneers, organized in March, 1874, for a brief career. Only those who had been in the county prior to the last battle at Owens Lake, in January, 1865, were eligible to membership. The officers were Patrick Reddy, president; J. B. Rowley and Thomas Passmore, vice presidents; J. J. Moore, secretary; R. A. Loomis, corresponding secretary; T. F. A. Connelly, treasurer; John A. Lank, D. D. Gunnison and John Lubken, directors. Other members included John Lentell, V. G. Thompson, James Shepherd, John Shepherd, John B. White, William J. Lake, C. D. Begole, Joseph Fernbach, Thomas W. Hill, John C. Willett, Thomas May, William L. Moore, George W. Brady, Paul W. Bennett, Jacob Vagt, John R. Hughes, and probably several other "taboose-eaters" not listed in available records.

An incident of 1873 was the rejection of election returns from Round Valley, Bishop Creek, Fish Springs and Lone Pine precincts, for informalities too gross for even the easy-going authorities of that period. What difference, if any, it made in the result of the county election is not known, nor does the action appear to have stirred up any special comment.

A different sort of election was held September 18, 1874, in Bishop Creek and Round Valley. The Independent Order of Good Templars had lodges in Bishop Creek, Independence and Camp Independence — the latter composed entirely of soldiers—and their members had much to do with solidifying sentiment against the absolutely wide-open conditions then general in Inyo as well as elsewhere. Local option was submitted to vote in the precincts named. Bishop Creek voted eighty-two against license, twenty-six for; Round Valley was nineteen against, six for; totals, one hundred and one against license; thirty-two for. This pioneer housecleaning effort was in vain; the Supervisors discovered that the election should have been brought in the Supervisor district, and that the Bishop Supervisor district included part of Big Pine precinct, where no election was held. At that election, as often later, the ladies took an active part by serving a feast during the day to voters.

March 1, 1875, the first six-times-a-week mail service between Owens Valley and Aurora, then the nearest communication, was begun. Up to then the settlers had been fortunate to get word from the outer world, considerably delayed, as often as three times a week, and sometimes no better than weekly.

Through all that period county finances were in deplorable condition, scrip selling as low as forty cents on the dollar. Its fluctuations offered a field for some small speculation, and citizens who could spare the money made its buying profitable. The county did not profit much from such conditions. An example was a bridge contract on which the bidder's offer was to do the work for $2,000 if paid in gold or $4,866.66 if paid in scrip.

Orders for abandonment of Camp Independence were received by Captain Alexander B. MacGowan on July 9, 1877, and before sunrise the following morning, the garrison, Company D, 12th Infantry, began the long march to the railroad south, later to go to the front as part of General Miles' force in the Nez Perce war in Idaho.

Departure of the soldiers was witnessed with deep regret. Citizens felt that the Indian situation was not wholly free from possibilities of trouble. Reports occasionally came in of friction in the desert regions. To the credit of Inyo Indians be it said that as a rule it developed either that the reports were baseless, that white men were chiefly at fault in the matter, or that the troublemakers were renegades, outlawed by Piutes as well as whites.

A movement was started at Bishop for organizing a company of the State National Guard, as a precautionary measure. It was found to be barred by reason of an already full list of authorized companies. Other efforts of the same kind were made in after years, with equal lack of State encouragement.

D Company had been at the post four years. In the beginning it was made up of a hard lot of individuals. On two different occasions they had clashes with citizens. One of these occurred on the night of December 31, 1873. A party of soldiers went into Independence, between two and three miles from the barracks, and made a general round of serenading. During the evening their potations at the town's bars were numerous. Toward midnight they approached a hall wherein a dance was in progress. The doorkeeper refused to admit them, on account of their intoxicated condition. They insisted, and the first comer was "sent to grass" by the doorkeper's fist. A general and wholesale melee ensued. Fence pickets were the worst weapons used, and many bruises were inflicted before the affair ended.

Those men were but part of the company, however. The more sober element soon afterward organized a lodge of Good Templars at the post, and pridefully sustained it during their stay. The toughs deserted or finished their time, and replacements improved the general average. When the post was abandoned there were many civilian friends to bid the departing soldiers farewell. How the company improved was shown by a guardhouse average of one man incarcerated each day during 1873, one each four days in 1874, one each thirty days in 1875.

It was a telegraph operator in the company who promoted the first telegraph line built in the county, in the fall of 1876. It ran between Independence and the fort. Its construction tried the ingenuity of the builders; its wire ranged from the finest copper to heavy iron; its insulators were mostly bottle necks—of which there was no scarcity. Only the instruments and batteries would have been approved on a regular system, but the line worked.

Early history and occupation of the post have been detailed in the chapters of Indian War history, up to the arrival of Company C. Nevada Volunteers, in April, 1865. Quite naturally the army uniform always excited lively interest among the Piutes. The arrival of a new body of troops at Camp Independence or a march from there by any considerable detachment invariably caused anxious apprehension and inquiry by Indian residents.

From the spring of 1865 to the final abandonment the place was always garrisoned. When the volunteers were mustered out, Col. John D. Devens' command of one company of cavalry and one of infantry succeeded them. Next came Captain (then Brevet-Major) Harry C. Egbert, with Company B, 12th Infantry. Egbert was in command when the fort's buildings were tumbled over by the earthquake in 1872. When the rebuilt barracks were completed the soldiers gave a grand open-house entertainment for the whole countryside. Among the decorations on this occasion were shields bearing the names of Civil War battles in which the company, including many of the veterans who were still under its colors, had participated. As the list included Gaines' Mill, Cedar Mountain, Antietam, Fredericksburg, Chancellorsville, Gettysburg, Wilderness, Petersburg, Malvern Hill, Cold Harbor, Five Forks, and others of less historic prominence, and the company was also at Appomattox at the closing scene, it will be seen that B Company had a record in which its pride was justified.

The last of this garrison, led by Lieut. Dove, just promoted to a captaincy, left for San Diego June 30, 1873, and thereafter found occupation protecting Arizona telegraph lines from marauding Apaches. Egbert, who was a lawyer of ability, resigned his commission, for a time engaged in practice as a partner of Patrick Reddy at Independence, and finally went to New York. On the outbreak of the Spanish War he tendered his services to the Government, served through the Cuban campaign, and was sent to the Philippines wearing the two stars of a major general. He was killed while leading a charge against the enemy. To his widow, doubly stricken by this and the insanity of her son soon after he had received an army commission, Congress voted a general's pension. Pioneer Inyoites felt a special and personal interest in one who had taken much part in local affairs, and who was designated by an appreciative friend as "the gentle, brave and gallant Harry Egbert."

MacGowan's command arrived five days before the departure of Dove and his company. Having no other opportunity for activity, MacGowan was ever ready to go a bit beyond the strictest construction of regulations in making his men a force for law and order. At one time his company was marched into Independence to protect the county jail against an expected lynching attack, which, however, did not materialize. At another, he took the field in pursuit of bandit Vasquez. A detachment was once sent to Round Valley as an object lesson to insolent Indians. Many scouts were made, and many tables of distance measurements were compiled by the company.

On abandonment of the post, settlers in the vicinity were permitted to obtain government title to the farms on which their homes had been made for many years. Previously, bills had been introduced in Congress at one time or another to meet the case, but no relief had been granted.

A movement was also inaugurated to make the well planted and beautiful post grounds the site of a county high school. It would be flattery to the California high school system of that day to call it crude; it was practically non-existent, except as each community might devise ways and means of its own. It was proposed that the Government be asked to deed the Camp Independence grounds to Inyo County, for the purpose mentioned, and a bill to that effect was introduced in the House of Representatives. Introducing bills in Congress is one of the easiest things that many Representatives do; the proposition never got beyond that stage, and was soon forgotten.

CHAPTER XXXII

FURTHER WAYMARKS

In the spring of 1885 a stock show was given by William Rowan, at Bishop. This led to the formation of an association for giving county fairs, the first of which was a one-day display on October 1, 1885. It was so successful that the county's representative in the State Assembly, A. J. Gould, was asked to further a bill to include the counties of Alpine, Mono and Inyo in a district to receive State aid for agricultural fair purposes. The bill became law, and an appropriation was made for its benefit. The Bishop organization was ready for business, having incorporated and bought grounds. While its recommendations for the fair directorate were being considered, a representative from Independence secured the Governor's appointments of a board favorable to locating the site of the fair at that place. The Eastern Slope Land and Stock Association, as the Bishop organization was called, maintained its stand, while the Eighteenth District Fair Association was also active. For several years rival fairs were maintained. Finally an adjustment was made, and thereafter fairs were alternated between Bishop, Independence and Big Pine. When State aid was no longer given the district organization languished. Bishop continued to hold fairs on a local subscription basis, until the purchases of land, and withdrawal from cultivation, by the city of Los Angeles put an end to the possibility of encouraging further agricultural development.

The Nevada Mission Conference of 1885 was held in Bishop, the first of a number of such gatherings convening there or at Big Pine. Its principal local effect came from the adoption of a resolution declaring for the establishment in Bishop of a school of higher education. The institution was erected on a subscription basis, and completed after a term of the school, named the Inyo Academy, had been held in the Methodist church. The cornerstone was laid September 30, 1886, and the building, at that time "the largest and finest in the State east of the Sierras," was occupied the following year. Several classes graduated under instruction of the teachers, who were paid by the church. The control of the school was in the hands of a board of local citizens, and it was never a denominational institution in any way. However, the fact of the church's fostering care had caused some of the original subscribers to repudiate their subscriptions, resulting in litigation; and the same objection was used to hold the attendance at an unprofitable level. The Academy ran at a financial loss until the Conference, unable longer to carry it and to care for the debt which hung over it, abandoned the effort. It was the beginning of higher education on this slope of the mountains. Its local supporters, principally, were in the lead of advocates of something better for the young people; and when it became obvious that the Academy could not continue, a plan for a high school under State laws was launched. At an election held February 25, 1899, it was defeated, 145 to 121. The matter rested thus for two years, during which there was further hope of the Academy reviving. This proving vain, in September, 1901, a public meeting was called and nearly $3,000 was subscribed as a guarantee fund for the payment of a high school teacher. School was opened in a room of the Bishop grammar school, and received a good attendance. A new campaign was begun, and March 29, 1902, the Bishop union high school was established by a vote of 176 to 72. Having set down the real beginnings of higher education in this region, there is small need to detail the subsequent purchase of the Academy property and the growth of the school. An effort was made, at one time, to vote bonds for a $40,000 building; the school's backers were disappointed at its defeat, which, in view of the almost metropolitan plant which has since become necessary, they now accept as a providential result. A $200,000 structure is now in use.

Big Pine was but little later in establishing a high school, and Independence and Lone Pine did likewise. Each district has shown its complete sincerity by voting bonds sufficient to provide housing and other facilities in accordance with the advanced development of educational ideas. This is true of grammar schools as well as of high.

Another step in accordance with modern findings was the consolidation of Warm Springs and Sunland grammar school districts with Bishop, at an election held June 14, 1921. The same advanced move has since been made in other districts of the valley.

The beginning of Owens Valley's systematic development as a dairy region dates from 1892, when the Inyo Creamery was incorporated and a plant constructed at Bishop. Of itself, the venture was not a success, due to mistakes of management rather than to any other cause; it was immediately followed, however, by installation of private plants of the same kind, which succeeded. Ultimately the business passed to a re-incorporated company, which under skillful management has won an established and leading place among Inyo enterprises.

Fire broke out in a vacant building in Independence on the afternoon of Wednesday, June 30, 1886. No fire fighting apparatus was available, and the flames ran unchecked until thirty-eight buildings in the central part of the county seat had been swept away. Practically all business establishments, some residences and the county buildings were lost. The total damage was estimated at $160,000.

Though the courthouse was burned, nearly all county records were saved through the presence of mind and the energy of two ladies, Mrs. R. L. Peeler and Mrs. J. S. McGee, who carried books and documents to safety during the hours that the men of the place were doing what they could to end the damage.

County officers soon established themselves in whatever locations were available, and county affairs went on without interruption.

An effort to move the county seat to Bishop was started. Petitions for an election were strongly signed and presented to the Board of Supervisors. District Attorney Laird advised the Board that though the headings of the different signed sheets of paper were identical, the fact that all signatures were not on one and the same sheet would prevent the whole from being considered as "a petition" within the meaning of the law. As no single sheet contained anything like enough names to justify an election, Supervisors refused the petitions, and proceedings for rebuilding at Independence were begun. On October 7th a contract was let to M. E. Gilmore for erecting the new structure for $11,458, a price afterward reduced, through changes, to $10,000. The building was accepted February 10, 1887.

County seat removal had come up and had been disposed of before, usually on some question of signatures on petitions. Later, a campaign of that kind was begun by people of Big Pine, and submitted to vote at the general election in 1908. It was lost by a vote of 670 against to 456 for.

From the coming of the white man, one of the chief sources of trouble with the Piutes was their securing liquor. In two instances at Bishop, this evil became so pronounced and so utterly beyond the law's control that citizens organized independently to cope with the condition. One organization known as the "C. P. S."—Committee of Public Safety—destroyed liquor stocks found in houses occupied by Chinese, and briefly improved the situation. The most thorough step in this direction, however, was by an organization known as the "145." This body included nearly all the prominent citizens of Bishop. Its name was in imitation of the famous "601" of Virginia City fame; as a matter of fact, the assumed numerals more than doubled the actual number of men in the movement. It held meetings and deliberated over the methods to pursue in getting rid of offenders. The worst of these was a man named Coronado, who held forth in a cabin arranged so that he passed out his goods to buyers without being seen, and never when more than one was present. He maintained an effective watch by means of flocks of dogs, whose alarm gave warnings when necessary. Law officers made repeated attempts to catch him; but while moral certainty could be confirmed, the exacting requirements of legal proof were not available. Coronado was notified by the spokesman of the 145 that he was to wind up his affairs and leave. He asked for and was given more time. Finally patience was exhausted, and the 145 resolved on starting him. Late one night in midsummer of 1901 he was playing cards in the saloon where he bought his liquor stock, and was called to the door by a committeeman who spoke Spanish. He was seized by a competent force, and a pistol that he drew was prevented from doing damage by a 145 thumb placed beneath its hammer. He was taken to his home, his horse hitched to a buggy in which Coronado was placed and with a guard he started off through the clear starlit night. He went on across the Sierra and did not return. Six other culprits left on notice. No drop of blood was shed by the 145, and its action materially lessened the Indian whisky traffic for a long time thereafter.

This "Land of Little Rain," as styled by a former Inyoite, Mary Austin, expanded and developed agriculturally as irrigation facilities were extended or better utilized. Earliest settlers found ample room for home-making along natural watercourses. A decade passed before pioneer farmers seriously took up the irrigation of tracts not thus easily watered. A ditch from Fish Slough to reach lands above Laws was one of the earliest of projected and completed smaller private enterprises. The McNally Ditch, serving the Laws vicinity, the Bishop Creek Ditch, for tracts between Bishop and Owens River, the Owens River and Big Pine Canal, for Big Pine lands, and a ditch for irrigation in the vicinity of Lone Pine were all projected during 1877 and 1878. The first and second were slowly but steadily pushed to completion by the labor of the projectors. The Big Pine enterprise, after the expenditure of considerable effort, remained idle until in 1902 it was reinvigorated and finished the following year. That for Lone Pine was never built. Various other enterprises, to the number of about twenty, were begun after those initial undertakings. A map of the whole array showed the Owens River Canal, begun in 1887 and covering the western side of northern Owens Valley, and the Inyo Canal, starting the same year and irrigating tracts east of the river and nearly as far south as Lone Pine, as the most widely separated co-operative enterprises. A colonization enterprise named the William Penn Colony had been launched in 1885, to develop the area in the vicinity of Owenyo. The colony and the Inyo Canal were the first enterprises in the valley to be obliterated through purchases by the city of Los Angeles.

There were many lean years in Owens Valley. Decline of Cerro Gordo, Panamint and Darwin, and gradual slackening of other mining camps within the territory accessible by teaming from the valley had brought a stagnation not offset in any other way. The building of the railroad in 1883 had not greatly bettered the situation, for only a few varieties of products could profitably withstand its long and time-consuming service and high freight charges. A further depressing factor came in the rapid fall of the price of silver, causing the suspension of mining properties which had been operated on a small scale.

A new era in Inyo began with the growth of the newer mining camps of southwestern Nevada. In the summer of 1900 Mr. and Mrs. James L. Butler discovered the croppings of the Mizpah mine, the beginning of Tonopah. Goldfield's discovery and growth soon followed. The rapid upbuilding of those large camps gave a fresh impetus to mining throughout the region, an advance in which Inyo districts shared. Far more important in effect was the creation of nearby cash markets which demanded the best efforts of the agricultural lands of Owens Valley.

In April, 1902, citizens of Bishop organized the Bishop Light and Power Company to supply local needs—the county's first electric enterprise. Its plant, starting in September of that year, was successfully managed until absorbed by the Nevada-California Power Company. This latter concern, backed by Colorado capital, saw in the growth of Tonopah and Goldfield a market for power, and in the tumbling torrents of Sierra streams an opportunity for its cheap production. Power locations on Bishop Creek had long been held by different locators, who had merely renewed their filings from time to time. Those sites were secured by the new enterprises. Generating plants were built, and transmission lines extended, first into Nevada, then southerly almost to the Mexican line, until now the longest power lines in the world carry the energy of Bishop Creek from Mono County on the north into Arizona and Imperial Valley on the south. ,

In addition to buying out the locally organized power company, the Nevada-California Power Company acquired the Hillside Water Company holdings. The latter concern had acquired storage rights on the creek's headwaters, of value to the electric plants. More or less of friction over water matters developed; on the one side, the farmers who had used Bishop Creek water for decades; on the other, first the Hillside Company, then its successors, the power interests. Temporary adjustments tided matters over until, unable to secure water enough for their crops, a delegation went to South Lake, or Hillside Reservoir as termed by the company, and on June 11, 1919, raised the gates sufficiently to release a reasonable flow. No property was damaged in the proceeding. This led to an effort on the company's part to enjoin the water users from interference with the storage. By agreement, the whole controversy was referred to A. E. Chandler, former State Water Commissioner, both sides agreeing to accept his decree as final. After an extensive hearing, in which practically every water user supplied from Bishop Creek was called to testify, arbitrator Chandler reached findings substantially sustaining every contention of the farmers. This was followed by a formal decree allotting to each tract of land within the affected area a specified amount of the normal flow of the stream.

The progressive spirit of the people of Bishop, who had bettered their condition as circumstances permitted, brought about the incorporation of the place as a muncipality. One of the chief purposes in view was the creation of a better water supply for domestic use and fire protection. A census was taken by the Women's Improvement Club to determine that the requisite population of 500 persons lived within the boundaries set. The census-takers managed to list 540. An election was held, and incorporation of the little city was voted sixty-three to thirty-six, April 24, 1903. W. W. Watterson, F. K. Andrews, George A. Clarke, G. L. Albright and J. C. Underwood were chosen as the first Trustees, with W. W. Yandell as Clerk, D. W. Pitman Marshal, and M. Q. Watterson Treasurer. Proceeding with the utmost care, the board did not complete its arrangements for a water bond election until the following summer. On September 6, 1904, bonds to the amount of $44,000 were voted for the construction of water and sewer systems, the three propositions receiving from 119 to 125 affirmative votes to 6 to 8 negatives. Many other advances have come since— further improvements, the creation of first a local telephone system, then its extension through the valley, then connection with the outside world; the establishment, March, 1902, of the Inyo County Bank, as the first in Owens Valley, and subsequently of others; and different items each of importance, but only incidental as compared to the first daring step of assuming municipal responsibilities and heavy outlays by a handful of people.

How the people of the northern part of the county had voted to close the saloons, under local option laws, in 1874, has already been told. It was not until 1896 that another attempt of the kind was made through election, the entire county being included in the territory which it was proposed to make "dry." The ordinance lost by only 56 votes, but the matter was again allowed to rest, until the latter part of

1909. As a result of the later agitation, in which all the older communities of the county had a part, the County Supervisors agreed that they would be governed, in the matter of adopting a prohibitory ordinance, by the action taken by the town of Bishop. "Wet or dry" was the issue in the municipal election in April, 1910, and the dry candidates won by a vote of 200 to 125. In anticipation of the result, and subject to possible repeal, the county had already adopted a similar ordinance, and the adoption of a dry ordinance by the Bishop authorities confirmed the matter.

Under the provisions of a change made in the State revenue laws of California adopted in 1910, Inyo County was deprived of that part of its income which came from the taxation of railroads and other public service property. Certain provision for reimbursement was made by the amendment itself. Though this lost revenue was rightfully due to the county from the State, it was a neglected issue until County Auditor Thomas M. Kendrick, knowing the facts thoroughly, made its collection a personal purpose. While attorneys were employed, the writer believes it but just to say here that success in the whole matter was principally due to Mr. Kendrick. A bill reimbursing Inyo County to the amount of $100,382 became law, the sum being a large part, but not all, of the total due.

With this money on hand, and with a surplus in the treasury, the Supervisors felt justified in proceeding with the construction of a new courthouse. A contract for $158,700 was let to William McCombs & Son, April 10, 1920. The building, accepted in November, 1921, would be a credit to a much larger county than this. It is worthy of note that the undertaking was completed without either bond issue or increase of taxes, the latter as a general rule being among the lowest levied by any county in the state.

There was much of local interest in the history of the decade beginning with 1921. To items of development, such as might be told of any progressive and ambitious community, little space need be given. Such a classification would include organization of farm bureaus and their auxiliaries, which were energetic in furthering agricultural interests; general advance in orchard planting, and other details characteristic of wide-awake, growing communities. Fraternities, schools, churches, co-operative organizations and clubs were thriving. Fine public buildings were erected; high-class highways were constructed. Though progress had a brake upon it, in the form of the Los Angeles menace, there still remained hope and public spirit that justified the final sentence of the closing chapter of the first edition of this book, mentioning "the spirit that will enable the future writer to dwell more on the details of achievement than on the hardships of pioneering."

But as the years advanced, the destruction of Owens Valley as a homeland was foreshadowed. How it came about and is being accomplished will be told in subsequent chapters.

CHAPTER XXXIII

INYO'S GOLD STARS

Inyo bore its part in the Great War. Not only did its young men answer as their country called, but some of them did not wait for that call. Some volunteered, waiving exemptions; others, before this nation became an active participant, went across the Canadian line and joined the British forces to help end the menace of the Kaiser. No complete roll of those who went to fortress or field from this county, or who, belonging here, joined the colors from other localities, can be had. There were five hundred or more, in all, from our small population. Some we sadly laid away in our own cemeteries, in their uniforms; some sleep in foreign lands. The roll of Inyo soldier dead includes these:

Thomas E. Climo
Abraham Diaz, Jr.
Roy W. Fitchett
Arthur W. Frish
George Benjamin Hogle
Fred A. Humphreys
Joseph Konda, Jr.
Herbert Landin

Joel Henry Lawrence
Fred E. Lewis
J. L. Linde
Oren E. Parrish
Grayson Wilkerson
Oliver Wingfield
Frank A. Wodicker

These were our greatest sacrifices. In money, the county did more than its share. Each bond offering was largely oversubscribed; the third loan brought out $170,000 to take up $128,000 worth of bonds. The first drive, a call for the Y. M. C. A., brought three times what was asked; the first Red Cross call, for $1,300, yielded $10,000; and when the next call was made for $6,000, President G. H. Dusenbery and Secretary H. R. Kearns and their assistants made Inyo one of the first counties over the top with a total of more than $38,000.

CHAPTER XXXIV

BETRAYAL OF OWENS VALLEY

RETROGRESSION REPLACES PROGRESS—SETTLERS PLAN WATER STORAGE
—RECLAMATION SERVICE WELCOMED—SERVICE HEAD'S INTEREST
ON BEHALF OF LOS ANGELES—FRUITLESS EFFORTS TO SECURE IN-
VESTIGATION

Residents still hoped for the continued development of Owens Valley when the first edition of this book was published, eleven years ago. The Los Angeles blight had checked the growth but had not yet brought paralysis, nor did it for three or four years thereafter. Within that period Bishop constructed a quarter-million dollar high school, an American Legion hall, a Masonic temple. Hopeful co-operative associations continued; one built a large warehouse at Laws, from which to ship its anticipated future crops. Other communities likewise added to their advantages.

The valley has since been driven to a status unique in California—that of facing a hopeless future. It is unbelievable that such a valley can revert to primitive waste; but the evil already done was equally unbelievable a dozen years ago, and changes are continually for the worse. Private greed combined with municipal ambition to needlessly ruin one of the most attractive homelands of the West. Inyo has been made a sacrifice to maladministration, incompetent plans and management, evil intentions and performance. It is entitled to have the facts known. While one writing of matters within his own time and contacts is open to charges of bias, this record rests on undeniable details which speak for themselves. Inyo County has invited the most rigid inquiry into a situation in which not a year, much of the time hardly a month, was uneventful. Space limits exclude all but the more important details; with the hope that the recital may not prove too

338 THE STORY OF INYO

tedious, that much is due to an issue of which California and sometimes a much wider field has long heard.

Reliance for the official correspondence quoted in this chapter is principally on findings by Mr. Andrae B. Nordskog, of Los Angeles, in reluctant departmental files in Washington, for the use of which obligation to Mr. Nordskog is acknowledged. He widely disseminated these matters, in communications to the California State Senate and subsequent publication, and without challenge.

And now to the record:

Owens River, draining 2,800 square miles of watershed, could not, in late summers of years of average precipitation, fully supply the numerous irrigation canals which drew from it. Seasonal shortages came when with the upper canals receiving less than their established shares of water the river channel was dry fifty miles above its mouth; and at such times a system of proportional allotment was in use. "Made," or return, waters from midvalley streams, springs and underground sources restored some flow to the lower channel.

But there were seasons of mighty waste. In high-water periods of late spring and early summer the lowlands were flooded, and larger tributaries, especially Bishop Creek with a maximum flow exceeding 20,000 inches and sometimes approaching 30,000, were far out of bounds. The ungraded roads became fords in places, and bridges but islands between sweeping currents.

The answer, storage to equalize the flow, was clearly indicated. Enterprising citizens located eight reservoir sites and sought government permits before the Reclamation Service ever professed to look to Owens Valley as a possible field for its activities. The record is anticipated in saying that these sites were willingly abandoned to the Service when it came, the claimants preferring government development and believing that their prior rights would be restored if the Government decided not to proceed. One commentator says: "These ranchers were naive, unsophisticated people; that is, they had faith in the Federal Government."

National legislation in 1889 provided for appropriations "for the purpose of investigating the extent to which the arid regions of the United States can be redeemed by irrigation," such work to be controlled by the Geological Survey. In June, 1902, a reclamation fund was established for "examination and survey for and the construction and maintenance of irrigation works for the storage, diversion and development of waters for the reclamation of arid and semi-arid lands" in the public-land States. The sole purpose of the Reclamation Service should be borne in mind.

In June, 1903, J. C. Clausen, of the Reclamation Service, came into Owens Valley, under instructions from J. B. Lippincott, supervising engineer for California, "presumably to look for an irrigation project" as Mr. Clausen afterward phrased it. Beginning work in July, he recommended withdrawal from entry of lands within the scope of the project. Accordingly 21,000 acres, surrounding prospective reservoir sites, were withdrawn by the Interior Department that same month; 436,480 acres in August, 58,000 in October and 50,000 acres the following January, a total of 565,480 acres.

The plan received enthusiastic welcome, most of all from men who had made storage locations. Their applications being still pending, they had no established rights to turn over, but expected recognition of their priorities in case of the Government abandoning the field. They went further; on official statements that it would be advantageous to show the people's attitude toward the proposed project, they circulated petitions asking that it proceed, and obtained the signatures of about 90 per cent of owners who would be affected by it. This was in effect, if not in direct terms, an agreement that established enterprises would be placed at the disposal of the Service.

Several of the prior locators always maintained that their rights had been directly relinquished to the Service. Mr. Clausen has written that he has no record or recollection of such direct relinquishments, but that

Whenever an application for a reservoir site was made in the regular way it went to Washington, was referred to the proper bureau, and said bureau would in turn refer it to the city, and of course the city's recommendation was always adverse. In this way the city was given everything and the private parties nothing, and of course all pending applications even if filed before were held up and disapproved. This all amounted to a forced relinquishment.

While this principally related to a later period, it included also the efforts made to revive the first locations.

Mr. Clausen continued as project engineer throughout the detailed investigations. He was not and is not considered a party to the course then taken by the Service; on the contrary, he was deeply anxious for the project's success, and expressed indignation at the use of his reports by Los Angeles before they were forwarded to Washington, while Owens Valleyans were denied information. Soon after the project was killed he resigned.

Thos. H. Means, soil expert, reported:

Owens Valley seems to have many peculiar merits to favor it as an irrigation project. Among these may be mentioned abundance of water power, fertile soil, genial climate, nearby markets for all agricultural products in Tonopah and Goldfield and a possible outlet to Los Angeles in the near future. . . . Agricultural methods compare favorably with those in average California.

Clausen planned a reservoir in Long Valley, toward the head of Owens River, with a dam 140 feet high, to impound 260,000 acre feet of water; canals skirting the Sierra and White Mountain ranges, on the west and east sides of the valley, commanding all the land; and drainage of certain areas. He estimated the water supply in average years to be 508,286 second feet of surface water, 46,820 second feet of return water at Fish Springs, this including water developed by drainage, and 9,859 second feet of minor storage, a total of 564,965 second feet available for irrigation. With duty of water placed at four second feet per acre, this supply would provide for lands in use and irrigate 106,241 acres of new land. Cost estimates were $750,000 for the dam, $208,800 for canals, $500,000 for drainage, $400,000 for laterals, $36,000 for land purchases, and other items to a total of $2,293,398.

The cost per acre was placed at $21.58. Twenty-eight such projects were then being built or considered by the

Reclamation Service. The most expensive cost $86 an acre; the average was $30.97. Only two cost less per acre than would the proposed Owens Valley project.

Fred Eaton, of Los Angeles, had been a summer visitor in the valley. Observing the flood waste, he had formed a vague idea as early as 1892 of turning it to profit. When that idea took concrete form is unknown.

Neither is there definite knowledge of when Lippincott became an active factor on behalf of Los Angeles. He and Eaton were on Owens River headwaters in August, 1903, the month after investigations in Owens Valley were announced. Clausen, mentioning this occasion, said: "Lippincott and I were talking business all the time, and Eaton was listening to everything we had to say, and this is probably what Lippincott wanted to be done. Eaton was of course taking in all the data. This was in August, 1903." Eaton, like the others, was an engineer.

Lippincott reported to the Secretary of the Interior, September 17, 1904, that Los Angeles desired to divert water to that city. February 10, 1905, he wrote to F. H. Newell, Chief Engineer of the Service:

There is possibility of our not constructing the Owens Valley project, but of our stepping aside in favor of the city of Los Angeles. It seems to me that the town should pay the cost of this work of sounding at the dam site, etc.

He proposed a plan of managing some of the outlays so that "these bills would probably not appear at all in the Washington office." Newell replied on February 17th that it would be wise to have an understanding that a reasonable amount of money be placed at the disposal of the reclamation engineers to be expended on work in California as an equivalent for work that may have been done that may be for the benefit of the city of Los Angeles. This discussion of finances shows that incubation of the city scheme was already well under way.

Eaton began buying or taking options on Owens Valley lands in the fall of 1904, and continued the following spring. His most important purchases were riparian lands along Owens River and a large area which would be

flooded by the proposed Long Valley reservoir. This gave
him ownership of fifty miles of river frontage, and control
of the proposed reservoir site. He went to the Independence
land office with a letter from Lippincott instructing him to
report on a power line and with maps which he states were
furnished him by T. B. Rickey, a large land owner. S. W.
Austin, Register of that land office, wrote to the Secretary
of the Interior July 27, 1905:

In the spring of 1905 Fred Eaton accompanied Lippincott to the
proposed site of the reservoir in Long Valley. . . . Mr. Eaton returned to the valley, representing himself as Lippincott's agent in
examining right of way applications for power purposes which had
been filed with the Government. He had then in his possession
maps which had been prepared by the Reclamation Service. [As
noted above, Eaton disputes this.] He expressed a positive opinion
that all lands withdrawn under the reclamation project would be
restored to entry.

In April, 1905, Eaton began to secure options on land and water
rights in Owens Valley to the value of about a million dollars. In
June and July most of these options were taken up and the said
purchaser now owns all the patented land covered by the government
reservoir site in Long Valley, and also riparian and other rights
along the river for about 50 miles. The well known friendship between him and Lippincott and his having represented the supervising
engineer for the Government made it easier for these rights to be
secured, as the people were all generously inclined toward the project
and believed Eaton to be the agent of the Reclamation Service. Mr.
Eaton's own statement was that he had bought these lands for a
cattle ranch. On the purchase of well improved lands in the William
Penn Colony he stated alfalfa lands would be allowed to return to
desert conditions. The men who had charge of the lands in this
colony after a conference with Eaton advised them (the owners) to
sell, as they would be forced to "sell out or dry out." To other
owners Eaton is reported to have said that the reclamation project
would be dropped within five or six weeks.

About this time letters were received at the land office stating
that it was understood in southern California that these water rights
were being purchased for carrying water to the city of Los Angeles.
This was corroborated by the fact that Eaton had tried to purchase
the Haiwee place, on the route of the pipe line to Los Angeles; and
further that a surveying party was making contour maps and finally
admitted they were in the pay of Eaton.

Abandonment of the project at this time will make it appear
that the expensive surveys and measurements of the past two years
have been made in the interest of a band of Los Angeles speculators.

In a letter addressed to President Roosevelt August 4, 1905, Austin said:

Mr. Lippincott, while drawing a large salary from the Government, was employed by the city of Los Angeles to assist in securing water for the city. . . . With his connivance Mr. Fred Eaton purchased all the patented lands within the Government's reservoir site and riparian lands along Owens River. As these matters came before this office I am now stating what I know to be true.

Now, Mr. President, will you in justice to the Owens River project and the people of this district see that this matter is thoroughly investigated?

Thomas Ryan, acting Secretary of the Interior, wrote to Mr. Austin August 30, stating that the letter to the President had been referred to him, and said:

The charges made against Mr. Lippincott are of so serious a nature that the Department cannot afford to ignore them. . . . It is the purpose of the Department to go to the bottom of this matter and ascertain the exact facts, whatever they may be.

On the same date acting Secretary Ryan wrote to the Geological Survey demanding to know whether Lippincott had protected the Government by priority action in acquiring added lands for the reclamation project in Owens Valley, or whether he had let the city of Los Angeles grab them. The reply to this is unknown.

Arthur P. Davis, second in command in reclamation headquarters, wrote to his chief, F. H. Newell:

Apparently some property owners have sold him (Eaton) property much cheaper than they otherwise would, owing to his supposed power of condemnation in the Reclamation Service. I think we cannot clear the skirts of the Reclamation Service too quickly or completely.

Eaton presented his plans to the city, and in May, 1905, the deal for purchasing his property and options was made; he retained the Long Valley lands, and cattle which had been acquired in buying that range, and granted to the city an easement for the lands necessary for a reservoir to be created by the construction of a 100-foot storage dam. The understanding is that he originally put $30,000 of his own money into the proposition, but that later funds were supplied by Los Angeles.

Lippincott wrote in November to the Director of the Geological Survey:

If the people of Owens Valley believed that Mr. Eaton was acting as an agent of the Reclamation Service, I don't consider that I am responsible for the fact. Mr. Eaton was warned by me against appearing in that position and says he has not done so. At the first intimation that some parties in Owens Valley imagined he was I wired him to make a public denial, which he did.

Newell found it well to caution Lippincott, in writing to him November 3:

The letters called for contain a number of phrases which I should prefer not to go directly to the Secretary. In fact, in going over your official correspondence I find many expressions which might well be omitted.

One wonders as to the subject matter of such phrases.

In the meantime the great scheme had become public. The inner circle, the San Fernando valley investors, and co-laborers in the plan, had not taken the people of Los Angeles into their confidence, and it was said that even the city council knew nothing of what was in the wind. But on a morning of July, 1905, the *Times* told the story, or as much as was judicious to reveal. There had been some leaks, so that the revelation did not come as a complete surprise; but that was its first public avowal. It was news in Los Angeles as well as in Owens Valley.

Los Angeles papers were liberal with predictions. Grass would grow in the streets in Owens Valley, and bats and owls would inhabit the county courthouse, they promised. Their predictions have not all come to pass, but they well reflect the disposition of the men then in command.

The revelation served to recall strange facts of preceding months. Confirmation of the part played by Lippincott was given with more candor than discretion by the *Los Angeles Times*:

United States Engineer Lippincott and his assistant, Mr. Perkins, have lent valuable assistance in getting title to land in Owens Valley. It is through Mr. Lippincott that the water board secured its concessions from the Government. He also arranged for the employment of three government engineers to select the route for the canal.

These government engineers have been working for four months. They have mapped out the line from Charley's Butte to the San Fernando Valley.

Without Mr. Lippincott's interest and co-operation the plan never would have gone through. Any other government engineer, not a resident of Los Angeles, undoubtedly would have gone ahead with nothing more than the mere reclamation of arid lands in view.

Official Los Angeles was no less appreciative. The water board minutes state:

The superintendent suggested that inasmuch as the department had received valuable assistance from the Reclamation department of the United States Government in connection with the procuring of a water supply from the Owens River Valley, a letter should be addressed to Mr. F. H. Newell, Chief Engineer, acknowledging such assistance and reporting progress to date, as that department is holding in abeyance some work it had designed in that valley pending our action.

As instructed, Clerk Vroman, of the board, addressed a letter to F. H. Newell June 5, containing the following:

Fully recognizing the valuable assistance rendered the city of Los Angeles by the United States Geological Survey department through your intercession in its efforts to obtain an additional water supply from the Owens River Valley, we deem it necessary in order to show our good faith in the matter to keep you informed of the progress being made by us. All our actions in this business will be held open to the scrutiny of the department at all times.

In the course of a suit brought in Los Angeles, Vroman testified that the letter had been sent, and while a copy had been made, such copy had been destroyed "in order that it might not be used to the detriment of the city and those who had aided it."

Notwithstanding these facts, W. B. Matthews, attorney for the water board and participant in all that went on, made this remarkable statement to the resolutions committee of the Sacramento Irrigation Congress two years later:

There was no collusion, and Mr. Lippincott was excluded from all knowledge of the project on account of his connection with the Reclamation Service.

Newell informed the same committee:

These charges have cut me and cut deep. No matter has ever been more carefully and openly investigated.

The simple fact that no Owens Valleyan was ever called on to furnish evidence of any kind concerning the many charges against Lippincott is in itself proof that no such "careful and open" investigation ever was made. Newell certainly indicated no zeal in meeting the Inyo charges, for the Service or for himself. However, the ghost would not down. As late as 1913 Secretary of the Interior Lane became inquisitive, otherwise Newell would not have written to him:

So far as I am advised, Mr. Lippincott gave his full time and earnest attention to *his duties in the Reclamation Service in good faith prior to July 1, 1906.*

There is temptation to further abandon the role of historian for that of commentator, but the mess is left for the reader's own conclusions. The views of some other reclamation officers will be noted further on.

Before any public action was taken on the Owens River project, Clausen was sent to Yuma, where other reclamation work was in progress. "They had a meeting there four or five days after they got my report," (on Owens Valley), said Clausen. "Mr. Lippincott knew that I had my heart and soul in Owens Valley. Mr. Newell was there and Mr. Lippincott made his report. Mr. Newell said: 'I do not care to tell him,' referring to turning down the project, and wanted Lippincott to tell me of it."

As customary, a board of engineers was appointed to pass on the question. Its members were D. C. Henny, L. H. Taylor and W. H. Sanders. The latter came into Owens Valley July 24th, Henny not at all. Coming was unnecessary, for the end was already determined. Henny had wired to Newell June 20th:

Lippincott telegraphs San Francisco office decision reached; hold preliminary meeting Owens Valley immediately, but suggest that final action be not taken until we hear from you.

On June 21st Newell wrote to his assistant, Davis:

It would be preferable to wait until the city of Los Angeles makes a formal request to turn the work over to the city. Such a request will probably be coupled with the statement that the city will refund to the reclamation fund the cost of the work accomplished. If this is done we will be in a far better position than for our engineers to take the initiative in withdrawing from the project.

Lippincott informed the engineers July 26th that Mulholland, Los Angeles engineer, Matthews, attorney,

Eaton and Newell had sat in conferences discussing the abandonment.

The board of engineers met in San Francisco July 27th and 28th to "consider" the project which had been settled already. Clausen presented a strongly favorable report which was not disputed. Lippincott advocated turning the business over to Los Angeles. The board went through the farce of finding the project feasible but subject to conditions which might make it otherwise. The most important was that if the "set of men" who had purchased the riparian lands would not yield the project would be infeasible. The "set of men" had by then become the city of Los Angeles, secure from condemnation proceedings; this was not mentioned.

A supplemental report was made by the board three days later, to declare that Eaton had no government authority in his actions. "We consider purchases made by Mr. Eaton antagonistic to the interests of the Owens Valley reclamation project and the Reclamation Service."

Henny wrote to Arthur P. Davis August 2:

It will be apparent to you that we have confined ourselves to the subject matter in hand, and that we did not consider Mr. Lippincott's connection with the city of Los Angeles was under investigation. In Mr. Lippincott's case he has represented two interests which are clearly antagonistic, and has allowed the U. S. G. S. and the Reclamation Service to be made use of for the private purposes of the city of Los Angeles. This is of course a very delicate matter, and one which I believe Mr. Newell and yourself had a full understanding of. It is a matter that came up for private discussion among the members of the board, but which did not seem necessary or desirable to touch upon in either of the two reports above mentioned.

It cannot have been the object of the Reclamation Act to make withdrawals under it merely for what is claimed to be general public policy, and what in effect may be the favoring of the interests of one public body as against those of another public body or a private corporation.

Henny added, in a footnote:

I have little doubt regarding an attractive offer likely to be made to Lippincott by the city of Los Angeles, possibly as a reward for past services. I further learn to my surprise that Mr. Perkins [Lippincott's assistant] wants to be placed upon a per diem basis so that he may become chairman of the Los Angeles water commission. All these connections and alliances I think are vicious and must bring disrepute upon the Service.

Maintaining the repute of the Service was important enough to justify a special report on the detail of whether private citizen Eaton had or had not acted with official authority, but when it came to officer Lippincott's having represented antagonistic interests, a vastly more important matter, private discussion sufficed; it was not "necessary or desirable" to refer to it officially.

Davis wrote, in reply to Henny:

This matter is at best a very delicate one, but would have caused little or no embarrassment *if we had adhered to the law* which requires our engineers to abstain from outside practice.

Davis wrote to Newell August 24th:

Lippincott stated that the expense of the Owens River project was $12,000. Lippincott's own accounts show that the amount is $13,887.26. He has charged nothing to Owens Valley account for office expenses, salary, etc. The facts show clearly Mr. Lippincott has been biased in distribution of expenses.

He expressed the belief that undoubtedly there were other expenses not known to the Bureau where Lippincott had directly charged to other projects or other funds matters which should be borne by the Owens Valley project. He thought it would be impossible to unearth these without the co-operation of the supervising engineer, and added that he could tell Newell of many things of similar nature. "Enough is known," he wrote, "to inspire caution and lead to such examination of past charges as may now be feasible." When this special favor to the Owens Valley project began would be an interesting detail to know.

In the final surrender of the project to Los Angeles, the latter was required to pay $14,000 for work done by the Service. Mr. Nordskog's investigations in Washington revealed an Interior Department finding that over $26,000 had been spent on the project.

Complaints, protests and charges against the management of reclamation affairs in Owens Valley poured into the Interior Department, from valley organizations and individuals, but without effect, beyond acknowledgment of receipt. One letter from an humble worker in the Service, a rodman on the survey south from the valley, said: "I feel sure an impartial engineer would never have turned this project down." Arthur P. Davis replied to this, informing the complainant that "Mr. Lippincott's interest was recognized by this office in appointing a board of engineers to consider the project, from which board he was omitted." The flood of comment relative to the supervising engineer seems to have made some impression on Davis, for in the letter of August 24th already quoted he wrote to Newell:

I also desire to withdraw my endorsement from the recommendation that the salary of Mr. Lippincott be liberally increased on condition that he give up his private work.

That is, it had been proposed that Lippincott receive additional pay if he complied with the plain command of the law. The letter continued:

I am convinced that Mr. Lippincott is too blind to the public interest and so biased by private and selfish considerations that it will be impossible to secure loyal services from him, and I believe the only safe way for the Reclamation Service is to encourage him to devote his time to private practice and give up his connection with the Reclamation Service excepts perhaps in a consulting capacity.

Among the inquiries received by the Service concerning Lippincott and the reported intention of abandoning the Owens Valley project was one from Senator George S. Nixon, of Nevada, dated August 2, 1905. Davis replied to him:

So far as this office is informed no official request for abandonment has been made. . . . Thanking you for calling this to my attention, etc.

Note the careful wording. With his knowledge of the "delicate situation," and the many charges that were being received, Mr. Davis's gratitude for the additional inquiry may be doubted. Senator Nixon was no more able than were Owens Valleyans to get the facts.

Nothwithstanding Mr. Ryan's assurance that "the matter would be sifted to the bottom," Davis's opinion of the "delicate situation," and Newell's later statements, nothing was ever done to "clear the skirts of the Service."

Instead, such efforts were resisted or evaded. Congressman Reeder, of Kansas, impelled by Inyo friends, asked in 1909 to have the subject investigated. Newell replied that "nothing specific" had ever been supplied to the department. Washington attorneys asked the Interior Department in 1913 whether any charges were made that during the time J. B. Lippincott was in the employ of the United States he was also in the employ of the city of Los Angeles. They asked also for the privilege of making copies of papers, including any reports or decisions made in connection therewith. An Assistant Secretary denied the requests.

Lippincott was superseded in charge of the Owens Valley project in March, 1906, by L. H. Taylor. He still retained an official status, however, until July, when he accepted a month's pay and went to work for the city which had paid him and his partner, O. K. Parker, over $4,500 for reports on water supply.

Taylor found nothing to do. The project had been killed a year earlier, in all but official announcement and restraint on the Owens Valleyans. The Los Angeles city council went through the formality of providing, November 11, 1906, the request for abandonment which Newell had thought best to have before formally acting. Eaton had stated in October that the reclamation project was headed off. A Los Angeles report in December stated that the reason the project had not been abandoned was because such action would open the way for claims of power enterprises. The formal proclamation of abandonment was made in July, 1907.

Easy disregard of laws doubtless prompted Lippincott in writing to Newell, June 10, 1907:

We desire, *notwithstanding the provisions of the Act of Congress,* to have a right of way covering all the Long Valley reservoir site, prior to an absolute abandonment of the Owens Valley project by the Reclamation Service.

A Federal grand jury in 1921 thought it worth while to indict a Riverside County man for "having alienated the confidence of the Mission Indians in the Government," a more serious matter, it would seem, than alienating the confidence of some thousands of citizens in an important government branch.

Years after the experience of Inyo with the Reclamation Service officers, the Fall-Doheny scandal stirred the country. Referring to it, in a speech in June, 1931, President Hoover said:

The breaking down of the faith of a people in the honesty of their government and in the integrity of their institutions, the lowering of respect for the standards of honor which prevail in high places, are crimes for which no punishment can ever atone.

CHAPTER XXXV

IRRIGATION OR MUNICIPAL USE?

WHOLESALE LOCATIONS—BILL FOR AQUEDUCT—SMITH COMPROMISE
IGNORED—PRESIDENT, DECEIVED, OVERRULES SECRETARY—IRRIGA-
TION AND NOT MUNICIPAL SUPPLY THE LARGEST USE OF WATER
TAKEN FROM INYO—VALLEY'S RUIN WHOLLY UNNECESSARY

Announcement of Los Angeles plans started wholesale claiming of water rights, especially on Owens River. The total thus filed on was several times as much as the stream ever carried. Friends as well as foes of Owens Valley were active in this. One of the first filings was made in August 1905 by S. W. Austin and Wm. Rowan for 200,000 inches of water at Charley's Butte, near the proposed aqueduct intake. This appeared to be important, for Eaton approached Austin with a request to abandon the filing. It was reported that an offer of $5,000 was made for the desired transfer; whatever the inducement, Austin stated that the claim was for the benefit of Owens Valley and was not for sale; it would be turned over to the Reclamation Service if the latter went ahead in the valley, otherwise to the Associated Ditches, free of cost in either case.

One John F. Dickson, of Portland, Oregon, set up a claim to the generous amount of 500,000 inches.

Only one of the valley claims proved to be more than a desperate gesture. Galen J. Dixon, White Smith and John H. Bulpitt, on behalf of the Associated Ditches, filed on Fish Slough, a river tributary. Money spent on engineering investigations showed that the storage would cost from $50,000 to $100,000. These outlays for data served to keep the claim alive until a further government withdrawal tied up the project.

The aqueduct undertaking was skillfully presented to the people of Los Angeles. Civic ambition naturally played an important part, and it was expertly guided by the group of wealthy men who had optioned the great San Fernando Valley acreage. A drouth was manufactured for campaign purposes; there was a scarcity of water for lawns and gardens, and while they withered and died the flow that should have kept them alive helped to flood the sewers. Bond issues, first of $1,500,000 and then of $23,000,000, were voted overwhelmingly.

In June, 1906, Senator Frank P. Flint, of Los Angeles, introduced in the United States Senate a bill giving his city sweeping privileges in acquiring in fee simple an aqueduct right of way, reservoir sites and public lands. It passed that body without opposition. Congressman McLachlan had introduced the same bill in the House, but there it found rougher going. It was referred to the public lands committee, of which Sylvester C. Smith, representing Inyo County, was a member; and it had also to secure the approval of the Secretary of the Interior.

Owens Valleyans conceded the just right of Los Angeles to such water as might be required for municipal and domestic use, but pointed out that it could be secured without destroying Owens Valley. Los Angeles engineers stated that in twenty years the city would need 2,500 inches more water than it then had. The aqueduct was being planned to carry 20,000 inches, and this excessive amount convinced the Owens Valleyans that irrigation of outside areas was one of the chief purposes. Congressman Smith, making this statement, elicited a shrewd denial from the secretary of the Los Angeles Chamber of Commerce, who said the city charter "would not permit bonds to be issued to supply water except within the city."

Smith replied that an understanding could be reached, in that case. He proposed that the reclamation storage proceed; that existing water rights in Owens Valley be recognized; that 10,000 inches, or four times the anticipated need, be allotted to Los Angeles; that reclamation of new lands in Owens Valley be next in order; and that any further amount of water be turned over to Los Angeles.

Los Angeles lobbyists in Washington had the support of Newell, to which was added that of Gifford Pinchot, comrade of the President. President Roosevelt was assured by city representatives that San Fernando Valley was a natural reservoir, and that the use of water for irrigation there was in fact storage to provide against possible dry years. It has been stated that Senator Flint assured the President there was no intention to use the water for agricultural purposes, but a prohibition on irrigation would prevent its use on small garden tracts. He might have added (if he knew) that it would also upset the plans of the chief promoters. Congressman Smith wrote that when he pointed out the amendments he desired the committee promptly accepted them, and that Secretary Hitchcock coincided with his views in every particular and took a firm stand for allowing Los Angeles water for municipal purposes only. But the Lippincott-to-Newell-to-Pinchot play outweighed all others with the President, who directed that limitation on the aqueduct be stricken out. It was so done and so became law.

As Smith's bill proves, Owens Valley offered no objections to the taking of part of its surplus for proper use by the city. Its protests were at the injustice of taking a large amount of water from Owens Valley acreage to irrigate farm lands in another watershed. Though Los Angeles ably deceived the President on that point, there is no longer pretense of denial.

Mullholland, testifying in later litigation, referred to the storage of water in San Fernando Valley as an "absurd notion."

He stated that the per capita daily consumption of water in larger European cities was 25 to 30 gallons; in a number of American cities, 55 gallons; in Los Angeles the year around, 110 gallons. Engineer Thos. H. Means reported that the Owens Valley water supply would furnish 130 gallons per capita daily to a city of 4,700,000.

Attorney W. B. Matthews stated, in an authorized article in 1908, that the water supply planned would provide water for a city of a million and in addition would irrigate 75,000 acres and also supply other cities.

A Los Angeles paper said in 1911:

What to do with the surplus, after every need of the city, no matter how small, had been supplied, was a question which confronted the engineers.

Sworn testimony in a later year was that the distribution to San Fernando ranches amounted to 18,000 inches; that the proportion that went to the ranches as compared with that used by the city in all other ways was as three to one, and that at times the ranches got the entire flow. Mulholland said he owned land in that valley, and was one of the officers who helped to set the rate of one cent per inch per hour for use of the water. Attorney Matthews admitted that revenue from the water did not pay sinking fund charges.

It was proved in the same suit (the Ford-Craig case) that in a given year 68,000 acre feet of water was wasted into the ocean, after having been used in the San Francisquito power plant. Mulholland explained that the water was thus disposed of in order to avoid waterlogging San Fernando Valley lands. And this was before there was interference with Owens Valley irrigating canals.

In 1912 Los Angeles unsuccessfully tried to interest the city of Monrovia in taking some of the aqueduct supply.

San Fernando irrigation was given the color of compliance with the city charter requirement, against bonds for water outside the city, by annexing 169.89 square miles of that valley.

That wholesale irrigation was a chief object is indicated by a report by engineers Hill, Sonderegger and Lippincott in 1924, giving figures of requirements of not only the huge area which by then constituted the city but also of San Gabriel Valley, the southern coastal plain, the western coastal plain, the Inglewood-San Pedro region, Pomona Valley and San Francisquito Canyon. They estimated the requirements in 1950 for Los Angeles county and its cities. They showed that the Los Angeles use alone in that year would be 564,500 second feet—of which 248,000 second feet was assigned to irrigation.

Apologists for Los Angeles point to the great development that has taken place in San Fernando Valley through Owens River water. It has a number of fine towns where once was little more than desert. Its agriculture runs into millions of dollars value, and its worth, according to ex-Commissioner W. P. Whitsett, has increased $300,000,-000. They tell us it was necessary to sacrifice Owens Valley to bring that about.

THAT IS UNTRUE. *The same results could have been attained without ruining Owens Valley.*

How? By the practical, sensible and far cheaper plan of conserving flood waters, instead of relying on taking the surface waters from Owens Valley.

Editor Frederick Faulkner, of the Sacramento *Union,* came in person, of such high interest was the controversy at that time, to learn the truth of the situation. After an impartial investigation, he published a series of scathing articles arraigning the city's procedure. In one he told of engineers' findings that the Long Valley site would support a dam of any construction; that one 165 feet high and 525 feet long would impound approximately 350,000 acre feet of water; and further:

Proper conservation of the water coming down from the various streams in the valley would have produced a total volume sufficient to have kept under cultivation the 80,000 acres of first-class farming land and still have given Los Angeles twice as much every day in the year as any day since the aqueduct entered service. These are facts of record from government engineers and the city's own engineers.

This, you will say, was the report of a casual observer, not an expert engineer. We quote the final report of the aqueduct, official document:

If this (Long Valley) reservoir should be constructed, its storage capacity would be 340,980 second feet. This would call for a dam 520 feet long and 160 feet in height. Its province would be to hold over a water supply from years of excessive flow for such years of drouth as may occur once in a generation. The capacity of the Long Valley reservoir would be sufficient to furnish a continuous flow of the full aqueduct for a period of 427 days, and of the Tinemaha reservoir with a 40-foot dam for a period of 159 days.

J. C. Clausen, engineer who made the reclamation investigations, reported that the average flow of the river at Charley's Butte (the intake of the aqueduct), for the years 1907 to 1922 inclusive, plus the inflow from various sources between there and the Haiwee reservoir, was

sufficient to supply the capacity of the aqueduct if such waters had been under control. . . . The record plainly shows that due to non-control in abnormal years those waters above the capacity of the aqueduct wasted into Owens Lake and were there lost to all beneficial use by evaporation.   ,

In the Mono Power suit, to be mentioned later in this narrative, in which the city tried vainly to condemn property that Mulholland had airily waved aside, Mulholland and Van Norman both testified that construction of the Long Valley reservoir was necessary to maintain the desired flow in the aqueduct. But to the day this is written, twenty-seven years after the disclosure of the great scheme, that reservoir is non-existent.

Van Norman's testimony, supported by documentary showings, was that in one abnormal year, 1912-13, there was a surplus of 400,000 acre feet of water; and that from 1908 to 1920 there had been a loss of 635,000 acre feet due to lack of storage. That waste would have filled the aqueduct to its extreme capacity for more than two years, without considering the normal river flow or any other accessions to the water supply, and without interference with Owens Valley farming or water supply.

The mean discharge into the aqueduct from Haiwee reservoir from June, 1919, to June, 1924, was 248 second feet, instead of the 400 second feet it could carry; yet with that percentage of a full aqueduct the southern wants seemed to be well supplied. Los Angeles, using its natural supplies, took care of its excessive daily consumption, and the San Fernandans continued to grow and wax fat.

These are some of the facts that are available to one outside the pale of official and intimate information; perhaps complete opportunities for investigation would disclose others still more convincing. Back to the narrative of events:

Moves and countermoves went on briskly, if not merrily. Owens Valleyans desired above all else that the people of Los Angeles understand the facts, that an amicable arrangement be worked out in "open covenants, openly expressed," confident that there should be some solution permitting the continued progress of the communities of the valley. But that public learned only what the dominant coterie wished them to know, and accepted it avidly. Misrepresentations and falsities were frequently in print, while Inyo was permitted no rebuttal. One paper, the *Evening News,* was fair and pointed out facts as they were. The prevalent hysteria was so skillfully directed against it that within eight months of the passage of the aqueduct bill the paper suspended. Congressman Smith asked the *Evening Express* the privilege of defining his position and views; that was refused.

The general ignorance of the situation was exemplified by a published article by Prof. Larkin, noted scientist, who in a glowing tribute declared that "Owens Lake will be as a never-ending source of water for the majestic city." There are many Angelenos as uninformed even to this day. As recently at 1930, Commissioner Strasburger stated to this writer that until two days before he was sworn in (in the week of the conversation) he supposed the aqueduct was supplied by Owens Lake, and not from a point thirty miles above. The incident parallels the old story of the newly appointed Secretary of the Navy who on first going on a ship exclaimed: "Why, the darned thing's hollow!"

So prominent a leader as the *Los Angeles Times* asserted:

If the wise men of Bishop could have their way the great early flow of Owens River would go to waste for all time.

This of course ignored progress made by settlers toward reclamation and the project the city had killed.

Candidate Barlow, opposing S. C. Smith for re-election, thought it good politics to declare:

Owens River is now flowing under desert sands and does no living man, woman or child any good. It never can be utilized in that country because as everybody knows the formation is lava and alkali, and if you had a thousand feet of water for a thousand years you could not raise a mustard seed.

And such sometimes get to be lawmakers!

One city delegation after another visited the valley, ostensibly to independently investigate the issues raised. Not one was permitted to accomplish that purpose, each being scrupulously chaperoned by a city water leader and kept from contaminating contact with those who had valley facts to present.

Capitalists organized the Los Angeles and Owens Valley railroad company, filed on water power for electric operation, and made surveys. Dummy locators for the city made subsequent claims blanketing the railroad filings, but such later locations were set aside by the General Land Office as being the result of collusion. One Dr. Houghton, a city councilman, introduced in the Los Angeles governing body a resolution reciting that

Whereas, certain individuals are contemplating building an electric railroad, acquiring rights of way and water privileges in connection with the said Owens River enterprise,

it was the sense of that body that

the city council will not be able to prevent tar and feather methods of dealing with such enemies of the public.

Obviously, "the public" included only supporters of the aqueduct scheme, in Houghton's opinion.

This proposed railroad's application for rights of way across the public land was pigeonholed in Washington; the Southern Pacific, filing a like application at a later date, was given the preference.

The L. A. & O. V. Co. went ahead as best it could, up to the time for letting a contract for hauling the immense volume of freight to be used in aqueduct construction. Though the new company was informed in advance that no bid it could make would get the business, it nevertheless made an offer to haul the freight at an average rate of 3¼ cents per ton mile. The Southern Pacific bid was 5¼ cents, which, later, was reduced to 4½ cents. Both bids were defective in some particular, the L. A. & O. V.'s fatally so, it appeared. Six years later an independent investigating committee reported that the aqueduct builders had paid excessive freights.

Candidates for Governor of California in the election of 1906 were Gillett and Bell, regular party nominees, and Langdon, independent. Gillett and Bell pledged their support to the Los Angeles program; Langdon said only that he would investigate and be guided by his findings. While Inyo's vote was no more than that of a city ward, it showed its appreciation of fairmindedness by being one of the two counties in the State to give Langdon a strong plurality, though foreseeing his defeat.

Seeking special legislation for Los Angeles advantage began in the Legislature of 1907, and has been a fairly constant fact in succeeding sessions. The most important at that time proposed to give cities the right to condemn all waters, power plants or other property that might be desired for their use. The bill was defeated.

Congressman Sylvester C. Smith was up for re-election in the campaign of 1908. The Democrats of Inyo showed their appreciation of his loyalty to his constituents by crossing their party line to give him formal indorsement. Los Angeles sought his defeat. Editors Otis and Earl, of Los Angeles, kept the wires hot preceding the Riverside County Republican convention, urging that indorsement be withheld from Smith. The effort was useless, and Smith was given a heavy vote of approval by that county as well as by others in his district.

CHAPTER XXXVI

PINCHOT TAKES A HAND

HYSTERICAL CONSERVATION—AGRICULTURAL LANDS WITHDRAWN AS
ALLEGED FOREST TO HAMPER SETTLEMENT—"YES" IRRIGATION
CONGRESSES—SQUARE LEAGUES OF FOREST WITHOUT A TREE

Having disposed of the reclamation project, and having secured Congressional sanction, the city's next move was to prevent further settlement in Owens Valley. Formal abandonment of the reclamation plan had been accommodatingly deferred but finally had to be made, thus opening to entry withdrawn lands except certain areas withheld under the aqueduct bill to permit selection of rights of way.

Gifford Pinchot was then Chief Forester. "Conservation" was a battlecry of the national administration. Prodigal waste of natural resources called for sane attention, and the new movement was indisputably timely. But in the stages of novelty it ran so far toward hysteria that there was danger of all being conserved for the future with little regard for necessities of the present.

The Forest Service law under which Pinchot was appointed said:

No public forest reservation shall be established except to improve and protect the forest within the reservation, or for the purpose of securing favorable conditions of water flow, and to furnish a continuous supply of timber for the use and necessities of the people of the United States; but it is not the purpose of these provisions, or of the act providing for such reservation, to authorize the inclusion therein of lands more valuable for the mineral therein, or for agricultural purposes, than for forest purposes.

The constitution of the State of California declares:

The use of all water is hereby declared to be . . . subject to the regulation and control of the State.

Pinchot, who has stated that he did what he could to help Los Angeles, was able to read into his authority the power to assist the city by preventing settlement. He has

since asserted that "the end justifies the means." So might
the highwayman say as he blackjacks his victim into help-
lessness; the end itself is not justifiable. As Henny, writing
of the Reclamation Service, had said, "It cannot have been
the purpose of the Act to favor any political body as against
another political body." Nevertheless, as Newell and Lippincott had seen fit to disregard limitations, legal as well
as moral, on their authority, so did Pinchot indirectly
infringe on the State's prerogative of controlling its waters,
and clearly ran counter to his official duty by checking agricultural settlement by unwarranted forest withdrawals.

A foretaste of what was coming was a departmental
order February 20, 1907, withdrawing land for "forest
additions" from township 2 to township 13 south, M.D.M.,
and from 30 to 37 east, except such lands as were already
withdrawn. Additional withdrawals were made at intervals, covering the whole of Owens Valley. "Protecting the
purity of the aqueduct supply" was one of the alleged reasons, though that was not a matter within Pinchot's
province; but even this pretense became ridiculous on the
inclusion of tracts below the aqueduct level. Pinchot stated
that the withdrawals were approved by the California Congressmen. Smith appealed to each of them present in the
House, by name (McLachlan of Los Angeles being absent), and each denied Pinchot's statement. A commentary
on the wholesale withdrawals was given by Senator Flint
himself, in the course of a visit to Independence. Asking
Register Dixon, of the land office there, about the location
of the withdrawals, miles of treeless grass lands were
pointed out to him. "It's a (profane) shame," said Flint.
Such withdrawals were afterward criticized by the California Supreme Court as being unconstitutional.

An outgrowth of the newborn attention to reclamation
was the National Irrigation Congress, with the slogan
"Save the forests, store the floods, reclaim the deserts,
make homes on the land." Its 1907 session met in Sacramento September 2, and to it harassed Owens Valley appealed for a degree of justice.

Complaints from many quarters were being made, directed at both the Reclamation and Forest Services, and the administration sent its most active defenders to repel boarders. Pinchot and many others of the higher-up officials attended. Inyo was represented by a large delegation, journeying at individual expense—which was probably not true of the government men. While many complaining regions were represented, the charges from Owens Valley were so direct and definite that all protestants were styled "Owens Valley kickers" by the press, which gave them much attention.

The Inyoites circulated a broadside outlining their complaints and charges, as a basis for the resolutions which they sought to have the Congress adopt. This document, placed in the hands of every delegate, did not refer to a spade as an agricultural implement; its charges and allegations were a direct challenge to the services, in unmistakeable terms. The resolutions for which indorsements were asked were, in brief:

That indorsement be given to the appeal for full and impartial investigation of alleged official irregularities and violations which the broadside definitely set forth;

That if the result of such impartial investigation appeared to justify, a better method of handling reclamation matters be recommended to the Congress of the United States;

That the Irrigation Congress indorse the Inyo request for restoration to entry of lands withdrawn as forest if investigation should prove that such classification was improper.

The afternoon given to the resolution was the session's most spectacular period. Official denials and certificates of good character, such as have been mentioned as being provided by Mathews and Newell, and by Pinchot; the prominence and power of the valley's opponents; and the skillful use made of the fact that one of the valley's spokesmen, though fighting the battle as a citizen and property owner, had served as an attorney for men who had made a power location; these facts made the defeat of the "kickers" a foregone conclusion. Some of the delegates afterward said that Inyo was right, but they were not in position to support it. Committee chairman George C. Pardee, ex-Governor, summed up the situation by saying that the Congress could not afford to open the door to complaints. One of the delegates said there was but one project where no wrongs were alleged. Several coast papers commented in vein similar to that of the San Francisco *Call:*

Several hours were devoted to the exciting procedure, but in the end the powerful pro-Roosevelt sentiment prevailed, and the resolutions asking the United States Congress to investigate the charges against the Reclamation Service were laid on the table. . . . Gifford Pinchot, chief forester and personal friend of the President, vouched for the good intentions of the Reclamation Service and the characters of Newell and Lippincott. Anybody who plays tennis at the White House can have anything he wants from these people, and the "kickers" had no more chance than a snowball. Due credit must be given to the farmers for the good battle they put up. They did not mince words.

The Irrigation Age, published in Chicago, later commented strongly on the administration control of the Irrigation Congress, and said it had many letters of complaint along the same line. The Congress, it appeared, was merely a "yes" organization, with the purpose of patting the backs of the powers that were, and not for suggestions on behalf of the people for whom the service was created.

A year later the Irrigation Congress met in Albuquerque, New Mexico. Inyo officially named three delegates to attend: Superior Judge Wm. D. Dehy, Supervisor N. J. Cooley and W. A. Chalfant. Administration control there was less in evidence, but the purposes of the session, beyond adulation, was little more definite than at Sacramento. The Inyoites submitted resolutions, which were opposed by a Los Angeles man who had secured a place with credentials from New York. The prospect was for the matter being tabled, when an Inyoite handed to Judge North, California's member of the committee, an album showing views of attractive homes, crop-laden fields and miles of farm land in the Inyo "forest." Judge North told the committee that the Inyo men had made an 1800-mile trip and he believed they were entitled to a hearing. A grudging five minutes

was granted, during which the case was hastily outlined—
pioneer sacrifices, Indian warfare, reclamation of the
waste, building of communities, and their later blanketing
by declaring square leagues of open valley to be forest.
Realizing that anything accomplished must be very general,
the resolution offered was framed to declare that where
large tracts of land not forest or suitable or intended for
forest uses have been withdrawn they should be restored
to unrestricted legal settlement. Judge North had been the
mover in laying the Inyo resolutions on the table at Sacramento; but he now took a more friendly view, and moved
the adoption of the resolution offered. It was adopted by
a three to one vote. The committee then went into executive session to frame its report, the Inyoites retiring. In
that session Maxwell, the Los Angeles spokesman, succeeded in changing the resolution by inserting words which
he assured the committee made no difference, but which
nullified the Inyo purpose.

It will be noted that nothing in the declared purposes
of either the Reclamation or Forest Service hinted at taking water from its own watershed for the benefit of a
distant city, or at the destruction of one agricultural community for the benefit of another. It is equally true that
the Owens Valley withdrawals extended over great areas
on which the only trees were those that settlers had planted.
They well matched the case of a Nevada "forest" withdrawal in which the rangers had to carry their firewood
several miles, and a Nebraska case where not 300 trees
grew on 300,000 acres which were withdrawn.

Preceding the wholesale withdrawals in Owens Valley,
the Service sent an investigator, who reported against the
plan. He was followed by a Chief Inspector, who also
turned it down. It was not until a third examiner was sent
that Pinchot was able to get the report he wanted. This
third man may be judged by the following from his report:

Owens River and its tributaries supply power to one electric
plant and irrigate 35,000 acres of land worth $20 an acre with water.
Mining is of small importance and is confined to a mine in the
vicinity of Mammoth.

Pinchot did not escape criticism. Smith of California declared in the House that "this is not a government by legislation; it is government by strangulation." Mondell of Montana was no less vehement in his denunciation. In July 1909 Pinchot and Newell were called to account by the Secretary of the Interior, who set aside some of the withdrawals on the ground that they were without authority, and that thereafter such withdrawals must be made in accordance with law. President Taft upheld the Secretary. The Transmississippi Congress in 1909 resolved that forest lines should be made in accordance with forest laws.

During the period of extreme Pinchotism, the Los Angeles water management was the arbiter of settlement in Owens Valley. Homesteading in forest reserves was still in effect, in form; it was met, in this case, by referring applications to the Los Angeles officials, and each was accepted or rejected according to their decree.

Pinchot was summarily dismissed from office January 7, 1910, by President Taft, for refusing to conform to Presidential orders that all departmental communications to Congressional committees must be made through the department head. Some improvement in policy began, including abandonment of 6,000,000 acres of Pinchot's withdrawals in western States. Assistant Forester Potter visited Owens Valley and agreed with local people on the elimination of lands suitable for agriculture. Various changes of lines were made from time to time, the most important being under a Presidential order February 23, 1911, directing the restoration of more than 275,000 acres of land in the Owens Valley area to entry. This however was but a promise, for a time; by the statement of attorney Matthews, of Los Angeles, that city council continued to control the situation until at least January of the following year. For months thereafter restorations were held up on the assertion that action was pending on power applications; the fact that the proposed sites were at higher elevations than the wrongfully withheld lands was a minor matter.

Newell still stayed with his Reclamation Service place. In February 1913 the House committee on expenditures asked for an appropriation to investigate this department, and recommended the ad interim removal of Newell and two subordinates from office. We have no record as to what was done about investigating. It was not until December 1914 that Secretary Lane finally eliminated Newell as head of the Service.

CHAPTER XXXVII

THE COILS TIGHTEN

LOS ANGELES BEGINS TAKING UNDERGROUND WATER—ABERDEEN CASE — TAXATION CHANGE — AGREEMENT MADE BUT NEVER KEPT — AQUEDUCT COMPLETED—CITY WANTS MORE GRANTS—FAILS IN CONDEMNATION

During the first decade of this century, the settlement of Aberdeen, in the central part of Owens Valley, gave promise of attaining some importance. It had only small streams, and the settlers depended on pumping for their water supply. A ditch was constructed from one of the creeks for a portion of the land. That creek also irrigated ranch property nearer the river, then owned by Los Angeles. The ranchers proposed to store the surplus run-off, and to cement their ditch to prevent the large waste from it through seepage. They were notified that such action would not be permitted. This, occurring in November 1911, was the first indication of city intention to take underground waters.

At a later time the Aberdeen people found that the water level in the wells was lowering, endangering their holdings. They took no protective steps, however, until 1924, when a farmer sued to close the wells then operating, because of their asserted interference with the Aberdeen wells. This case, heard by Judge Owen, of Kern County, was won by the city, on the ground that the ranchers had failed to prove the interference charged. The decision said that if the court believed that the city wells were responsible, the injunction would be issued, for "neither legally nor morally has any one the right to take water from under ten acres of land at Independence to irrigate ten acres in San Fernando." This case is somewhat notable in the record as being an instance of a decision favorable to Los

Angeles. There were other similar suits, as will be set forth later; in those the plaintiffs were better fortified with proofs of their allegations.

Though the aqueduct was nearing completion, Los Angeles had a Congressional bill introduced in 1913 to extend for four years its privilege of preferential selection of lands for rights of way for aqueduct and power purposes. Sylvester C. Smith, Inyo's Congressman, had been stricken with the illness which caused his death the following January; John E. Raker took over his interests in the law-making body, and successfully resisted the adoption of this new concession.

A "people's board" of Los Angeles men made an independent investigation of aqueduct matters in the summer of 1912. Its extended report declared that the whole project had been launched without sufficient investigation of nearer and less costly sources of water supply, and that 12,000 inches of available water in the vicinity of Los Angeles had been ignored. It charged that certain citizens of Los Angeles had immensely profited through having obtained control of San Fernando valley lands in anticipation of water being placed thereon. The report recommended that suit be brought to recover Owens Valley watershed lands which it charged had been wrongfully retained by Fred Eaton, and expressed a belief that unless such action was taken their acquisition would ultimately cost the city $500,000. It condemned efforts of the administration to prevent its investigations. Job Harriman, a candidate for Mayor of the city, elaborated on the San Fernando detail, alleging that Otis, of the *Times,* and Earl of the *Express,* had in 1903 taken five-year options on San Fernando valley tracts, and that chief engineer Mulholland had also become an owner there.

Municipally-owned property was exempt from taxation, by constitutional provision. Framers of that exemption never imagined a situation such as was then arising in Inyo county, in which a city was acquiring large amounts of property remote from its own borders, and thus under constitutional provision removing it from county revenue pro-

duction. While Los Angeles might have resisted successfully the collection of taxes on such property, it did not, but
paid them with the reservation of a protest. This peculiar
situation led Assemblyman George A. Clarke, of Inyo, to
introduce, in the Legislature of 1913, a constitutional
amendment, limiting municipal exemption to property
within the boundaries of the proprietor municipality. Los
Angeles legislators joined in support of this just change,
which was later confirmed by popular vote.

Owens Valley had repeatedly sought to obtain a clear
assurance of Los Angeles intentions, so that the disturbed
affairs of the valley might be settled and a basis for future
plans reached. Many promises and conciliatory talks had
no result until on April 5, 1913, a conference was held in
Bishop. Los Angeles was represented by Wm. Mulholland,
W. B. Matthews and John Shenk, candidate for Mayor;
the valley ditch companies by T. M. Kendrick, Harry Shaw,
Fred Eaton (who had become a city opponent), George
Collins, George Watterson, C. W. Geiger, U. G. Smith
and C. E. Bell, and attorneys S. E. Vermilyea and W. B.
Himrod. The following points were agreed to by both
sides:

The valley people to store water on Big Pine Creek and
elsewhere north of Fish Springs to supply existing ditches;
to have the right to drain their lands into Owens River; to
pasture stock on the watershed without interference by the
city; to irrigate all land that would be made dry by Long
Valley storage.

The city to assist in adoption of the Clarke taxation
amendment; not to interfere with underground waters; to
withdraw opposition to reopening public lands for settlement; to admit rights of existing ditches, including that of
pumping them to higher lands.

These matters were to be stipulated in a friendly suit,
to be brought by the city. After an irritating delay, for
which customary dilatoriness was the kindest explanation,
the suit was filed. It was promptly halted when an injunction was sought by a Los Angeles citizen who alleged that
the authorities proposed to "give away the city's birth-

right." The injunction was not ordered, neither was it contested. The agreement drifted along, unconfirmed, while Los Angeles ignored its points until it became impossible.

Suits were brought by companies engaged in reclaiming minerals from the waters of Owens Lake, to stop diversion of the river into the aqueduct, on the ground that their business was being damaged by lowering the lake level. These actions, brought in the Inyo Superior Court, brought motions for a change of venue, it being alleged that Judge Dehy, owning riparian lands many miles north of the aqueduct intake, was therefore disqualified to act. Denial of the change of venue was sustained by the Appellate Court, but reversed by the Supreme Court. A Tuolumne County judge refused the injunction, holding that the plaintiffs had neglected their remedy at the proper time.

The aqueduct was completed in October 1913. It was 233¼ miles long, and cost approximately $24,600,000. Omitting smaller details, it included 60 miles of open canal, 97 miles of concrete conduit, 43 miles of tunnels, and 12 miles of steel siphons.

Four years passed without material change in this subject that was never wholly quiet. Engineer H. A. Van Norman brought forward, in April 1917, a proposal that the city proceed with its Long Valley storage, allotting water to the ditches. The valley people saw in this the surrender of whatever rights they might still retain. Non-fulfillment of promises to ratify the agreement of 1913, as well as the vagueness of the suggestion, ended this plan.

Los Angeles began sinking wells for underground water, in January 1918. That year the ditch companies besought the Government to take up storage in Fish Slough, which was still held by the people, as a reclamation measure. The earlier applications of valley locators were still pigeonholed in Washington. Nothing ever came of this effort.

Los Angeles went to Congress for more grants in 1919. City representatives assured Owens Valley citizens' meetings that the new bill was not harmful to their interests, as it sought only to rectify errors in the description of the aqueduct right of way and to grant right of way for a power line from Long Valley. Inyo had the bill held up in committee until investigation could be made. It proved that new grants were asked. Telegrams notified W. B. Matthews, in Washington lobbying for the bill, that Inyo would oppose it until the city had confirmed its agreement reached in Bishop in 1913. Matthews replied that "the city stands by the agreement and will promptly formally accept and stipulate same." Galen J. Dixon and George Watterson were sent from Inyo to attend the public lands committee hearings, and they, with Edson F. Adams, owner of power locations on Owens River, obtained such changes that the bill was made to conform to the stated purpose and was unobjectionable. It died in the final days of Congressional filibustering. It may be added that the City Council of Los Angeles not only failed but refused to confirm Mathews's promise.

Power-right contentions have been a complicating factor in the situation from the first. Not only have such locations had a bearing on issues of water storage; they have also come in conflict with the wish of the city to control the power sources of the region, and the broad question of municipal ownership, a live issue in Los Angeles. Owens Valley has been indirectly concerned with these matters, which appear throughout the long record; and thus the power fight has become a proper part of this history even though some of its scenes have been beyond the county's borders.

The rise of Tonopah and Goldfield, in Nevada, created new fields for electric power. Within a hundred miles were Sierra streams, on which several hopeful but undeveloped locations had been made. Capital began investigating possibilities. Two or more locations were made on Owens River; others on Bishop Creek and elsewhere, antedating the passage of the aqueduct act of 1906. With contentions betwen rival locators we need not be concerned; suffice it to say that the final clearing up of the situation left two private interests in the field.

Edson F. Adams, Oakland banker, was chief owner of the Owens River and the Mono power companies, with recognized locations in Owens River Gorge. Men working on these locations had been ordered by J. B. Lippincott to desist, early in the reclamation undertaking, with threats of arrest if they did not vacate. Colorado capitalists organized the Nevada-California Company, with Bishop Creek as its chosen ground, and the Silver Lake Power and Irrigation Company, to develop power in Mono County. The Silver Lake figured in litigation, but was ultimately eliminated. The Nevada-California in time became the Southern Sierras. Beginning with one modest plant on Bishop Creek, and acquiring the Bishop Light and Power Co., it ambitiously expanded and grew into a mammoth corporation. It secured the upper hand in rights of way to Nevada camps, over the Adams enterprises. To the latter, this reverse together with Reclamation Service interference proved serious, but their location rights were maintained by performance of legally required work.

In this situation, Mr. Adams sought to market his holdings. No agreement was reached with the city of Los Angeles; it has been stated many times that Chief Engineer Mulholland discouraged negotiations, with the remark that when the city wanted the rights it could pick them up cheaper. Fred Eaton was more farseeing, and by request of Adams he interceded. He offered the Adams holdings for $475,000, less a $50,000 payment he was to receive for making the sale. Eaton offered the property to Los Angeles for the net cash price, but the offer was scorned.

By September of 1919 the Southern Sierras company had completed its building plans then in hand, and with a view to expansion began to consider the river gorge. Preliminary surveys proved the desirability of the property, and on December 10, 1919, after the Eaton sale effort had failed, a 60-day option was obtained from Mr. Adams by the power company. Final surveys were completed in January 1920, and company president A. B. West was authorized to conclude the deal. The option was taken up on February 4, and Southern Sierras men were elected as officers of Mono Power, in preparation for a formal transfer.

Los Angeles officials heard of the deal, or suspected it from observation of the surveying parties. The city belatedly moved to head off transfer of the property it had waved aside, and to secure the holdings for itself. The property transferred included a mile of the river below the proposed Long Valley dam. Two days after the sale was made, city authorities voted to bring suit to condemn the Mono Power locations. A special messenger was dispatched to Bridgeport, county seat of Mono County, to file the complaint. He reached there on Saturday, after the county offices had closed.

News of the city move reached president West in Riverside the evening of the day it was voted. He and other Southern Sierra leaders were attending a ball, part of the program of the company's annual gathering of officers and employees. A hasty conference was called in one corner of the ballroom, and future moves planned. Delivery of the Mono Company deed the next day made the Southern Sierras the legal owner of the disputed ground.

While it was considered the delivery was sufficient, it was thought best to have the deed recorded at the earliest possible moment. Fred Cats, superintendent of transmission, was asked if he could have the deed in Bridgeport the first thing Monday morning. The roads, then little improved, were deep under snow in the Mono country, and the journey was difficult. Cats replied that it was for the officers to tell him what was to be done, and it would be. He and Roy Hill left Riverside at 3 o'clock Saturday afternoon, by which time the rival messenger was already at Bridgeport. The power company automobile broke down in the snow, forty miles from the destination. Company men at the Cain ranch, in Mono Basin, had been notified of his starting, and when Cats and Hill failed to appear, Guy Montague set out to meet them. Cats said afterward that the lights of Montague's car were the most welcome sight of his life.

They worked through the snow that night and reached Bridgeport Monday morning. They found County Clerk Delury at breakfast, and at 8 o'clock he went with them to his office. Affixing $500 of war stamps was necessary. Cats had taken with him 164 $1 stamps and 168 $2 stamps, and was busy sticking them on five pages of the already filed deed when the Los Angeles representative, who had enjoyed a good rest, appeared with his papers. The Mono Power Company had nothing left to condemn; and condemnation of a utility already supplying current for the same uses which Los Angeles proposed was a different matter from shutting off one whose service was only prospective.

Suit was then brought against the Southern Sierra Company and the case was transferred to the Federal Court of Judge Van Fleet, in Oakland. That jurist's rulings strongly favored Los Angeles. Under his instructions the jury found accordingly, and set the price of the river property at $525,000. This was a compromise between the $250,000 to $300,000 valuation to which the city's experts testified and the $800,000 to $900,000 claimed by those of the defendant company. The company appealed to the Circuit Court, which set the verdict aside, denying the right to condemn. Appeal was taken by the city to the United States Supreme Court, which sustained the Circuit Court, and the case ended in 1923 with the company in possession.

Under orders from their superiors, men working for the city sought to hamper power development on the river during the litigation, by fencing the only way of access to the scene, by trying to undermine a grade reaching it, and by blocking it with boulders rolled from the hill above. An injunction was obtained to end such interference.

The company completed its plants in the gorge, thus increasing greatly the ultimate cost to be paid by the city in case of its acquiring that important interference with its river control. Its Long Valley dam, when built, must permit a legally awarded flow of water sufficient for operating the plants, so long as they are held by an adverse interest. Development of the Los Angeles hydroelectric plans for the gorge is restricted by the Southern Sierras holdings. The final price which may be paid sooner or later will amply demonstrate the error of Chief Engineer Mulholland's idea of economy in that instance.

It appears that another tactical and financial error was made when the city failed to carry through a plan for buying those holdings together with the Southern Sierras Mono Basin property. Negotiations reached such a stage that in 1930 the water board asked for and won a $7,000,-000 bond issue for the purchase, along with other bonds. Again the board's advisers decided that the longest way 'round was the shortest way home, and again undertook condemnation, this time for the Mono Basin waters owned by the company as well as others. This was promptly met by a countermove, in which the power people organized a company for the purpose of conveying Mono Basin water to southern California cities outside of Los Angeles. This matter is still in court when this is written. Judicial decisions are not to be anticipated; but predictions are not lacking that by the time Los Angeles acquires the sought-for holdings the sum voted must be greatly increased— another demonstration in the long series of acts that have cost Los Angeles taxpayers sums needlessly large.

Mayor Porter, speaking at Mono Lake in 1930, advised the people there not to go to the expense of hiring attorneys, as Mono owners and city men could "put their feet under a table" and settle the whole matter. Familiar with Los Angeles promises, the Monoites were not surprised that no opportunity for conference ever came, or that they were required to contest the suit involving them all. This action, transferred to Tuolumne County, has never been pressed and still awaits trial. The suit that Porter told the Monoites they would not have to defend is still a cloud on their property.

CHAPTER XXXVIII

UNCEASING MENACE

DISCUSSION OF DAMS — EATON-MULHOLLAND FEUD — INJUNCTION
SUITS NEVER PRESSED—IRRIGATION DISTRICT—CITY TRIES CUTTING
OUT CANAL—CAUSELESS SUIT PREVENTS BOND SALE—LOCAL MEN
ALLIED WITH CITY—WHOLESALE BUYING

Conferences were held in Los Angeles in January 1921, the valley being represented by W. W. Watterson, J. C. Clausen, C. A. Partridge, H. H. Beckman, C. A. Trowbridge and George Watterson; Los Angeles conferees were Matthews, Mulholland, Van Norman and E. F. Scattergood. The outcome was a document to which only two of the Inyo ambassadors, Partridge and George Watterson, assented. It provided that the city would store water in Long Valley by erecting a 100-foot dam, to be begun within one year and finished within three; that the storage would discharge an average of 300 second feet during the irrigation period, ranging from 256 in April and September to 483 in June and July; that in case of emergency conditions cutting down the supply a board, one member appointed by each party and the two to select a third, would amend the schedule; the citizens to use the water outside of prescribed boundaries. Additional storage to the amount of 15,000 acre feet might be built by the city on tributary streams; if the city should not provide such additional storage the citizens might do so. No agreement was reached at that time; substantially the same idea was to come up two years later, in referring to which some of the valley reasons for disagreeing will be mentioned.

A cycle of continuous dry years began with the winter of 1920-21. Light snowfall in the Sierra accurately foretold a subnormal flow in the streams, and necessarily that the aqueduct, for which the normal run-off surplus in preceding years should have been stored, could not depend on surface streams.

During January of 1921 the Reclamation Service again sent investigators into the valley. They were financed by Los Angeles, and access to their maps and findings was denied to Owens Valleyans. It was afterwards concluded that this inquiry was connected with a plan later suggested by the city, that it be permitted to drill and pump wells on the farms, to replace the surface water it wished to take. No guarantee of maintenance of a water supply was offered.

Continued drafts on the underground water supply in the vicinity of Independence were beginning to affect the farms there. The County Farm Bureau petitioned the County Supervisors to proceed by injunction to stop operation of the wells. Objections to this move were on the ground that it was a matter for the injured individuals to take up, and the Supervisors voted 3 to 2 against proceeding. Probably had the matter been pressed at that time there would have been a different story now. Some suits were brought by property owners, and in each case the litigation ended by Los Angeles buying the affected property.

Many statements had been made of the Los Angeles intention to construct a dam 150 or 160 feet high for Long Valley storage. Engineering reports had been favorable to that project. Los Angeles applied to the State, December 12, 1916, for a permit for a dam of that height, and renewed that application June 4, 1923.

But in the meantime a personal feud had arisen between Chief Engineer Mulholland and Fred Eaton. The latter, it will be recalled, had reserved for himself the lands in Long Valley except for granting an easement for so much as would be submerged by a reservoir created by a 100-foot dam. Mulholland, despite all favorable reports, declared that no dam of over 100 feet height should be built, his assertion being that the character of the hills made that the safe limit. He was the absolute dictator of city policies regarding the aqueduct and allied questions—and this statement is not a word too strong. Consequently, though the city representatives said that footings would be put in for a 150-foot dam, and though their permits were for such a structure, the Inyoites felt that the intention was for the lower dam only. It is to be understood, of course, that the higher construction would necessitate flooding a large part of the Eaton holdings, therefore requiring their purchase. The statement was attributed to Mulholland that the city would never buy that area while Eaton lived.

J. C. Clausen was then engineer for the Owens Valley interests. He advised against acceptance of the proposed 100-foot dam, showing that the irrigation requirements of the still privately-owned land amounted to 233,941 acre feet per year, with 169,288 feet of that total needed during the warmer months. Storage with a 100-foot dam would amount to 68,000 acre feet, while one 150 feet high would store 260,000 acre feet. Clausen showed by preceding years that with the 100-foot dam the water supply would have been inadequate in seven of the seventeen years of which he had record, while with the greater storage it would have been short in but three years out of twenty, this also taking into consideration a full aqueduct supply. Under an award of a constant flow for the power plants in the gorge, some flow besides irrigation and aqueduct requirements would have to be released at certain periods; besides, Los Angeles proposed to construct power plants of its own, taking water through a bypass tunnel—another item of constant drain on the storage, regardless of other uses.

Los Angeles preparations for constructing a dam for the reservoir went ahead, and produced a somewhat peculiar local situation. The irrigators, convinced that the proposed 100-foot dam would be unsatisfactory, threatened injunction proceedings to prevent interference with the river's natural flow unless a higher dam were built. Eaton, on the other hand, would not permit a 150-foot construction unless the city bought his holdings. The controversy continued until 1923, when on July 30 the Eaton Land and Cattle Company filed a complaint in Mono County against the city of Los Angeles, enjoining the construction. The city filed a demurrer, and extension of time for pleadings was stipulated. Nothing further was ever done in the case. A precisely similar suit was filed April 30, 1930, but service on the city was never made. Owens River Canal Co. et als vs. Los Angeles was a case filed, transferred to Alpine County, and still unheard in that court. None of these suits was ever pressed to a hearing; the sometimes heard statement that the ranchers obtained an injunction against construction of the dam is erroneous. Los Angeles spent about $200,000 at the dam site, it is stated, and the amount of work done seems to justify the statement. The Los Angeles *Times* put the outlay there at $1,300,000. During the later years the city acquired such areas, as well as such control of the objecting Owens Valley companies, that legal interference with its proposed 100-foot dam would be impossible; but it has done nothing further toward the chief storage project. It constructed an earth-fill dam at Tinemaha, on the river a little north of the aqueduct intake; that is a wholly negligible fact, since the storage would be small and because the structure as built was largely a failure through leakage.

Owens Valley defenders brought forward the frequently suggested plan of organizing an irrigation district, which should become legal owner of all rights of diversion from the river. The plan was carried, 596 to 27, at an election December 28, 1922. Attorney Matthews, of Los Angeles had expressed himself as strongly favoring the district, so that the city would have a single organized body with which to deal. From the valley standpoint, the chief merit was in grouping all water claims under one control. The city's encroachments by purchase had reached such proportions that its gradually becoming the principal owner was probable; many, in fact, were convinced that its ultimate acquisition of the entire valley was sure. It was felt that unification of all interests was a necessary protective step. It was planned that each of the ditches should transfer its rights to the district, for agreed compensations. Options were given by several of the principal local companies. An election was held in August 1923 which by a vote of 702 to 80 decided to issue $1,650,000 bonds, of which $150,000 was to be used for constructing works for distribution of the river flow, the rest to be paid to the companies.

September 18 of that year the Round Valley irrigation district, with a similar purpose in that area, was voted.

Local opponents of the district included George Watterson, L. C. Hall and Wm. Symons. In March 1923 they obtained options for the city of Los Angeles on lands watered by McNally ditch, in the vicinity of Laws. Hall was credited, after that buying had progressed, with having boasted that he had "cut off the left arm of the irrigation district." Other lands and rights east of Owens River had been or were then secured, placing that territory wholly under Los Angeles control. The McNally company rescinded its agreement to convey its water to the district. The city replaced the company officers with dummies of its own selection, and the remaining irrigators under the system were powerless.

Sale of the district's bonds was subject to approval by State authorities, and was so approved despite efforts to prevent. The men named persuaded two others, Charles Winters and Fred Heitman, to bring suit to enjoin the sale, guaranteeing them against expense. It was commonly assumed that Los Angeles prompted this move, but any connection with it was officially denied.

Sale of the bonds was advertised, and buyers for the whole were in Bishop when the Winters-Heitman complaint was served on the district board. This stopped proceedings. The suit was promptly thrown out of court, but it had served the purpose. While the bonds were readvertised, the litigation had frightened away earlier prospective buyers. A month later, a bid for $471,500 of the issue, at a large discount, was accepted. The sum paid would have purchased the Bishop Creek and Owens River canals; it was never so used. Its misuse or disappearance, after its receipt by the district treasurer, was revealed by the crash of the Inyo County Bank.

All at once it developed that the district could not acquire ditch company stock, Attorney-General Webb bringing forward a constitutional provision forbidding ownership of stock by any public corporate organization. This law was completely disregarded by the city of Los Angeles in acquiring valley ditch companies, dummy boards being put in control. In the McNally case, the irregularity was corrected February 28, 1924, by having the directors vote to sell the canal as a whole for the price of $175,000.

Hall, Watterson and Symons, who had turned against Owens Valley, were unsparingly condemned by farm bureau resolutions and otherwise. The feeling in the case of Hall, fanned by his defiant utterances, culminated in a party of men entering a restaurant where he was eating dinner, on the main street of Bishop, one evening in August, 1924, seizing and putting him into an automobile, and releasing him some miles farther south with an injunction never to return.

Los Angeles submitted an agreement draft in July, 1923, proposing that the river flow be distributed, 67 per cent to the ditches west of the river, 33 per cent to the city lands in the McNally area and south, that portion however to be permitted to pass on down the channel to the aqueduct. This was promptly objected to by the Big Pine and Owens River company, receiving its supply below the McNally lands. Its position was that the latter tracts were entitled to their share, but any water not used on them belonged to diversions lower on the streams; that the established diversion point could not be changed. It maintained that position and took the water. Los Angeles had bought something it could not get.

W. F. Hines, president of the Big Pine company, coming to Bishop to attend a meeting at which the situation was to be discussed by city and valley men, rode along his canal. Its headgate was at the point of a long U-like bend in the stream. He found a force of city workmen with scrapers and shovels cutting a new channel across the base of the bend, through the silt bottom land. Once started on the new course, the river would soon wash out a new and permanent bed, leaving the ditch wholly without water. Hines promptly stationed a crew of riflemen commanding the scene to enforce his order stopping the work.

That same month a small storage dam at the lower end of Convict Lake, from which ran a stream watering Eaton's Long Valley lands, was dynamited by men acting under city orders. This was not the first forcible interference on the city's part; in 1920 its representatives had torn out a dam put in by the Forest Service on Rock Creek, causing an effective protest by that governmental branch.

Los Angeles now began wholesale buying of lands in the neighborhood of Big Pine, again securing control of water-distributing corporations through the expedient of dummy directors. Had this action preceded the distribution proposal, the latter probably would have been accepted. It would not have saved Big Pine from destruction, but it might have made a verity of the city's announced intention of "keeping 30,000 acres green." At that juncture, also, with the McNally area eliminated from those requiring water, Los Angeles could have gone ahead with its 100-foot dam without interference.

Declarations made by Los Angeles representatives that no lands would be bought in the northern part of the valley had been thrown overboard long before. Purchases in the vicinity of Laws were soon followed by a wholesale onslaught on property west of Owens River. Every trick and device and misrepresentation was used in the campaign. A city representative boasted that his office knew the financial status of every owner in certain territory, if mortgaged when his mortgage was due, and other facts.

Unavoidably the valley's credit had been badly shaken. The Inyo County Bank carried all the loans it could. Dry years and the uncertain conditions had been hard on the farmers. National and State banks, formed for farm relief, decided to withdraw from this field, though their agents recommended loans. Even the State's Veteran Welfare Commission refused to consider loans to worthy ex-soldiers, simply because of their location in Owens

Valley. Every source of assistance, of its own volition or because of sinister influences, turned against Inyo County. The mortgaged owner could find no relief, and in many cases had no alternative but to sell to the city and get out with what he could save.

The "checkerboard" system of buying was employed; an obdurate owner would find that neighbors who had shared with him in maintaining an irrigation system had sold, and the whole burden was to become his. There were cases where owners were told that their neighbors had optioned and were thereby induced to deal, only to find out too late that the story was untrue. These and other devious methods were denied by city officials, who disclaimed authorization of any but straightforward dealing; but if true that did not change the effects of what their agents had done, to which affidavits were made in some instances; neither did it change methods.

Among the many court actions of the period was one brought by the irrigation district to condemn some of the ditches, this formality being understood to affect only the legal title and not the actual use of the water; also one by which Los Angeles sought to gain full control as against some users, on the ground that being a riparian owner it was entitled to have the stream flow past its lands, though the same complaint frankly stated an intention to divert the stream into the aqueduct. None of these cases, brought in 1924, were ever pressed to judgment.

Effort after effort was made by Owens Valley's people, during the trying years, to have Los Angeles announce a definite program, whatever it might be, so that the future might be planned. The lack of such an understanding was one of the most injurious facts of the whole controversy. Frequent requests for arbitration were made. Mulholland, absolute in dictatorship of the Los Angeles policy, unrelenting in antagonism to the Inyo people, was immovably opposed to any plan savoring of arbitration. Ultimate circumstances, when his grip had somewhat loosened, forced steps which were in fact an arbitration, but under another name.

In June, 1924, the Los Angeles Chamber of Commerce named a committee headed by C. S. Whitcomb to learn the grievances of the Owens Valleyans. They visited the valley and briefly investigated, and prepared a report which was never given out. Perusal of that report shows the only reason for such secretiveness to be in its disagreement with the policy the water board wished to follow. Its points most objectionable to the water board were a suggestion that the city purchase all property at just and fair compensation, that differences be adjusted by disinterested arbitrators, and that the economic life of the valley be preserved as far as possible.

A special committee of engineers examined the Long Valley reservoir site in the summer of 1924, and reported that with proper storage the water supply would be sufficient to keep the aqueduct full and to irrigate 30,000 acres of Owens Valley land. Thereupon the water board declared "keeping 30,000 acres green" to be one of its purposes, this in an official pamphlet issued in January, 1925—a statement not repeated in subsequent propaganda. Knowing the failure of many promises, Owens Valleyans placed little reliance on such assurances, particularly as the buying campaign did not end.

During this period (exact chronological order is not being followed in all these details) the water board decided that a board of arbitration, long sought by Inyo, might be advisable. It proposed that the city name an arbitrator; that one be named by the Inyo Supervisors; that the two select a third. The water board proposed also that the Inyo selection must be approved by the city, a suggestion that was refused.

CHAPTER XXXIX

CITY LAWLESSNESS EMULATED

AQUEDUCT DYNAMITED—ALABAMA SPILLWAY SEIZED—STATE OFFICER
INVESTIGATES — PRESS SYMPATHY WITH INYO — ARBITRATION
VAINLY SOUGHT—REPARATIONS ACT—LEGISLATIVE COMMITTEE
CONDEMNS LOS ANGELES—CITY'S GUARDS AND DETECTIVES—BANK
FAILURE

Examples of violence set by Los Angeles
representatives, in tearing out dams in Owens River
tributaries and in trying to divert the river so as to deprive
an irrigation canal of its flow, were not imitated by Inyoites
until May 21, 1924, when a small blast of dynamite was
exploded against the aqueduct wall a short distance
northwest of Lone Pine, doing slight damage.

The second overt proceeding became almost a "shot
heard round the world," for news of it was published not
only all over America but also in European papers. During
the forenoon of November 16, 1924, a large party of
citizens, unmasked, went to the Alabama spillway, four or
five miles from Lone Pine. A solitary watchman offered
no resistance, nor was any personal force employed.
Possession was taken of the water gate mechanism, and
the aqueduct flow, estimated at 14,000 to 15,000 inches,
was turned into the spillway, to make its way back to the
river.

City men appealed to Sheriff Collins, who appeared on
the scene and began listing the names of the persons
present. He was given full assistance, in requests to "put
my name down," and information that a typewritten list
would be furnished to him if desired. Superior Judge Dehy
issued a temporary restraining order against interference
with the aqueduct, but shortly afterward dissolved it of
his own volition after consulting decisions affecting his
authority to act in the matter.

The citizens held the spillway for four days. Those first on the scene were replaced by others, in such numbers that the place took on the appearance of a large picnic. No arms were displayed, and the general understanding was that none were taken there. Los Angeles men came and were courteously received. Their declarations were similar to that of a British commander in an early Revolutionary skirmish: "Disperse, ye rebels," and were no more effective. They were informed that when Los Angeles began to make good on its promises it could have the spillway. Sheriff Collins appealed to Governor Richardson to send militia to disperse the mob, stating that 100 unarmed citizens had taken the spillway, that not enough citizens could be secured to remove them, and that they would surrender possession to any miiltary force, without bloodshed. This request was denied.

The seizure was made on Sunday. W. W. Watterson, of the Inyo County Bank, arrived from Los Angeles the following Wednesday with copy of a resolution in which the Los Angeles Clearing House Association pledged its best efforts to bring about a settlement of the troubles. With this, and having attracted the State's attention to the valley's unhappy situation, the citizens withdrew. It may be added that the Clearing House Association took no further action.

This affair was generally supported in the valley as a publicity move. No harm was done to persons or property; the only loss was of water, an infinitesimal part of as much as the water board was running to waste through its San Franciscquito power plant.

Governor Richardson sent State Engineer W. F. McClure to investigate the situation. That officer submitted a report of a hundred printed pages, embodying his findings, statements from various Owens Valley organizations, and a great deal of comment from California newspapers. The press, outside of Los Angeles, was practically unanimous in sympathy with the Inyo people. McClure's findings are too voluminous for extended quotation here; a few sentences will suffice:

Whatever notions of justification, censure or excuse that may be formed by readers are to be gathered from a statement of facts and a reading of valley history during the past eighteen or nineteen years.

The people of the valley are not anarchists, criminals or thieves, as has been stated, but on the contrary are ordinary industrious American citizens.

The valley people claimed that the language used (in the aqueduct authorization bill) would permit "the municipality of Los Angeles to use the surplus of the water thus acquired beyond the amount actually used for drinking purposes for some irrigation scheme." (Quotation from letter of President Roosevelt to Secretary of the Interior.) The irony of the situation is that that is just what has been done.

The irrigation district contains 53,900 acres. The city has purchased in excess of 24,000 acres within the bounds of the district, mutilating it so as to make operation impracticable.

A fresh effort was made by the valley people to induce the city to submit the whole issue to an impartial arbitration; this like earlier endeavors of the same kind was fruitless. In conferences, city officials admitted that business interests of the valley had been damaged, but said that Los Angeles had no legal power to pay compensation. To meet this objection, a bill was passed by the Legislature known as the Reparations Act. In resisting its passage, the same individuals who had admitted local loss through the removal of many families set up the claim that Owens Valley was more prosperous than ever before. Pursuant to this law, a large list of damage claims was submitted to the city; it was anticipated that each case would be considered on its merits and awards made accordingly. The officials who had deplored their inability to settle for any damages declared that payment could not be made until the validity of the law had been tested—a position recognized as reasonable. But Attorney Matthews went further, in declaring that even if the law were upheld by the Supreme Court even then the claims would not be paid. There were too many valley men who feared prolonged litigation, and the matter never got into court.

The water board adopted resolutions in July, 1925, that it would buy about 15,000 acres of land in the northern part of the valley, setting a price however that was about

58 per cent of the demands of the owners. Later that year, it employed a board of appraisers, Geo. W. Naylor, chairman of the Inyo Supervisors; V. L. Jones, County Assessor, and U. G. Clark, ex-Assessor, and these men, each working for a compensation of $50 per day, prepared estimates for it. The appraisement was unsatisfactory and claimed to be inequitable in many cases, but was accepted for fifty pieces of property contained in what was called the Young pool. The price paid for 2,730 acres of land, situated in the West Bishop area, was slightly over $1,000,000.

The city had now begun to drill wells on its Bishop area lands, making the statement that the water thus brought to the surface was to be used in irrigating those tracts.

Blasts were fired in two of the city wells on the nights of April 3 and 4, 1926, neither doing great damage. These shots were attributed to the refusal of the city to meet the terms of owners, for property on which the difference of valuation was $141,000 in a $2,500,000 deal.

Frequent denunciations of Los Angeles officials in the Inyo papers led to an effort to pass a press gag law for the county's special case, but it received little legislative support. The Owens Valley *Herald,* unbridled in its charges against the officials, challenged the latter to libel suits; that step was considered in a star chamber session of the water board, but the latter refused to adopt a course that would have put the whole issue into the courts, and thus before the people of the State.

Another blast shattered the aqueduct near Lone Pine May 12, 1926. Majority public opinion which had approved the spillway opening, did not support these repeated occurrences.

Assemblyman Dan E. Williams introduced a resolution in the Legislature in February, 1927, asserting that Los Angeles had adopted a policy of ruthless destruction in Owens Valley, and calling on it to either restore the valley to the agricultural status it had up to 1923, or to make settlement including proper compensation for business damage. In resisting this, Attorney Matthews, who had admitted to Inyoites the serious effect that had occurred, asserted that "for the most part Owens Valley was more prosperous than it had ever been." This was met by concrete figures, showing decreases in schools and in many lines of business. Under the resolution, Assemblyman Isaac Jones of San Bernardino, T. W. Wright of San Jose, Frank Mixter of Tulare, E. G. Adams of Merced, H. L. Patterson of Kern, Van Bernard of Butte, H. S. Crittenden of San Joaquin and R. S. Anderson of Shasta, disinterested men recognized as among the ablest in the Legislature and from widely separated counties, were named as a committee to report. The following extracts are taken from this committee's findings:

We wholeheartedly support this resolution because we believe that the policy of the city of Los Angeles in the Owens River Valley in Inyo County, and the methods adopted by that city in carrying out that policy, are against the best interests of the State of California. . . . Lands purchased by said city in Owens Valley are being rapidly devastated of orchards, buildings and improvements. . . . That said lands are being rapidly returned to their former desert state. . . . We believe that if the city of Los Angeles had purchased available dam sites and reservoir sites and had also tapped the Mono Lake country it could have constructed water works which would have irrigated Owens Valley and still have supplied the needs of Los Angeles. . . . This is one of the most serious problems confronting the State, and as such resolution is at this time of unusual importance, we have given it our most sincere and earnest support.

The Assembly adopted this 43 to 34, three members not voting; at least two of the three were known to be favorable. Of the negative votes, 14 were from Los Angeles, 13 from San Francisco which city was similarly involved in its Hetch Hetchy water enterprise. Assemblyman Williams wrote to Governor Young that several of the negatives expressed their approval of the resolution but said they had to vote otherwise.

Governor Young, after consultation with the water board (the people of Owens Valley not being represented), proposed that test suits be brought to determine the case. This was refused by valley representatives on the ground that the city purpose was to tangle the valley up in a snarl of litigation, which it could prolong indefinitely and during which it would refuse all attempts at settlement, while the communities perished.

Dynamiters gave the aqueduct little rest during June and July of 1927, six different blasts occurring. The most serious in effects was at a canyon near the southern border of Inyo County, where dynamite or the subsequent rush of water, or both, carried away more than 450 feet of large and heavy steel siphon. Los Angeles officials who had given the press of that city many statements as to their knowledge of the guilty parties were summoned before the Inyo grand jury, but denied possessing the information attributed to them.

An immediate effect of this lawlessness was the placing by Los Angeles of armed guards not only along its property but also on the highway. For a time, until effective protests availed, these irregulars made a practice of stopping and searching passing automobiles, where the drivers would submit to that practice. Even such precautions did not prevent repetitions of the dynamiting. It was charged that some of the guards themselves were responsible for minor blasts, in order to make their jobs last.

Another consequence was the flooding of Owens Valley with so-called detectives, whose presence was speedily known and provided community amusement rather than anything more serious. Suspected citizens were watched with sleuth-like vigilance, but not skillfully enough to be of value. Even their rooms when they visited Los Angeles were entered and their property searched.

District Attorney Hession assured the city that all evidence that might be gathered would be given the fullest consideration. The efforts of the city's large company of investigators were barren of practical results. Six arrests were made, on evidence of such little value that the accused were promptly freed by the court. There was no later dynamiting.

As if harassed Inyo had not already enough to bear, now came financial disaster.

Clerks in the office of the State Superintendent of Banks observed that while the Inyo County Bank reported a credit of about $190,000 with the Wells-Fargo Bank of San Francisco, the latter reported the amount to be about $11,000. An examiner came to Bishop at once. At noon August 4, 1927, the following notice was posted on the doors of the Inyo bank, including its branches at Big Pine, Independence and Lone Pine, and the First National Bank of Bishop, in the same ownership:

We find it necessary to close our banks in the Owens Valley. This result has been brought about by the past four years of destructive work carried on by the city of Los Angeles.

This was signed by W. W. Watterson, president of the Inyo County Bank, and M. Q. Watterson, cashier. Another placard stated that the State Bank Superintendent had taken charge.

The public could not credit that the difficulty would be of serious moment, believing that it was some matter that would soon be adjusted. Few such institutions in the State had such general confidence. The bankers had been leaders in public activity, promoters of every movement for moral or material advancement. While they had open enemies, even those had no anticipation of the calamitous situation that was revealed as examination of affairs continued. Much more than a million dollars was unaccounted for; and besides, the affairs of several large corporations were involved, directly or indirectly, to a still greater total. These included the Natural Soda Products Company, which was a wreck when the Wattersons took it over years earlier and built it to a great business; Coso Springs Company, Tungsten Products Company and Watterson Bros. Incorporated, operating hardware and farm business and securities of the other concerns.

The brothers were prosecuted on thirty-six counts, by District Attorney Jess Hession, with Judge Lambert of Kern County presiding. Philip Carey, an Oakland attorney, conducted the defense. His efforts to bring anti-Los Angeles feeling into the case were excluded as irrelevant. the defendants stated that it had not been their purpose to take and keep the missing funds; they were trying to maintain Inyo industries to offset the loss of business due to the work of Los Angeles. They did not contest the showing of facts. Many of the jurors had been close personal friends of the accused. Though some wept as they voted, a verdict of guilty on every count was returned, and in due course the law's penalty was pronounced—one to ten years on each count, the sentences running concurrently. Parole was granted in March, 1933.

Ranch owners in the vicinity of Lone Pine brought suit, which became known as the Dearborn case, in 1928 for an injunction against operation of the aqueduct, because of the drying up of their lands. The court, Judge Lambert of Tulare, set damages to be paid by Los Angeles, but denied the injunction unless the city should fail to pay the damage awards. In that case the injunction should become effective, stopping all pumping in the valley south of the aqueduct intake from wells which had been operating less than five years. These cases were settled by purchase of the injured property.

CHAPTER XL

THE END OF THE TRAIL

CITY INVITED TO MAKE CLEAN SWEEP OF DESTROYED VALLEY—ARBITRATION AND APPRAISALS—CITY ELIMINATING POPULATION—ANOTHER LEGISLATIVE INVESTIGATION — WHERE THE WRECKER IS HAVING HIS WAY

By 1929 the most optimistic foresaw the gradual decline of valley towns. An earlier count had shown that already some 325 families had moved from the valley. Loss of so many from among the supporting population had seriously affected local business. The prospect was only for continued emigration and continued decrease in business; moreover, incentive for progress was gone. This led to a general conclusion that the best course would be for Los Angeles to make it a clean sweep by buying the towns. A proposal to this effect was made to the water board, and the idea approved. A conference was held in Bishop, at which H. A. Van Norman, for Los Angeles, agreed with local business men to purchase real estate, improvements, and business equipment, stocks of merchandise not to be considered. A little later, President John R. Richards and others of the water board visited Bishop, and repeated the assurances.

In anticipation of complete local control by Los Angeles, consideration began to be given in that city to the method of governing Owens Valley, the result of which was a legislative bill looking toward annexing the towns to Los Angeles. Like many other interesting measures, it failed.

In conferences with city representatives, it was agreed that in determining prices for town property the valuations as of 1923 should be taken as a basis, to which should be added a reasonable allowance for the growth that would have occurred but for Los Angeles becoming a factor. Valley people formed what was named the Committee of

Ten, consisting of two representatives from each valley town. Those selected by their fellow citizens were J. L. Gish, Carl Nellen, Laws; B. E. Johnson, C. H. Rhudy, Bishop; A. G. Barmore, George Warren, Big Pine; Jess Hession, Geo. W. Naylor, Independence; Mrs. E. H. Edwards, J. C. Morris, Lone Pine. This committee took complete charge of further negotiations.

Los Angeles put appraisers in the field. Bishop as a municipality had employed J. G. Stafford, a recognized coast authority, to appraise Bishop property for assessment purposes. The Los Angeles figures were so far from agreement with the Stafford list that a third set, known as "the Rhudy-Johnson set-up," was worked out by the Bishop representatives, taking into consideration a growth curve of 8 per cent per year as ascertained from a survey of ten Southern California counties.

Meeting in Independence September 14, 1929, President Palmer, of the water board, Engineer Van Norman, A. J. Ford and E. A. Porter, for Los Angeles, discussed with the valley committee the prices to be established. Lone Pine proposed that prices be fixed by taking the county assessment roll and multiplying it by an agred ratio, as had been done in many ranch cases. This was rejected. After a lengthy session, Judge Palmer proposed that the Los Angeles appraisal be taken with increases as follows: Laws, 34½ per cent; Bishop, 40 per cent; Big Pine, 30 per cent; Independence, 25 per cent; Lone Pine unchanged. The Bishop members stated that they would not recommend acceptance to their constituents, but in practical effect the proposal was accepted. There were inequalities which it was agreed should be adjusted by reviews.

To go back and pick up other threads of this involved story: Mrs. Edwards and others of Lone Pine won a sweeping decision by Judge Lamberson, of Tulare County, in 1929, forbidding the city's taking from Owens Valley any water in excess of what it had been diverting five years earlier, and from taking water from any wells not operating for the same length of time. A writ of supersedeas was sought, a technicality of delay. No decision has been given by the Supreme Court in this case, the city having purchased the property of the plaintiffs and ending their interest in it.

During that summer arbitration, under the name of an appraisal board, was agreed on as a means of settling prices for such ranch property as might be offered, principally that known as the Keough pool, watered by the Owens River Canal. Valley owners named W. R. McCarthy as their representative; Los Angeles named A. J. Ford. The ranchers submitted a list of names for the third selection, any one of whom would be acceptable to them. From this list Los Angeles selected C. C. Teague, but he was drafted, about the same time, by President Hoover for national duty. The next choice was E. D. Goodenough, of Ventura county. The two partisan members went over the area thoroughly, each making his estimate of value. The compiled results were submitted to Mr. Goodenough, who spent more than a month in making his own investigations. Thirty-eight pieces of property were included in this enumeration. After some demur, the Goodenough appraisal, mainly favorable to the settlers, was accepted by Los Angeles and valley people. One by one the several properties covered by it were bought by the city.

Following the virtual agreement on the general plan of town purchases, Los Angeles submitted offers to all real estate owners, and in case of acceptance furnished an option to be signed. This option was sweeping in its terms, embodying provisions inconsistent with the agreements reached, particularly in this: Assurance had been given to the Valley Committee of Ten that the purchase of property would be independent of the issue of business damage, and those who claimed reparations would still be free to bring such suits if they saw fit. But the sale agreement submitted required the seller to dismiss all claims for damages, not only (properly enough) as to the real estate sold, but all of any nature whatsover, involving any property then or thereafter owned by the individual, within the watershed, or any other liability charged against the city. This was modified by written-in agreements in some cases, but was insisted on as a general rule. Los Angeles refused to confirm its earlier promise to buy business equipment.

Town buying began and has continued until at this time Los Angeles is the actual owner of most of the property in every town as well as in the ranch areas.

In a conference between city and valley representatives, the latter asked if it were the intention to eliminate a permanent population from the valley. The water board officially replied, in writing:

It is not our desire to eliminate any permanent or continuing population in Owens Valley.

When those who proposed to sell their homes learned that the terms on which such places could be leased back required annual rental of six per cent of the sale price, plus all taxes, the occupancy to be on either monthly basis or lease subject to cancellation at short notice; and when tenants of wholly habitable dwellings were notified to vacate so the places could be torn down, they were justified in questioning the sincerity of the answer. Nor was that questioning lessened when renters of ranch homes, simply as homes, were notified to get out or have their buildings torn down about them, or when those wishing to rent were told they could not have domestic water, let alone any for small gardens. When they learned, through sworn statements in a Los Angeles hearing, that the same management which dictated this policy had leased to a southern California sportsman 6,400 acres, estimated to be worth $150,000, for five years at a rental of $450 annually—less than one-third of one per cent per year— estimates of that sincerity were not improved. The further revelation that the city had laid almost a mile of 12-inch pipe line, costing over $7,000 of which less than $3,000 was repaid, in order to keep ponds filled for attracting wild ducks, made it appear that the use of drinking water for households had been given undue importance. An independent investigation in Los Angeles led to the cancellation of this favoritism, after a large investment had been made.

State Senator J. E. Riley introduced a resolution, which was adopted 27 to 8, for appointment of a committee to investigate the Owens Valley situation. Senators J. M. Allen, C. C. Baker, Bert A. Cassidy, Nelson T. Edwards and Thomas McCormack were named by Lieutenant Governor Merriam, presiding. After visiting and holding hearings in Owens Valley, they reported that the options required by the city were unreasonable in terms, that business losses should be reimbursed, and that Los Angeles should acquire any further property by negotiation rather than by condemnation.

Suit was brought, 1931, by the Hillside Water Company, a Southern Sierras subsidiary, to stop operations of city wells which were draining its farm lands, like others in the valley, of their underground water. The municipality of Bishop and West Bishop farmers joined in the suit as intervenors. On a motion for change of venue, or rather for change of magistrate in accordance with State law, the Los Angeles attorneys stipulated against the selection of a Los Angeles judge or one from San Joaquin valley. Judge Pat R. Parker of Mono was named by the State Judicial Council, and in the early part of 1932 was referred to in Los Angeles legal filings as a fair and impartial judge. But when the trial was imminent, exceptions were taken to Judge Parker by the city. A test of the matter before an outside court brought a decision qualifying Judge Parker, to which the city replied with an appeal. This reversed the decision. When the matter was called in the Supreme Court, May 4, 1933, Los Angeles secured another 15-day delay. When that time expired the Supreme Court of its own motion vacated all proceedings, and Judge B. C. Jones, of Lake County, was named by the Judicial Council to preside. Los Angeles continues to use every legal resort to prevent a final decision, but it is hoped by all concerned except Los Angeles that it will soon be settled.

Delay—delay—delay, has been the city's method, the nearest approach to a settled policy it has shown. One set of candidates after another has gone before the city's electorate with promises to "clean up the Owens Valley matter;" and each of the successful ones has followed in the same small-politician tracks of his predecessors.

It has been claimed by Los Angeles officials seeking to justify their course that liberal prices have been paid for Owens Valley property. Considering land and buildings only, and with some exceptions, that is true. But while Los Angeles has secured realty that is merely incidental to its real purpose. The finest farm in the valley is of no more value to it than a town lot, so far as realty alone is concerned. It is buying water, surface and underground, worth thousands of dollars an inch according to its own engineers; and it is buying freedom from interference with its stripping Owens Valley of such water. Every seller parts with not only his surface holdings and appurtenant rights; he expressly abandons and cancels any and every other present or future claim against the city of Los Angeles. If he sells a town lot, the printed agreement he is called on to sign precludes his defending the water rights of his 160-acre farm if he has one. This requirement has been modified in some cases, but is on the form presented to him. He is virtually banished, if his living depends on the soil, for he cannot thereafter acquire Owens Valley property with water rights assured to him. He has signed away any privilege of defense.

The question is sometimes asked if there may not be an ultimate restoration, when Los Angeles gets its Colorado River water; if the city may not, by resale, restore farming and get back some of the millions it has spent. It seems incredible to the casual observer as well as to residents that a valley of such fertility, matchless climate and superb attractions shall be condemned to desolation. Only the future can reveal. The most optimistic cannot paint a future that will mean much to those who made Owens Valley what it was. If there is to be a coming back, it must be well into the years ahead when those who have given Inyo their devotion are beyond its enjoyment.

There were some in every community willing to sell and move on. There were more who were less willing but compelled by financial necessity or especially alluring offers to sell; and others whose courage was unequal to continuing in communities where shrinkage and not progress was anticipated, weary of seemingly endless contention, and seeing in the future only litigation or conquest by an infinitely more powerful opponent which had been able to turn even the national government to its own unjust purposes.

Not least in importance in consequence is a succession of dry years. Los Angeles had a canal with no means of filling it except variable and failing surface streams and later the wells which are now exhausting underground storage. Having in its ambition spread over a great area, the city finds it easier to destroy the welfare of Inyo County than to abandon the farm irrigation which it disclaimed to President Roosevelt, or than to provide the storage which it should have if for no other reason than a common-sense step for its own good. Los Angeles has some reservoirs to equalize the aqueduct flow. Haiwee is the chief of these, holding 63,800 acre feet; all others together hold less than half as much. But all combined are unimportant toward storing summer floods, and are where they cannot help Owens Valley.

Family after family departs sorrowfully, seldom with expectation of finding another Owens Valley but at least with the consolation of being away from a field in controversy for a generation. Some of those who leave were born and raised on the acres they have sold. In some cases their fathers or their grandfathers had cleared those lands amid the dangers of Indian warfare. This was the home of their hearts; the land and people they understood and loved. The mere payment of so much per acre or so much per lot, and of the cost of the boards and nails and paint in their dwellings, did not compensate for what they surrendered. One writes from a new location—his third since leaving Inyo—that he has not seen a happy day since he left; another, that come what might, the Owens Valley home would not be sold for any figure if it were to be done over again. Such expressions are many.

The sincere work of years is being undone. On tract after tract acquired by Los Angeles orchards have been uprooted, whether fragrant with bloom or golden with fruit when devastating tractors ruthlessly seized them. Thousands of acres, once spreading fields of green alfalfa or richly productive fields of grain, have been abandoned to the encroaching sagebrush. Dwellings, whether humble or pretentious, have been wrecked, or stand as the sport of the elements, unless fire has already has its way with them. Homes which echoed to the music of children's voices and sheltered the toiler at his day's end are windowless and their doors swing in the breezes. Lawns about them have vanished; the perfume of their gardens has fled. Their portals are no longer shaded, and the avenues leading to them are bordered by gray stumps where venerable trees once welcomed feathered songsters and were part of a beautiful landscape. Even the roads giving access to the homesteads have been plowed up, in some cases, to make the work of obliteration the more complete. Districts which settlers brought from sage-grown waste to productiveness and charm are on their way back to the primitive. Railroad sidetracks over which once rolled carloads of produce are becoming but streaks of rust in a wilderness from which all inhabitants have gone. The very sites on which stood the schools are bare, in some once thriving districts. And this in a land brought from savagery to civilization by the toil and blood and lives of high-class American citizens. Their pioneering was rewarded by being stripped of the protection of the laws designed to promote just such settlement.

These are facts to be observed along any valley highway. What many outside observers have found might be cited in corroboration. Some of the most influential papers sent representatives to learn the situation at first hand. "The Valley of Broken Hearts" was the title of a series of articles in the San Francisco *Call*. Some of the most forceful criticisms of Los Angeles were printed by the *Record,* of that city. World-known Will Rogers last summer informed the nation:

Ten years ago this was a wonderful valley with one-quarter of a million acres of fruit and alfalfa. But Los Angeles had to have more water for its Chamber of Commerce to drink more toasts to its growth, more water to dilute its orange juice and more water for its geraniums to delight the tourists, while the giant cottonwoods here died. So, now this is a valley of desolation.

Going to show that the *Call* titled its articles understandingly, the continually disturbed mental condition prevalent in Owens Valley accounted for at least two suicides and one case of insanity.

News comes that Manzanar, once a fruit growing and shipping point of importance, now owned by Los Angeles, is to be deprived of its water and lights. Its remaining orchards are doomed; its settlers must move. Another school and community destroyed.

And while farms revert to the wild, what of the towns? Some of the same decay is theirs, but figures better serve to show their plight. Business done by three reporting Bishop concerns fell from $242,000 in 1924 to $180,000 in 1926; of four houses for an average of four years, from $439,000 to $288,000. The American Railway Express did about 66 per cent as much business in 1926 as in 1924. One house did 25 per cent as much business with farmers in 1926 as in 1922. A seed retailer bought less than one-sixth as much from wholesalers in 1925 as in 1922. The largest of three dealers in farm implements sold 140 pieces of machinery in 1922; when 1926 came two dealers had quit, and the one remaining sold only four pieces, of which two were for outside the valley. Of the eleven school districts once neighboring Bishop, four have not a single family left, another contains but one school child; within another year or two other districts may lapse. The business figures were of seven years ago, meeting W. B. Matthews' claim of Inyo's prosperity because of its benevolent assimilation by Los Angeles. To-day the showing would be far stronger, for some then in business have given up the sad struggle. Los Angeles alone is responsible—but it refuses to compensate for the evil it has wrought.

The dominant genius of the whole undertaking was William Mulholland, whose attitude was typified by his

remark (here expurgated) that there were not enough
trees in Owens Valley to hang its people on. It must be
said of him that he is not open to charges of deception. To
him the Inyo people were outlander enemies to be
conquered; he left the methods to competent subordinates.
The nominally controlling water board served as his rubber
stamp, up to the time when the chickens of different
engineering failures came home to roost at his doorstep, and
when the tragedy of the San Francisquito dam sent out its
flood to take hundreds of lives and to wash down to the
clay feet of the city's almost defied idol.

Mulholland passed from the picture, so far as Owens
Valley was concerned, and internal politics took hold. The
water board became more independent, but continued to be
named with little regard for fitness or understanding of the
important matters in their care. By the time a member
learned what it was all about, if he tried to do so, he was
liable to be displaced by some one else whose views on
municipal ownership or some other local issue were more
acceptable to the ruling faction. Tribute is due to one
notable exception: Judge Harlan G. Palmer. Appointed to
the board, he conscientiously studied the problem and was
arriving at a fair solution when some unrelated issue
displaced him. Such frequent changes account for but do
not excuse the weathervane ways of the city in its Owens
Valley activities. A line of procedure on which the board
might agree, after much effort on the valley's part to
inform its members as to facts, was good only during the
uncertain tenure in office of its members. Even most of
those who came to Owens Valley and learned some of the
facts returned to their council rooms to again become yes-
men for the dominant anti-Inyo influence. One would
think that any sincere intention of carrying out promises
to "clean up the Owens Valley situation" is treason to Los
Angeles.

The whole shameful perpetration is a crime against the
people of Inyo County; against the people and taxpayers
of Los Angeles; against the State of California; against
the just administration of the nation's laws. Not because

the city came to Owens Valley for more water; that could have been arranged, though little of such water finds its way past the lands which the foresighted promoters sold. All that was right could have been won at far less cost in millions and in good repute by a definite program of honest, aboveboard dealing. The campaign began with wrongful use of government functions; it continued in the engineering folly of creating a $25,000,000 aqueduct without sanely providing for its supply; and it was carried on unscrupulously.

With adequate storage of flood waters there would have been little occasion for interference with the streams that were the very life-blood of Owens Valley; there would have been no destruction of homes and farms; Owens Valley towns would have continued to grow; there would have been water for all; millions of dollars would have been saved to the city; and Los Angeles would not have created for itself a repute that generations may not forget.

Mary Austin, wife of the Austin who first protested to the Government about the peculiar acts of Lippincott, saw the beginning of the calamity as a resident of Independence. In her autobiographical "Earth Horizon" she briefly sketches it, and thus tells of her seeking guidance as to what she could do:

She called upon the Voice, and the Voice answered her "Nothing." She was told to go away—and suddenly there was an answer; a terrifying answer, pushed off, delayed, deferred; an answer impossible to be repeated; an answer still pending, which I might not live to see confirmed, but hangs suspended over the southern country.

Many have commented in Inyo's defense, often in language more vivid and less restrained that these pages have shown. Morrow Mayo, who was for six years a Los Angeles reporter, now an author, declares in his recently published "Los Angeles":

Los Angeles gets its water by reason of one of the costliest, crookedest, most unscrupulous deals ever perpetrated, plus one of the greatest pieces of engineering folly ever heard of. Owens Valley is there for anybody to see. The city of Los Angeles moved through this valley like a devastating plague. It was ruthless, stupid, cruel and crooked. It stole the waters of the Owens River. It drove the people of Owens Valley from their home, a home which they had built from the desert. For no sound reason, for no sane reason, it destroyed a helpless agricultural section and a dozen towns. It was an obscene enterprise from beginning to end.

While these proofs are being read, the California State Senate has adopted, without a dissenting vote remember, resolutions excoriating the course of Los Angeles. Even if you declare that the opinions heretofore given are inspired by prejudice, you cannot deny the facts, given without misstatement, on which these opinions are based. And if you choose to set aside facts, you must still admit that when the highest legislative body of the State deviates from legislating and without an objecting voice condemns a municipality there must be a strong reason. This was the third time the matter had been taken up in the Legislature, and the third time that condemnation had been voted.

It will be recalled that two legislative committees had visited Inyo, in both cases made up of men chosen to reach fair judgments in the dispute. In each instance every man became a champion of Owens Valley. The second committee, in 1931, was headed by Senator James M. Allen, of Yreka, in far northern California. That committee made certain recommendations, in the interest of justice. But the opinion of unbiased judges weighed as little in amending the conditions as dictates of right and fairness had done. This led Senator Allen to introduce a resolution, briefed hereinafter. In speaking for it he scathingly reviewed the whole issue. He was followed by Senator Thos. McCormack, of mid-state Solano County, and Senator Edwards, of Orange County, neighboring Los Angeles; both these had been members of the 1931 committee. Other speakers for the resolution included Senator J. M. Inman, of Sacramento; Senator Dan E. Williams, of Tuolumne; Senator Andrew Schottky, of Merced. Thus prominent representatives from counties far apart voiced the knowledge the whole State has of what Los Angeles has done toward ruining one of its once growing home regions. While the southern city is making records in other ways, it has made another in being the only municipality in existence which has come in for such legislative criticism.

The resolutions, adopted April 28, 1933, recite, in more than 1300 words, a merciless review of Los Angeles-Owens Valley affairs. They show that objectionable policies have not changed; that Los Angeles citizens voted $38,800,000 for the express purpose, among others, of settling the whole matter; that though nearly three years have passed since that mandate, it has not been complied with; that Inyo owners have been and are being ruined by the city policy; that the Mono condemnation suits are not being pressed but remain as a cloud on property; and others of the facts that have been detailed. The Senate therefore demands that Los Angeles close up these matters without delay or show cause why it cannot, and if it fails to do so that the Legislature "bring all powers of the State to bear upon the situation and exert every means within its power to end for all time this episode which is one of the darkest pages in our history and which has resulted in the utter destruction of one of our richest agricultural sections."

APPENDIX A

OFFICERS OF INYO COUNTY

COUNTY JUDGE

Oscar L. Matthews appointed by Governor 1866; 1868-1871, A. C. Hanson; 1872-1880, John A. Hannah. Office abolished by new constitution.

SUPERIOR JUDGE

1880-1890, John A. Hannah; 1891-1896, George M. Gill; 1897-1908, Walter A. Lamar; 1909 to present, Wm. D. Dehy.

SHERIFF

1866, W. A. Greenly, resigned December, 1867; 1868-1869, W. L. Moore, resigned November, 1869; 1870-1871, A. B. Elder; 1871-1873, Cyrus Mulkey, resigned May, 1874; J. J. Moore appointed, served to end of 1875; 1876 to February 10, 1878, Thomas Passmore, killed in discharge of duty; 1878 to July 3, 1879, Wm. L. Moore, killed in discharge of duty; J. J. Moore appointed to complete term; 1880-1882, J. W. Smith; 1883-1884, S. G. Gregg; 1885-1886, J. S. McGee; 1887-1888, S. G. Gregg; 1889-1890, J. R. Eldred; 1891-1894, J. S. Gorman; 1895-1902, A. M. Given; 1903-1906, Charles A. Collins; 1907-1910, George W. Naylor; 1911-1914, Charles A. Collins; 1915-1922, Frank Logan; 1923-1926, Charles A. Collins; 1927 to present, Thos. F. Hutchison.

CLERK, AUDITOR AND RECORDER

1866, Thos. Passmore, resigned May 6, 1867; S. P. Moffatt appointed, then elected, serving to end of 1871; 1872-1874, M. W. Hammarstrand; 1875-1877, W. B. Daugherty; 1878, John Crough, who served until March, 1884, when he suicided in Clerk's office; Thos. Crough appointed for remainder of 1884; 1885-1886, Wm. L.

Hunter; 1887-1890, P. H. Mack; 1891-1892, John N. Yandell; 1893, D. J. Hession, who served until his death in February, 1900; J. E. Meroney appointed, and served by election until end of 1905; 1907-1914, Wm. L. Hunter, Jr. Offices of Clerk, Auditor and Recorder segregated effective January, 1915. Jess Hession served as Clerk 1915-1918; Dan E. Williams, 1919-1922; 1923-1930, Louis H. Bodle; 1931 to present, Mrs. Dora Merithew.

AUDITOR

Position segregated from office of Clerk beginning 1915. T. M. Kendrick filled the office from then until fall of 1930, when he resigned and Louis H. Bodle was appointed.

RECORDER

Position segregated from office of Clerk beginning 1915. W. L. Hunter, Jr., served from then until his death February 4, 1920. Mrs. Mamie Reynolds, then appointed, is the incumbent.

ASSESSOR

1866-1867, John T. Ryan; 1867, A. C. Stevens resigned, L. A. Talcott appointed; 1869-1871, Geo. W. Brady; 1872-1873, J. F. Dillon; 1873-1874, Wm. J. Lake; 1875-1879, J. F. Dillon; 1880, Thos. May, who absconded May, 1881, with a shortage of $1,279. J. C. Irwin appointed; 1883-1886, John C. Irwin; 1887-1898, P. A. Chalfant; 1899-1914, W. W. Yandell; 1915-1918, Vivian L. Jones; 1919-1922, U. G. Clark; 1923-1926, Vivian L. Jones, who resigned; A. A. Brierly appointed, and by election now serving.

TREASURER

1866-1867, John Lentell; 1868-1869, A. N. Bell; 1870-1871, Isaac Harris; 1872-1879, Henry M. Isaacs; 1880-1886, Geo. H. Hardy; 1887-1892, J. J. Moore; 1893 to December, 1902, W. T. Bunney, who absconded; 1903-1906, Irv H. Mulholland; 1907-1927, A. P. Mairs; 1928 to present, J. E. Shepherd.

DISTRICT ATTORNEY

1866, John Beveridge, failed to qualify; Thos. P. Slade appointed, resigned August, 1868; Pat Reddy appointed, failed to qualify; P. W. Bennett appointed. Beveridge elected 1869, failed to qualify; Bennett again appointed; 1872-1873, E. H. Van Decar; 1874-1875, R. B. Snelling; 1876-1877, P. W. Bennett; 1878-1879, R. B. Snelling; 1880-1886, J. W. P. Laird; 1878-1888, P. W. Forbes; 1889-1890, Geo. M. Gill; 1891-1898, P. W. Forbes; 1899-1910, Wm. D. Dehy; 1911-1914, F. C. Scherrer; 1915-1918, P. W. Forbes; 1919-1929, Jess Hession, who resigned; H. W. Guthrie appointed, elected for present term.

SUPERINTENDENT OF SCHOOLS

1866, Josiah Earl; 1868-1869, C. M. Joslyn; 1870-1873, J. W. Symmes; 1874-1875, Geo. H. Hardy; 1876-1882, J. W. Symmes; 1883-1886, Charles H. Groves; 1886-1894, J. H. Shannon; 1895-1898, S. W. Austin; 1899-1902, H. C. Hampton; 1903-1922, Mrs. M. A. Clarke; 1922-1925, A. A. Brierly; 1926-1929, Mrs. Ruth W. Leete; 1930, present term, Mrs. Ada W. Robinson.

CORONER

1866, B. D. Blaney; 1867, A. Farnsworth, place declared vacant and John A. Lank appointed, serving to end of 1873; 1874-1875, A. Wayland; 1876-1877, J. D. Blair; 1877-1878, John A. Lank; 1879-1882, V. G. Thompson; 1883-1884, G. W. Brady; 1885-1888, Wm. F. Matlack; 1889-1892, Thos. Parker; 1893-1894, H. H. Howell; 1895-1898, I. J. Woodin; 1899-1902, I. P. Yaney; 1903 until his death March 2, 1916, H. H. Robinson; M. M. Skinner appointed; 1918, Milton Levy, resigned, Cris Carrasco appointed and now serving by re-election.

TAX COLLECTOR

Position segregated from Sheriff's office beginning 1907; 1907-1910, J. E. Shepherd; 1911-1914, C. I. MacFarlane; 1915-1918, U. G. Clark; 1919 to present, Mrs. Jessie C. Miller.

APPENDIX B

ALTITUDE OF PEAKS

Altitudes of peaks neighboring Owens Valley are sometimes a matter of controversy. In listing for convenient reference a trifle of information, it is found that observers differ in several cases. Gannett's Dictionary of Altitudes is a publication of the United States Geological Survey; so are pamphlets giving the results of spirit leveling, and so are the U. S. G. S. quadrangle maps. There are instances in which no two of these, all from the same authority, agree in statements. North Palisade, or Mt. Jordan, is given as 14,250, 14,275 and 14,282. One puts Mt. Williamson at 14,500, another 14,384; Mt. Tyndall, 14,025 in one tabulation, is 14,386 in another. In the list below the quadrangle figures are used where available. A few peaks in other States are included to show the relative rank of the highest points of the nation.

Mt. Whitney 14,496
Mt. Elbert, Colorado 14,421
Mt. Blanca, Colorado 14,390
Mt. Williamson 14,384
Mt. Shasta, California 14,380
Mt. Harvard, Colorado 14,375
Mt. Rainier, Washington 14,363

According to available figures, these are the seven highest in the continental United States. There are nearly fifty over 14,000 feet. Disregarding many peaks less known, some other altitudes are as follows:

White Mountain Peak (ranks twentieth) 14,242
Mt. Sill 14,198
Pike's Peak, Colorado 14,108
Middle Palisade 14,049
Mt. Langley 14,043
Mt. Muir 14,035
Mt. Barnard 14,003

Mt. Humphreys 13,972
Mt. Morgan 13,739
Mt. Tom 13,649
Mt. Montgomery (White Mountains)................................13,465
Basin Mountain 13,229
Mt. Emerson 13,226
Kearsarge Peak 12,650

APPENDIX C

DEATH VALLEY NOTES

As indicated in the first chapter of this book, the topographic extremes of the United States proper are both within the limits of Inyo county. Mt. Whitney lifts its head nearer to heaven than any other spot. Death Valley sinks further toward the orthodox nether regions than any other; deeper below the sea's level, and is at least not surpassed on earth in its power of torment for the human atoms who may fall within its clutches.

Possession of the ill-famed sink is not a matter for boastfulness. Neither is it necessarily a reproach, for aside from the fact that it is a mineral treasure house, it is so far distant from Owens Valley's fertile farms and comfortable homes that if Death Valley and all its neighborhood were taken from our map Inyo would still have a greater area than any one of several of the Atlantic States possesses. Bishop is farther from Death Valley than the width of the State of Connecticut, and there is plenty of room to outline a new Delaware between the most contiguous points of Owens and Death Valleys. The territory had to be under some jurisdiction, and it was wished upon Inyo.

A distinction is made: "Death Valley" is a rather broad term taking in a large area of desolation: "Death Valley proper" is much smaller. The broader term is applied not only to the more noted central portion but also to arms or branches known as Lost Valley, Saratoga Springs, etc. This larger region extends fully 130 miles. "Death Valley proper" is the region of dread, and is fifty or sixty miles long. This more restricted part is below sea level, and for more than forty miles is floored with a saline marsh from one to six miles wide. These great beds change their appearance according to the observer's view point and the time of day. In the morning, seen from the east, and in the afternoon, seen from the west, they are gleaming white; reverse the hours and positions and they become a shady gray. This is due to the shadows of an uneven surface.

On the west the Panamints, on the east the Funerals, are the valley walls. Telescope Peak, seen from the valley, is majestic indeed, for it stands shoulders above the range to its left and right, and has an elevation of 11,045 feet above sea level. The observer in the valley is some 200 to 300 feet lower than where tides ebb and flow, so there is offered the greatest difference in elevation in the country. Whitney stands much higher, but is seen from a valley that approximates 4000 feet above the sea, and the contrast is less. The Funerals, also called Grapevine or Amargosa in different places, rise from 5000 to 9000 feet. The Death Valley face presents a varied coloring, white from strata of borax, gray, green, yellow, and other hues. It is a country of striking scenery.

Geological aspects of that region are interesting to the thoughtful layman as well as to the expert. Sidney H. Ball, of the Geological Survey, gives the name of "Pahute" to the primeval lake that once served the area. This is believed to have covered the country from north of Goldfield to south of Death Valley, and ninety miles east and west. Rugged islands rose in it here and there.

"The climate must have been moist," says Ball, "and the presence of fossilized wood in the lake beds shows that trees flourished near the shores. The lake was for the most part fresh. The Pahute lake was destroyed in part by the increasing aridity of the climate and in part by deformation. Volcanic flows and explosive eruptions of rhyolitic material occurred at various times during the existence of the lake. The deformation blocked out the mountain ranges as they now appear and formed many of the enclosed valleys by broad folding and warping. Death Valley was at this time first outlined, though it was depressed later.

"In Tertiary, probably early and middle Miocene time, Death Valley did not exist. Amargosa and Panamint ranges were low, and their southern portions at least were covered by a lake which extended well into the present Death Valley south of Salt Creek. In late Pliocene time, however, Death Valley was probably a closed basin occupied by a sheet of water. . . . The folding of the Amargosa and Panamint ranges does not alone account for the valley, as it appears to be a block dropped down between the bounding ranges by faults."

A geological survey report claims that Death Valley is one of the best watered parts of the desert. Water—mineralized—is close to the surface of the marshes. The Amargosa River, running around the southern end of the Funeral Range, turns toward the southern end of Death Valley, but rarely carries water enough to reach the sink. It is said that it has not carried sufficient volume to discharge into the sink since 1850. Generally its bed is a dry wash, with water in a few places only; but when a cloudburst occurs within its drainage it may become a raging torrent for a few hours. Willow, Furnace and Honepa creeks are other streams of considerable flows which are lost in the sands within a few miles of the springs from which they start. However pure the waters of these streams at their heads, they soon become impregnated with minerals.

The Geological Survey lists forty-eight springs and wells in the area north of Saratoga Springs and between the boundary ranges. Persons familiar with the country say that not more than half the water is listed, and that there must be at least a hundred such places. Most of the water holes are small, yielding but a few gallons in a day's seepage. Saratoga Springs is a pool twenty-five feet in diameter and four feet deep. While most of the springs are charged with minerals, those above sea level are considered safe for use. The "poison springs" do not contain arsenic, we are told by a survey authority, but are charged with Epsom salts and Glauber's salts, and are fatal only because the victim, usually weakened in condition, drinks their water without moderation. Usually the springs are hard to find, and even old-timers in the vicinity have been known to hunt for two or three days before coming upon the coveted water supply. Indians indicate water holes by placing white rocks conspicuously on larger rocks, in situations where they can be readily seen.

What Death Valley has cost in human life will never be known. The starting point, so far as known, was with the unfortunates of 1849, as related in this book. Probably not a year since the white people began coming to this region has passed without adding to the list. In one short period covering a few years the known fatalities numbered twelve. It is said that during 1906 thirty-two bodies were found. How many were lost and not counted in such records will never be known; how many started out on a "short cut" and, with no one to inquire as to their safe arrival, got no farther than the bottom of that pit no one can guess. Near the Furnace Creek ranch is a graveyard with thirteen mounds. Generally the dead are buried where found. One writer has maintained that gases from the marshes has had something to do with some of the deaths, but no scientific investigator notes any fact in confirmation.

For all its ill repute, there is much of interest in the noted spot. It is not a place of poisonous atmosphere. Its dangers lie in disregard of the warnings of experience; in foolhardy or ignorant braving of its furnacelike heat at the wrong season. Every nook in it has been explored; trails and roads cross it; mining is done in its mountains; gardens produce profusely in the valley itself. But to the end of time it will justify its name, and men, heedless of what is told them, will perish in its burning sunshine.

It is a place of paradoxes. During some parts of the year it would serve as a veritable health resort. While rain is scanty and seldom falls, the skies shed rivers at times. It is the hottest place in America, but is often shaded by snow-capped peaks. Men die there from lack of moisture, but waterfowl tarry in Death Valley on their migrations.

DEATH VALLEY CLIMATOLOGY

The United States Weather Bureau sent an observer and assistant to Death Valley in 1881. The assistant, R. H. Williams, was unable to stand the terrific heat, and left; John H. Clery, observer, stayed through the five hottest months.

During May, June, July, August and September the average temperature was 94 degrees. The highest in May was but 105; each of the three following months the thermometer reached 122, and in September the top mark was 119. The July average, night and day, was a trifle over 102. These maximum temperatures run about the same as in the hottest places in India, Arabia, Lower California and northern Mexico, but Death Valley keeps it up for a longer period. This is the judgment of the Weather Bureau. Reports from other sources seem to indicate that Mr. Clery happened to make his visit in a cool summer. The writer has been informed by a transient Death Valleyan that the mercury in a common thermometer reached the top of the tube, 132 degrees, in the shade at the Death Valley ranch. It is said that a record of 137 was made by a thermometer on the north side of the house at the Furnace Creek ranch. Observations made by common thermometers are rightly open to suspicion, so better evidence is given by a tested thermometer used by a surveyor who ran lines in the valley in 1883. He kept it in the shade and hanging over a stream. It repeatedly registered 130, and for forty-eight hours in one stretch 104 was its lowest.

The effects of such conditions are striking. Meat killed at night and cooked at 6 in the morning had spoiled at 9 o'clock. When meat is fresh killed, cut thin and dipped in brine, the sun cures it in an hour. Eggs can be roasted in the sand. Fig trees thrive in the genial air of late winter and early spring, but their fruit never matures. Furniture warps, splits and falls to pieces. Water barrels lost their hoops within an hour after emptied. One end of a blanket that had been washed dried while the other end was in the tub. Near where these tests were made is a flat rock upon which is lettered: "Hell, 8 miles; Nowhere, 150 miles."

A thirty-year resident of that country noted that he had known the mercury to stand at 128 and 130 at midnight. He relates that he once thought to take a refreshing bath in water from a pipe in the valley. The

stream that fell upon his skin was so near scalding that he
gave it up as too hot for even a well-baked "desert rat."

The air is not only hot; it is kiln-dried. It is understood,
of course, that we write of the extreme conditions, at the
hottest season. Most of the wind, of which there is enough,
comes from the west and south. The Sierra, Owens
Valley and the ranges between Death Valley and the coast
extract the wind's moisture to nearly the last degree. The
glaring wastes and sun finish the job. Clery found
remarkably low percentages of humidity during his stay.
Men who dug a ditch at the Furnace Crek ranch slept in
the running stream with their heads safely pillowed above
water.

It is this extreme dryness of the air that helps to wind
up the lost man. The moisture is drawn from his body
rapidly; his drinking supply is drawn upon, the more
excessively if he is unacquainted with the dangers. When
the heat overcomes him, and insanity comes, as seems to be
usually the case, his first tendency is dig for water if he
be desert-wise. One experienced desert habitue who had
become lost was picked up just in time to save his life.
He had started to tunnel through the Funeral Range to
reach Greenwater, with only his fingers for tools. In
another case—typical of many—if the victim had had the
same instinct, he might have lived; for when those found
him dug a grave close by in which to lay his body they
struck water within 18 inches of the surface. One rescued
man had tied all his clothing into a bundle and was carrying
it on his head, under the impression that he was wading
through deep waters.

Bodies of those lost in the lowlands decompose very
rapidly, as a rule, regardless of whether they lie on salt
or borax fields or on the sand. In the higher places they
are more likely to wither and mummify, to a considerable
extent.

An experienced "desert rat" tells of hearing a man
lecture for an hour on how to avoid the perils of the desert;
a week later the lecturer was rescued from the fate he
had been warning against. One man about to perish cut

his palate with his knife so that the blood dropped on his tongue and kept it from swelling. A teamster for the borax company started for a spring, and he and his mules all died on the road.

While moisture is customarily very much missing, there are times when it comes copiously indeed, in the form of cloudbursts. They are most to be expected in the hottest weather. One who saw such an occurrence thus describes it:

Right in the clear sky appears a cloud, black and ominous, streaked with fire, growing with wonderful rapidity, and eventually sagging down like a great sack. The cloud is always formed above the mountains, and after a time its bulbous, sagging body strikes a peak. Floods of water are released on the instant, and in waves of incredible size they roll down the cliffs and canyons. Precipices and peaks are carried away, gulches are filled with the debris, mesas and foothills are covered. The face of a mountain may be so changed withis an hour as to be scarcely recognizable, and even the lighter storms rip the heart out of a canyon, so that only jagged gulches and heaps of broken rock are found where once, perhaps, a good trail existed.

A Death Valley pioneer tells of sleeping near the mouth of Furnace Creek Canyon, with a "bug hunter"—desert for entomologist. The scientist, unable to sleep in the hot air, gave his attention to a roaring in the canyon, along toward midnight. To his surprise, the space between the canyon walls suddenly grew white. His comrade chanced to waken, and the bug sharp asked him what ailed the sky. One look sufficed to cause the desert denizen to yell "Cloudburst. Climb!" And climb they did, just in time to escape a wall of water which was estimated to be not less than a hundred feet high.

It has been stated herein that winds are plentiful. Though generally of but a few hours duration, their velocity is often from thirty to fifty miles an hour. In that country this stirs up sandstorms which must be seen, or experienced, to be fully appreciated. One observer says he awoke one morning to find the air full of a whitish haze. To the west the landscape was blotted out by a dense brown fog—blown particles of earth. A Death Valley sandstorm seen from the mountain top is a strange spectacle. The huge pit of Death Valley is full of tumbling clouds of dust, billows that roll and change with every instant. After such a storm the sky shows generously the evening sky-markings which as children we held to be caused by the sun "drawing water." After a sandstorm there are such fan-like shafts, made by suspended dust in the upper air. "Sharp squalls," says one writer, "plunged down the canyons and gulches, and there gathered the dusty forms in their arms and went whirling away in gigantic waltzes. It is no wonder that the Arabs of this desert country, the Piutes, believe in witches and supernatural powers in the air."

At times the lofty whirligigs become what the desert men call sand augers. Slender in form, the sand auger is a column of dust rising thousands of feet into the air with a faint cloud of dust at the top and a slight spread at the base. Wherever it touches as it travels across the land there is a sudden stirring, a commotion of whatever is loose and easily moved, and while it is being watched the sand auger moves on across country and perhaps vanishes completely in a few seconds.

During such storms the dangers of being abroad increase. The scorching blast takes the lives of men even though they have full canteens.

Sidney H. Ball, of the Geological Survey, remarks that the Piute name for Death Valley is "Tomesha," meaning "ground afire." Those Piutes sometimes have graphic descriptive powers.

Fog is one of the unexpected winter phenomena of the valley. One writing of it tells of being on the mountain when the valley was fog-filled from floor to rim-top. Moving white clouds rolled about, raised, lowered, divided into vast chasms and reunited, at times disclosing narrow sections of mountain or valley, at times resembling a vast sea. The writer has seen a like wondrous display there.

DEATH VALLEY FLORA AND FAUNA

It might be supposed that such forbidding natural conditions as exist in Death Valley would preclude possibility of much variety of animal or vegetable life. It is therefore surprising to learn that at least 182 varieties of plant life have been listed. The majority of these are arid flora; some are marsh plants, including two kinds of trees as well as shrubs and smaller plants, found where there is a fairly abundant water supply.

The standby tree of the desert is the mesquite. It flourishes where water is abundant, and may also be found where water is many feet below the surface. It sometimes attains a trunk thickness of eight inches or more, though its usual appearance in Death Valley is that of a great bush. It bears a bean-filled pod, on which animals will browse and which are not without value as sustenance for human beings. It is thorny and spreading, and like many other trees when neglected usually grows a closely set mass of stems. About such groups the sandstorms pile up dunes, sometimes completely covering and smothering the tree. The roots spread nearly as much as the tops, and make better fuel. When a desert resident wants wood, he may get it with a shovel, by digging instead of chopping. It is said that as much as five or six cords of wood have been dug out of a single mesquite mound.

The yucca, familiar on western deserts, seldom appears in Death Valley though found in the arid country in every direction from there.

Arrowweed, one of the reliances of the Indians, grows in wet places, to a height of six feet or more. Greasewood, creosote and other desert bushes are found.

A little round gourd is found in some of the canyons. "Desert apple" it is called, but its thin meat contains little hint of the fruit for which it was named.

The large number of plants listed as true arid flora, growing away from any water except the scant and infrequent rains, include three kinds of grass, retaining some vitality the year round. A very few of these species are not found anywhere except in Death Valley. All are stunted and of a color in keeping with the harsh surroundings, during nearly all of the year. There is a short period in the early part of the year when parts of the surface between the hills and the marshes are golden with flowers, which soon succumb to the increasing heat. Many colors are seen there and on the slopes and hillsides, living their brief span before the sun withers away all evidence of their having been.

The marshes are not alone in being without vegetation. There are occasional stretches of sand as bare as a floor. In still other places the surface is covered with small flat rocks, whose dark colors are believed to be the result of intense heat and light during a long period. The chance for plant life there would appear to be much the same as it would be on a sheet of iron; and yet the writer has found tiny flowers rooted in bits of soil on such surfaces.

The animal kingdom is represented by no less than 150 forms, varieties and species—this without counting the jackasses which roam the hills by hundreds. These are the progeny of escaped or abandoned animals.

Mountain sheep are the largest game in the bordering mountains, which are among the chief habitats of those now rare animals. For years they were one of the reliances of the Indians, and annual slaughters were the rule. Thirty are said to have been killed near Furnace Creek in one year, as the culmination of an extensive Indian campaign. They travel well worn trails, across which the Indians build low stone walls as blinds. The sheep do not look up while eating, but when alarmed they run to the highest points, a trait which Lo turns to his advantage. The sheep campaign of 1891, mentioned above, was preceded by such preparations in the way of blind-building that the few whites thereabouts concluded that the walls were for the purpose of guarding mineral deposits of great value. It developed that feed and not fighting was the purpose.

Waterfowl, migrating to and from far-off haunts, frequently tarry briefly at the little pools, Geese, swan and ducks are among the visitors. Their rests in the crystallizing vats at the old borax works sometimes brought them to grief, for on cold nights they became so weighted down with crystals that they could not fly.

"Bellerin" Teck's planting of quail at Furnace Creek throve, and those beautiful birds became acclimated to the conditions of the little oasis, and withstand the fearful summers.

Bats abound in some sections, and one of the observations of Dr. S. G. George, heretofore quoted, comments on the quantities of bat guano accumulated in such places. Badgers, gophers, skunks, foxes, coyotes, snakes, bugs of different kinds, flies and gnats are among the things found. A special variety of mouse exists there. The trade rat is found in Death Valley as well as elsewhere in the West. This little animal has a certain standard of honesty; he will carry off articles that he can handle, but will invariably replace them with something else. A camper left a box of dried fruit open during his absence; when next examined, the fruit was gone, and in its place was an assortment of chips. Another found that his collection of matches had been replaced by pebbles. Once a box of cartridges was emptied by rats and something else substituted; the cartridges had been carried into a temporarily unused stove, where they would have provided a surprise for their owner but for his accidental discovery of them. It seems that frequently, as in this case, Mr. Rat had no particular use for the goods; he merely wanted to keep busy. There is a kangaroo rat, but whether identical with the trade rat no desert man has been able to tell us. The kangaroo rat has a body four to six inches long, and with a stout tail serving the same purpose as that of the Australian mammal for which the little beast is named. The animals show no fear of man, sometimes eating from the hand if given the opportunity.

The chief desert rattlesnake, and the most vicious, is the sidewinder, a reptile from twelve to eighteen inches long. It has been known to be disagreeably familiar around camp, crawling into bedding or other places where its presence is by no means desired. A former desert freight driver tells of seeing them in balls ten to twelve inches in diameter. It takes several snakes of whiplash size to make a mass of that size. In traveling the sidewinder goes with the snake motion, but with half their length in the air and weaving from side to side.

A little desert terrapin is also found. Common lizards reach comparatively huge proportions in those surroundings. Specimens fifteen or sixteen inches long are reported. The most unique form of the family is the chuckwallah— chawalla in Indian. It is a lizard, heavy-bodied, fat and stumpy as to tail, and weighing up to three pounds or more. They are said to be good eating—the writer takes this statement on faith. Casual visitors will no doubt prefer bacon; still many desert people learn to like chuckwallah meat. The Indians are less squeamish about details, and roast the reptiles just as caught, feathers and all.

The adjacent mountains contain many song birds, and great numbers of mocking birds. A Death Valleyan relates that one year the water holes in a certain part of that country dried up. One morning a miner found a dozen or more young mocking birds helping themselves from his water supply. He filled a tin with water and gave it to them. Every morning thereafter for weeks they came, perched upon the bed or table, and coaxed for water, showing not the least fear. On another occasion a returning miner found a mountain swift in his bean pot, making a meal. He tossed a stone in its direction; the bird jumped out and to one side, looked fearlessly at the man, and then back into the pot. It was allowed to finish its dinner.

"Death Valley: the Facts" (Stanford University Press) treats this subject comprehensively.

INDEX